EMBERS: BOOK 1 OF THE EIRE EMPIRE

C. J. Shaffer

r631

This story would never have happened without a dear friend's help.

DSC, you have my eternal gratitude.

Noble Houses of the Eire Empire

Diamond Houses:

Von Sinclair

Von Anker

Von Chen

Von Dearworth

Emerald Houses:

Chi Nirvana

Chi McMurdo

Chi Colombia

Chi Viktoria

Chi Devi

Chi Ibrahim

Chi Alves

Ruby Houses:

San Cannes

San Wo

San Cixi

and twelve others

Sapphire Houses:

Kun Haldis

Kun Fernandez

Kun Jakarta

and twenty-one others

Key Characters:

House Haldis:

Lord Boston Dublin Kun Haldis

Sir Baghdad du Haldis

Sir Chang du Glydenfeldt

Madam Malaysia du Eberhardt

House Nirvana:

Lady Clarisse Bern Chi Nirvana

Lady Katalia Vermont Chi Nirvana

Lady Menodora Vermont Chi Nirvana

Jordana Vermont, the Lady Chi Nirvana

House Sinclair:

Lady Aspen Dakota Von Sinclair

Lord Wallace Delaware Von Sinclair

Lord Huntington Dakota Von Sinclair

Sherah Dakota, the Lady Von Sinclair

Other Houses:

Augustine Sinclair, the Lady Von Montana

Lady Jane Eiravati Chi McMurdo

Lady Mairwen Torianna Von Chen

Lord Istanbul Feliciano Chi Colombia

Lord Charles Dhaka Kun Jakarta

Nobility SpaceGuard Ranks

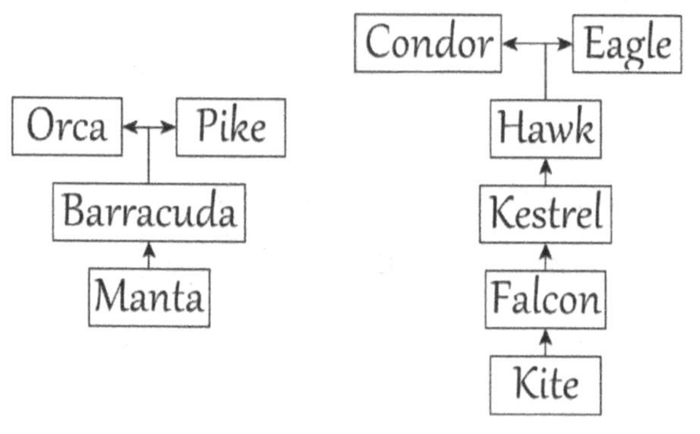

Commoners SpaceGuard Ranks

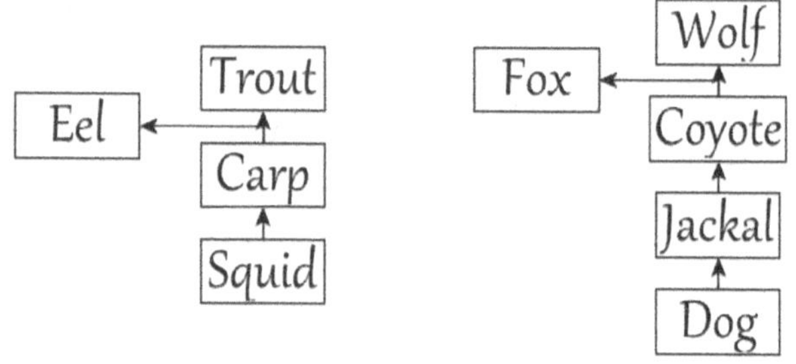

PART ONE

CHAPTER ONE

Dustbowl

BOSTON

In the moment, decisions that set in motion the fall of an empire are small things, hard to see. The largest of rivers begin as puddles you wouldn't bother stepping over. Like everything involving people, it started small. Personal. Intimate, even. It involved people whose names won't be remembered by History, trying to do the right thing. Operating on instinct.

The fall of the Eire Empire began as such, on a planet that was, technically, not even part of the Empire, a seething dust bowl where humans barely clung to life, losing a long war against a planet eager to grind them into its dust. The socio-economic factors, the cultural zeitgeist, the inevitable tide of events--all these would come later.

For now, there was just the drop.

Boston Kun Haldis fought his stomach, trying not to vomit into the tight confines of his helmet. His whole world was the shrieking, shaking confines of their small gumdrop as they plummeted toward the alien planet.

The seven Wolves around him didn't even grunt under the strain as the g-forces mounted. It was a steep entry, nothing like what he had experienced in the month of training his grandfather had managed to provide before he shipped out.

"You sure this is how you want to play it, Falcon Haldis?"

It was so strange to be addressed by his rank. "Yes, I am." He was proud it came out sounding only a little strained.

"We should just level the village and save ourselves the trouble," the older man grumbled.

"Sir Glydenfeldt—"

"Chang."

Boston reminded himself that even though he was in charge, fifteen-year-olds did not curse out Wolves with twenty years of service. Before he could respond, the gumdrop danced violently as the atmosphere grew denser, and Boston bounced inside his armor, not yet tall enough to feel its cushion around him. It would do; it would have to.

"Chang, then. Yes," Boston said when he'd caught his breath. "We have no idea what happened on this planet. It is premature to assume—"

"This is only going to go one way."

"Falcon, is there any sign of the *Dakota* yet?" One of the other Wolves called out on a different channel. Boston lost a few seconds fiddling with the controls, trying to figure out how to respond.

"No," Boston replied, cursing that he couldn't identify the Wolf's voice by name. He'd only met this flock a week before, and now, they were dropping on an untamed planet. It was insanity, but it was necessary.

He braced his forearm with his other hand, trying to

steady the small screen on his wrist, reading quickly. "The *Lee* got a whiff of a distress call on the last orbit, but nothing they could decode. They will need another rev to know if the *Dakota* really is down there."

Chang grunted on their private channel. Boston waited for another recrimination, but none came, so he focused on keeping himself still in the chair as they raced downward. Their gumdrop was a shooting star as it descended across the sky. The air tore apart before them, leaving a gaping wound across the face of the planet.

The engines reached a crescendo of breathless shrieking, fighting to be louder than the relentless thundering of the air. Boston tensed, knowing what was coming. His ejector seat fired, catapulting him up into the dark night.

The fall was nothing, just a blink of an eye, and then suddenly, he was on the ground, splinter in his hands. That, he had practiced.

He gazed out into a black void. The gumdrop behind them provided the only light, leaving the night outside their circle of civilization oppressive and dark. Nothing moved, nothing rustled; there was just bare sand devoid of trees or brush.

Satisfied for the moment that there was no threat in front of him, Boston glanced to his side and saw Chang in an identical pose. It was rare for a colonial to attack a Wolf pack directly, but it happened. Especially on worlds that had not yet been taught the consequences.

Chang made his way over, the IFF overlay in his helmet painting him green. Chang's rank—a roaring wolf—appeared superimposed above his head.

"Area secure. Ready to move," the old Wolf said. "If you would care to wait here until we've—"

"No."

The Wolf froze for a few seconds. Boston could imagine the scowl he was receiving, but he didn't care. He refused to be one of the Falcons that waited, safe, away from the battle, for the Wolves under his command to do the hard work for him.

Without waiting for a reply, Boston started loping toward the village to their north. The other Wolves fell in around him, and they bounded into the night.

CHANG

The boy broke into a run as soon as they saw the village burning.

"Slag," Boston cursed, panting. "Our shock-wave!"

"Boy, wait!" Chang yelled, but Boston was ahead and accelerating.

"Get the people out and stop it spreading. All we can do." Boston gave the order on the pack channel as he jumped over the wall dividing the inside and outside of the village. Chang tore through it, not bothering to stop, trying his hardest to keep up with the boy.

There was screaming coming from the huts.

Chang noted the the crowd of villagers as he tore his way into the burning hut, following his HUD after the boy. The inside was the pitchest of black; even with his helmet lamps turned on, the smoke was opaque. His helmet did its best, flickering between settings, trying to cut through the swirls of smoke, but nothing seemed to do the trick.

Chang found a body first—hot, immobile on the floor, the face and chest sickly wet, and left it. There was more screaming ahead, even in the gloom.

A wall of flames crashed down in front of him as one of the roof beams gave out. Chang felt the impact on his back, but his armor held. Suddenly, his helmet was bathed in warnings, but he crashed forward through the curtain into a clearer pocket.

It was getting harder to breathe as the temperature in his armor skyrocketed.

Boston stumbled out of the gloom, a writhing body over his shoulder. Boston's armor was flashing red in the HUD, but he was moving.

"Damnit boy, what are you doing?"

Suddenly the woman was in his arms, and her screams doubled. She was barely even a weight in his arms.

"I need to get the rest of them," and he disappeared back into the flames.

"Damnit," Chang cursed under his breath, and took the nearest exit through what remained of a wall.

BOSTON

Only once he was sure no one else remained to be found did Boston pause to study the village. They'd dragged the living and the dead out into the square where the other colonists could minister to them. There weren't many—less than fifty—but the entire village was out in the square now, split between staring in fear at Boston and the rest of the Wolves and wailing over their fallen.

"Done playing hero?"

Boston glared at the old Wolf. "We did this."

Boston couldn't see the man's face but thought he might be shaking his head. "This isn't why we are here."

"I—" Taoiseach damn it all, Chang was right. There was a member of the *Dakota's* crew here—a noble, or a noble's implant, still transmitting after being trapped on this rock for sixteen years. Boston glanced around the tiny village again. No one was waving like they'd just been saved. No one was trying to make contact. The villagers kept their distance warily, walking close only when they had to.

"Anyone see the survivor?"

Chang's silence was the only answer.

"Fine." Boston turned and approached the largest group of colonists. A few shrank back from him in fear, but the man in front—one of the few who had been trying to deal with the fire when they'd arrived—stood his ground.

Boston keyed his external speakers. "We are from the SpaceGuard cruiser *Robert E Lee*. There is a member of a lost exploration ship here. Do any of you know where she might be? Lady Atlanta?"

Boston stared at the man in front of him. His rib cage was visible through gaps in his vest, but there was no fear in his eyes. A cool calculation, perhaps, but no fear.

"*Gamise sto, daimon.*"

Boston blinked. "Ever hear that language before, Chang?"

"Can't say I have. Did you really expect them to understand Standard?"

Boston bit back his first angry answer. "If the survivor had been living here for sixteen years, she could translate for us."

Chang harrumphed and glanced around. "I don't think there's anyone else here. They must have killed her."

Boston's helmet chimed. "Haldis here."

"Give me a status report, Falcon."

Boston gulped. Lord Ducane had a reputation as a harsh taskmaster, and Boston had seen nothing in the few weeks he'd been with the ship to disprove it.

"All the fires are put out, and we got everyone out of the buildings. Six dead so far. A couple burn-throughs in the pack's armor, but otherwise everyone, is combat-effective."

Cool silence answered him.

"Am I to understand you have been rendering aid to the village?"

The bottom dropped out of Boston's stomach.

Something wasn't right. The Pike's words were clipped even tighter than normal. "Yes, Lord."

"Put me on the pack channel."

Boston tapped his wrist controls. "Done."

"Pack, listen up," Ducane said, his voice low and rumbling. The Wolves stopped what they were doing, waiting.

"We found the *Dakota* on the last rev and sent 2nd pack down. The crew had been slaughtered. Brutally, according to Chelsea. No one left in one piece, bones smashed. Must have happened right after landing. Any sign of your survivor?"

"No, Lord." Boston's voice cracked as he said it.

"Pity. Best we can do is avenge her, then."

The sinking feeling in Boston's gut was like they were falling toward the planet again.

"What are your orders, Lord Ducane?" Chang asked. His hand was already reaching for the long-barreled splinter rifle slung across his armored back.

"As far as we can tell, you are standing in the only populated part of the planet. Whoever did this, they are standing in front of you. Put them down."

Ducane clicked off, leaving a ringing in Boston's ears.

The villagers knew. The moment Boston was able to focus on them, he saw the look. A thousand years separated from Earth, a different language, but some things were universal. Like the way you tensed before a fight.

"On my mark," Chang said, calm, like it was nothing, as the Wolves designated their targets. "Mark."

Pandemonium reigned from the first shot.

Chang's immediately dropped the leader. The man detonated like overripe fruit, throwing a wave of blood and organs in every direction. Boston couldn't move, his whole body betraying him as a second round of cracks from the other Wolves' splinter rifles blasted out around him.

The villagers scattered. They dove into huts, some screaming, some just running, getting as far away from the slaughter as they could, as quickly as they could. All except one. A girl, only a year or two younger than Boston, stood rooted to the spot, staring down at the pieces of what had been the leader of the village. She was covered in blood, a tiny island of calm in the sudden chaos. But then, she turned to look at him and, without a second's hesitation, charged.

Boston tried to get his rifle unstowed in time, but the girl was too fast. She jumped at him, a tiny knife raised. It skittered off his armor like nothing, but she tried again and again, beating her other tiny fist against his armored skin until it sprayed blood. She was so sickly thin, he could barely feel her weight.

"Falcon! Kill that thing and let's get on with it!" Chang shouted. Suddenly, he couldn't take it. His rifle fell to the ground.

Boston snatched up the girl with one hand and sprinted out into the dark.

BOSTON

She screamed at him the entire time. For five minutes he run, pushing his armor as fast as he could, as hard as he ever had before. He left the gumdrop behind him after only a minute and continued into the night of the desolate planet, desperate to get away from the killing. The girl kept up her assault on his armor, even after he slowed to a stop. Her dark hair was streaked with blood, and more sprayed from her hands as she struck him again and again.

"Calm down!"

The girl broke her sob to shriek, *"Patera, pou eisai!"*

When no response came, she resumed her efforts to punch through his armor.

He could still hear the thunderclaps in the distance, growing less and less frequent as the Wolves finished their job.

"What do you think you're doing, boy?"

Chang stalked his way around Boston, brushing past him like he was an errant pup. The old man moved with the confidence gained from forty years on the battlefield. He picked up the girl with one hand, holding her at arm's length.

"*Daimon!*" the girl screamed and began attacking Chang's arm to no avail. She clawed at the armored gauntlet, streaking it red.

"She would not have even been alive when the *Dakota* was attacked!" Tears streaked down Boston's face, and he scratched futilely at the outside of his helmet.

"And just what do you want to do, boy? Let her live till she starves to death?"

The weight of Chang's hand crashed down on Boston's shoulder. "Killing her now's a mercy."

Boston couldn't breathe, tears and gasps choking his throat.

"You'll learn, boy," Chang sighed. "If you can last, that is."

Chang drew his splinter and pressed it against the struggling girl's forehead, his other hand wrapped around her chest. "Hold still."

Boston closed his eyes and heard the click of the trigger. But no blast, no crack of lightning. Just the girl screaming.

"What the rotting slag?"

Boston opened his eyes again and watched Chang pull the trigger again, and again, nothing happened.

Chang continued cursing his rifle, probably flipping through menus, trying to find the problem, but Boston studied the girl. There was a long, ropy scar visible on her arm. She may have been older than he first thought, just malnourished.

"Chang."

"Give me a second. I'll—"

"Look at her eyes."

Chang froze for a moment and then flipped on his hand light. Violet eyes reflected back at them, clear and squinting through the bright light.

"She is a half-breed. The daughter of the survivor."

Chang growled, but released his grip on the girl a micrometer, and the girl responded by throwing an unintelligible curse at them.

"Taoiseach forsake it all, that's the last thing we need."

The rest of the Wolves had begun to assemble around them, six other hulking figures in bulky armor. The largest of them had a real wolf pelt glued to the outside of his armor, fully embracing the mythos that came with the rank of Wolf.

"Joliette!" Chang barked "Get me something to put this whelp under for the trip up to the *Lee*."

All sounds of one-sided combat had faded into the night, which was now silent except for the struggling girl's anger. Joliette withdrew a syringe from her med kit and approached.

He had to look away, wanting to be anywhere else as her screams reached a crescendo and then ceased.

"Falcon, call for a lifter. And go get your damn splinter!"

BOSTON

"Let me be clear, Lord Haldis. Identifying the girl is the only reason I am not throwing you off my ship and sending you back to the Terra."

Boston stood at attention, shivering in his sweat-soaked fatigues, but he refused to cower. Lord Ducane was on his feet, pacing the plush carpet of his office on the *Lee*. He hadn't even raised his voice, but his anger still cut like a whip.

"You risked your Wolves to render humanitarian aid to those animals," Ducane continued. "You refused to follow my orders. And you ran, leaving your pack in a combat situation."

"Begging your pardon, Lord Ducane, but the boy was just trying to spare the girl harm."

Boston started at Chang's voice and eyed him as best he could without breaking his position. Chang had somehow come out of the lifter with starched fatigues, the old bastard.

The Pike glared at Chang. It was a lie; he must be able to see that!

"As I said, that is the only reason you are getting another chance, Lord Haldis."

Boston nodded ever so slightly.

"I confess, when your grandfather asked me to take you on, I expected more. Son of the Hero of Camelot, trained by a decorated retired Wolf. I expected you to have more backbone than this!"

Boston shrank into himself as the tirade continued.

"Do you even want to be in the SpaceGuard?"

"Yes."

Ducane raised an eyebrow, but before he could say anything else, the door behind them slid open, and a middle-aged woman stepped in, manta rays flashing silver on her collar. She glanced sideways at Boston before stepping around him.

"Lady Vermont. How is our guest?"

"Sedated. They woke her when she got to the ship, but she started throwing things and had to be restrained."

Ducane tutted. "Poor thing. I keep asking myself what kind of life she must have led, surrounded by all those colonials, raised as one of them. Do we have any clues to her parentage?"

"I had her blood analyzed," Lady Vermont said. "She is the daughter of Lady Atlanta Caesonia Von Sinclair, third in command of the *Explorer Dakota*. Her father, though…" The Manta shook her head sadly. "I am afraid it appears our young Falcon was correct: Her father must have been one of the colonials down there. She is indeed a half-breed. It may have been more merciful to kill her."

"As much as it pains me to add another Sinclair to the galaxy, we did the right thing." Ducane said, "Still, Caesonia was far smarter than I ever gave her credit for. She managed to get the implant into her daughter, ensuring we would know to save her when we finally found them."

"You knew her?" Boston asked despite himself.

Ducane gave a wry smile. "I did, when we were both younger. Before Sinclair was taken over by Lady Sherah."

"How did you know she was a half-breed, Lord Haldis?" Lady Vermont asked.

"Von Braun's disease," Boston said with only a small stammer. "Violet eyes have only been observed in half-breeds—when the DNA of one parent has been mutated by centuries of interstellar flight and the DNA of the other has not."

"That was quick thinking. Well done, Lord Boston, realizing what she must be before the Wolves ate her."

Chang coughed loudly, sending his snow-white mustache quivering. Boston fought to keep his face straight and glanced back at the elderly Wolf.

Lady Vermont ignored the tension, if she noticed it at all. "The banquet is scheduled for 1800 hours tonight... assuming you still want to go through with it?"

"Of course. A young noble rescued from the clutches of colonial oppressors. A legion of those oppressors eliminated. No Wolves lost. Today was a good day for the Empire!"

"Just so," Vermont said with a nod. "Shall we get underway?"

"Yes, yes" Ducane waved, sitting down. "Paradise, as we discussed. We will be able to find someone to take her back to Sol there."

Vermont nodded and left without another word. Boston remained braced, waiting.

"If anything like that happens again, I will send you back to Sol in disgrace," Ducane said, not looking up. "You have a very limited amount of time to change your course, Falcon. I suggest you use it to do everything you can to learn what it means to be a member of the SpaceGuard."

Boston's throat was dry. In fifteen years of being entertained by stories of his father's and grandfather's exploits, the slaughter of innocent villagers—when they still didn't know anything about what had happened down on the planet—had not featured.

Still, what else could he say?

"Yes, Lord Ducane."

"Dismissed."

CHANG

Chang held his tongue as they stepped out into the cold corridor. SpaceGuard ships were always cold, but he was feeling the chill more than usual. He ached all over—not the pleasant soreness that came from good exercise, but something stiffer. Older.

Chang shook his head to clear it and focused on

Boston. The kid kept it together, though, walking without hesitating. That kind of chewing out would be hard to take, especially when so new to the service, but damn did the boy need it. Wet-behind-the-ears little welp.

All of a sudden, the boy stopped dead in the middle of the corridor. "Yes?" Chang asked.

"How do you do it?"

Chang glanced around, but the rest of the flock was occupied. They wouldn't likely be troubled. "Do what, boy?"

"Not see them as people."

Water glimmered somewhere on the boy's face as he turned quickly, trying to keep Chang from seeing it. Something pulled in Chang's chest, but he ignored it, focusing on Boston.

"They are people, lad. If they were animals, the job'd be easy."

"Then how can you not care when—" Boston started, puffing up his chest.

"I was with your dad, the day he died."

The boy deflated like Chang had slapped him. "What? I never—"

"I don't like to talk about it. But..." Chang took a breath. "I watched him hesitate. Watched him not take the shot, because he wasn't sure."

"He was a hero." The boy's voice was suddenly so small and confused, it pulled at that muscle in his chest again, but Chang had to ignore it.

"He was." Chang clasped his hand hard around the boy's shoulder. "He was. He took the next shot. The one that saved the Taoiseach, the one he knew would cost him his life. But he didn't have to die. He could have come home to you, if he'd just..."

Chang could still feel his lungs bursting, his legs

screaming as he tried, tried so hard, to reach Baltimore, but…

He shook his head, clearing away the memory, and focused on the life he could still save. "When you put on the armor, every colonial is a threat, Boston. That's what the job needs. That's what the Taoiseach demands."

"But—"

"No buts." Chang looked him as dead in the eyes as their heights allowed. The unkempt black hair was the same as Baltimore's. "I promised your mother I wouldn't let you make the same mistakes. So, you need to promise me—you take whatever compassion you feel toward them, and you bury it deep. Do it, or I send you home."

"I—"

Chang held up a finger and waited. Waited for the tiniest of nods; the boy couldn't even say it out loud yet.

"Good enough. We've a lot of work to do before we get to Paradise, and you need to make things up to the captain. We could try…"

Chang led Boston into the Wolves' den, one arm still around his shoulders.

CHAPTER TWO

Sol

BERN

Ten years passed, and the Eire Empire spun ever closer to its fall. But THE END was not yet inevitable. There would come a moment when it tipped just a little too far and could not tip any further, but that was some time off yet.

An empire, it has been said, is a pump for wealth. It concentrates the currency of the day, be it gold or kilowatt-hours, in its center, and teaches its constituents to do the same. As long as the pie grows, as long as the wealth that drives the engine continues to flow, all is well.

But it is an unstable system. This makes it easy for small disruptions to grow.

Lady Clarisse Bern Chi Nirvana had the small tram car to herself as it raced around the ring of Castle High. Half-palace and half-capital city, it sailed serenely through space, hovering high above the slate gray, abandoned planet Earth.

At least, it was usually serene. Today, she could feel the tension in the estate like a drawn bow, a coiled spring wrapped around the ring. She wouldn't have thought it possible to have such a unified mood, but here it was.

It was her first House War, after all.

Bern forced herself to focus on her slate and not on the tram car hurtling her toward the epicenter of today's crisis. Nirvana was a large house, and a standing army of analysts, policy wonks, and social climbers kept her and the other professional members of the house well-supplied with news and gossip. It was mostly research on the opposition, the other houses, but her cousin Katalia featured rather prominently. Bern, a measly four-hundredth in line, was mentioned far less often. Still, it was occasionally useful to get an idea of how she was perceived. Not pleasant, usually, but useful.

The tram dropped her on the lowest deck of Castle High, where the cargoes landed and gravity was lightest. She spared only half a glance for the cavernous room with its large receiving docks and containers hanging suspended in their cranes. Her focus was on the small crowd of Terran workers camped in front of the machinery.

The foreman, a squat woman built like a brick, got to her feet as Bern approached, already shaking her head. "My Lady, it's no use. Nothin's moving today."

"And things were going so well between us."

Tacna snorted. "Von Anker says our contract is being negotiated, and until it completes, we can't move any other houses' goods."

"As if Von Anker had anything to move." Bern pointedly drew Tacna's gaze to the nearly empty docks.

"Me and the boys are just supposed to sit and wait."

"Tacna, how long have we been working together?"

"Too rotting long. I should've retired years—"

"Is there really nothing you can do?"

Tacna glared up at Bern, black eyes hard. "My hands

are tied."

"I can arrange to supplement your retirement fund..." Bern suggested, reaching for her slate, but Tacna's face went slack.

"Unless you plan to adopt me and my whole family, don't bother. Anker'd throw us out on our collective rotting asses if I took Nirvana money. The only way to get goods moving is to close that contract."

"Slag," Bern said under her breath as Tacna retreated back into the crowd of porters gathered around a dice game. To cover, she pulled out her slate again, tapping at it to give herself time to think. Anker needed these contracts; management of the Castle High's imports was one of the last true monopolies they held. What could they be thinking?

"Good sol, cousin."

Bern glanced up from her slate at the ethereal woman that had appeared at her elbow.

"Good sol, Aspen." Taoiseach above, the last thing she needed was a witness to this. Not least a witness from House Sinclair. "How can I help the great and mighty House Sinclair today?"

Aspen's laugh was a silent, breathless thing. "Nirvana has nothing we need today, but thank you for the offer. Are we still at this insufferable charade?"

Bern rapidly tried to think of a response to her banter, but pivoted as she saw Aspen glance toward the porters and their dice.

"Do you have cargo you are trying to rescue, too?" If Sinclair joined with Nirvana in a protest, that might —

"Shipping is rather the point of the Empire," Aspen said, and Bern resisted a childish urge to stamp her foot. Fencing with Aspen, while good for her reflexes, was rarely productive. "To impede that so callously with so little gained is almost blasphemy."

"An interesting hypothesis."

Aspen shot her a rare smile. "A pity that testing it would cause so much disruption."

The fact that Aspen even considered testing it was enough to turn Bern's stomach, but Aspen had already moved on, contemplating the dockworkers with an icy chill. "Still, it seems best to deal with this problem directly. Before we tackle the rest of Von Anker."

Bern could only imagine what dealing with Von Anker would look like. House Wars had felled even the great diamond houses before. "You might find this one beyond even your considerable powers of persuasion."

"There is no such thing."

Aspen glided away, bare feet silent against the metal deck. Bern followed, wary. For all her recalcitrance this morning, Tacna was a valuable contact, and Aspen had never known mercy.

"Madam Foreman," Aspen said as Tacna rose to her feet. "You have some Sinclair family cargo that has been languishing here for more than a week."

"Could be."

Aspen nodded primly. "I would like it to be unloaded and in transport to the family apartments within the hour."

"That'd be sporting, even if I was inclined to take orders from you."

Aspen's face didn't change a micrometer. "I am sure you and your men are up to the task."

Tacna chuckled under her breath. "Sure they are. But—"

"I can even provide you some motivation."

Aspen bent double, dropping her head close to Tacna's. Bern suddenly couldn't hear a word being said, but she saw the blood drain from Tacna's cheeks, leaving her ashen. They whispered for a moment before Aspen drew back, face just as placid as before. "Will that suffice?"

Tacna swallowed heavily. Bern even thought she caught sight of tears in the hardened woman's eyes. "Yes, Lady Sinclair."

"Cousin! Would you care for me to unstick your cargo, too?" Aspen called without looking back.

Bern considered the offer for a microsecond. "What will it cost me?"

"Nothing today."

Bern needed the win. "Do it."

Tacna nodded sharply. "It'll be done."

"Good," Aspen acknowledged, nodding ever so slightly to Bern. "Foreman, do tell Lord Von Anker that the cargo will flow while he negotiates his contracts. If he has questions, he can discuss it with me."

Bern watched in awe as Aspen padded her way back to the tram station. And hoped fervently this wouldn't hurt too badly when the bill came due.

BOSTON

"Sometimes, I think it would be better for us if we just gave up on Asgard," Amman said quietly on a channel only they shared.

Boston regarded the world through his armor's viewscreen. Like so many other worlds, the poorly understood art of terraforming had not yet succeeded here, and the planet—barely hanging on when the Empire found it—was still barely hanging on. The constant rain had turned the land into a swamp and kept it in that state. For the six months he'd been posted on Asgard, the rain had never once let up.

"Pull the colonials off, shut down the terraformers, and let the dark have this world again," Amman continued.

The Hawk and Boston wore identical armor laced with Chen colors. The mud had done its best to wash that out, too.

"We would be out of a job. And Chen would be out of its best source of phosphines in the eastern half of the Empire."

Amman sniffed like he might argue, but just said, "Come on. We should get this over with."

They hiked along the ridgeline to where the village had been carved into the rock of a cliff face. You had to, here; otherwise, everything you built just sank into the mud or was washed away.

The rest of the flock was already there, getting people organized. Chelsea was particularity enthusiastic, shouting over his armor's speakers.

"Surprised you made it down for this," Boston asked without asking as they joined the line of Wolves on the edge of the perimeter. As a Hawk, Amman was technically in charge of all the SpaceGuard on this Taoiseach-forsaken rock. Though, a larger planet would have had a higher-ranked Guardsman in charge.

"Our dear Lord Under-Governor, beloved of all his subjects, insisted that I be here in person to make sure his message went over well. He will be here before long."

"Ah."

A Fox, distinguishable from the wolves around him by the litheness of his armor dashed up and saluted Amman, fist on chest. "Lord Chen, we are ready."

"Double wound?"

"Yes, Lord."

Amman dismissed the Fox with a wave. "Wait for my signal."

Switching back to their private channel, Amman said,

"Hopefully, the little slag will be on time."

In the privacy of his helmet, Boston enjoyed a chuckle, but he kept his eyes swiveling, trying to spot any problems in the crowd. Things had been restless everywhere on the planet lately, but here most of all. For the moment, there was just sullen anger, beaten down by the rain.

"This needs to go smoothly," Amman said after a few minutes. "We are trying very hard not to make an enemy of Chi Colombia right now."

Boston blinked. Amman was a Chen, the same family who had patronage on all of Asgard.

"Meaning what, exactly?"

Amman sighed. "Sending the little twerp home in disgrace will not make the family happy."

While they waited for the under-governor, Boston circulated through the flock as they kept careful guard. After ten years with them, he knew every Wolf by name, could read every movement, even through their armor. Chelsea, a foot taller than everyone else, was cracking jokes. The way three of the Wolves all paused at the same time, chuckling together, gave him away.

Chang was last, sweeping a row of carved dwellings again. They had strict orders to get everyone assembled before the under-governor arrived.

"Any surprises?" Boston asked as they passed. Protesters had been showing up more often these days, sent by someone going by the name Ember. An agitator. A troubling development on a world like this.

"Nothing. Smooth op, for once."

"Mmm."

Eventually, the lift fans became audible, and Boston and Chang made their way back to the little square at the base of the village. Without needing to discuss it, they stopped at corners together to check them, varied their pace with practiced ease. Their movements were effortless, which just gave Boston more time to worry.

The mood at the square had soured. The crowd was restless; standing out in the rain for twenty minutes would do that to anyone. The under-governor had chosen to bring four colonial porters with him from the capital, each holding the corner of a tarpaulin over him, making things worse.

Lord Istanbul Chi Colombia was only a little older than Boston. He was built broad, like a carrot, with wide shoulders and a narrow waist—a dashing if incompetent cavalier. His tunic faintly shone neon red, the only splash of color as far as the eye could see, and it drew every eye to him. As intended, Boston was sure.

Istanbul said a few inaudible words to Amman and then cleared his throat. Hidden speakers brought his voice to the whole clearing at stone-vibrating intensity.

"Subjects of the Empire of Eire, I have a solemn duty to discharge today," Istanbul started. There was nothing solemn about the man. Gleeful enthusiasm radiated from him, enough to make Boston's stomach turn.

"No one has confessed to the horrible crimes committed here only a month ago. No loyal subjects of the Empire have been able to ferret out the perpetrators. Murders."

"'E got what was coming to him!" came a shout from somewhere in the crowd.

"So, it falls to me to mete out a just punishment to this village."

Boston stiffened and glanced at Amman standing next to Istanbul. It was absolutely not in Istanbul's power to decide to levy collective punishment like this. He must have consulted with the governor's office. He must have.

"As per my authority as under-governor, I have

decided that this village is to be razed to the ground, the malice here stamped out."

The only noise was the rain. It should have been impossible for that large a crowd to be that silent. It was the kind of silence that beat against Boston's ears and made him unsnap the splinter from its holster across his back.

"Let the Taoiseach's will be done!" Istanbul extended a hand.

The explosives lit in order, just as the Foxes had designed. It didn't take much—small charges in absolute terms—to send the entire carved facade of the village collapsing in on itself. Boston's sonic filters cut in, making the stone fall in silence, but he could feel the rumble, the ground shaking as the rock slid and toppled off the cliffside, leaving the square untouched.

Istanbul had gone slightly pale, watching the explosions from such a close, unarmored distance, but he rallied as the echoes of the blast fell away, leaving the rain to splatter down on a new collection of stones.

The crowd got to its feet slowly. Boston could see injured, the red of blood momentarily bright before it was covered by swirling dust and rain.

"Let that be a warning to everyone who would dare raise a hand against a Noble of Eire!" Istanbul declared, his voice shaking slightly. "Now, go. Disperse among the nearby villages and—"

It was a single shriek. A single, bloodcurdling, wordless shriek, buried deep inside the knot of colonials, and the crowd surged forward.

Boston didn't hesitate. His rifle was out in his hands before they had made it more than a few steps, and he squeezed the trigger without thought.

BERN

Full-size hummingbirds did a hectic dance in Bern's stomach, but she refused to let any of that discord break her calm appearance as she maneuvered her way through Castle High.

She recited her arguments as she traced the careful path to Montana's townhouse, ticking them off on her fingers. How Montana would be better off saving her resources for a better time. How discretionary spending, such as it was, was falling. How she needed to find a more secure support system. The arguments all made sense... until Bern imaged Montana's reactions to any of them.

The little townhouse she was destined for had nothing to mark it as special from the outside, just the scarlet-and-silver pattern on the door that marked it as owned by a small, unimportant house, but Bern paused at the threshold, readying herself. Her hand at the door was enough to get her access, and Bern slipped in.

The room was comfortable enough, fashionably done up with colorful tapestries in earthy colors, but it was dominated by detritus. A pair of low divans were submerged under sheets of bubble wrap and canvas; the door to the kitchen completely blocked with lumber. Crates loomed like icebergs, their tops off, spilling packing material on the floor.

And then, of course, in the center of it all was Montana.

Augustine Sinclair, the Lady Von Montana, was one of those who, like Katalia, managed to look beautiful without trying. Shorter than most nobles, with dark brown hair and elegant, if understated, features, she was up to her knees in packing materials at the moment, attacking one of the unopened crates with vigor. She wore a simple shirt and pants with a pattern Bern didn't recognize. It was something more likely to be found on a common Terran shopkeep than a diamond-ranked woman running her own house, but the outfit managed to have a charm all its own. She'd left her hair down, and it draped fetchingly over her shoulders, slightly unkempt from her exertions.

"I see your cargo made it up."

Montana snapped around, revealing her best feature: a pair of violet eyes. One of the many things she'd received from her colonial father that made her unlike anyone Bern had ever met.

"Your doing, I assume?"

Bern nodded, reveling in Montana's simple presence and letting no hint of that reach her face. "I did run into your cousin, though. Our cousin."

"Which one?"

"Aspen."

Montana's tool skittered off the top of the crate she was trying to open, leaving her leaning on it ungracefully. "Her," Montana panted before attacking the crate again. "I thought I was done with her when I divorced. And yet."

"And yet," Bern repeated, raising an eyebrow. "You know, there are people we can hire for this."

"This is far more fun," her friend grunted, and with a heave, the top crate's lid bounced up. Montana's face was flushed with triumph, a slight sheen of sweat making her olive skin glow.

"I can see that. Hang on." Bern reached out and uncoiled a scrap of packing material that had become tangled in Montana's tresses.

"How did that get there?"

Bern shrugged. "These things can happen when you decide to take things into your own hands, dear." Her brow furrowed. "What is this?" Bern took another step forward and ran a hand over the fabric of Montana's forearm. "Did you import this?"

"Maybe."

"So soft! What is it?"

"Bamboo fibers."

"Is that an animal?"

"A plant. Like a tree, but smaller. I found this small area of Asgard where they grow it a few years ago. I fell in love."

"I can see why. Are you going to sell it?"

"No, it costs too much. Even change-fabric is cheaper once you factor in how much it would take to grow a reasonable supply of it. I will have to stick to selling art…for a while, anyway."

"Too bad." Bern ran her hand along Montana's upper arm again. "This feels divine."

Montana caught Bern's hand in her other and squeezed it gently before removing it from her shoulder. Bern sought somewhere to put her eyes and dropped them to the crate in front of them. A painting had been revealed—all soft, muted colors, pastels of a group of people. A dignified, if rounded woman in blue and scarlet was holding a mostly nude baby, walking on what appeared to be clouds. There was something peculiar about them, unreal, but that distracted her attention from the figures in the background, which appeared to be more children. Though these had wings.

"Is this…?"

Montana picked it up gently and nodded. "A painting of a copy of a photograph from Earth."

"And pagan," Bern spoke over her. "And illegal."

"Mhm."

Bern waited for an explanation as Montana gently moved the painting to rest on a free scrap of table. "Already sold."

That made her blink. "How much?"

Montana named a scandalously high figure, and Bern immediately understood. "And how much of that was consumed in bribes getting it here?"

"Less than you think. Imported from Kazakhstan."

"I may make you into a shark after all," Bern said with pride. "And I am increasing my cut."

Montana smiled back, but her face shifted. "But you came here to tell me something. What was it?"

Bern did her best to lean herself elegantly against a crate. "You can guess."

"Clarisse, I can't stop."

"Not stop," she corrected gently. "Just… delay things. A little."

"No."

"Augustine…"

"A House War is coming?"

"The House War is here." Her slate was in her hands without thinking. "The docks were a mess, and it took far more than it should have to get your crates moving. Jordana is planning on having the Nirvana Bank restrict lending, raise interest rates, and convert its investments to cash, if we can, before the market crashes."

"So?"

"No one is going to spend anything on art now! There has not been a House War in a generation. No one knows what is going to happen. A recession is the best we can hope for. It could be far worse."

Montana didn't care, Bern could see.

"You can just do what you have been doing, sell directly: build your reputation."

Montana shook her head. "It will not make enough."

"It makes enough to live on, and —"

"And that is not enough!"

Bern tried to see past her friend's anger but couldn't.

Montana could be like that, her anger coming and going like a comet on a hyperbolic trajectory, barreling through the inner system in sudden glory before sweeping away just as quickly.

"What is it you want to do, Augustine?"

"I want to go home."

Finally, Bern understood. And her heart broke.

Montana smiled the tiniest of small smiles. "Worry not. It will be a short trip. But I have to know."

Bern wanted to lunge across the space between them and wrap the other woman in her arms, but she resisted. With difficulty.

"We read the reports together. They—"

"They were written by slobbering Wolves who didn't care what they were leaving behind!" Her whole being radiated anger. "Fucking SpaceGuard, writing for the medal. They knew no one would ever go back and check. Well, I intend to. I am going to go back there and prove we had nothing to do with the deaths of that survey crew."

"We could just wait," Bern tried again, but Montana shook her head violently.

"Every year, it will get harder to figure out what happened. No. Ten years is long enough."

"Chartering a whole liner—"

"I know what it costs," Montana insisted with that streak of boldness, of fire, that made her magnetic. "This is too important."

She would not be moved—not that Bern had really expected her arguments to work. But she'd had to try. If Montana was determined, it was all Bern could do to try to help. And be there when it all came crashing down. Her plan couldn't work, but Montana was her own woman. She needed to learn that for herself.

"I will help you as much as I can. Organizing, keeping

track of your finances, whatever I can do."

Montana reached out and squeezed Bern's hand. "Thank you. Really, Clarisse. You have no idea what it means to me."

"I have some."

BOSTON

"Recalled!"

Blood and mud still splattered the front of his armor. Sometime during the flight back to the capital, he'd removed his helmet, and Boston still regretted it. All the Wolves stank and would until they got their armor off. Chang was off somewhere trying to find a press strong enough to yank apart Chelsea's damaged chest piece.

Amman had found time to change out of his armor. He nearly vibrated with indignation but nodded. "Your next assignment finally came through."

Boston froze. "Olancha?"

Amman nodded again. "Baghdad finally did it."

It was the crown jewel of the Empire, the largest colony, deep in the south. He could have sung.

"Finally!"

"I want to ask you not to go."

The room seemed to shrink a little as Boston refocused on Amman. "Are you serious?"

"Boston, we could you use here."

"After that? The under-governor just nearly got us all killed for some political stunt!"

"And he will be on his way back to Castle High in disgrace just as soon as I can get an audience with the governor," Amman said, hands up. "Please, Boston, he will not be a problem for long."

"What happened to not pissing off Chi Colombia?"

"Like that matters now!"

Amman had been an excellent superior,. They'd been

friends, even. But Olancha! It was the dream posting, a place where the SpaceGuard was actually needed, not just prison guards.

"We need your help finding Ember."

Boston grimaced. "You do not need me for that. When someone finally turns him in, you can send in a pack or two. This is Olancha we are talking about!"

"I know." He sat down on the small bench in Boston's quarters, shaking his head. "I know."

"Baghdad must have pulled in so many favors. Dearworth owes us nothing."

"And you can hardly offend them," Amman said tiredly. "Not right now."

"Not offending Chen is just as important."

"Chen will be fine." Amman dismissed his comment with a wave of his hand. "This was me asking."

Suddenly, Amman was on his feet again. "Pack your gear. The *Emperor Savoy* seals locks in the morning, Find yourself a lifter and get up there."

"If I could bring you with me…"

"Ha," Amman grunted. "Chen and Dearworth are far from that close, even if we are better than Nirvana and Sinclair. Go with my blessing. But go."

<h3 style="text-align:center">BAGHDAD</h3>

Baghdad Kun Haldis, head of House Haldis, took a bite from what should have been a truly excellent steak to buy time.

He could afford steak. With only two blood members, Haldis could afford to spend on such luxuries, but he rarely allowed himself it. So, he'd jumped at the chance to eat at Castle High's best restaurant on someone else's dime.

Despite that, it tasted like nothing. The blandest algae couldn't have tasted worse. This was close to the worst thing that could have happened.

Jame Riyadh Von Dearworth sat across the table. Harder and older than when they'd served together in the Olancha campaigns, he commanded the SpaceGuard now. Nominally.

"I assume someone in your family objected?" Baghdad asked, finally.

Riyadh twitched his head, eyes meeting Baghdad's levelly. The one thing Riyadh had never done was shirk what he considered his duty.

"It is as good an assumption as any." Riyadh sighed heavily, and polished the corner of his mouth with a silk napkin. "In truth, I try to stay out of the family politics. But Governor Aadvik let me know that Boston's services were no longer required on Olancha."

"His liner was due to leave yesterday evening."

"It did," Riyadh confirmed. "I was informed this morning."

There was no way to contact a liner while in flight. Boston was hurtling back toward Sol, expecting a hero's welcome before continuing his travel south to Olancha. Now…

"A calculated insult?"

Baghdad would never have asked someone else that out loud, but Riyadh was different. Which was probably why he had been blindsided by his own house.

"To you, to me, to Haldis in general, all and none." Riyadh sighed again. "Taoiseach forsake them all, anyway."

Riyadh tossed back the rest of his glass and raised his middle finger for another. Baghdad remembered the day he'd lost his index.

"What can be done?"

"I am so tired, Baghdad. Tired of trying to keep this

pack of dogs moving in the right direction. Not one of them remembers what we are trying to do out there! Certainly not put house politics above the mission."

Baghdad sat back slightly, re-evaluating the commander. He looked tired. It was perhaps the first time Baghdad could remember seeing him look thus, outside a foxhole.

"We still need you to show them the way."

"I know. No rest for the competent." Riyadh shook his head. "I am confident you will find something for Boston, old friend. But you will have to do it alone. One Falcon, however capable, is not worth a fight at the moment."

"Are things that bad in the colonies?"

"Things are that bad here." Riyadh's slate chimed, and he got to his feet and offered a hand. "That is all the time I have, but I owed you telling you in person."

Baghdad shook the hand on automatic and contemplated his plate long after Riyadh had left. The House War would break into the open any day now. Baghdad ran down his list of options, silently weighing them. The diamond houses had the most planets, the most alliances, the most chances.

Haldis had survived this long by being independent, though it had been difficult to resist becoming a vassal to a major house. Any of them could provide what Haldis needed, but the price would be steep.

Baghdad grimaced to himself and began to plot their way through this latest mess.

CHAPTER THREE

Homecoming
BOSTON

Baghdad was waiting the moment Boston stepped off the liner on Port Chittagong.

After so long in the colonies, Boston couldn't believe the number of people crammed into the space. Port Chittagong was the largest estate orbiting Earth, larger even than the Taoiseach's palace, Castle High. Chittagong was more than half a mile across, but in the moments after a liner docked, it was as crowded and noisy as any colonial market.

The sound, though—voices echoing in the metal wheel—told him he was home.

"Come, now. We've work to do," Baghdad said, making Boston refocus.

Baghdad set off into the crowd, setting a blistering pace even with his cane, and Boston followed him, swinging his bag over his shoulder.

Boston didn't have to check to make sure Chang was following; the tirade of curses under his breath was enough. Chang never enjoyed returning to Sol.

They hadn't managed to make it more than a few paces into the crowd before a woman's voice called out, "Lord Boston!"

Boston turned and was immediately engulfed by the fashionable traveling dress of Lady Eiravati—and then, by her hungry mouth. He kissed her back with vigor and managed to get one arm around her back for balance. Chang sighed somewhere behind them and took Boston's bag off his shoulder, letting him wrap the young woman in another arm.

She released him reluctantly, panting breathlessly, and stared up at him with hazel eyes flecked with mirth. "I just had to see you and say au revoir!"

He kissed her by way of reply, and she rose on her toes for him.

"You know, I may be at Terra for a while," he said once she let him breathe again. "We might find time to meet for a drink."

She giggled like wind chimes in his ear. "I will think about it. I want to give my husband a chance, at least. Who knows, though?"

"As you wish," Boston said and meant it. But he chuckled in that low-pitched rumble that he knew Eiravati appreciated.

Eiravati giggled again and licked her lips. "Next time, I trust you will introduce yourself promptly! Rather than make me wait half the voyage for you."

Boston couldn't help but grin. "Of course, my Lady."

"Good man," she said with a coy smile. "Now, I do need to be going."

She disappeared into the crowd as quickly as she had appeared.

Baghdad was far ahead of them by now, but Boston knew the way. The family limo would be parked at the same small, out-of-the-way dock it was every time he came home, rare as they were.

Suddenly, Boston's footsteps were swallowed up by plush carpets and elaborate hangings, significantly more refined than those in the more public areas. There were even red upholstered chairs sitting every few feet along the corridor, arranged like sitting rooms next to every hatch.

Baghdad had already stepped into the limo, but the smartly dressed, ebony-skinned young Terran in Haldis livery was immediately recognizable. The boy did his best to keep a straight face but lost it the moment Boston roared, "Hannigan!"

Hannigan covered the fifteen or so feet to Boston in a mad run and slammed into Boston's chest, setting him back on his heels. Boston clapped the young man on the back. "By the Taoiseach, Hannigan, you must be a foot taller than when I last saw you!"

Boston held the boy at arm's length, studying him critically. He had the slightly pinched look of a boy doing a lot of growing in a short amount of time and was thin as a weed, shooting up toward Boston's height with a thin, wiry frame. "Since when does your grandmother let you out of the estate?"

Hannigan smirked. "I'm almost at my majority. She doesn't have a choice. Either she gives me interesting things to do, or I'll join the SpaceGuard next year."

"I bet you would make Wolf in less than ten years."

Chang growled, but he tousled the boy's hair affectionately anyway. "Twelve, I think. He needs to put on a few more pounds before he'll be able to make the best use out of Wolf armor."

"We'll see."

"Boston!" Baghdad barked from the confines of the

limo, and Hannigan stepped back, still grinning.

"Coming, Grandfather." Boston glanced around, looking for the expected fourth member of the party. "Can you tell your mother we are ready to shove off? Or did you hire a pilot?"

Hannigan grinned wider.

"Slag." Chang shot Boston an imploring look. "You're not going to let him fly, are you?"

Boston shrugged. "He got the limo out here from the estate, apparently."

"We're all going to die," Chang sighed even as he marched up and into the limo.

"After you, Lord Kun Haldis." Hannigan waved a hand.

"Careful, you," Boston said, laughing, and stepped into the limo.

BAGHDAD

Baghdad reluctantly dropped into his favorite armchair, massaging his hip. Despite the pain, he preferred to be on his feet, though he could stand it for shorter and shorter periods. Hannigan and Boston were still reminiscing, so out of habit, he pulled out his slate. He tolerated the social reports from various gossip columns, describing every detail of the various parties the younger generation spent their time on. He read business prospectuses, transcripts of earnings calls, anything he could get his hands on. Even a few briefings from the colonies he wasn't supposed to have.

Boston entered the room with his customary energy, arm in arm with young Hannigan. His grandson had finally finished filling out, and the three years since they'd last seen each other had apparently been good to Boston. He was as tall as his father, though none of them were tall by the standards of nobles, and the boy had taken the time to part his close-cropped black hair to the side.

"Take us out, Hannigan."

As usual, even that was enough to excite the boy. "Yes, Baghdad." In a flash, he was gone to the cockpit.

Boston made his way to the drink cart and poured one for himself and one for Chang, then settled on the divan across from Baghdad. The mirth had deserted his grandson.

"I know they took Olancha away," Boston said quietly, facing his drink. "We got a bit of news when we got to Aztlán."

"I'm sorry, boy."

Boston waved a hand, shaking it off. "Where am I headed instead? Back to Asgard? They still have not been able to track down—"

"Filled."

Boston nodded, expecting it. "Then where?"

"Here. For now."

Boston looked dumbstruck.

The limo disconnected from Port Chittagong, and suddenly, they were weightless. Baghdad gripped the handle of his seat, keeping himself steady, and managed to snatch his suddenly drifting whiskey glass in his other hand. Then, the engines caught, and gravity returned, heavier than before.

"Here?" Boston finally asked. "Why?"

"Finding another posting for you has proven... difficult. With the House War, the price in favors has risen dramatically."

"The Guard doesn't need Falcons somewhere?" Chang asked.

Baghdad shook his head. "Recruitment has been down for years. The Guard officially wants to put you on the beach, half-pay."

Boston shivered at that, and Baghdad sighed heavily. He'd always known it would be a tough sell.

"You are going to need to settle down and produce an heir at some point. This is as good a time as any."

Silence greeted his statement. Boston's mouth had dropped open slightly, his warm black eyes wide.

"You aren't serious," Chang said.

"I am."

"No, you are not," Boston spoke up.

The limo's engines lit, pressing all of them back down into their seats, necessitating another pause while they each shepherded their glasses back into a semblance of order.

"Boston—" Baghdad started, but the little wretch cut him off.

"No, Grandfather, we had a deal. Thirty-five—that is what we said."

"We did, but that was before—"

"What would I do? Sit on my ass and—"

"And focus on running this house!" Baghdad regretted shouting as soon as it left his mouth, but the boy could be so naive. "I spend all my time trying to navigate through this morass we call an empire, and I could use your help."

"Baghdad..."

"If we are to get through this House War in one piece, we need allies," Baghdad said. "And I refuse to tie us to one of the big houses. I've worked too hard for too long to keep us our own house. We could have sold out. But I made sure we didn't. And that costs. We need to be strong enough on our own so they can't crush us in a long weekend. And that means a marriage."

"No," Boston said stiffly.

"Boy."

"I said no."

Baghdad stared down his grandson, seeing every bit of himself and his son in the boy, refusing to give an inch. The silence stretched as neither of them yielded. Baghdad cast around again for another idea, another way of ensuring the house his son had earned with his life would survive.

"There is one thing we might try, then. There is one person more influential than the rest of the houses put together."

"The Taoiseach."

Baghdad nodded. "Getting him to interfere won't be easy, though." Baghdad checked his slate. "Tomorrow night, we're invited to the Founding Day festivities. The Taoiseach will be there, and I can get us an audience. Asking for a boon like this, though…"

"Alright." Boston finished his glass. "Better than nothing."

CHANG

The Founding Day celebration filled the Taoiseach's Great Hall, the largest open space on Castle High. It was everything Chang had missed while in the colonies, a target-rich environment poised for the taking. That he'd get to enjoy, as soon as their business was done.

Chang walked a careful step behind Boston as the boy glanced everywhere, trying to take it all in. Baghdad didn't give them a moment's pause, though. Hopefully, this business with getting their new assignment would be done soon, and they could enjoy what Chang sincerely hoped was a brief stopover. As entertaining as this sort of thing was, more than a night of it at a time wore on him.

"Lord Kun Haldis!"

Chang's eyes darted toward the source of the shout, then relaxed a millimeter as Pike Ducane stepped out of the crowd. The years had not been kind to their former commander; he was thinner, as was his hair, with none of the bearing Chang expected from the man. Still, he was dressed impeccably in his SpaceGuard blacks with the Pike crest on either shoulder.

"Lord San Wo," Baghdad greeted the Pike with a deft incline of his head. He greeted him as one house lord to another, unlike Boston, who saluted.

"I wanted to give you one last chance to be reasonable."

Chang's eyebrows rose, and Baghdad's back stiffened. "We have been, Lord."

"After everything I have done to help House Haldis over the years, you—"

The low, sonorous notes of bagpipes interrupted, and Chang swung to face the raised dais across the room where the Taoiseach would appear. After a pause, he strode out to the edge of the dais, his face projected into the corners of the room, magnified so he glowered down at the crowd from three or four directions.

"Lords and Ladies, Sirs and Madams," the Taoiseach began, "welcome. We are here, as I am sure you all know, to celebrate the one-hundred-and-ninety-sixth year of our Empire. Almost two hundred years ago tonight, Adele Van Eire accepted the surrender of the last of the Jovian colonies and made Terra one again.

"Before Adele's rise to power... those were dark times, indeed, far beyond the memory of even the oldest and wisest gathered here today," the Taoiseach continued, voice gathering strength. "But each of us should try, here and now, to picture what those times must have been like. Humanity was separate. Disjointed. Meager little pockets, eking out meager little existences in separate little estates. Built into asteroids, scattered to the outer planets, looking down on a Mother Earth abandoned, uninhabitable after centuries of democratic excess. Her people, humanity, had fled across the stars, abandoning her for new worlds, leaving Earth to die. Only the faithful remained here at Terra. And they had fallen so far.

"Can you even imagine it?" the Taoiseach asked, looking around. "To think our great, galaxy-spanning Empire started there. But start there, it did. And when Adele Eire was born in the outer reaches of the solar system, when she saw her true purpose revealed, she did not hesitate. She would bring all the tiny pockets of true Terrans together, and a golden tide spread to encompass the entire system—every planet, estate, and hollowed-out asteroid. She conquered them all, with treaties, alliances, economic might, and the thunder and crash of Wolves and forced decompression.

"And as Sol swelled, free from divisions, from tariffs, from inefficiencies, humanity—for the first time since the fall of Earth—humanity prospered. And their old stories were reborn, the dream of taking back Earth, shaping the world back into what it once was.

"When her daughter, Empress Venus, discovered the secret knowledge of interstellar transport on Luna, all Terrans were given another duty. Slipping the bounds of light, they could travel not just to the stars, like the Forsakers, but back again. We would reclaim those pitiful humans who had lost hope and left the mother-planet. We would bring them back under one true rule. With open arms where we were met with open arms and with fire and fury where we were met with reticence, we would drag them back, out of the dark and into the light!"

Scattered clapping started in a corner of the hall, and Chang raised his hands to join in after only a small delay.

"And we have succeeded. Wherever our ships fly, we see only worlds that have heard the call of the mother-planet and given up their bounties toward making Earth great again. Every human, be it noble, Terran, or colonial, is united in the dream of returning to the mother-world. In the seven generations since Empress Venus led us away from Sol, there has never been a moment when Adele's dream of reclaiming Earth was closer to a reality.

"But our task is not yet complete. There is much left to do, many more hard roads to travel, before her dream is a reality," the Taoiseach continued. "On this, the anniversary of our Unification, all of us must recommit to achieving that dream. Recommit ourselves. Our families. Our fortunes. All to accomplishing this dream."

The scattered clapping started again, louder than before.

"Thank you all again for being here tonight. Please, enjoy yourselves. Celebrate our renewed dedication to the reclamation of Earth."

The moment the Taoiseach had stopped speaking, Ducane drew closer and continued, "And after I was able to take Boston, an untried Falcon, into my command."

"That debt has been paid."

Boston stepped forward like he might speak, but Chang rested a hand gently on his arm.

"The Taoiseach is going to take the *Lee* away from me."

"I can't give you funds that don't exist."

"It has been in my family sixty years.;" It came out as a whisper.

Baghdad shook his head. "I am sorry, Rio. We can't help. Leave the *Lee* behind and get your house in order." His tone was harsh, but not cruel. "Get your house in order, and you can get it back. Eventually."

Baghdad took another step forward, and Chang towed

Boston behind Baghdad. They had an appointment to make.

BERN

Bern did her best to tune out the crowd around them, but it was more difficult than usual. The Great Hall was packed for the Founding celebration, and almost every house was present in a riot of colors. But instead of people-watching or politicking Bern kept her attention focused on Montana and her increasingly futile attempt to make a sale.

"You really want me to invest in someone who sells this poorly?" Katalia asked into her champagne glass, her voice pitched low enough that only Bern could hear her.

Bern flushed, crackles of anger in her stomach, but breathed through it. Katalia, as blunt and indecorous as she could be, was rarely wrong. "I believe in what she is trying to build."

"Of course, darling."

Bern ignored the disappointment emanating from her cousin and focused on Montana. She had many things going for her. Bern had chosen a lavender dress with a high collar for her friend—simple, elegant, and of the more conservative bent that Montana generally consented to wear. It was stunning and got her enough attention from the ruby-wearing noble Katalia had pointed out. But she was losing him, descending into lecture even as Bern watched.

"Is she good in bed, at least?"

A strangled squeak left Bern's lips, causing Katalia to burst into a peal of laughter. "Oh, Bernie. Not even that far along?"

"Apparently not." Now, her face was burning.

"As much as I wish I could help..." Katalia said.

"Kat, please."

Katalia raised an eyebrow. "Low blow."

Bern almost never used the pet name she'd had for her cousin when they were little, though Katalia seemed incapable of calling her anything other than 'Bernie', especially in public. Bern would do anything in her power to make tonight go well, if she could.

"You have it bad, I see."

"Should you, perhaps, be focusing on your assignments?"

Katalia threw her head back and laughed, a tinkling sound that drew every male eye within a hundred feet. "There is a Falcon that just got in from Aztlán that I mean to speak with. You have the much harder job."

Bern spared a glance for the group she'd been assigned to get close to. Lord Erland Von Dearworth was still chatting amiably with some lower-ranked nobles, waiting for her. For the moment.

"Do I need to remind you what Jordana will say if you miss the mark? Again?"

"I remember," Bern said tiredly, but still, she hesitated. Montana was still trying, in vain.

The butterfly's wings of sparkles around Katalia's eyes twinkled. "Why not pay for it yourself? She would be very appreciative, I am sure."

Bern gripped her calm with bloodless fingers and glanced toward Lord Erland again. "Menodora and Jordana refuse to let me play with this kind of money."

Katalia tutted. "You are far better at it than I."

"Nevertheless."

"This probably will not help you get her into bed. She seems far too proud for that."

Bern bit back a stronger retort. Her cousin, as dear as she was, could be painfully aggravating at times. "How often am I wrong?"

"Almost never." Katalia turned to look back at Montana, who was striding back toward them, dejected but determined. Bern trusted her shadowcasters to keep her gaze hidden; she couldn't help but drink in every detail as Montana approached. The way the lights shown through her hair, almost like a halo. The way her olive skin seemed to glow. Her makeup's simple elegance.

"Did you succeed?" Katalia asked, her voice pitched light and airy. It was the voice she used when she wanted to deceive.

"No," Montana said immediately.

"Oh? Well, the San Vanderbilt have never been known for their taste. Better luck next time, Augie."

"If you have made your decision…"

"Almost," Katalia said. "Though I am torn. Bernie has given me all the logical reasons, and someone else—like my mother or my sister—might believe them. But not me. I know Bernie better than that. Now is not the time to be taking risks on side projects, and yet, you convinced her to talk to me anyway. Why is this so important to you—and by extension, her?"

"Clarisse has always been too good a friend to me."

Katalia waggled a finger back at Montana. "I know why this is important to Bernie. Why is it so important to you?"

"Have you ever traveled the colonies?"

Bern stayed quiet.

"Just to Eden. Not my scene."

"Well then, you won't have seen the bazaars. In nearly every capital city, where the lifters touch down, there's this huge market for people trying to sell things to the Terrans getting off the liners. Sometimes, they've traveled for months just to meet the liner schedule.

"They're always small things. Trinkets. Slaved over.

Sometimes beautiful. On Lanka, there was a man with some of the finest metalwork you have ever seen. I could tell that he spent weeks on each one. He put so much thought into matching a gem to a piece. They were all coppers and tins, quartz and topaz, hematite, maybe just a hint of silver.

"I bought his whole stand. It was pocket change. But the look in his eyes when I did?" Montana shook her head and broke off. "I want to be able to make a difference for people. And this is the best way I know how."

Bern had to tear her eyes away from Montana to study her cousin, but Katalia was far more disciplined. Bern couldn't tell much from her expression, even knowing her for almost her whole life.

"Noble," Katalia finally said.

"I try," Montana said and made a minuscule curtsy.

"However, an art gallery does not seem to fit with the rest of my assets at the moment," Katalia said with sudden finality, letting the air out of Bern's hope. "I wish you luck, though. If you will excuse me, I see someone I need to talk to."

Katalia pranced away without a backward glance, so she missed the flash of anger in Montana's face before it was schooled away behind blandness. Still, her tone was cutting. "Spiteful witch."

"Katalia treats that as a compliment."

"Spiteful or witch?" Humor returned to tickle the corners of Montana's mouth.

"Both."

BOSTON

"Baghdad, the Lord Haldis, and his grandson, Boston Dublin, heir to House Haldis, and factor!"

The bottom dropped out of Boston's stomach as the herald announced them and he took the last two steps onto the large dais containing the throne.

"Remember, let me do the talking," Baghdad whispered faintly before dropping to one knee. Boston followed microseconds after him, and he heard Chang grunt as his knees hit the ground.

The gold-skinned herald stepped back, her eyes black with shadowcasters, and then, the Taoiseach stepped into her place. Boston's shadowcasters had to dim as the man stepped into view, so bright was the halo of the ceremonial armor the Taoiseach wore. It was brushed gold, glowing with an undisclosed science.

Command radiated from the man. He was tall, with flaming red hair and a chin that could have taken an orbital strike without dimpling. He too wore shadowcasters, dark enough that his eyes appeared as two bottomless black pools set into his ruddy face.

"Rise, House Haldis."

Boston sprang to his feet and offered an arm to Baghdad, who growled slightly but took it. His grandfather had changed into his old Wolf's uniform, the twin of Chang's but with twice as many campaign ribbons across his chest.

"Welcome, welcome," the Taoiseach said, pacing a step and spreading an arm wide. "We are all grateful you were able to celebrate with us tonight. I had heard your liner was almost delayed coming from Aztlán?"

Boston found his voice with only a moment's hesitation. "It was nothing that the technicians could not settle quickly."

Baghdad gave the barest nod.

"Of course." The Taoiseach turned a micrometer toward Baghdad. "He is everything you promised, Lord Haldis."

"Thank you, your grace."

"And is that Sir Glydenfeldt I see still by your side?"

Boston turned a quarter degree, enough to see Chang nod sharply, one step behind him.

"One wonders… if Sir Glydenfeldt had been standing closer to your father, defending mine, might your father still be alive?"

"Either I would have saved Sir Baltimore, or I'd be dead with him," Chang answered stiffly.

Taoiseach Dublin nodded sagely. "I suspected. Are you happy to be back at Terra?"

"Your grace, I am happy to serve wherever the Empire requires." Boston ignored Baghdad's suddenly urgent gaze and plowed on, "Though I seem to have found myself without a posting in the colonies."

Discord creased the Taoiseach's placid face. "The colonies," he dismissed with a gesture. "The colonies are cowed. There is no glory left to be won out there. No, Lord Boston, here is where you belong. Helping us retake Earth from the mistakes of our ancestors."

"Of course, your grace. But—"

"When does young Boston take over the stewardship of House Haldis?"

If Boston could have made the deck open up and swallow him, he would have. If he could have jumped naked, into a pit of howling wolves—real ones—he would have. He might even have traded away his Falcon crest to be anywhere else.

Baghdad recovered, making it look effortless. "Not too much longer, your grace. Boston wishes to concentrate on his career in the Guard for the moment."

"Lord Baghdad, you have been a wonderful leader of your house these last twenty-five years," the Taoiseach said with a wry smile. "However, it is your son's blood that my father blessed, not yours. Boston is the inheritor of that legacy, and it is his destiny to be elevated to the head of the house. Hopefully, while he is still young enough to enjoy it."

"Of course, your grace," Boston said, earning a fiery glance from Baghdad. "I know one day, I must take over the house and leave the Guard behind, but surely—"

A heavy gauntleted hand descended on Boston's shoulder. The heat of it was hard to stand, but Boston locked his knees and bore the friendly gesture. "My boy, it does you credit to want to serve. To follow in your father's footsteps. You have a different destiny, though. I can see it. And that destiny is here at Sol." The Taoiseach smiled, and Boston could feel the heat of it. "I have a solution, my son. Herald, fetch me Lord Delaware Von Sinclair."

"Here, your grace," a portly lord called from the base of the dais, where he was already waiting. He bulged from his uniform in all the wrong places, putting his golden buttons under visible strain, and wore his gray hair slicked back. Still, gold Pikes lay on his collar. A SpaceGuard cruiser was his to command. "How may I be of service, your grace?" Delaware asked as he ascended the dais. He glanced sideways at Boston and Baghdad, skipping to the sapphire gems they both wore.

"Have you found a new Falcon to take over duties on the *Cortés*?"

"Not yet, your grace. I am still waiting for the right candidate."

"We would appreciate it if you could take on young Boston here. He has just returned from Asgard and is in need of a posting."

Delaware's silence lasted just long enough to be notable before he nodded. "Of course, your grace." He turned to Boston, for the first time acknowledging his existence. "Report to the *Cortés* on Monday."

Boston's heart fell. A posting in the capital? With even less to do than Asgard. It—

"Thank you, your grace," Baghdad said quietly, grabbing Boston's arm. "We won't take any more of your time."

"Now, go enjoy the festivities. Your family has much to celebrate tonight."

"Yes, your grace," Baghdad repeated. With a sharp glance at Boston, he turned and marched off, Boston and Chang following in his wake.

CHAPTER FOUR

Nirvana

BAGHDAD

Baghdad fumed and set a blistering pace across the ballroom, his leg pounding with every step. The boy trailed behind, getting distracted now and again by the plethora of partygoers around them.

At the edge of the room, there were small sitting pods, barely a few feet across but quiet and restful. Baghdad threw himself into one, tossing his cane angrily onto the seat next to him. "You stupid boy."

"Grandfather, I—"

"I told you to let me do the talking!"

Boston settled into the seat opposite Baghdad without answering but met Baghdad's glower evenly.

"You can't blame the boy for trying," Chang said. He stayed standing, keeping his head on a swivel, making sure no one drifted close enough to overhear.

"I can, and I will. I knew that position was open! And Sinclair set a price for it. Now, we've gone around them, run to the Taoiseach to fill the seat they offered me." Baghdad shook his head, a crushing weight on his shoulders.

He could tell Boston was rattled. "What do we do next?"

"You do nothing. We might be able to bluff them, make it seem like we have more backing than we do. The two of you go find something to entertain yourselves. I need to think."

"Are we really giving up on finding a posting in the colonies?"

Baghdad gave him the harshest look he could muster. "Boston. The Taoiseach has spoken."

He held the glare until the boy nodded. But he apparently couldn't resist another question. "And Ducane?"

Baghdad sighed heavily. "He owed a debt to a Sinclair bank. And now, a Sinclair Pike will replace him on the *Lee*. Hopefully, he can save his house, or this House War will have claimed another."

"The Taoiseach will not help him?"

"The Taoiseach only cares that the ships are paid for."

BOSTON

A thought had been bubbling away in some corner of Boston's head, and after they separated from Baghdad, he finally gave voice to it, "Who do you expect has the assignment for Olancha?"

Chang's reply was immediate. "Baghdad told us not to get into trouble."

"Are we?"

Chang tugged at the ends of his mustachio, thinking. "It couldn't hurt to find out, I suppose."

"Right. Battambang?"

Chang agreed, "Battambang," and started craning his neck to try to find him in the crowd.

They headed toward the edge of the dance floor that

was brightest. Battambang, fop that he was, wouldn't be far from it.

The great ballroom of Castle High was the largest room Boston had ever seen, large enough that he could see the floor curving up and away before it reached the far wall. The colors of the Eire Empire were everywhere—scarlet, emerald, and gold. Crystal chandeliers gave the entire room a shimmering quality, twisting slowly as if in a breeze. They made the lights of the room below never quite still. Thousands must have been gathered under the lights amid marble statues twice the height of a man. The revelers were dressed in every color under the rainbow, from somber suits to tight-fitting body suits and togas.

"Would you look at that," Chang said.

Boston followed his gaze. Five women were all clustered together a little way away, deep in animated conversation. All of them had donned multicolored dresses that sparkled with lights. Long and flowing, a few had trains that touched the ground while still clinging tightly to the torso, a mix of styles in between.

The closest woman noticed his gaze and raised a sparkling eyebrow that disappeared into her brilliant scarlet bangs. He nodded to her and then bent at the waist in a small bow. The woman smiled seductively, eyes fluttering under impossibly long eyelashes. She dropped one of her hands, and her fingers disappeared behind a fold of her dress. Her fingers twitched and suddenly, the tremendous folds at the bottom of her dress seemed to vanish. It had been a flashy purple but was now sheer, and he was treated to a view of her tremendously long and graceful legs. He let his gaze rise until he caught her eyes again. They sparkled in a mischievous expression.

She winked at him, and then, the dress was back, now

a light blue shade.

"I think I just witnessed a miracle," Boston said softly. He inclined his head once more to the lady, and she laughed and then curtsied. Then, she turned her back, returning to her group of compatriots.

"Ah," Chang said, his voice more than a little hoarse, "I hoped change fabric would still be in fashion."

"Change fabric?" Boston asked, following the group with his gaze as they flounced away.

"It was everywhere few years back. I've missed it out on the rim," Chang explained. "Tactical flexibility, Boston. We aren't the only people to appreciate it."

"I see." His eyes roved the room, and now that he knew to look, he could see a few dresses that seemed to be slowly changing color.

"There," Chang said under his breath. Boston followed his gaze and found them.

Battambang was immediately recognizable. His slim frame was draped delicately in a toga festooned with slowly changing patterns of orange and green. He'd also applied a fair amount of eyeshadow—orange in one eye, green in the other. Rubies glittered along the strap of the toga thrown over his shoulder.

But the woman he was chatting with was far more interesting. She was short—uncommonly so for a noble lady—with olive skin made glowing by a lavender dress. He couldn't see her face, as it was hidden behind long dark brown tresses, but he was sure it would be just as beautiful.

"I'll just watch from here," Chang said, grabbing a drink from a passing cart.

Boston nodded and approached the small knot where Battambang was holding court, arms wide as he made some inaudible point.

"Boston, old boy! Come, come, you can settle a debate for us."

The group parted for him slightly, and Boston stepped into the circle. "Lord Boston at your service."

Battambang's voice was just as brittle as Boston remembered, but he made sure it didn't set his teeth on edge. "You just returned from Asgard, did you not, Lord Boston?"

"Via Aztlán, yes."

"Visiting the colonies has always been a dream of mine," Battambang's companion mused, her voice high-pitched enough to almost get a wince from him. Even through his shadowcasters, her dress was blinding, probably because it was barely there. Only by hiding beneath the bright lights did she maintain a modicum of decency. "Lady Sikasso Kun Fernandez," the young woman said, offering her hand for Boston to kiss.

"A pleasure."

"Until you arrive," Battambang said. "After a day, you will find them far too dirty and humid for your tastes."

Sikasso pouted.

"There are seventy-five different colonies," the tanned woman who had caught his eye broke in, "and the difference between them is literally light-years."

Battambang tittered behind a demure hand. "As I believe you have said."

Boston glanced between the pair. "Lady ..." Boston started.

"Montana."

"Lady Montana is quite right," Boston continued. "Olancha, Camelot, Eden... the climates and temperaments of colonies are as different as summer and winter."

"Winter?" Sikasso repeated.

"A season," Lady Montana replied softly. "When the whole climate changes based on how far the planet is tilted from the sun."

"It can be quite dramatic," Boston explained. "The autumn winds on Paititi are unique to behold, with the trees bowing in the breeze. And the summers on Camelot, when you can feel the weight of all that air above you..." He shook his head, remembering a hundred nights spent sleeping under the stars.

"The storms on Ram Setu..." Montana interjected.

"Oh, Taoiseach above, the storms!" Boston agreed. "The whole sky is lit up with electrostatic discharges for hours. You can read by them!"

"It all seems frightfully dangerous," Sikasso observed. She batted eyelashes that must have been three centimeters long.

"It can be. Living in space has a few advantages, after all. Food cooked over an open-air fire, though, or living under the open sky..." Ge trailed off. "Well, it is quite something."

Sikasso remained unconvinced, her lips pulled into a pout. "It still seems like quite an investment."

"Well, then," Montana said, "perhaps you should just bring a piece of the colonies to you? I am sure we can find something that would appeal to you."

Battambang tittered again, "Oh yes, Lady Montana. Your... charity."

"Not quite a charity, but I do try my best to support local artists."

"What kinds of art?"

"All kinds of things. Message me, and we can arrange a time for you to look through the collection," she said, offering her small plastic card. "I just received a lovely shipment of statues from Olancha."

Sikasso took it, glancing at the card with interested. "I will think about it, Lady Montana."

"Speaking of Olancha, Bat, who is taking over the vacant flock there?" Boston asked.

"Eying your next assignment, Lord Haldis?" Montana asked. "Eager to get back out there and throw your mass around?"

Boston blinked. "I would not have put it that way."

"Perhaps you should. Excuse me," she said and turned away, latching onto another group that was passing.

"She is like that," Sikasso said. She stroked Boston's sleeve lightly. "Pay it no mind, Lord Haldis."

"I had thought you were assigned to the capital, Lord Boston. On a Sinclair ship, if I heard right."

Battambang's smile redoubled as Boston's slipped. He was good.

"Oh, just trying to keep an eye out," Boston lied to no avail.

"Regardless. I believe it was Lord Istanbul."

BERN

Somehow, Montana had disappeared into the crowd, and despite Bern searching the more remote corners, she'd yet to find her. She was certain she wouldn't have left without messaging. And yet.

Katalia, at least, was easy to find. Bern admired her cousin's technique out of the corner of her eye as she strode the perimeter of the dance floor. She'd found her Falcon, and as expected, he was putty in her hands, whisking Katalia around the dance floor with vigor. He was even Katalia's type: nicely defined jawline, slim frame, with just the right hints of muscles.

Katalia always had the easy course to follow.

Finally, Bern caught sight of Montana, watching the dance floor with a dazed expression. She was so engrossed, she started when Bern touched her arm.

"Everything alright?"

"It's him," Montana said. She gestured at the same Falcon currently dancing with Katalia. "Haldis. He was in command."

Bern appraised the Falcon again. It was surprising to find someone so blood-soaked so carefree.

"Younger than I would have thought."

"He was only fifteen at the time," Montana said.

"Have you talked to him yet?"

Montana looked shocked. "Absolutely not."

"But he could tell you what happened! He could tell you why—"

"Fuck."

Montana bolted from Bern's side back into the crowd behind them. Bern turned, intending to follow, but Katalia waved from the dance floor and approached.

She had draped herself all over the lord, who didn't seem to mind. Still, he kissed her hand pleasantly enough and seemed to keep his eyes to himself as they approached.

"My cousin, Lady Bern," Katalia said by way of introduction. "Have you had the opportunity to meet Lord Haldis?"

Bern shook her head that she hadn't.

Katalia continued, "I wondered, Lord Haldis, if you could tell her the story you just told me."

"Of course," Haldis started. "It is only a small thing, though."

"No, you were very brave."

Bern kept her gaze focused on Katalia, confused, as Haldis spun a tale of daring and danger, rescuing a dozen Terrans from flood-waters and hauling boulders to divert a rushing river. It was interesting enough but completely irrelevant. Until the end.

"Where did you say this was, Lord Haldis?"

"Aztlán. We were some of the only Wolves on the planet, laying over on—"

Katalia caught Bern's eye. Even through shadowcasters, her smug grin came through.

"So, the mines were completely destroyed?" Bern asked, smiling too now.

Boston shrugged. "They would have to have been. This was a few months ago, but still. That kind of thing takes time to repair."

"Does it?"

Boston nodded. "The complex was the work of a decade. It will not be easy to replace."

"Well, Lord Haldis, thank you for the thrilling story," Bern said, the wheels already turning in her head.

"Going to call it a night?" Katalia asked, fake indifference dripping from her words.

"You know, I think I will go back to the apartments early. I have a lot of things to prepare for tomorrow."

Katalia's grin took up half her face. "Good for you. I think Lord Haldis and I will stay a while and celebrate."

"Celebrate what?" the young lord asked.

"Oh, a family matter. Unless you would like to try the Falcon out on the dance floor, Bernie?"

"Not tonight."

CHANG

Chang sipped his coffee and kept a watchful eye on the alameda, hunting for his quarry. Something still didn't make sense about the situation they were in. House War or no, Istanbul never should have ended up in charge of a pack again.

What little sleep he'd gotten had been in his uniform, but it was a Sunday morning. Anyone who'd complain about his appearance wasn't likely to be awake yet.

Chang barely glanced at his food when it was brought out. Anytime now, the little rat would walk by, and he needed to be ready to—

Chang pounced the second he saw Fisk, bounding over the low railing that divided the cafe from the rest of the alameda and grabbing the old man's arm in an iron fist.

Fisk had lost something over the years; his kick to Chang's knee was barely enough to make him stumble and nothing to make him let go.

"Happy to see you, too, Fisk," Chang said as he dragged the thin man back toward the cafe.

"Glyd, you bastard," Fisk spat, still struggling. "Just what do you think—"

He dropped Fisk into a seat, then took the one between him and the door.

Seated, Fisk finally stopped trying to get away. He stared glumly at the mangled croissant on the table. "Did you have to be so rough?"

"Hand it over."

Fisk's eyes, already too big for his head, went wide in innocent wonder, but he palmed a thin blade onto the table without breaking the expression. How Fisk had lasted this long was beyond Chang, but he could be useful.

"Do you still have a spike in the Dearworth house core?"

Fisk's innocent expression didn't waiver a millimeter. "Don't know what you mean, Chang."

"Yes, you do. You knew how to find Governor Durban. You knew exactly where their bruisers were going to be on Atlantis. You have something on them."

"If I did, it'd be very illegal. And not something anyone would admit to in public."

Chang smiled. "How'd Istanbul Chi Colombia get assigned to Olancha?"

Fisk chuckled and tore a bit off Chang's half-eaten pastry. "Not asking the easy ones, are ya?"

"If it was easy, I wouldn't have come to you."

"Dearworth and Colombia have a little alliance," Fisk said. "Keeping it in the static for now. Colombia needed something to make this kid look good, and Dearworth supplied the posting. Had to do something, after the trouble this schmuck got into on Asgard. Heard he was fired as an under-governor," Fisk said darkly. "Colombia can't afford to look weak right now, and Dearworth needs its allies in fighting shape."

Chang growled under his breath. That'd be almost impossible for them to turn around. Even if Istanbul was a terrible flock leader on Olancha, it looked good enough. The Wolves and the other Guard would carry him.

"Can I go now?"

"One little scrap isn't worth me forgiving you."

Fisk's ears perked up, and he settled down in his chair slightly. "Forgive me? Like I won't have to watch the shadows for you anymore?"

"Give me something I can use on this kid."

Fisk chuckled "You really must not want to spend the next couple years on Castle High!"

Chang rested his fists on the table. "You really don't want me spending time here, either."

Fisk shook his head. "I got nothing. I definitely don't have a spike in the Chi Colombia core. That'd be where all the juicy is stuff. I'd tell you if I did."

"Taoiseach damn you," Chang muttered.

Fisk took the moment of distraction to spring to his feet and bounce over the fence onto the alameda proper.

"Be seeing you, then," Chang called to his retreating

back.

BOSTON

The first nights back on an estate were always hard. What little time he had to sleep was spent fitfully. There was neither the steady rumble of a ship in flight, where every fitting hummed with the same subtle vibration, nor was there the reassuring solidity of a planet. It was something in-between. Wrong.

Hence, coffee. Boston took another long drink and glanced around the bar. The old Wolf was still off somewhere, hopefully getting more sleep than Boston had. Still, it wouldn't do to call Hannigan before they were both ready to leave Castle High and head back to the Haldis Estate. Katalia had been effusive in her disappointment, but she'd ushered him out a half hour ago, having to get ready for some family meeting.

"Black coffee, no stims," a voice at his elbow said.

Boston eyed the woman who was suddenly perched on the stool next to him in the otherwise deserted bar. He couldn't recall seeing her the night before; he would have remembered. She was a study in white, porcelain, with almost translucent skin, white gold hair, a white dress accentuated by red and blue trim. Diamonds sparkled at her neck.

"Did you have an enjoyable evening, Lord Boston?"

"I did indeed, Lady Sinclair."

She gave him the barest hint of a smile. "Good."

Her voice maintained that ethereal quality, like they weren't really there and had wandered into some strange dimension. It was quite an effect, that had to be purposeful.

"I myself did not have an enjoyable evening. It seems that our dear Taoiseach—with the best of intentions, of course—assigned a provincial lord to one of the Sinclair cruisers over the heads of all the people we were considering for the job. It has thrown quite a few of our plans into disarray."

"I imagine that must be trying."

"It is indeed."

"What do you intend to do about it?"

"Well, there is an interesting question," she said and turned to face him for the first time. Her gaze was far sharper than her tone; Boston felt her looking through him, down into his bones. "First, I need to figure out why it happened."

"The Taoiseach was probably doing someone a favor." Boston thought desperately. Dammit, had Baghdad decided to bluff them? "A posting on a Guardship here at the capital might be seen as a sign of the emperor's favor."

"It might. But those positions are often bought and sold for a high price or given to close friends to shore up close alliances."

Boston drank his coffee and let that comment lie.

"Then again," Aspen said after the silence stretched a moment. "Some of it depends on the man put in that position. On how cooperative he can be."

"Cooperative."

"Indeed. Of course, he may not even want the position. That may be a way to resolve matters to everyone's satisfaction."

"I thought you said the Taoiseach appointed this Falcon?"

"The Taoiseach is easy." The Sinclair woman waved her hands. "Simple enough for everyone involved to decide it is not the best fit. Especially if the lord did what was initially suggested and focused on leading his house. Of course, that would have certain expenses. But the friendship of House Sinclair could alleviate many of those burdens."

"A posting on a cruiser is that valuable to House Sinclair?"

"It has value to others. And thus, value to us."

Boston had consumed far too little coffee for this conversation, but something began needling him. Sinclair was here, asking him to refuse the position. They couldn't block him, not without pissing off the Taoiseach. It was up to him to name his price.

"I think you might find that the only thing that would tip the scales would be a better assignment. Something worth the risks of refusing a gift from the Taoiseach."

The ghostly Sinclair woman's smile grew thinner. "Favors like that can be arranged, of course, but they come with… strings. Sinclair has several planets that might be excellent worlds for a young man to make his name. But all of them have their Guardsmen assigned, and displacing someone… Well. That is a very expensive proposition. But Tartarus or Kvenland both come to mind."

It was so tempting. Both worlds had populations in the hundreds of millions. They were massive, crowded worlds constantly in need of calming influences. But Baghdad was dead set against selling themselves to a great house, and Boston was sure that's what these attached strings would be. Significant, likely perpetual, servitude to Sinclair.

"It might be safer, then, for this lord to follow his Taoiseach's command."

The woman withdrew slightly and downed the last of her mug. "It might at that. Initially."

She slid to her feet. Standing, she towered over Boston, a wraith about to snatch away his soul. But then, her face was back to the placid nothingness she had worn for most of the discussion. "How disappointing, Lord Haldis. Either way, I think if the lord made his decision before reporting for duty on the *Cortés*, it would all work out for the best."

"I will think about it."

"Good. And if you change your mind, Lord Haldis, do not hesitate to reach out."

Boston rose to his feet and bowed to the woman. "That might be difficult, as I do not yet have your name."

"How silly of me. I forget how new you are to Sol." She gave him another of her smug smiles. "Aspen. Ask around, Lord Haldis, you will find me easy to reach."

CHAPTER FIVE

Risk

BERN

Bern wiped the sleep from her eyes and made sure her hair was pulled into neat waves. She hadn't slept much, just catnaps here and there when she could stand no more, but it was enough.

She made sure to get to the family dining room ahead of everyone else and laid out her prospectuses, still warm from the paper-bonder. Hardly anyone used hard copy any more, but Jordana liked it. Not that she didn't have the presentation loaded on the house core to be projected if needed, but it helped. As much as anything helped with Jordana.

Family started to trickle in a few minutes before the planned start time, and Bern settled at her place near the foot of the table. Hardly anything was real wood anymore, but this table was, nearly petrified with age and gleaming without a single blemish. Bern had supervised a cleaning crew uncounted hours ago, making sure that was so. She picked open a random page in her document and studied it as the room started to fill. She could recite every page, but it made her look more normal than simply waiting.

"Why are these meetings so rotting early?" Katalia asked as she dropped into the seat next to Bern.

"Go sit with your mother." Bern didn't raise her eyes from the document she was pretending to read.

"I will have you know that I probably got less sleep than you did." Bern risked a glance out of the corner of her eye. Katalia was in her nightgown, yet again.

"You could have at least ordered me a scone."

"It is at your place." Bern nodded toward the head of the table.

"Thank you, darling." Katalia rested a hand on Bern's shoulder for just a second and headed to her seat.

The room was beginning to hum, and Bern spared a glance around. Yes, most of the family that would care was already here. They just needed—

All conversation ground to a halt as Jordana Vermont, Lady Chi Nirvana, marched into the room, her heels clacking against the marble floors.

"Ah, Taarush, you made it back from Eden. Good to see you," Jordana murmured, clasping Taarush's shoulder on her way up. Taarush responded with a small, silent smile nearly as wooden as the table, but she hardly slowed her pace. By the time she reached the head of the group and turned, every place was filled, and the servants had closed the doors of the room and dimmed the lights.

Envy and trepidation warred in Bern's stomach as she watched the calm, unflappable way Jordana surveyed the house, her gaze everywhere at once.

"Menodora is away today, so we should get started," she began. "Clarisse, I believe you requested to present business first?"

Her tone was flat, conveying no dissatisfaction or ire. Still, Bern readied herself for an uphill battle. Jordana was impossible to impress.

"Yes, Jordana. Last night, we were made aware of a potential opportunity. The Sinclair tungsten operations on Aztlán have apparently been severely curtailed in the last year. This provides us with a significant, near-term opportunity to break their monopoly on the Taoiseach's contracts. If we move quickly enough, we can secure a significant new revenue stream."

She was rushing, she knew it, but the blank looks around her gave her nothing.

"How?" Lady Koichi asked, fifth from the head of the table.

"By securing the rights to take over patronage of Okeanos from San Wo."

Murmurs ran around the table.

"Securing San Wo's only planet will not come cheaply," Bern continued. "We will need to pay off the other creditors. However, the benefits outweigh the costs significantly."

Koichi scoffed, but Jordana held up a hand, and silence fell again. "Take us through it," she commanded with hardly a glance down at Bern.

Bern's stomach churned, but she made her pitch. How Okeanos's position made it perfect for them to exploit. What Sinclair's likely countermoves would be.

It was difficult to see how her presentation was landing everyone was well-versed in keeping their feelings controlled. Even among the family.

"How do we know the mines are not producing?" Jordana interrupted, and Bern's heart sank. Something in Jordana's tone boded ill.

Still, she rallied. "We have independent confirmation from two sources. First, Sinclair has placed orders with three Chen companies for a complete refinery system, with expedited delivery. They broke up the order and the shipping locations to disguise it, but it is enough to completely replace the assets we know they had on Aztlán. Second, we have a report from a SpaceGuard officer who witnessed the aftermath of the destruction."

"Katalia, are you sure Lord Haldis can be trusted?"

To her credit, Katalia barely flinched as Jordana proved why she led the house. Bern had never mentioned Haldis, but she knew. "This is Clarisse's lead, Mother."

"And yet, you are the one who kept half the east wing up last night with Lord Haldis." Jordana's face allowed no argument and might as well have been frozen in vacuum. "I would prefer your… more intimate assessment."

Katalia hesitated only a moment, catching Bern's eye, defeated. "Haldis is no friend of Sinclair," she finally said. "They may be playing us, but they would be playing him, too."

"A glowing recommendation."

"We can limit our exposure by asking for the Taoiseach's permit to import tungsten before we buy Okeanos. However, that will tell everyone else how valuable it is at the same time," Bern said, trying to regain control of the meeting.

Pages flipped, as more people began studying her proposal. Bern began to hope as people found the number of zeros she predicted.

Jordana ignored the proposal and focused on Bern from across the room, her slate-gray eyes measuring her, stripping away the layers of self-confidence that she projected for everyone else.

"This will do nothing to decrease our tensions with Sinclair," Jordana observed. "In fact, it might be called an escalation, directly challenging one of their monopolies."

"The reward is too significant to pass up."

Jordana smiled thinly. "This coming from the young woman who counseled reconciliation."

"I counsel whatever makes the most business sense." Bern did her best to maintain her composure. "This is worth doing, even if it did not embarrass Sinclair."

"That is just a bonus," Lord Daumantas observed to general chuckles, sitting two seats beneath and across from Lady Koichi.

"I am convinced," Jordana said, bringing all conversation to a halt. "We will proceed."

Shock washed over Bern. For as much time as she had invested in the proposal, in the negotiations with San Wo in the middle of the night, in the careful checking of every scrap of research they had, she had never expected Jordana to agree. And so easily!

And then, it all came crashing down. "Katalia, see that it happens."

The begining of a grin slipped off Katalia's face. "What?"

Jordana pulled herself up slightly in her chair. "I want you to handle this acquisition. Clarisse has found the opportunity, and now, I expect you to turn it into a reality."

"Exactly. Clarisse found this opportunity," Katalia said quietly.

"And you, my youngest daughter, will secure it. Is that a problem, Clarisse?"

All eyes swiveled to Bern. She wavered against the table, fingers going white against the pristine lacquered surface. "No, Jordana, of course not."

Jordana's face didn't change a micrometer; she'd known there was no other answer forthcoming. "Well then. Katalia, take a week at most and then brief us on your progress. Excellent work, Clarisse. If this works, we will need to make sure you are rewarded in some small way. Now, what is next on the agenda?"

Bern slowly took her seat as Taarush stood and began briefing the family on the rising tensions with the colonial workforce on Eden. She could feel Katalia's eyes on her, but she dared not show anything other than placid interest.

BOSTON

The orbitals above Earth fairly glittered with the assembled structures of man. Despite the wide variety of planets conquered by the Eire Empire, most of its population still lived here, floating in their estates, both large and small. With Earth largely uninhabitable, everything was done in space. From algae farms in orbit around Venus, to scientific outposts on the dark side of Luna, and to hydrogen mines around the Jovian worlds, generations were born and died without ever setting foot on a planet. Everything mankind needed to survive was found in one of the estates.

Including sport.

Chang eased himself closer to the glass next to Boston, and Boston repressed a bubble in his stomach. The observation gallery that ran down the axle of the polo court was in zero g; it had to be, but it made him uncomfortable. He missed the press of gravity.

"Do you think Istanbul would agree to a swap?"

Boston nodded. "The capital would be more to his liking, anyway. Only a few days here, and already, I am sick of it," Boston said, watching the doors to the locker room. A match had just ended. "Nothing but parties, waiting around, and bland food."

"There's more to life than the colonies, you know, boy."

Shocked, Boston turned to Chang, but his face was

more inscrutable than usual. "Are the planets spinning backward? What did you just say?"

Chang grinned. "Oh, I hear you, boy. I'd much rather be out there. But Baghdad is right: Eventually, you'll need to settle down. Even Baltimore… there."

Istanbul stepped out onto the court, dressed in the latest fashion of workout singlet and accompanied by another young lord.

"My father stayed on duty even after he married Vienna."

"Your mother understood how much it meant to him. And I know he intended to come home after you were born."

"Either way, it is a long way off."

Chang looked dubious, but Boston ignored him, watching Istanbul miss two passes in a row. "We should head down."

"Alright."

They settled in to wait for Istanbul at the exit to the court, Chang doing his best to lean nonchalantly against the wall. Boston paced, unable to settle.

They heard Istanbul before they saw him, all big booming laughter and back-slapping. Chang stepped behind Boston, deferential at least when there were others around, and they waited.

"Lord Istanbul! Might we have a moment of your time?"

Istanbul glanced their direction as he exited the ramp and exchanged a glance with his partner. "No, you go ahead, Digby. Save me a seat at the bar. This will not take long."

Boston's stomach turned, but he refused to yield without even trying. Istanbul swaggered up to Boston, appraising. "Lord… Haldis, was it?"

"Yes, Lord Istanbul. I was flock leader for—"

"I remember." Istanbul glanced around, but they were reasonably alone. "Go ahead, say your piece."

"Begging your pardon?"

"I assume you are here to barter for your posting back?"

"Actually, I wondered if you would consider a simple trade. I have an assignment here at the capital, serving under Delaware Sinclair on the *Cortés*. I thought you might prefer that to sailing all the way to Olancha."

Istanbul snorted. "Oh, did you now?"

"I am not sure I follow, Lord Istanbul."

"Obviously. Do you have any idea how much money this assignment is going to make me?"

Boston blinked. Of all the arguments he had considered, that was not one he thought he was going to have to deal with. "My Lord?"

"Olancha is worth a fortune! I am finally going to get a chance to sink my teeth into a world, and you want me to trade it to stay here? Sol will be here when I come back, richer and ready to enjoy it."

Boston gaped at Istanbul. "You want the Olancha assignment so you can make money off it?"

"Of course. Why else would anyone put up with the colonies?" Istanbul shook his head. "I knew your family was antiquated, but honestly, Haldis, grow up."

"How did you even manage to arrange it?" Boston couldn't help but ask.

Istanbul shrugged. "I left after you but still got here before you. Been here over a month, which was plenty of time to get you booted out of the job. It is exactly what you deserve, after what you did to me on Asgard."

Boston gaped. He hadn't expected Istanbul to remember him, much less hold him responsible for that mess.

"Oh, you play as a good soldier, Boston, but honestly. Recalling me just a week after your flock eliminated a village I was trying to relocate? It was a pathetic attempt to shift blame, but I was able to explain the whole situation to Lord Dearworth."

"You miserable fool." Boston shook his head, hardly able to believe the man standing in front of him. "The Olanchans will eat you alive."

Istanbul inflated with rage. "I am going to finally bring these colonists to heel! Like you never could, Haldis. You are nothing, just like your father. He—"

Boston's fist collided with Istanbul's smug face before he realized he'd thrown a punch. Istanbul was launched backward and landed sprawled on the metal deck, cursing.

Instinctively, he was already moving forward, but Chang wrapped an iron grip around his withdrawn hand, stopping him cold. Boston glanced back, and Chang's face was set in a warning.

"What the slag are you doing, Haldis?" Istanbul spat, blood landing on the deck.

"Let me help you there, Lord Istanbul," Chang offered, grabbing Istanbul by the shoulder and dragging him upright. Chang was able to keep himself between Boston and Istanbul, even as Boston's rage faded into regret.

"You will pay for that," Istanbul hissed, red showing from perfect teeth. "Slag, the whole lot of you. Jumped-up commoners."

"I am sorry you were injured playing polo, Lord Istanbul," Chang said. "I think you should be getting to the medics. We wouldn't want that nose to stick crooked like that."

Without another word, Chang turned, grabbed Boston by the arm, and dragged him in the opposite direction.

BERN

Electricity still burned in Bern's stomach as she paced through Castle High.

It unsettled her. Her plan was an attack on House Sinclair, no matter what else it also was. It was all so petty, and yet, here she was.

For all Castle High's size, it still felt rather small sometimes. Like now, as Aspen turned a corner and made her way toward Bern.

"Good sol, cousin," Bern said, making sure no sign of her inner rancor appeared in her voice.

"Good sol. Going to visit our divorcée?"

"There is very little that escapes you."

Aspen nodded at the compliment. "If you could remind her that my offer stands whenever she wishes to take it, I would be most appreciative."

Montana hadn't mentioned anything about an offer from Sinclair. Not that she would have necessarily; she was always a very private person.

"I will convey the message."

Aspen smiled the smallest fraction. "I knew I could trust you to be sensible, cousin. If only we could convince our families that things need not be so acrimonious between us."

"There is much we could do together if our families stopped focusing on petty things," Bern agreed. "On both sides."

Aspen's tenuous smile vanished. "True enough. Take care."

"Fly safe." With a final nod, Aspen resumed her languid walk down the corridor, gliding on silent footfalls.

Montana's townhouse was only one more corridor away, and Bern pressed the buzzer rather than let herself in.

"I told you the answer was no," Montana said before the door was even open.

"I assume that was meant for Aspen?"

Montana sagged against the door, her long dark hair unkempt. "It was. Come in."

The living room was tidier than the last time Bern had been there, but not by much. Bern rapidly took in the remains of the night before; the lavender dress shredded and tossed over a couch, Montana's obvious hangover, packing material corralled into odd corners, as if Montana had been pacing.

"Are you alright, Augustine?"

"Yes," Montana snapped. Bern raised an eyebrow, but let her friend have a secret for the moment. "Did you end up enjoying the rest of your evening?"

"Not the words I would have used," Bern admitted, and the whole story poured forth, including how the meeting had gone. How conflicted she felt about adding fuel to the fire.

She could feel Montana's suppressed judgement but all she did was take Bern's hand and squeeze. "I understand family."

Bern squeezed back. "What did Aspen want?"

"Nothing. Empty threats, as usual."

"Aspen usually makes very well-researched threats." Bern earned a glare for her trouble.

"Magistrate," Montana said, adding a liner's worth of sarcasm to the title. "On Kvenland."

Elation and trepidation warred in Bern. Something must have shown in her expression, because Montana slumped into a seat on the divan next to her. "Worry not, Clarisse. I have no intention of taking it."

"Why not?" slipped out before she could control it. Rallying, Bern continued, doing her best to make it sound natural, "It could be a great opportunity for you."

"Mmm," Montana said through pursed lips. "Joining the system that is oppressing the people of Kvenland. Having to sit in judgment of them."

"You could make things better. A magistrate has broad powers." Bern wasn't quite sure why she was arguing this particular point, as the thought of Montana leaving created a vast gulf in her heart.

"On a Sinclair planet?" Montana shivered. "I would accomplish nothing. They just want me out of the way, to stop embarrassing the family."

"Perhaps. However, it would solve some of your financial difficulties."

Montana's violet eyes, unencumbered by shadowcasters, flashed. "The gallery will solve that, too."

"Augustine."

"Last night was a setback, nothing more."

"How many more months of savings do you have?" Bern asked gently.

"Enough."

"At least tell me you decided to reach out to that Falcon. Finally get some answers."

"No!"

Bern waited, trusting that her patience was stronger than Montana's.

"He killed them," she said finally

"He did," Bern agreed. "But he saved you too. Made sure you survived the chaos, at least." Montana shook her head profusely. "Just talk to him! I am sure he will be able to tell you more than what you know."

"I'll think about it."

Bern could have cheered. She was making some small progress on getting Montana off this quixotic quest and focused on her life here. It wasn't much, but it was something.

BOSTON

Boston lay in bed, staring at the ceiling, unable to sleep.

Baghdad hadn't been pleased when he and Chang related their brief discussion with Istanbul. His reaction wasn't unwarranted. They'd gone in without much of a plan. What had they expected? It had been ill-advised and brash.

Boston could feel the jaws of the cage closing around him. Come tomorrow morning, when he presented himself to Delaware, that would be it. He'd be trapped here in the capital, likely for years. Eventually, Baghdad would succeed in tying him down to the house. And his career would be over.

His slate chimed, and Boston pulled it from the bedside. An out-of-system ansible call was about the only thing it could be, at this time of night, but he was surprised at the name.

"I thought you were not speaking to me, Amman," Boston said once the connection opened.

"I was never good at following the rules. I suspect it is why I ended up stuck out here."

"How are things on Asgard? Cleaning up now that Istanbul was tossed out?"

"Unfortunately not." It was hard through the low-bandwidth connection, but Boston thought he could hear the strain in his voice. "Things are quite a bit worse, actually. Ember has been more active. There have been protests. More deaths. Your old packs are in the thick of it."

"Slag, Amman. You have my sympathies."

Static crackled on the line.

"I know, Boston. I know."

The silence stretched, tugging at Boston's guilt.

Amman shouldn't have to be going through that alone. He should have had another noble to shoulder the burden with. But because of Boston, he didn't.

"I need a favor, Boston," Amman started. "With everything going on, we are not getting the support we need. There has not even been a liner passing through the system since Istanbul left."

"What can I do?"

"I know you are on your way to Olancha, but—"

"Istanbul took that assignment out from under me. I am going to be stuck on Castle High, working for Sinclair." Boston waited, long enough to wonder if they were still connected. "Amman?"

"Still here," he grunted. "Slag, Boston. That burns. I would have tried harder to get him cashiered if I would have known he was going to—"

"No way you could have known."

Amman chuckled slightly. "Well then, it might be easier for you to help me, then."

"What do you need?" Boston asked again.

"I need to know where the closest other packs are in case I need to call for help."

"Call for help?" Boston repeated, confused. It was hard to imagine a situation that had gotten so out of hand that Chelsea and the rest of the Wolves couldn't handle it, bloody though it would be.

"Yes."

Boston waited for an explanation, but one never came.

"Amman?"

"I am just trying to be prepared," Amman said finally. "And the family is not… they are keeping things from our superiors, not wanting to be embarrassed. Things are worse—worse than I could have imagined when you left."

"I never would have if I had known."

"But you did."

That hurt.

"Once I report to my new command, I will find out who is nearby and send you their details."

"Thank you, Boston." Amman sounded like a weight had been lifted from his shoulders. "I should go. This call has been expensive enough as it is. I will send you an address where you can send the info."

The link closed without further fanfare. Boston stared at the blank screen for a few long minutes, unsettled. The morning—and reporting to his next command—couldn't come soon enough.

CHAPTER SIX

Duty
BOSTON

Boston did his best to keep his hopes up as they reported aboard the *Cortés*, but it was harder than he would have liked. The lethal cruiser was hard docked to Castle High and looked as though she spent most of her time there.

"Looks like a boring assignment," Chang muttered as they walked through the ship, being ushered to the Pike's day cabin.

"Quiet," Boston hissed, even though he agreed. What did a flock of Wolves assigned to the capital even do?

Before he had an answer, he and Chang were standing at attention in front of Delaware Sinclair's broad desk. The Pike barely looked up as they came in. He was busy studying a slate that was dwarfed by his meaty hands.

"I took the liberty of reviewing your record, Falcon. I have read worse, but not many. A shame you have not served with a Sinclair ship before. I would have liked a fitness report I could trust."

Boston stayed silent, braced at attention.

"Colonial princesses kidnapped and rescued,

avalanches, hostage exchanges," Delaware tutted, paging through the reports. "I think you have a flair for the dramatic, Lord Haldis." He gave Boston a sharp look.

Boston refused the bait and met the Pike's raised eyebrow with a blank expression.

"At least you can follow orders. Go ahead and speak, Falcon."

"Thank you, Lord. I—"

"It is clear to me that you spend a great deal of time showing off in the colonies. And I will not tolerate that."

"My Lord, I—"

"No, no, Falcon." Delaware held up a hand. "You are a junior officer from a junior house, serving in the capital. I will not have you making this ship and my house look bad because you want to show off."

Boston opened his mouth to defend himself, but Delaware waved a finger. "Ah!"

Delaware turned his eyes back to the slate. "I served in the colonies once upon a time myself, Falcon. Good officers follow procedure, rather than their gut. Falcons like you get their men killed."

"I have not lost any Wolves serving under me, my Lord."

Delaware's gaze was merciless. "Not yet, Falcon."

Boston was able to bite back his retort. And Delaware could tell Boston could see the tightening of his lips, the blood rising in his face.

"While under my command, you will comport yourself with decorum and with a minimum of flair. Is that clear?"

"Yes, my Lord."

Delaware was interrupted by the door sliding open behind them. Aspen Sinclair stepped in wearing SpaceGuard blacks, looking slightly more solid than she had before. She took a position at Delaware's elbow like she belonged there, face just as impassive as he remembered.

"Lady Aspen is my second-in-command," Delaware said, "and she has the details of your first assignment."

A slate appeared in Aspen's hands, and without a flicker of recognition, she rattled off instructions. "We have been asked to inspect the liner *Hikawa Maru* when she arrives in-system tonight. No police were available, apparently, so as usual, it falls to us to clean up their mess. You can monitor the proceedings with us from the bridge."

Boston almost thought better of it, but the words were on his tongue before he could take them back. "My Lord, I would prefer to accompany the Wolves, if I may."

Delaware pursed his lips in disapproval.

"I will not ask my Wolves to do anything I am not willing to do myself." And cargo inspections were the worst of assignments, usually handed out as punishments to flocks who needed to be brought down a peg.

Delaware gave him another long glare and finally waved his hand. "Fine, Lord Haldis. You are dismissed."

Boston turned to leave, Chang on his heels, but Delaware's voice called again from the doorway. "Oh, and Lord Haldis, I expect you to be in the proper uniform when I see you next."

Boston glanced at Chang, noting the blank patches on his shoulders where the ship's crest usually went. His were bare, too. "It will be done, my Lord."

BERN

Bern glanced around the throne room with interest, checking for any unfamiliar faces. The room buzzed, as it had almost every day since the House War broke out, but there were no currents that said anything in particular was going to happen today.

Other than in her heart.

Bern kept an eye on Katalia, seated in the front row with the other petitioners. She was unflappable as always, chatting animatedly with Lady Eiravati. Bern envied that poise; while she knew she wore a placid expression, her stomach roiled.

A soft swish of fabric announced someone dropping into the chair next to her. Aspen nodded coolly and did her own scan of the room, while Bern inwardly cursed. Aspen was the last person she wanted to try to hide this from.

"Why hello there, cousin."

Bern nodded back politely and willed the proceedings to start, but she wasn't that lucky. The head table was still half-empty, with no sign of the Taoiseach or a herald in his stead.

"Odd tidings of late," Aspen said, her head on a swivel as well.

"Things have been unsettled for a few months now."

"True," Aspen said with a wry twist of her lips. "I meant more specifically the last few days. Almost as if there is a shoe that has yet to fall."

Bern couldn't help glancing toward Aspen's bare feet. "That must be a new experience for you." It was good that they'd managed to keep news of the Okeanos deal quiet. The contracts had been signed the night before.

"Indeed. I hate not knowing things. It makes me..." Aspen pretended to struggle for the word and finally made a show of settling on "anxious."

Bern believed none of it. "Perhaps you should talk to someone about that."

"I chose to talk to you today."

Another few members of the Privy Council wandered in and took their seats. As soon as things started, Bern would be free, but until then, she had to tap dance.

"Did you hear that there was a riot on Genovia? Unrest over a new population-control policy." Bern offered a useless tidbit that embarrassed Dearworth and nothing more.

Aspen inclined her head a micron. "I did hear that. Strange. Genovia has been settled a long time."

Bern controlled her flush, thinking of their own problems on Eden. And it had been settled far longer.

"Something does seem to be tilting the colonies out of balance," Aspen mused. "I wonder if they can sense our unease, like any good pet. But—" And Aspen turned the full force of her piercing glare on Bern. It made her conscious of every hair out of place, every wrinkle in her dress. "—I was hoping you might tell me what inspired your cousin to be the first presenter this morning. Katalia is not an expected name on the rolls of petitioners these days."

"Katalia keeps her own council."

"As if anyone in your family moved without endless meetings, briefings, and paperwork. No, I think you are well-aware."

Bern raised an eyebrow. "And if you got advance notice of her petition, what would be the point? A few minutes' advantage?"

Aspen smiled. "Oh, there is much one can do in even a short time. And you owe me a favor, cousin."

A jolt of cold ran through her stomach, but it only took milliseconds for her to decide. "I do. But not this."

Aspen raised an eyebrow. "Oh? I could be very appreciative."

Bern shook her head.

"And here, I thought you were eager to carve a better place for yourself."

"I would have thought you were better at reading people than that."

Aspen nodded appreciatively. "Perhaps I did underestimate you."

A horn filled the room, cutting off further conversation. The Taoiseach approached the head of the horseshoe table and raised his voice. "Welcome, citizens of the Empire of Eire. We will now open the floor to petitions on how to improve the Empire."

Katalia was on her feet before the Taoiseach had ceased speaking, and took the small, raised platform. "Your grace, today, I would like to talk to you about tungsten."

BOSTON

After stowing his gear, Boston made his way to the Wolf den. Though she was slightly smaller than the other ships he'd served on like the *Lee*, *Barca*, and *Caesar*, the Wolf den was in the same part of the ship, just ahead of the engines.

The Wolf den had the strange feeling of being cramped and spacious at the same time. Bunks were stacked four-high against the walls, enough for the full complement of twenty-four Wolves. Overheads and piping twisted above, like knurled roots of a tortured tree. The ceiling was a few hands higher than in a normal corridor as it was meant to accommodate their height when in armor. Corridors led to the ports that housed the gumdrops.

The central rec room was crowded with all manner of equipment, including a couple of small tables with Wolves packed around them, playing cards. Behind the bunks were the ranks of armor stands, and twenty-four sets of gleaming armor observed the rest of the room.

"Slag, Falcon!"

Boston had to give the Wolves credit; they noticed him

duck into the room immediately and were scrambling to their feet a second later. Someone had trained them well—at least well enough to avoid an irate commander. The table and cards crashed to the ground, along with a chair or two, but in impressively good time, there was a double line of Wolves standing at attention in front of him.

"At ease," Boston called out as soon as the crashing faded, letting them relax at least. He glanced along the line of Wolves for a moment, trying to pick out the seniors, and his eyes immediately landed on the woman near the center. Her informal ship suit didn't carry rank insignia, so he couldn't be sure, but he was reasonably certain she had been the one to spot him enter, too.

"Pack leader?" Boston guessed, holding eye contact for a second.

"Pack Second Dunkirk. Rotting pack leader is in the head." She jerked her head over her shoulder.

"I'm here," an other Wolf gasped, sprinting out from the side corridor with his belt still in his hands. "Pack Leader Voyen, at your service, my Lord."

"Thank you, Sir Voyen," Boston replied, doing his best to memorize the man's face. He was a little older than Boston and of the same slim build that made him seem dwarfed by his second. "In his wisdom, the Taoiseach has assigned me to be your new Falcon. I am looking forward to working with you all."

"Rotting finally," Dunkirk muttered under her breath.

"How long have you been without a Falcon?"

"Three months, Lord," Voyen said quickly, with a sharp look in Dunkirk's direction. "Lord Delaware was waiting for the perfect candidate." Voyen answered the next question on Boston's tongue.

Boston grimaced and glanced back at Chang's non-expression. "Well, it seems he found me. We have a mission tonight?"

Voyen nodded. "Inspection of the *Hikawa Maru*."

"I would appreciate if you could brief me." Boston nodded. "Everyone else, by all means, go back to relaxing. There will be plenty of time to get to know each other tonight on the ride out. Is there a conference space?"

Voyen nodded smartly. "This way, Lord."

BOSTON

The cargo inspection was exactly as excruciating as Boston had expected. Chang waited until the two of them were alone in a container before beginning his tirade of invective again.

"What a miserable excuse for a Pike," Chang finally finished.

Boston ignored him. He had stopped trying to get his friend to cease complaining about the standing orders dictating how they searched the liner over an hour ago. "We should start with this one," Boston said, indicating a crate on the left side of the container and pulling out the XRI kit.

"This is the worst way to search an interstellar," Chang grunted, but he grabbed the other end of the reader and pulled it into place.

Boston glanced at the reading and shook his head. It was exactly as it should be. Exactly as the last hundred crates had been. "On to the next one."

He turned off his helmet pickup and consoled himself with grunting loudly as they shoved the heavy crates around the inside of the container. Wolf armor wasn't designed for cargo handling—or for microgravity. The biofeedback mechanisms were tightly wound, precisely calibrated. It gave Boston the strength to lift thousands of kilos in normal gravity, the dexterity to squeeze a splinter trigger with the utmost precision, and everything in between. But it took a lot out of you.

The armor amplified his strength many times over but in order to access the armor's full power, to lift the most the armor could lift, it required the wearer to use their full strength, pushing as hard as they could against the armor so the armor knew how hard to push against the outside world. A cargo-handling suit would have let the wearer lift an elephant without breaking a sweat, but a cargo handler couldn't have used a pen without breaking it. A Wolf could.

"Come on. We have a schedule to keep," Boston chided, as he lagged moving to the third crate.

"That's another thing," Chang growled. "Who sets a time per container? Two minutes? It's a travesty."

"Yes, Chang, I know."

He pushed himself to keep moving, and Chang matched him with no external signs of hesitation, though Chang had to be hurting as much as Boston was. Every container was the same, but with only about two minutes to search each, they had to rush every moment.

An empty container was roomy enough for two even in armor, but they were packed to the brim with individual crates. They had to get inside, unstack a few crate—which could be filled with anything from linens to rocks—run the XRI against three randomly selected crates, compare the report to that on the shipping manifest, restack the crates, squeeze back into the service corridor, and pull themselves out to the next container. It was backbreaking work. The containers weighed nothing; the liner's engines were off, so they floated. But the crates still massed the same, still needed force to get them moving and stop them from moving, and there was precious little purchase.

"You didn't have to follow the standing orders."

"Of course I did."

"Delaware never mentioned them, and you could have just claimed to not have read them. We were on the damn boat for less than two hours."

Safe in the knowledge that the Faraday cage of the container blocked the rest of the world from hearing their comms, Boston replied, "The Wolves would have mentioned it."

"Bah. Easy enough to breeze past."

"And how exactly would that help endear me to Delaware?"

They heaved a crate together, momentarily stopping conversation.

"We might find something if you had."

"Opening the hatch," Boston said and then did just that. The moment Boston stuck his head out into the service corridor, his helmet beeped with updates on the rest of the flock. Most of them had finished their containers and were waiting, pressed against the walls of the service corridor, allowing just enough room for Boston to slip between them.

"Anyone find anything?" A chorus of nos answered him on the flock-wide channel, though he didn't recognize any of the voices yet. He scanned the little lights, one for each Wolf. Each of them had checked in. "Alright, next spoke."

Boston led the way back down to the spinal corridor that ran through the ship, turned sixty degrees, and headed down the next corridor. Eight new containers awaited them.

"Falcon Haldis, are you monitoring this channel?"

Boston perked up and tabbed through the channels available in his headset. "Haldis here," he answered, trying to place the voice.

"Wolf Nevada, Lord, comm tech," the Wolf answered

before he could ask. "We just had a call from the dockmaster over at Port Chittagong. He has some... irate nobles demanding their cargos an' wanted someone to come and explain the situation to them."

"Of course, Nevada. Pass back that I will be right over," Boston replied, then switched back to his private channel with Chang.

"Better you than me," Chang said when Boston explained.

"Keep them moving. Help out where you can."

"Of course."

ASPEN

Aspen made herself a cool pool of calm amid her brothers' rage, refusing to let the tumult of their argument distract her. She devoured every article, every post, every snide comment on Nirvana's coup, cataloging as many of the reactions as she could. Not that the comments mattered for themselves; what the reactions revealed was the important thing. Where their support was strong, where it might be weakening. And who immediately seized the opportunity to get in swipes of their own.

"I tell you, we cannot stand for this!" Ambroos continued and slammed his fist on the table. "Grandmother, Nirvana has gone too far this time! We must respond!"

Huntington, arrogant buffoon that he was, nodded along with Ambroos, sending his jowls quivering. "Absolutely. I say we revoke docking rights for their fleet on our worlds. Let them try to find cargo for their liners elsewhere."

To her credit, Lady Sherah didn't immediately respond, but Aspen had been around the old woman enough to know when her control was slipping. A concerted attack by the three of them, while trapped in the most secure room in the estate, was getting to her. Jamshad sat silent and useless as always, but even Grenada had lost her temper and was fuming from the foot of the table, occasionally reading aloud sound bites.

"I want to hear from Aspen." Sherah finally interrupted the two shouting blowhards, and all five of them turned to look at her.

Aspen ignored the half-jealous, half-contemptuous looks and focused on Sherah. "Nirvana has done us a favor."

Explosions of incredulity was the response, but Sherah hissed, and eventually, the room was blessedly silent again.

"Explain."

"The tungsten contracts were profitable enough," Aspen said, dismissing the half a billion crowns they brought to the house each year. "They were, however, hardly existential. Deposits run out, and Azatlan had a few years left at most. Now that they have taken the contract, we no longer need to rebuild."

"Cede the entirety of the market?" Ambroos was aghast.

"Why not? If we announce we are no longer going to compete, everyone will rush to get a piece. The price will free-fall, and Nirvana will end up with barely enough to cover their expenses."

"And yet," Huntington said, rumbling out of his stupor, "Nirvana has publicly stolen the contract from us. Whether or not they gain from it is not the point. Our image is the point. The erosion of our unsullied reputation. We must respond."

"We can think of something."

BOSTON

Hikawa hung high above Earth next to Port Chittagong,

where the tendrils of Earth's gravity were the loosest. The trip across was short, and Boston spent most it divesting himself of his armor and continuing to read the files on each of the Wolves under his command. Many of them had served on the *Cortés* for years, though it had only been a Sinclair ship for the last five years. Chi Devi had sponsored it for the thirty before that.

The leech docked in the industrial section of the port, skipping the grand passenger entrances that Boston had traversed a few days ago. A few dockworkers glanced up at him as he walked through to small office area, but he was able to follow the sounds of shouting to the dockmaster's office without trouble.

"I tell you, this is intolerable! A personal attack on our house, no less!"

Boston brushed fingers through his hair in a vain attempt to get it to lie flat once more and stepped into the small room.

The Terran dockmaster, a small man in a simple if colorful purple and orange uniform, sighed in relief as Boston entered and pointed a finger in his direction. "Lord Istanbul, this is the SpaceGuard officer in charge of the inspection. If you could—"

Istanbul took a step back when he saw Boston and raised one hand to his face, where there was still a bruise on his jaw. The dockmaster went silent immediately and left the two of them staring at each other.

"This was your doing?" Istanbul asked, voice low.

Boston bit back his second, third, and fourth curse before settling on, "I had nothing to do with it." The last thing he needed to do was antagonize Istanbul more. Not when a formal complaint on his first day could be ruinous.

"Punishing me for not accepting your 'trade'?"

"You think I could have arranged an inspection on my

first day?"

"Only if you were smarter than I gave you credit for," Istanbul said. Boston could feel the appraisal in Istanbul's gaze, for the first time, really considering him a threat. "*Hikawa* was inspected before she left Eden. And yet, here you are, causing hours of delays for every container."

"You have done cargo inspections before, Stan. You know how hard it is to search a liner quickly."

"I do, and I have, Haldis. But you know that this is not the way to do it quickly!"

Boston shrugged. "All I know is Pike Delaware said we were to take our time inspecting her."

"Delaware Sinclair?"

"Yes."

Istanbul rubbed the bridge of his nose and muttered, "Rotting diamond games," under his breath. "Fine I will give you the benefit of the doubt, Boston. What can we do to get my cargo released as quickly as we can? Dearworth and Sinclair are obviously playing a game, but there's no need for us to get caught up in it, is there?" Istanbul gave him a bright smile that was too tight at the edges. There was no sincerity there, and Boston wasn't even sure if he was supposed to think it sincere. "Houses like ours need to stick together. Otherwise, the diamonds would be running everything, eh?" It was as if he expected Boston to forget the insults he'd hurled moments earlier.

The dockmaster was carefully ignoring them, tapping at his slate, but probably drinking in every word.

Boston shook his head. "Sorry, Stan. You know how it is, having to obey orders even though they are the least well-thought-out slag you have ever heard?"

"I suppose I will have to talk to your Pike myself, then. Comm code?"

Boston rattled it off with only barely concealed malice.

"And best of luck to you, Stan."

Istanbul's face was a rictus of false politeness, but he nodded, said "Good sol," to the dockmaster, and stepped out, already pulling a comm from his vest pocket.

The short dockmaster waited a few seconds for Istanbul's footsteps to fade before bounding to his feet and clasping Boston's hand in his own. "Thank you... Lord Haldis," the man wheezed, sweat dripping down his neck.

"Istanbul would ruin anyone's day," Boston agreed, withdrawing his hand as soon as was appropriate. "It was the least I could do."

Recovered slightly, the dockmaster waved his hands over his desk and studied the readout for a moment. "Do you have any idea when you'll be complete, Lord? I have several other complaints to deal with already."

"Was the inspection not scheduled ahead of time?"

The dockmaster pursed his lips. "No, Lord, it was not. We were notified this morning that *Hikawa* would not need one, then that changed when your flight was on the way. But it isn't unusual these days for these things to be... last minute."

"Great." Boston wondered just what game he was in the middle of. It could be a powerplay between Sinclair and Dearworth. "Allow me to let you get back to work, Sir."

The dockmaster glanced up, and what little color had returned to his sallow cheeks vanished. Boston steeled himself for another explosion from Istanbul at some new slight, but it was not his voice that said, "You," in a decidedly uncommon accent.

Boston turned slowly. It was not, in fact, Istanbul. Lady Von Montana stood in the doorway in a simple, if becoming, set of work clothes. Her hair was up this time, braided into a pair of rings that encircled her head. She was still wearing shadowcasters, which made her look like she had just come from a party. Even Istanbul hadn't been that vain.

"I suppose I need not wonder why my cargo is being delayed. Again. As if being inspected at Asgard, El Dorado, and Eden were not safety enough, I now find you rummaging through my life. Again."

"Lady Von Montana," Boston said quietly. "Why above Earth would I want to inconvenience you in any way?"

She blinked at him. "You really have no idea who I am, do you?"

"A beautiful woman I would enjoy getting to know better," Boston said. "Beyond that, no. And I can assure you, tonight's delays have nothing to do with you."

Her face grew harder, her mouth bending into a grimace. "Of course they do. Not enough that I am ridiculed for trying to provide the smallest scrap of perspective for our rule. Not enough that I need meticulously crafted licenses for every single atom I import from the colonies. But I need to submit to these constant harassments."

"We are searching the entire ship, Lady Montana." A headache was beginning to pound in the back of his skull. "At this moment, I doubt we even looked at one of your crates. It is all random."

"Random. Ha! It's never random."

"Lady Montana, I have already had to deal with another noble feeling personally attacked by this routine operation. This has nothing to do with you."

She shook her head. "You are going to tell me that Aspen has nothing to do with this?"

Boston blinked. "Lady Aspen is second-in-command of my ship."

"I knew it. Gods, that wraith just can't—"

Istanbul chose that moment to slide into the room, the same fake smile plastered on his face. He glanced through Lady Montana, dismissing her in an instant, and focused on Boston. "I just finished with your commander. He and I were able to… straighten everything out."

"Oh?"

Istanbul looked slightly pained. "Well enough, anyway. Now, Lord Haldis, let my cargo dock! I have a long night ahead of me, and I want this settled."

Montana snapped her mouth closed and glanced between them, eyes narrowed, weighing each word.

"How exactly did you work things out?" Boston asked.

Istanbul shook his head. "You made me deal with the Pike. No coming back to the till asking for more now, Haldis."

Boston felt his mouth go slack. Had Delaware accepted a bribe? But that would—

Istanbul clapped his hands, momentarily startling Boston. "My cargo, Haldis!"

Boston shook his head, goggling at Istanbul. "Until the Pike says to close things up, I have to—"

"Fine." Istanbul's face grew redder. "I look forward to being able to return the favor when a Haldis liner docks at Olancha. Of course, Haldis would need to be running a liner first. Taoiseach damn you."

Istanbul glanced at Montana once more before departing, leaving a sucking silence in his wake.

Boston waited, reeling with the implications, and glanced at Montana. She shook her head at him. "That proves nothing."

Boston glanced back at the dockmaster and nodded to him. "Please call again if you have any more issues." He marched out, heading for the leech, leaving the still-irate Lady Montana behind.

And just as he suspected, before he got more than a few feet, his comm was blinking with a request from Lord Delaware.

CHAPTER SEVEN

Shadows
BAGHDAD

Baghdad watched as the fifth straight day of chaos reigned in the throne room below. He'd almost missed the start of it—Nirvana petitioning for a writ to import tungsten—for what it was. Then, the news from San Wo broke with their request that the Taoiseach transfer control of their last planet to Nirvana. And finally, there was the news of the Sinclair mines.

The throne room still buzzed with the aftermath. The galleries had never been so full for a regular day's business, yet here he was again, with everyone else. He was busy watching the grind of petitions, trying to spot the currents beneath the surface, reading the implications faster than those around him. And acting in the slivers of a moment he was able to discern them.

"And that is why, Lord, House Dearworth wishes to ask for a writ of import. Too long have the Taoiseach's contracts gone unfulfilled. If other houses are not able to supply it, our house would be glad to."

Baghdad reflexively checked the contracts again on his

slate. Dearworth was playing a dangerous game. At least, they would be pissing off Nirvana and Sinclair both and not taking sides in what would soon turn bloody. If it hadn't already.

All eyes in the gallery turned to Lord Huntington, the massive Sinclair representative on the Taoiseach's ruling council. He sat at the right hand of the herald who was chairing today; the Taoiseach rarely attended in person unless he was prompted that there was interesting business before the court.

Huntington was still for a moment, his bulk impassive, before he shifted slightly. "A few sessions ago, the Taoiseach ruled that more competition was needed in this market. Since little has changed over the last few days, Sinclair raises no objection to making the same decision again."

"Interesting," Baghdad hissed, leaning forward, his knees creaking.

Menodora, the Nirvana representative on the council, passed a fleeting glance toward Huntington, then spoke up herself. "I disagree, Lord Huntington. New players have entered the market. The Taoiseach granted a new writ just a few days ago. Another..."

"And yet, no deliveries have been made, no more contracts fulfilled." Huntington hurled Nirvana's words back at them, echoing Katalia's petition. "Has anything really changed?"

The herald at the center of the table nodded sagely. "No. We have not had a chance to see which houses will be successful in realizing their potential. Are there other comments?"

None of the other councilors made a comment, though the buzz from the galleries grew. Baghdad ignored the Dearworth scion standing at the podium and focused on

Lord Huntington, the only one of the group not acting as Baghdad had expected.

"Then, hearing no other objections, I will rule in favor of granting the writ," the herald said, setting off more whispers.

Baghdad sat through three more irrelevant petitions, considering the implications. If Dearworth knew that Sinclair wouldn't contest the writ, and they found themselves working together, it could be a major shift. And make things even more dangerous.

"Lord Kun Haldis?"

Baghdad blinked himself back to the present and glanced around. An elegant woman in soft pastels was standing at the edge of his aisle.

Baghdad was on his feet in what he would have called a bound in his youth but now was simply a mistake. Still, he bowed without wavering. "How may I assist you, Lady Ababa?"

She smiled slightly and offered her hand. "I wondered if I might take a few minutes of your time for business. I have a daughter the same age as your grandson."

"Of course. Please." He offered her a chair next to his. San Cixi could make a useful ally. "Let's talk."

BOSTON

"Thank you for sending the information, Boston," Amman said, voice wavering in and out of hearing.

Chang sat with him around the table reluctantly. Sleep still dripped from Boston's eyes, but aligning schedules between planets was rarely easy.

"I need more from you, Boston," Amman continued. "Things are... getting worse here."

"Tell us what's happened," Chang said through a mouth full of cereal.

"We are all under express orders not to talk about it."

Boston and Chang shared a look. "Are you in danger, Amman?"

"Not yet."

That was hardly comforting.

"Something is going on here, Boston. Ember is almost a religious figure to the crowds now, someone they chant about. And none of them—none—can tell us anything about him. Or they refuse to. But no one can stand up to this forever. They should be breaking, and they are not."

"So, what do you want us to do about it?"

"We need the police here. We need interrogators, someone who knows what they are doing."

Chang set his spoon down, ringing gently against the bowl. "Are you mad, Amman?"

"I know it is asking a lot, but—"

"The police commissioner is in your own damn house! Why do you need us to talk to her?"

"My family controls all communications in and out of the system!" Amman shouted right back. "They refuse to admit that we have a real problem out here! That we need help. There is no way for me to talk to her. You are there! You can talk to her and never mention me."

"What exactly do we tell her?"

A long pause. "I need to go. Do this for me. Just tell her what you saw when you were here and recommend sending the police here to investigate. Do at least that for me, alright?"

But he broke the connection before Boston could respond. Boston studied Chang's face over the small table, but the bushy moustache gave away nothing.

"I know you like Amman, but..." Chang shook his head. "Going to the police is jumping without a tether. We might not make it."

"We might do a bit of good, though."

BOSTON

They met Lord Dhaka in one of the many bars that dotted Castle High's outer decks. It was a high-class place, the kind that offered very private booths from the start and private rooms if needed.

Boston stood when the young man found them and waved him over. He was wearing a rather demure formal suit, one that didn't make Boston's shadowcasters click up at his approach, though his tie was a riot of clashing colors. Nothing marked him as member of the police, but Boston supposed they didn't like to advertise.

Dhaka held out a hand. "A pleasure to meet you, Lord Kun Haldis," he said and took the seat across from Boston.

Chang had the booth opposite them and kept his head swiveling, looking for anyone who wandered too close.

"Not Kun Haldis for a few more years, hopefully," Boston said. He tried to relax, but it was hard. There were so many stories about the police.

"Oh, yes, I suppose not. Still, you are the heir, so…" Dhaka shrugged. "Boston, then?"

"Boston will do fine."

Dhaka saluted with his glass slightly. "I have been meaning to reach out, actually, so I was glad to get the message from your factor. You first, though, Lord Boston. And I should ask, is this an official meeting?"

"Not to start with."

"Ah, yes," Dhaka said with a slight grin. "One of those. Well, we can talk off-the-record. Up to a point."

Boston waited for a moment, but there was no clarification about what point they might stop being off-the-record. He pressed on before his courage failed him. "I wanted to talk through some concerns I had. About Asgard."

"Asgard, Asgard," Dhaka said to himself. "Fourth-tier

world, Chen patronage, population just a hair under a half a million. Unremarkable. Correct?"

"Close enough. They had some… unrest."

Dhaka's expression didn't change. "Unrest is nothing uncommon."

"True, but…" Taoiseach damn it, how was he going to broach the subject? "This was more than I expected. And it does not seem to be getting the attention it deserves."

"Hurm." Dhaka's interest was clearly piqued. "You know our commissioner is a Chen. Most of us have Chen patronage in the office."

"Will that be an issue?"

"It depends on what you say next. And how public a report you want to make."

"I hope it does not have to go that far."

Dhaka gave him a look. "If there is something going on, it will be very public. If not," he shrugged. "The department refuses to take part in politics. Whatever our houses may be up to, we work for the Taoiseach."

"We all do."

"Finish your story."

"There is not much more, truth be told. We were never able to get to the bottom of what was causing things to turn sour, other than the usual. And I wondered if a police presence might improve things."

Dhaka studied Boston carefully, sharp eyes peeking out of his easygoing facade. "What was the problem exactly?"

Boston shrugged. "Some new leader stirring up trouble, but we were never able to pin him down."

"I see…" Dhaka muttered. He played with a splash of water on the table idly, his hands never still. "Did this leader have a name?"

"Ember."

Dhaka's hands stopped their idle playing. "You are sure? I will be quite cross if it turns out you were pulling my leg."

"Quite sure."

Dhaka was still for a long moment. "We will have a team moving as soon as we can find a liner," he said finally. "You have that long to recant without too many consequences."

"That is... fast."

Dhaka nodded. "This is not the first time I have heard of Ember. We have reports of him stirring up trouble from Okeanos to Valhalla. Caused a riot on Olancha last week, that the local militia could not put down on their own. The Guard stepped in."

"How..." Boston whispered. Ember was a colonial, barred from travel except for a rare few permits handed out every year.

"We will find out when we catch him. I will pass your report to Lady Torriana. Discreetly," Dhaka said before offering Boston a hand. "Thank you, Lord Haldis. As much as I wish you had better news, I appreciate hearing it." Boston shook Dhaka's hand and stood as the other sapphire withdrew. An ominous, "We will be in touch," were Dhaka's parting words.

Chang sidled into the booth, a pair of coffees in his hands as soon as Dhaka left. "So?"

Boston told him and watched Chang's mustache droop with every word. "Slag," was his summary at the end. "Didn't expect that. One of the religious cultists that's allowed to travel?"

Boston shook his head. "Only thing I can think of. That is easy enough to check, though."

"Yeah."

Boston took a sip of his drink. "A riot on Olancha over

it. Guard had to step in."

Chang eyed him coolly, wordless.

"That is supposed to be us."

"Aye, but that ship has sailed, Boston."

"Not for another few months." He'd checked the liner schedule. They had eleven weeks before Istanbul sailed for Olancha, eleven weeks before it was carved in stone.

"We tried to get you another posting, and now, we're stuck on the *Cortés*!"

"Not get us another posting," Boston said, dropping his voice almost to a whisper. "Just make sure Istanbul does not get it."

Chang blinked. "Revenge isn't worth the cost of that, boy!"

"Not revenge," Boston hissed. "Keeping Olancha from blowing up is the hardest job in the Empire! Do you really think Istanbul is up to that?"

"This isn't going to help Amman, you realize."

"If someone catches Ember on Olancha, it will."

Chang scowled but made no further argument.

<h1 style="text-align:center">BERN</h1>

"This space is perfect," Montana said, pacing the room.

Bern withheld comment and let Montana have her optimism. It was perfect that was the problem. Double-tall ceilings, a huge open space they could customize however they wanted. Perfect for a gallery that would have people flocking to it.

But Bern knew the price tag, and some calculations told her Montana could never afford it. Not without significant patronage that Bern couldn't hope to provide with her meager allowance.

"Don't you love it?" her friend asked.

"I think the last one is a better fit."

Montana's face fell. "No, you don't. You think I can

afford the last one."

"They amount to the same thing."

"How much is it?"

Bern told her, and it was high enough to make her eyes go wide. But then, determination set in. "We might be able to make that work."

Bern snapped her slate closed. "No, Augustine, we cannot."

"But—"

"You need to decide what is more important to you: a liner or the gallery." Bern waved a hand. "A month's rent here costs almost a tenth of what you need for the rental. Is it really worth that risk?"

There was no hesitation. "The liner."

It burned. "Are you sure, Augustine?" Bern touched her shoulder. "Remember, you still have no idea if anyone is waiting for you back there."

Montana pulled away, keeping her face hidden. "I thought you were against the gallery."

"I want whatever makes you happy."

Montana paused. "Then I need to go back."

"Have you at least talked to the Falcon?"

She didn't even acknowledge Bern's question. "Should we put an offer on the third place, then?"

Barely bigger than Montana's townhouse, it was at least in her price range.

"I think that's for the best."

BOSTON

Getting to know the *Cortés* took what felt like an eternity but was only a few weeks of drudgery and paperwork. He spent what time he could on board; the family estate held only Baghdad's ominous tutorials on the running of the house and hints of negotiations surrounding a marriage. When Katalia's and his schedules finally matched, he welcomed the distraction.

He found the place he'd been directed to easily enough, drawn in by the brighter glow from its patrons. It was a larger club than he'd imagined two stories with balconies crossing the space above them, but lit well.

"Lord Haldis!"

He spotted Katalia almost immediately; she was positively glowing in a Nirvana-green dress. The fabric was softly illuminated from within and flickered as if she was wearing nothing but flames. He made his way through the crowd to her with difficulty, noticing quickly he was one of the few not dressed in their house colors. Katalia held court in the center of a large green patch, though by the time he'd reached her, she had managed to secure a pair of stools next to the bar.

"Glad you could make it!" she purred and touched the sleeve of his SpaceGuard uniform. "Something to drink?"

"Please." He wanted nothing more than to forget the day he'd had.

Katalia motioned to the bartender, who broke off mid-conversation with a party halfway down the bar and nodded deferentially to Katalia when he arrived.

"Two double sunrises, mixed with whatever you have older than twenty years. Imported from Camelot, if you have it."

Without a glance in Boston's direction, the bartender bustled off.

Katalia's gaze was never still. Almost immediately , her eyes alighted on a small tray borne by another waiter. "Mhm, this place is one of my favorites. They always have a supply of DeeDee on hand."

"DeeDee?"

"Oh dear, you really have been doing without."

With a wave of Katalia's fingers, the waiter

approached and offered the tray.

Katalia selected one of the small confectioneries, and with pinched fingers, she pressed the chocolate to Boston's lips. Sweet, chocolaty goodness exploded in Boston's mouth, along with a host of other flavors he couldn't identify.

"Delicious," he admitted.

Katalia smirked and popped the other half of the chocolate into her mouth. She picked a few others from the tray and waved, dismissing the waiter. "Dearworth Delicacies. Imported from Olancha. Of course, you need to put up with the bragging about them, but they are worth it. Especially if someone else has done the bartering for them."

"Do you work with Dearworth much?" Boston asked.

Katalia's eyes narrowed slightly, focusing on him again. Boston wished he knew her well enough to read the expression locked behind her shadowcasters. "As much as anyone in the family, I suppose. We get along with them better than Sinclair, at least. What do you need?"

"It can wait."

She gave him a droll look. "Tonight is supposed to be my break from politics, I will have you know, Lord Haldis. You dance well enough that I am, however, willing to listen. Briefly."

Boston nodded. "Istanbul Chi Colombia is due to ship out to Olancha, for a posting with the SpaceGuard there. It would be best for the Empire if someone else had that assignment."

He could feel her appraising him, a chilling feeling like he was a bug under her microscope. "You?"

"Ideally, but not necessarily."

"Mmm. I will decline to help you get posted somewhere else. It would spoil all the fun I have planned.

What did Istanbul do to deserve losing out on his assignment?"

"I served with him on Asgard, and he proved more than once that this kind of posting is beyond his abilities. I have little difficulty imagining the amount of slag he will get himself into on Olancha."

Katalia pursed her lips. "It sounds rather like we would be doing Dearworth a favor, preventing them from taking on such an albatross."

Boston shook his head. "Olancha is important to the Empire, beyond Dearworth."

"Hurm" Katalia considered him again. "How altruistic of you."

Boston shrugged. "Istanbul deserves everything he would get, but the people around him do not."

The butterfly wings winked at him. "Fine, fine. You want Bernie, then."

"Who?" Boston asked, but Katalia had already slipped off her stool and darted into the sea of Nirvana colors.

Boston focused on nursing his drink and steadying his stomach. Anticipation and something a little like guilt warred in his gut. But Istanbul deserved it.

Katalia returned, towing her slightly taller cousin in her wake. "Lord Haldis, a pleasure as always," Bern said, offering her hand to be kissed. "Katalia tells me you have a character you want assassinated?"

"Oh, Istanbul has no character to be impugned," Katalia cut in.

"Istanbul Chi Colombia?" Bern's composure cracked a millimeter. Her lips pursed. "Truer words were never spoken."

"And yet, he has arranged an assignment for himself on Olancha," Boston said.

"Most likely because no one in his family wants the

liability of having him around and wanted him as far away as possible," Bern said, earning a sharp nod from Katalia. "And you want to keep him here?"

"Olancha is too important a post to waste on him. Istanbul will make a rotting mess of it."

Bern studied him with the same intensity that her cousin had applied minutes before. "Certainly... which will be very embarrassing for Von Dearworth and Chi Colombia both."

"You two negotiate I see someone I need to talk to," Katalia interrupted. She fixed Boston with a firm glare. "And I expect you to be finished when I get back. Otherwise, I may have to find someone else to dance with."

Boston watched her go, but Bern continued, "On Olancha, any incompetence will be much harder to cover up than on Asgard. The matter seems likely to resolve itself without intervention."

Boston could see the logic—not that it did anything for the torrent of despair that was desperate to escape. Why wasn't the need clear to anyone else? "He may end up causing a lot of people's deaths in proving that."

"Perhaps."

Boston waited, but nothing more was forthcoming. He was aware of how outclassed he was, but this was the only thing he and Chang had been able to think of.

"I suppose it is possible," Bern said quietly, "that I might be able to look into this. Not actually do anything, mind you, but investigate. See where there are cracks that might be exploited."

"Thank you, Lady Bern, I—"

"Not for free, mind you."

Boston caught himself. "Not even for a future favor? That is how these things are done, yes?"

Bern frowned "Not by me. I have something far more concrete I need."

"How… how might I be of service to House Nirvana?"

"House Montana, actually."

"Montana? Why?"

Bern's face gave nothing away. "My business, I am afraid. How much do you remember of your first operation as a Falcon?"

Boston shivered. There were nights when he still woke from memories of that hellhole of a planet, shivering, drenched in sweat. Heard the screams. Felt the heat all around him. But there was never anything he could do to make it better. To stop those violet eyes from boring through his skull.

"Falcon?"

He shook off the memories and studied Bern more closely. How much did she know? "Why do you ask?"

Her face told him nothing. "In exchange, you will sit down with Lady Montana and myself and tell us everything that happened. Everything you can remember. And bring us any reports you have access to."

"I do not particularly enjoy reliving that night."

Bern pushed herself off her stool. "And we do not particularly enjoy dealing with mundane matters like assignments on Dearworth planets, Lord Haldis. This is the price for looking into how you might cut Istanbul's assignment out from under him. Do you accept?"

It burned, cold snow on a bare hand, but Boston nodded. "I do."

"Good. I will be in touch with details. Do your research, Lord Haldis. Falsehoods will not be tolerated."

Lady Bern stepped away without another word, disappearing into the depths of the party. Boston contemplated his drink forlornly.

He didn't notice Katalia's return until she draped an arm along his shoulders, pressing herself against him. "I hope Bernie did not spoil you for the evening?"

"Only a little."

"Cheer up, Boston. One way or another, he will be gone soon, and we will not have to endure any more of his social climbing." Katalia chuckled behind a demure hand. "'The Bull,' indeed."

"Mmm."

"Come now, Haldis. Dance with me," Katalia whispered in his ear.

ASPEN

"And just when do we actually get to punish Nirvana?" Ambroos asked.

"Patience, brother." Aspen flicked her eyes over her slate, making sure everything was ready. "Pettiness is bad for business, too."

"Nevertheless," Sherah said.

The temperature of their small, secure room dropped fractionally, but Aspen accepted the rebuke. "We need to end this chaos before it erodes our margins any further. The way to do that is to threaten what Nirvana holds most dear."

"Her daughters?" Ambroos asked, only half in jest.

"Pharmaceuticals are essential to Nirvana. Camelot is their lifeblood. Threaten that, and they will cease to trouble us."

"How?" came quick as a whip from Grenada.

"First, we need them distracted."

CHAPTER EIGHT

Chaos

BOSTON

Boston sighed as he finished one requisition report with a flourish and then saw how many more were waiting in his inbox. Paperwork was the bane of his existence and somehow there was more of it on the *Cortés* than in any of his prior duty stations.

"Perhaps it is proportional to the distance from the capital," he said under his breath.

Boston pulled up the next form and stifled a yawn. He'd been waiting for Bern to make good on their deal, but so far, he'd heard nothing. In truth, the delay suited him perfectly; there was really nothing he wanted to do less than dredge up all those things from the past.

At least the *Cortés* was docked to Castle High. It meant his nights weren't nearly as boring as—

A klaxon filled his room, and the overhead lighting shifted from soft white to blood red. Boston's hands were over his ears by reflex. He counted, one, two, three more blasts of the piercing alarm, and then he was up and running for the bridge.

Bedlam greeted him, but the piercing alarm wasn't sounding on the bridge. Four Fish occupied it, and it took Boston precious seconds to sort through the voices raised over each other.

"Report, please!" Boston yelled to be heard.

"Everyone, quiet!" one of the Fish shouted. She was an older woman wearing Trout emblems on her collar. She spared a glance for her three fellows and then nodded sharply in Boston's direction. "Lord Falcon, we've received an emergency beacon from one of the enclaves down on Earth."

One of the wall screens snapped to life, showing a hazy outline of the land area beneath them. There wasn't much of it, of course, and what little remained above the water was poorly mapped. Gold dots of imperial enclaves were scattered widely across what was left; one of the dots flashed red.

"We're tied into the security systems at each enclave," the Trout explained. "Just in case the prims get restless. The emergency beacon is an inner-perimeter breach. They could be close to being overrun."

"Slag. Any word from the Pike?"

The Trout's face grew more pained. "Malaga, anything?"

The Eel at the communications station shook her head. "Nothing. I can't get any answer from Lord Delaware, Lady Aspen, or Lord Dursun."

"What's going on?" Chang asked from the doorway. The old Wolf was panting heavily, his tunic rumpled, but his eyes roved the room, looking for any source of danger.

"Trouble on the surface." Boston thought for a moment, studying the map. "Who is the senior officer aboard, then?" he asked the Trout.

"You, Lord." The Trout glanced around. "At least, no

one else has reported in."

Boston hesitated, but his eyes were drawn back to the flashing red dot. A whole enclave full of people under attack by the primitives that still occupied Earth. He'd heard rumors they were cannibals. Or they just didn't consider people from above the same species.

"Plot our predicted track on that." There wasn't any choice. "And the optimum drop point."

"Bishkek, Rico," the senior Trout snapped, and two of her Fish began manipulating their controls. A swept curve of their trajectory appeared superimposed over the map, crossing the same continent as the flashing dot.

Another alarm sounded from Malaga's station, a fast wail that was almost as quickly silenced by his rapid movements. "That's the building alarm. They're inside."

"Rot," Chang said, shaking his head. "They'll be massacred."

"Optimum drop point is in twenty minutes," Bishkek announced, glancing up from her station. "After that, we won't have access for another six hours."

"Chang, can we drop in twenty?"

Chang's mustache curled in a feral grin. "It's an hour by the checklist. But we can do it."

"Go." Chang's feet were blurring before the word was half out of Boston's mouth. He turned back to the Trout. "Stay here and feed us whatever intel you get about the situation down there. And keep trying the Pike. If you get through, let him know the situation."

"Yes, Lord." The Trout nodded sharply. "Do you think you can make it in time?"

Boston glanced across four expectant faces. "Of course we can."

BOSTON

The three gumdrops of Boston's command cut flaming

trails down through the atmosphere of the mother planet, and Boston gritted his teeth against the rattle of reentry. Their trajectory was steep, slowing just as much from the antigravity engines in the gumdrop's core as from the air buffeting them. The temperature of the gumdrop soared, making his armor work overtime to keep his temperature down. But it was the fastest way from orbit to the ground that didn't involve becoming a pancake.

"Anything new, Baku?" Boston asked, timing his words between jolts.

"Nothing," the Trout answered. Her voice was crystal-clear despite the noise around them. "Alerts from the enclave, but nothing to give us an idea of the size or makeup of the threat. Nothing at all from the Pike."

"We go in blind, then," Boston said. In the race to make ready to depart, he hadn't had time to be annoyed, but now, his frustration threatened to bubble over. "Slag, how can we have so little information?"

Chang grunted over the net. "We couldn't have waited and made the drop. Deaf and blind was always how this would go."

"Lord, we're about to go out of range," Baku said softly. "Is there anything else we can do for you?"

"Find the rotting Pike."

Boston ignored Chang. "No, Madam, you have been immensely helpful."

"Best of luck, Lord," Baku muttered, and then, she was gone. They were alone, racing toward the ground on pre-programmed courses.

BOSTON

Their plummet continued, and the jolts increased. Boston caught his breath as best he could, then switched to a channel shared by all the wolves. "We have an entire enclave down there under attack. When we get there, it will have been forty-five minutes since the building alarm went off. It could be bad.

"We are going to go in just as hard and as fast as we can. No one stops for anything, not a cup of coffee, not doors, not walls, until we get between these rotting prims and the people down there. Is that understood?"

A chorus of howls answered him, and Boston felt the pleasant rush of the hunt under his skin. After more than a month of being trapped in high society, the drop felt good. As good as anything this painful could feel.

"Still nothing from our waste-of-air Pike?" Dunkirk asked.

"Stow it, Pack Second," Boston said. "We will just have to settle this one ourselves. Just remember to keep your IFF up at all times. Aimed shots only, unless I give the word."

Grunts of assent answered him. Boston glanced at the drop clock. Still another four minutes until they hit the ground. The exterior cameras were hashed; whether from the dark, the rain, or the heat of reentry, he couldn't tell. It was as if they were falling through a void.

Lights flickered on in the dim gumdrop—the three minute warning before touch-down. Boston glanced around at the Wolves, but they were impossible to read in their heavy armor. He could have read the mood of his old pack just by their grunts as they fought the heavy weight of deceleration on their chests, but not these strangers.

They were all sitting facing outward, backs to the central hub of the gumdrop, waiting for impact. Long splinter rifles were held at the ready, waiting for the moment the seats below them would fire, launching them through the hull of the gumdrop and into battle. Less than a second after landing, the Wolves' boots would hit the ground ten feet from the gumdrop, ready to fight. Just the noise of a gumdrop landing was enough to incapacitate a crowd, if it was targeted close enough.

"What kind of Pike takes the whole command crew out to dinner and leaves no one in charge of the bridge?" Chang groused in Boston's ear.

Boston checked that they were on an isolated channel before replying. "One where the ship is tied up in dock and has not moved in years?"

The drop clock buzzed, and Boston switched back to the flock-wide channel. "Everyone, remember your deployments. Find the survivors as quick as you can."

Red lights flashed overhead—the thirty-second warning—and Boston tensed every muscle in his body, clamping down on the rifle, his knees together, ready to pounce as soon as the impact came.

And then it came.

The gumdrop slammed down from above, gravlock screaming to keep them from cratering like a meteor, velocity falling too fast to track. The moment the gumdrop crossed the safety threshold, Boston's seat accelerated him up and out, launched from the gumdrop and into the air.

He hit the ground with practiced ease, hitting, rolling, and coming up into a bounding gallop toward the enclave ahead, his rifle at the ready. He swept his rifle left, right, center, looking for anything that wasn't a friendly, but nothing appeared out of the gloom other than the gray buildings.

Seven of the Wolves—a whole pack—settled in behind him as they ran for the building. Meanwhile, 2nd and 3rd packs had landed equidistant around the enclave and were completing their own runs.

Boston checked the readout from the wall ahead and slowed his pace slightly. "Abuja, breaching charge."

Abuja, 1st pack's striker, lengthened her stride and withdrew a breaching charge from the bandolier in the small of her back. Boston stopped a few feet from the wall, rifle still on a swivel, as Abuja traced out the shape of the hole she wanted and placed charges at the four corners.

"1st pack in position," Voyen reported a few feet to Boston's rear.

"2nd, in position for breach," Gault reported over the same net.

"3rd, ready, going in the windows," Carla completed the trifecta.

"Go."

Boston was moving as the explosive charge detonated, weakening the wall just enough so when he hit it, it shattered under him. At his back, the Wolves flooded into the building, moving as fast as their armored legs could carry them.

The corridor was well-lit, though covered in dust, and Boston flew down it, trying to orient himself. They hadn't been able to find plans for the enclave anywhere, so they were flying blind.

"Got a kitchen here," Gault announced on the net. "Staff is hiding in the aisles. No casualties yet."

"Couple here. Some cuts from glass. Nothing serious."

"Nothing back here. Delivery docks clear."

Ahead, someone screamed. Boston pushed himself, heading for a nice pair of double doors. He didn't stop, but hit them at full speed, shattering them, and swept the room ahead.

It was a dining room, luxuriously appointed, large enough to seat several dozen. And inexplicably, there were people seated at the table. Others were slowly rising to their feet in front of him. There was even food on the table.

Boston did a quick sweep, but every one of them had an implant and glowed green in his HUD.

"Where are the prims?" he asked, taking off the voice

filters. "What rooms have been compromised?"

Stunned silence followed his question. On the net, Wolves were still announcing their findings, all negative. No bodies, no blood, no prims. No signs of a break-in.

At the end of the table, someone finished getting to their feet. Boston focused on that end of the table. As the dust and dirt of his entrance cleared, his stomach sank to the planet's core. Delaware's eyes glared daggers at Boston, his jowls quivering as he got to his feet.

"What in the Taoiseach's name are you doing?"

BERN

Bern was careful to keep her face placid as the disaster played out in front of her. The wine helped, a new vintage from Heaven she'd brought to create the right atmosphere. But nothing could have helped enough.

They'd hung tapestries in interesting colors to make the space feel larger. But it hadn't done a bit of good. The overhead was too low, claustrophobic, and they were tucked away three turns from the main promenade, far enough back that foot traffic was minuscule. It felt more like a forgotten aunt's storeroom than a gallery you would trust enough to buy art from.

And Montana knew it. She was far less adept at hiding her panic, her frustration, and the few potential patrons who waded in received the brunt of it. She could be quite charming, but only when she didn't think about it. When she did, the result was exactly as it played out in front of her.

Bern held the glass and bottle tightly as Montana threw herself onto the second rickety stool they'd rented. "Give me one," she said, reaching for a glass on the other side of the counter.

"Are you sure that would be wise?" Bern asked.

"Do you see anyone who wants to buy?"

"I suppose not." She poured a quarter glass for her friend.

Montana's hair had come out of its neat bun, fraying around the edges where she'd tugged it in her annoyance. It was oddly captivating, and Bern's gaze kept straying to it.

"This was all for nothing."

"Say nothing of the kind, Augustine!"

"A disaster."

"Well, it is that. However, it was not for nothing."

"I just lost so much money." Montana's voice was strained.

"We got your name out there. Now you can say you had a pop-up. We can get people interested in the next time."

"I can't afford to do this again!"

"We will find a way," Bern said, not quite believing it, but sensing how close Montana was to the brink. "We are not going to stop now, are we?"

Montana's eyes were shinning. "No, no we aren't. But, Clarisse—"

Bern rested her hand on Montana's, ignoring the sudden hammering of her own pulse. "We will find a way through this."

She didn't pull away. "I—"

"What entrepreneurs you look."

Bern's head snapped up toward the open door to their closet. Katalia leaned against the doorway in a figure-hugging pink concoction, eyes covered by shadow-casters. Despite the teasing lilt to her voice, there was no mirth in her face.

"Oh, what are you doing here?" Montana asked. She dropped her head onto her hands, refusing to look at Katalia.

"Sorry," Katalia mouthed and moved to stand over Montana's shoulder. "Believe me, I had other plans this evening. However, darling," Katalia patted Montana's shoulder, "you managed to get Bernie to turn off her slate. And it has turned into a rather exciting night."

"Slag." Bern's heart sank as she reached for her bag across the bar. "What has Sinclair done now?"

A small smile appeared at the corner of Katalia's face. "We are not exactly sure, but they dropped Wolves down to Earth at the last minute. Jordana wants everyone home, just in case."

"In case of what, exactly?"

Katalia shrugged. "Everyone has suddenly realized Sinclair has the only real soldiers in the capital. You do the math."

Bern thought rapidly, but it was a terrifying idea. Even if nothing ever came from it, Sinclair showing that they could drop two dozen Wolves on an enclave with zero notice was... troubling.

Jordana was right this was something they needed to discuss immediately. "I need to go, Augustine," Bern said softly. "Will you be alright?"

But Montana seemed just as galvanized by the news as Katalia. She was upright again, her wineglass forgotten, and fixed Katalia with a calculated gaze. "A Wolf drop? Haldis's Wolves?"

"Forget I said anything. Idle gossip. We should go, Bernie."

Bern nodded and allowed herself to be towed away.

BOSTON

Just getting the Wolves marshaled and back to the *Cortés* had taken hours. And then, Delaware had started on his rant. It still burned, having to stand there silent and take the abuse Delaware heaped on them. And for nothing more than doing their duty.

Boston's only consolation was that it wasn't public. The most common speculation was that there had been an unscheduled drill

Still, just telling the story to Baghdad was acid in his throat. Failure was a rare pill that Boston had to swallow. As were threats of being cashiered.

"I told you before, he can't," Chang said. "It was his fault for not leaving standing orders, as he should have. His fault for not informing anyone that the whole command crew would be out of contact. He didn't even make new watch bills! It's gross negligence on his part."

Baghdad nodded. "You did the only thing you could do in those circumstances. As commander of the *Cortés*, it is ultimately Delaware's responsibility."

Boston shook his head. "He was apocalyptic.

"It was sloppy," came from Chang, affronted, "castrating you in front of everyone."

"Or calculated to humiliate you," Baghdad agreed. "But how did this happen? What exactly did happen?"

Boston shook his head. "It was a sophisticated hack that sent us false warnings. As to why, Delaware has no idea. Just said he would raise it with the house leadership."

"The house? Sinclair? Not the Guard? Not the police?"

Boston nodded miserably. "Chang said it perfectly, Grandfather. Delaware must know this slag will land on him, too, so Sinclair is keeping it internal."

Baghdad leaned back in his chair, the leather creaking loudly. "That is a problem..." he said slowly.

"At least it keeps us from being embarrassed," Chang muttered.

"True, but it also keeps anyone else from finding out what happened." Baghdad took a long drink from his coffee, thinking hard. "Why would someone do this?"

"Embarrass Sinclair?"

"No one knows about it. And they won't. Sinclair will be able to keep the details quiet."

Boston's frustration peaked. "Then why do it?"

"I have no earthly idea. Which means someone isn't playing by the rules."

Boston felt a chill, as even Baghdad looked a little stricken. "That scares me."

"Me too," Baghdad agreed.

"All the more reason to get the police investigating! Critical safety infrastructure compromised. Imperial systems, not house systems. Someone should..." Boston trailed off and fixed Baghdad with a hard look. If he'd thought of it, then the old man must have, too.

"Someone should?" Chang prompted, glancing between them.

"Finish the thought," Baghdad said, smiling now.

"Someone should leak it. Force the police to investigate a public humiliation."

Chang snorted. "We'd be torn to pieces. Boston leading a charge of Wolves to no-where? He'd be a laughingstock."

"Which is why no one will believe we're the ones who leaked it."

BOSTON

It was worse than he expected. Every gossip columnist and professional journalist on Castle High latched onto the story. People asked if the Guard was too high-strung. There were rumors of inquiries. The Wolves were harassed in bars.

But somehow, that wasn't the worst of it. Not facing the snickers, not seeing his face plastered on screens over the station, not listening to the scandalized interviews of

the Terran staff, not the video of Delaware screaming at hi,
in the wrecked ballroom. No, the moment he dreaded
most of all was waiting for him in a private room of a
Castle High nightclub.

Lady Montana was seated when the hostess led him in
and made no move to rise. Or to offer him a chair. Even
here, the music thrummed distantly, and the lights were
set bright enough that his shadowcasters were still active,
washing out the displays filling the room.

He waited for her to speak, but nothing seemed
forthcoming. So, he drank her in instead. She really was
quite enchanting, with a skin tone dark enough that it
must take effort to maintain. That, or regular trips to a real
planet.

"Bern said you had something to tell me," she said
finally, breaking the silence.

"If you insist."

She looked up for the first time. "You act like you are
not proud of it. You seem to have a history of such bloody
engagements."

"Never by choice, my Lady."

She was impossible to read, still wearing her
shadow-casters. "You would never know it by reading
these reports."

"When was the last time you were completely satisfied
with a job you had done?"

"Rather frequently."

"Well then, I envy you. I wish I could say the same."

She was quiet for a moment and then gestured for him
to take a seat. "Tell me your story, Lord Haldis."

"What do you want to know?"

Her black eyes held no mercy. "Everything."

So, he told her. The words twisting his gut, he found
every memory he had of that night, every one of his

failures, and poured them out onto the table in front of her.

It left him feeling empty.

"So, that's it? You killed them all?"

"I killed none of them." It hurt to admit, burned to think of how young and naive he'd been. But she'd said to give her every detail. "I never fired that night. My first mission, and I… just…"

He could recall that terror, his hands trembling, the urge to run, the urge to save something, anything from that night.

"They beat that mercy out of you before long, I see."

"I was eventually able to grow out of being a child, yes."

Her knuckles went white. "And you never considered that that kid was right?"

"I—"

"Never mind." She drummed a hand on the table. "Your morality isn't why we are here. The entire village was destroyed, yes?"

Boston nodded. "No one was left alive."

There were tears dripping down her cheeks. Why was she crying? But you wouldn't have known from her voice as she instructed, "Tell me about the *Dakota*. The ship that crashed."

Boston's confusion deepened. "I never saw it."

"Tell me what you know, anyway."

Boston thought hard, trying to recall what the pack that had gone down to the *Dakota* had said. "It did not crash."

Now it was her turn to freeze and stare at him. "It didn't?"

"My Lady, what is this? Why—?"

"I am trying to figure out what happened to the ship."

Still mystified, Boston studied her again. He noticed

the diamonds on her bracelet. High-ranking indeed, but Montana wasn't one of the four diamond houses in the empire. "Did you have family aboard?"

"You could say that. Now, tell me what you know!"

"The *Dakota* landed fully intact. No one could find any damage to it, and the Fish went over it several times. The *Dakota* had landed, and the crew slaughtered by the colonists before—"

"They weren't!"

He felt her anger like heat radiating from a gumdrop after reentry, a bonfire of feeling held back by the barest veneer.

"How do you know that?"

The heat cut out in an instant as she retreated behind some wall, her face smoothing. "Because I do my research, too."

She tapped at her slate, and a crude survey map flashed up on the screen. There were only a few markings, which were hand-drawn over the map, but the village and the *Dakota* were both marked.

"The *Dakota* wasn't detected until the orbit after your Wolves dropped," Montana said, drawing in the orbit tracks. "That puts her crash site at least 1200 miles east. And there is no way the villagers you described could have traveled that far."

"I..." Boston studied the map, but it looked right. "I suppose not."

"Something else happened to the *Dakota's* crew. And I am going to find out what."

Boston buried any questions he would have asked. "I am afraid that is all I know."

"Fine." A slim drive skipped across the table toward him, and he caught it in one hand. "Bern said to give this to you."

Boston pocketed the drive. "Will there be anything else, my Lady?"

She shook her head and waved him out.

Boston made it all the way to the alameda, three doors down, before he realized who she had to be.

CHAPTER NINE

Revelations
BERN

Bern fumed at the end of the table as the family meeting dragged on and on. She studied her slate, unseeing, paging through tab after tab without reading. Things were getting worse on Eden. Again. Restlessness in the colonists and on a world just a few light years from Sol.

Far more interesting was the news that had broken this past week. It finally explained Sinclair's actions, their Wolves. And it filled Bern with a sense of dread. Things were spinning out of control.

"We need more support from the Guard," Taarush declared, raising his voice slightly to be heard over the muttering. "And soon, before things slip beyond our control."

Menodora shook her head. She was seated at her mother's right hand at the far end of the table, across from Katalia, in a formal ball gown. Tonight was the third family meeting called at the last minute in less than a week.

"What would you have us do, Taarush? We have

recalled the *Attila* and the *Bonaparte* from their patrol routes. That was hard enough without the entire court understanding the depth of your failure."

Taarush flushed. "Ember is stirring up trouble. It has nothing to do with our policies."

"Well, when the *Attila* arrives in six months, you can root him out and make him pay for it."

Bern watched her little cousin's hands tighten out of sight. She wished he'd asked for her help, but no, he was beyond such things now. "Six months is too long. We need to stamp this out before the harvest."

"We cannot bend the speed of light faster, Taarush," Jordana said gently. He was a favorite. "What would you have us do?"

"Send in the *Cortés*. She could be in orbit of Eden in hours."

A ripple went around the room. "The *Cortés* is a Sinclair ship," Jordana reminded everyone.

"The *Cortés* is a SpaceGuard ship."

Bern could have cheered. Taarush could be rash and stubborn, but he had a good head on his shoulders. Finally, someone else was brave enough to say it.

Menodora looked like someone had sideswiped her with a liner, but Jordana kept herself more in check, looking disappointedly down the table at Taarush.

"I am sure having to keep things together on Eden has been hard on you, Tarui," Jordana said. "We appreciate everything you have had to do. However, we will not make fools of ourselves for Sinclair— and the rest of the court—by admitting we cannot handle things ourselves. Especially not now. They would seize on our request, as innocent as it is, and use it to weaken us. No. You will find a way to prevent this from becoming a catastrophe. I have faith in you."

Bern watched Taarush war with himself, before common sense finally lost. He nodded, just once, and sat without another word.

"What is next?" Jordana asked, glancing down the table.

BOSTON

"Just don't mention it," Chang whispered in Bostons ear as they made their way stiffly down to the Wolf den. Starched tight, their dress uniforms were almost new.

The other Wolves were already there, and Boston walked down the line of them, looking for anything out of place, following a step or two behind Voyen, who was doing the same thing. Boston only found one medal that wasn't straight.

He had just enough time to finish his inspection before Delaware stomped in, pulling at his tie. He glanced in Boston's direction, nodded, and took up position next to the doorway. It might have been comical, except for the graveness of his face.

Boston found his own place in line and tried to remind himself that this was their idea. They'd released things on purpose so someone would investigate. This was better than the alternative of no one investigating. Still, the dread that settled low in his stomach was hard to ignore.

Bagpipes played over the ship's intercom, and then, Aspen led Lady Torriana Von Chen into the den.

The police commissioner was a trim, grey-haired woman only a little shorter than Aspen, but all breathing stopped when she entered the room. Snarling Tigers glinted from her shoulders, but they were nothing compared to her grim visage.

She didn't break her stride and took the center of the compartment like it was her ship, examining each Wolf and Lord Delaware alike. Boston felt like his entire soul was on display for her as her eyes glanced over him and along the line of Wolves.

Dhaka, in police silver and black, and two other Cats slid into the room after her, each of them performing the same assessment of the assembled Guard. There was no flash of recognition from Dhaka, though. He may as well have been a stranger.

"At ease," Torriana barked. It wasn't her order to give, but every Wolf obeyed it, standing at rest with a snap of two dozen boots hitting the deck at the same moment. Boston's feet were among them.

"The Condor Supreme has asked my Cats and I to help get to the bottom of this security breach," Torriana announced with no preamble. She was a woman who didn't need to introduce herself. "Each of you will speak to one of my Cats. You are to tell them everything and anything they ask. Everything that seems relevant, and anything that seems irrelevant. Our one and only goal is to determine how this ship's systems were compromised.

"It is probable that some of you share responsibility for this. It will not have seemed like a crime. It may not even have been worth remarking on at the time. However. The command codes for this ship were passed to those who had no need of them. And that did not happen by accident."

Torriana glanced to each of her Cats. "Cooperate, and the Taoiseach will show you clemency. Fail to do so, and we will assume you are complicit."

Silence greeted her words, not even the shuffling of fabric.

They broke them up after that, talking to each of them individually. Boston was called first and found himself leading Lady Torriana to the wardroom. With her eyes on the back of his head, a walk of less than a minute felt like an hour. He took a seat on one side of the linen tablecloth as the Lady Tiger sat across from him, and Dhaka blocked the door.

"Lord Haldis, you do not disappoint," Torriana started, making Boston jump slightly. She extended a hand across the table, and Boston shook it, surprised by the intensity of her grip. "And the stories about you have made that a great achievement, I must say. It is a pleasure to meet you, Lord."

"Thank you, my Lady."

"Dhaka and I very much appreciate you coming forward and telling us about Ember's antics on Asgard," she said, voice made of honey. "Even if those in my house failed to see the importance of coming forward, you did, and that makes you an excellent judge of things."

"Thank you, my lady."

"We will catch Ember before long, do not worry. Even if he is a Terran."

"What?"

Torriana's eyes flickered to Dhaka.

"Ember has been active on several worlds, stirring up trouble," Dhaka said. "And none of the permitted colonials fit his movements."

"Whoever it is, I will see them buried alive for this. Fomenting rebellion in the colonies! Hard to imagine someone would be that stupid."

Boston's head was spinning. Ember might be a Terran? How could they have missed that?

"Nirvana seems to have been spared the treatment. Did you know that?" Torriana continued, not giving him a moment to think.

"No."

"Did you give anyone from Nirvana access to the *Cortés*?" slipped out of her mouth like a cat pouncing.

"No."

"Are you sure? You have been sleeping with their third-in-line. Did she promise you something in exchange for a quick peek at her rival's business?"

Heat rose in Boston's face, but he shook his head. "No, my Lady."

"You might not have known it happened," Dhaka offered, giving Boston a kind smile. "Just leaving your slate unlocked when she was in the room could have been enough. Did that ever happen?"

"No."

"Can you really be sure, Lord Haldis?" Torriana asked. "It may have only taken one slip."

"I am sure, my Lady. I never take my Guard slate with me when I leave the ship."

"Hurm." She rolled her neck to one side, studying him. "What about that sympathizer you have been associating with. Lady Montana? Did she ever have an undue interest in the *Cortés*?"

Boston shook his head. "What would she have to gain?"

Torriana shrugged. "Not the question I asked."

Boston shook his head. "No, she never showed any interest."

Again, Dhaka broke in helpfully, "It would have been subtle, Boston. Anything from a serial number of a console, a restricted net access."

Boston shook his head.

"Fair enough." Torriana nodded.

For a full hour, the questions came. Sometimes hard, convoluted questions designed to trip him up; sometimes lightning-fast. And for that whole time, Torriana's eyes never left his face, hardly blinked, just bored into him through her halo of gray hair. He made it until the end—through all the questions about his slate, his Wolves, whether any of them had been acting suspiciously, whether any of them were disgruntled—before he broke.

"Whose idea was it to go public with the breach?" Torriana asked, and the answer was out of his mouth before he realized he'd said anything.

"Baghdad."

Horror hit him immediately, but Torriana's face didn't move a muscle. A dozen frantic heartbeats passed before her face cracked in a smile.

"Very good, Lord Haldis. I think I believe you."

Boston slumped on the table. He had one job, and he'd rotted it up.

"You did very well for such a novice at this."

"What happens now?"

"You mean, after you admitted to leaking classified information to the media? After you admitted to giving such embarrassing details about your own commander's failings to his house's enemies?" Torriana asked. "Nothing at all, Lord Haldis. For the moment."

He blinked. "What?"

"Lord Haldis, you are going to owe me," Torriana said quietly. "And if you ever do get word of anything, anything at all, related to this business, you will tell me. No matter if it is Lady Katalia or some random Terran you bump into on the street. You will not even wait an hour before telling me." Her eyes held no mercy at all. "If you do, we will destroy you."

It was said so plainly, so matter-of-factly, that Boston struggled to register it. But she was deadly serious.

"We have a lot of other people to interview," Dhaka said quietly.

"Yes, we do. Well then, Lord Haldis?" She offered her hand again. "Next time, do come to us directly. Rather than the media."

BERN

Bern tapped at her slate, not really seeing it, but needing something to cover her nerves. This just wasn't done, going to Jordana directly, but there was nothing else for it. She needed to know.

The door to Jordana's chambers slid open, and Katalia poked her head out. "She is ready for you." Katalia's gaze, with just the two of them, was full of concern. But Bern didn't let her mask drop. If she did now, there was no way she could get it back in time.

Jordana was eating at a small table in a nook of the room, Menodora at her side. There were only three chairs, and Katalia found hers before Bern found her breath.

"What is it, Clarisse?"

Her hands were damp on her slate, but Bern clasped it behind her back and soldiered on. "I trust everyone is familiar with Sinclair dropping a Wolf pack on one of their own dinners?"

Menodora chuckled under her breath. "It has turned into quite the embarrassment for them."

"It has."

"What of it?" Jordana asked, and Menodora's grin disappeared.

Here it was. "Was it us?"

A pregnant pause filled the room. Menodora and Katalia both turned to look at their mother, who reacted not at all, just dabbed at the corner of her mouth with a napkin. "If it was?" she asked after the silence had stretched to the breaking.

"Mother!" Katalia hissed quietly.

"I merely want to understand Clarisse's intentions," Jordana said smoothly.

"If it was not us," Bern said, "we need to say so.

Immediately. Public opinion already believes it was us. Sinclair just announced an embargo on Camelot. They seem to think it was us."

Menodora curled her lip. "They would have gone after Camelot eventually, either way."

"This is madness, Jordana. We need to be ending this House War, now, before the damage is irreversible. Our own estimates project revenue being down thirty percent this year!"

Jordana maintained her stoic expression. "What else would you have us do?"

"Talk to them," Bern said. "Do exactly what Sinclair showed they were willing to do with Dearworth; sit down and talk. Without cameras and without eavesdroppers. And solve this."

Jordana shook her head. "I understand, Clarisse. It sounds attractive, but how could we possibly arrange that? If it became public that we were surrendering to Sinclair..."

"We are not surrendering."

Jordana shook her head. "It may not matter. If they leak that we are, if they leak that we asked to meet first, even if that is all they announce... You understand what the consequences could be."

"How can we know if it is possible unless we try?"

She kept a careful grip on herself as the silence lengthened, and, Taoiseach forsake it all, Jordana actually considered it. Bern's slate chimed, so low only she could hear it, but she refused to break her gaze.

Finally, her composure cracked. "Find out what is possible." Jordana said finally.

"Mother—"

Jordana held up a hand, and Menodora fell silent immediately. "Clarisse, it is worth a chance at ending this.

However, if you are wrong, if Sinclair tries to betray us, I will deny we ever considered approaching them. And deny you had any backing from anyone here. Is that clear?"

Bern felt the estate turning around her for just a second. "I understand."

"Then leave us. And for all of our sakes, I hope you are right."

ASPEN

"And what do we do about this proposal from Nirvana?" Ambroos asked idly, spinning his slate in one hand.

"We take it," Aspen replied. "A way to get rid of these pointless games is a blessing."

"Hardly," Ambroos said. "We managed to sweep up three houses so far, and I have my eye on another."

"As I have said before, Ambroos, while effective, your methods are… fragile. Yes, we can pick up the assets for a song, but it takes time to turn them back into something worth acquiring."

Ambroos shrugged. "That is what you are so good at, sis. Fattening the calf. Leave the slaughter to me."

Aspen sighed and gave up on her brother. He might eventually see, but it was no longer worth her time to convince him. Sherah, though, usually could be counted on to see reason. Usually.

"Nirvana has proven too hardy for your usual methods to work," Sherah said.

Ambroos scowled, but he was smart enough to admit they were right.

"All the more reason to focus on growing the pie before we come back and try to smother them," Aspen agreed.

"Do you think your cousin is sincere?"

Aspen considered that and nodded. "Bern is very

focused on building Nirvana's financial standing. It makes her… predictable. Ending this fight makes the most financial sense for both of us. Therefore, she will do everything in her power to bring her family to heel."

"And if they have some contingency prepared?" Even before someone leaked it, the hack against their cruiser had been concerning. Concerning enough that Aspen had installed a second, more direct link from their enclaves to the bridge. If the *Cortés* was called, it would receive it.

"It would be nothing we are not prepared for."

Sherah's eyes glittered. "A pity for Nirvana they did not listen to Bern sooner."

"Pity Nirvana does not have a viper like Aspen of their own."

"Why thank you, Ambroos." Aspen offered him a rare, genuine, smile. "You say the nicest things."

BOSTON

Boston fidgeted in his chair, more than a little uncomfortable and stuck in another endless staff meeting in the small conference room on the *Cortés*. The chairs were stiff, his back was stiff the conversation was stiff, as Delaware prattled on about some perceived slight.

In the last few weeks, Boston and the flock had made fifteen drops down to Earth. All of them were planned exercises, part one of Delaware's punishments for the mess he'd made, but that didn't help the bruises. And the increased gravity, the bumpy rides to and from orbit, and the launch out of a gumdrop all left their marks on him.

"And then, later this week will be the family gala on the surface," Delaware continued. "I expect all of you to put in an appearance. This is our opportunity to show off for the house leadership, and we will do it with a united front."

Boston glanced across the table at Lady Maine, the

other non-Sinclair officer, but she refused to meet his gaze.

"Yes, even the two of you," Delaware said, and Boston glanced back at the commander. "Lady Maine knows that the San Zoila are always welcome. As for you, Lord Haldis, I think leaving you in orbit with me on the planet again would be tempting fate. You will be there." Delaware's tone brooked no disagreement.

"Of course, my Lord."

"Good. You and I can go over what a properly maintained security system looks like up close."

Boston nodded, not trusting himself to speak. Seven days of this, seven staff meetings, and seven blatant digs at his ability to command. Delaware was nothing if not persistent. The rest of the officers studiously ignored the exchange, looking everywhere but at him.

Boston made it through the rest of the meeting without losing his temper and without speaking. The needling was constant, and by the time he was able to excuse himself for the short walk to his quarters, he was fuming silently.

The small room already felt quite a bit like home. It was functionally identical to every other SpaceGuard cabin he'd enjoyed over the last ten years, and he'd finally started to be able to ignore the small differences. *Cortés* was still an unhappy ship, but the small piece of consistency meant the world to him.

"Still making you go to the gala?" Chang asked, leaning nonchalantly on the wall of the corridor, just outside Boston's room.

"Apparently," Boston sighed. "Baghdad still intent on coming?"

Chang nodded. "He says he needs to make sure you don't make a mess of things."

Boston thumbed the door open, biting back a retort. "Having his and Delaware's trust means the world to me.

And you?"

"I think I'll stay up here with the Wolves," Chang said, stepping inside. "Make sure they don't get into any trouble without any officer supervision."

"Forsake it all, this is going to be miserable."

"Probably. Shoot yourself in the foot?"

"Ha. If only. Leaving the Guard is starting to not sound so bad."

Chang dropped into Boston's chair. "Serving here at the capital will do that to you. But we'll be back in the colonies before too long."

Boston just shook his head. "Go get ready for the drop. I will be there in a few minutes."

Chang nodded but made no move to leave. "Things will get better, boy. I promise."

PART TWO

CHAPTER TEN

Games

Empires fall due to small decisions, personal decisions. But never alone, never in isolation. It takes many of those small decisions, many of those little, personal choices, to build a catastrophe and convert a whispered tremor into world-shaking potential.

It should be easy to avoid. Easy to not drive through hostile streets n an uncovered car. But it never is.

Even then, it takes a determined kind of blindness not to see the funnel cloud coming for you. Not to hear the roar of the waterfall just around the bend.

Empires give their consent to fall.

But then again, empires are just the shared dream of their members. And anything created by man can be destroyed by it.

BAGHDAD

Frequently, those who could hear the rumble, who would turn the boat around are not at the helm. And those that are at the helm, have grown unable to see and hear and react in time—if they ever could.

Baghdad Kun Haldis was not one of those asleep at the wheel, though he took the opportunity of the limo ride to Castle High to doze lightly. Sinclair had provided a shuttle service for the evening, saving him the trouble of having to rent a lifter. But it meant another stop, another wait.

"I swear, this one event will consume my entire day," Baghdad said under his breath.

Boston was the only one close enough to hear and chuckled under his breath.

His grandson was in fine form, flirting with a pair of noblewomen before they'd even reached the small waiting area. Dressing sharply was one thing Boston could do on his own, and Baghdad found little to critique. Tonight would make an excellent opportunity to introduce Boston to some potential matches. But only if Baghdad could prevent the boy from making any further messes.

"Boy, make yourself useful and go get me a glass of something." Baghdad gestured at the bar set up on the other side of the small waiting terminal.

"Tired already, old man?" Boston asked but headed off to join the queue anyway.

Baghdad felt a twinge from his bad knee and rested a little heavier on hia cane. This always happened when he had to stand for long periods; for whatever reason, that triggered the injury more than anything else.

Baghdad began a slow circuit of the waiting hall, picking his way between the revelers carefully, observing. Lady Ababa refused to meet his eye; she'd been ducking his calls ever since Boston had been made to look a fool. As had most of the families of eligible partners he'd found.

Baghdad made the turn around a row of chairs but had to step back as a woman cut him off. He wavered but got the cane down and rested both   hands on it to recover. "My apologies, my Lady."

"Watch where the hell you are going, my Lord."

"Of course. My eyesight isn't what it used to be," he hedged, taking the opportunity to study the young woman. Her tanned skin was striking against a lavender dress, and her face was framed by dark brown hair. Although her head barely came up to his chest, she carried herself with a forceful presence. The effect was marred somewhat by the grit of her teeth and the tension she obviously carried.

"Yes, Lady Montana, do be more careful!" one of the cluster of women she was conversing with teased. "Not all of us have your center of gravity."

The group tittered, and the young woman at his elbow flushed. "Thank you for the reminder, Lady Ahava. At least I have never had to worry about hitting my head on a doorframe."

Lady Ahava scowled and brushed a lock of hair behind her ear. Her hair coiled up into a tall spire added to her already impressive height.

The group's smiles thinned somewhat. "Is this one of your imports?" asked another woman with dark-brown skin and a light-blue dress. She darted forward and pinched the fabric of Montana's sleeve. "You know, you could wear an expensive dress to one of these."

"Some people enjoy the style."

"You know they fence the prims out of the enclave, right? You can dress to impress nobles," the final lady of the group said.

Lady Montana made no reply, and the group shook their heads sadly and headed away, Lady Daejeon's dress trailing behind her, prolonging the exit.

"You could drop your glass on the train," Baghdad suggested as it slithered past. "But it's probably change fabric, so it may not have the effect you want."

Lady Montana appeared to consider it for a moment before shaking her head. "No, I told myself I was not going to make another enemy tonight."

"Enemies are the sign of a life well-lived."

"That's what I keep telling myself."

"I take it you are Lady Von Montana, our resident importer of colonial art?"

"If you would like to get a jab in, now would be the time." Her voice was more tired than Baghdad expected.

"Not at the moment," he answered only a little behind his mark. "I'll let you know if any come to mind. I take it you did not succeed in making a sale?"

"It was a long shot, but San Cixi likes to make it look as if they have a long history of looting the colonies."

"You might try Lord Durban Von Anker," Baghdad said. "He was quite the collector when we served together."

"Von Anker is too strapped for cash right now to make major purchases," she said reflexively. Baghdad filed that away for later review; it was news to him. "What I really need is a contact with Dearworth. They are still trying to keep up appearances."

"You may have better luck once we get down there," Baghdad said, glancing around and not seeing a single diamond in the crowd. "The diamond houses seem to have made their own arrangements for transportation."

She offered her hand. "I will try that. Thank you for the tip." Then, she was gone, disappearing into the crowd.

The trip down to Earth was harder than he remembered. As a Wolf, he'd made combat drops into the middle of hurricanes and facing heavy artillery. Once he'd had to exit a gumdrop that took a hit when it was still a mile up. He fell the rest of the way with an emergency parachute on his armor. And yet, the sedate descent into the atmosphere of the home planet—in a lifter, no less—left him grasping both armrests with every jolt. By the time they were finally on the ground, Baghdad was almost panting, leaning heavily on his cane as the heavy fingers of a real planet's gravity gripped him for the first time in decades. Just getting out of his chair was a struggle, but he managed.

"Doing alright there, Grandfather?"

He nodded, not answering, and paced out into the night.

Gray clouds hung over them, as they did everywhere on the harsh remnant of the mother world. The air was heavy with water, making him sweat immediately, but it was clear and fresh. Just like he remembered.

"They provided boards. Excellent," Boston said as they made their way into the great ballroom. Spread around the edges of the room were small tables for four, each with its own Empire board. "Fancy a rematch?"

Baghdad considered and nodded. "It'll take long enough to get everyone down here. We probably have time for a game before dinner. Go find us a fourth."

Boston raised an eyebrow. "Have you already found us a third?"

"I think I know someone who would put up a good fight, yes."

Baghdad found Lady Montana already seated, chatting animatedly with a Nirvana scion. He announced his approach with a cough and timed his bow perfectly as she glanced up. "Good sol, Lady Montana."

Her expression was bemused. "You again, Lord?"

Not wanting to be rude, Baghdad glanced to her companion, who offered her hand. "Lady Bern Chi Nirvana."

He took it automatically and replied, "Good sol, Lady

Bern. Lady Montana, I wondered if you would give my grandson and I the pleasure of a game of Empire before dinner?"

Montana raised an eyebrow, clearly interested, but glanced at her friend.

"I have plenty to do to get ready," Bern assured her. "Go play. It will be fun."

"Why me?" Montana asked, switching her gaze back to him.

"I think you will be a good opponent."

"How can you refuse that?"

The Sinclair enclave was a shining beacon in the radioactive waste. On a world lit only by moon and lightning, it was a lighthouse, declaring to anyone who saw it the majesty of House Sinclair, the wealth, the riches. The power.

Usually.

Things stirred in the mist, creeping cautiously closer.

BAGHDAD

Montana placed the last piece of the board into place—a flat hexagon of marble carved with one of the game's insignia—in the center of the rock board. It would be an interesting game. She studied the board intently, her tongue unconsciously clenched between her teeth, mouth only open at one corner.

"Would you like to place the first nexus?" Baghdad asked.

She recognized the implied compliment—and trap—and her eyes narrowed as she analyzed him right back. Placing first was considered the most rewarding position, but also the hardest to be successful at.

"You may be giving me too much credit," she said quietly, but quick as lightning, she placed a nexus token and a shipping lane token.

He noted the direction, placed one of his own, and was gratified to see her brow furrow slightly in response. There were several zones that appeared rich, but he took pleasure in positioning himself well and being able to thwart her initial plans simultaneously.

"Why is this so often played at these events?"

"It goes back to Taoiseach Adele, if I recall," Baghdad said, spotting Boston and waving him over. "She was a student of the game. Always carried a board with her and played even when her armies were engaged in real battle. That's why it's traditional to never leave a game halfway through. She never did, not even during the final assault on the Hermian estates."

Montana nodded, clearly still concentrating on the board. She didn't even look up when Boston and his friend, another young lord in the silver-and-scarlet uniform of the police, took their seats.

"Who's your friend, Boston?" Baghdad asked, breaking the silence.

"Lord Dhaka, a Puma with the police." Boston smiled.

Montana's head jerked up at the sound of Boston's voice, and her face fell sharply. "You, again, Lord Haldis?"

"My grandson," Baghdad introduced. "Though I see he has already succeeded in charming you in his usual manner."

Montana glanced toward Baghdad. "You are the elder Lord Haldis?"

"Guilty, I'm afraid."

"Well then." She glanced back toward Boston, who picked up his second nexus token and placed it on the board. "I will quite enjoy destroying you."

"There's no room for sentiment in war," Baghdad cautioned.

Montana picked up her second station and stared at

the unfolding battlefield. "I will remember."

Then, the game began, and as Baghdad had predicted, it was a very interesting one—for all except Lord Dhaka. Lady Montana took a choke point early, successfully walling him into a rather poor corner of the map. He was making up for it, slowly, but the game was almost over.

Boston and Montana both obviously felt the end of the game coming too, with their restless hands and careful maneuvering. Her face was pleasantly flushed, eyes narrowed in intense concentration, while Boston dropped his feigned indifference and watched everyone's hands closely.

It was interesting to see how Boston flirted; he'd somehow managed to turn the game into a battle of wits between himself and Lady Montana. They'd ended up in a loose alliance against his own forces, but the two of them were constant rivals, managing to compete even while uniting whenever it was required to block him. They weren't going to be successful, but it was still a valiant effort. And, whether she realized it or not, her anger and disdain directed at Boston slowly disappeared over the long-fought game.

"I must say, I am surprised at how well you play the game, given your upbringing, Lady Montana," Lord Dhaka said, passing the dice.

"Sinclair ensured I received a classical education. That included empire."

"True, but I thought you would refuse to play."

"It is rather a social imperative, Lord Dhaka," Montana said as she sent a knight toward Baghdad's forces.

Baghdad chuckled. "True. But he is right, my Lady. You would be hard-pressed to find a better model for our empire."

"Do tell."

"You gather what regions you can into a single polity. And together, their resources allow you to enrich all the tiles under your control—more so than any one tile could on its own."

"The game conveniently leaves out having to suppress local populations. And having to force them to become part of this 'polity.'"

"It is a game," Dhaka said.

"And yet," Montana moved one of her pieces, "the four of us compete as equals in starting position, if in not skill. One of us did not start out with a thousand years' more technological development than the others. You might say it would be a boring game if one of us did. That would be my point."

"There are differences," Baghdad said. "But the central premise holds true. Humanity is stronger together."

"Whether humanity likes it or not."

The lady stared at her hand for another long moment, trying to make the cards turn into something more appetizing. With a sigh, she laid down a few more. "One more Random Occurrence, if you would."

She drew the top card from the deck and placed it face-up on the table. She didn't need to, but she must have known that keeping her hand hidden didn't matter anymore. It was a windfall, one of the rarest cards in the game, but not enough to let her win immediately.

"There are countless colonies that could have slipped away without the Empire's resources. When our explorers still flew, we found many worlds where humanity had tried—and failed—to take hold." Baghdad said. "The Empire provides medicines, technologies, sciences that have been lost."

"Arguments that humanity should trade, not that the

Empire should rule." She surrendered the dice.

Baghdad tossed them into the bowl, uncaring what they read. "My congratulations, my Lady. Your central authority would have defeated mine next turn, I think." He lay down most of his hand and added three more shipping lanes to the board. Wordlessly, Boston handed over the longest supply route token, and Baghdad slotted it into his standings, securing his win.

"It is a shame how much suffering had to be caused, building the Empire," Boston said quietly. "However, I think it is less than if all these worlds were left to wither on their own."

"A parent doesn't let their children starve just because they want to sulk in their room out of spite." Baghdad couldn't help a quick glance at Boston. "We have an obligation to bring all the scattered children of humanity back into the fold. Almost every colony would be poorer, hungrier, and smaller without the Empire."

He watched her carefully. It was clear she still didn't agree with him, but before he could continue, a steward in Chen livery approached the table. "Lord Baghdad? If you are done with your game, Lord Lincoln would ask you to join his table for dinner."

"Ha! Of course, I will be right there."

Baghdad left the youths arguing over the game.

BERN

Her preparations complete, Bern found Montana exactly where she expected; arguing over the results of her game with the dashing Lord Haldis. She dropped an arm around her friend and tapped her shoulder. "Time to eat." An impish desire struck Bern, and she glanced back at Lord Haldis. "Care to join us?"

He nodded, eyes locked on Montana. Arm around her friend, Bern led Montana toward the table she had selected. She glanced around, and yes, Menodora and Jordana were already absent. The rest of the family was gathered together at the front of the room so it wouldn't be noticeable. But it was starting.

But then, why was Katalia cutting her way across the floor, towing Istanbul, Eiravati, and a bottle of wine?

Bern separated from Montana and glared at her itinerant cousin as she approached. "You have somewhere to be," Bern said under her breath as Katalia leaned in for a kiss on the cheek.

"I brought the good wine!"

"Katalia!"

"Go." Katalia blinked, her trademark butterfly wings winking. "You made this happen. You deserve to be in that room. Jordana will be pissed at me, but who cares?" Then Katalia leaned away and said in a loud, carrying voice, "My cousin has been called away on family business. I will be taking over as entertainment director for the evening."

"Do you have to?"

Bern glanced at Montana, who looked positively stricken. Haldis was manfully waiting to push her chair in, but Montana hovered, concern evident even through her shadowcasters. It was almost enough to make Bern stay. Almost.

"I do," Bern said, trying to make it sound like an apology.

"Bern needs to go show those Sinclair bastards who is in charge," Katalia continued unhelpfully.

Montana nodded, just once, and then Bern was away. She'd made the plans for the summit, had negotiated every little detail with Aspen, made sure there was nothing that would distract Menodora and Jordana. Being there would let her be sure it would work.

The Sinclair guards didn't even look at her twice as she made her way to the secure conference room. Jordana was gathering her notes at one end of the table when Bern arrived in, flanked by Menodora and Lord Daumantas. She hardly glanced up when Bern entered. "That girl will be the death of me, I swear it."

"She is as headstrong as her mother."

"As long as you are going to be here, make yourself useful." Jordana studied another set of slates. "Find me the projections for Camelot over the next six months."

Bern nodded and joined Jordana at the end of the table. When Aspen arrived with her leadership, they would be ready.

Defenses were probed and found deactivated.

Alarms that should have rung went un-rung.

The survivors of Earth's harsh storms, rarefied oxygen, and constant bath of radiation pressed in.

It was not memory, for none of them had ever seen the inside of an enclave, but myth they sought. They carried an ancient resentment, passed along in story over generations. Tales of flight, abandonment, and terrible, terrible wrath.

The shadows pressed around the fire, seeking the warmth and light that had been denied them for so long.

BOSTON

Boston did his best to keep track of the conversation around him, but Montana was his whole focus. Meanwhile she did her best to studiously ignore him. Now that he was looking for them, he could see her mannerisms plain as day. The way she slipped up occasionally and spoke more like a Terran than a noble when she was excited, the strange style of her clothes. Her immediate defense of the colonies.

Eiravati sat to his right and occasionally tried to draw

him into conversation, but even that was difficult. It was hard to get a word in edgewise, with the three-way banter between Istanbul, Montana, and Katalia.

"Istanbul, this is forty-year-old port wine," Katalia said, waving her glass under his nose. She'd taken the bullet of sitting next to him but seemed unable to stop herself from needling him at every turn. "From Eden!"

The fop shook his head. "I understand and appreciate your generosity, my Lady. My family does not drink colonial wine."

"How can you be serious?"

"Our refineries have been fermenting algae around Venus for the last five hundred years, from strains my ancestors carried all the way from Old Earth. Unlike most strains in the colonies, they have not been tainted to grow on terraformed planets. Do you even know the name of the star that was grown around?"

"What does a star have to do with how it tastes?"

"Taste is not the issue. Purity is. Anything else is simply blasphemous."

"Blasphemy tastes divine, darling," Katalia said and drained the wineglass she'd poured for Istanbul.

"Here here," Boston seconded, and took a long drink from his.

Montana's remained untouched.

"I ought to have expected you to indulge in that swill, Haldis, but I expected you to have a more refined pallet, my Lady."

"My family recognizes quality, no matter the source. As well as its lack."

If Istanbul had expected a willing audience for his diatribe, he was sourly disappointed.

"Lord Istanbul, do you think that steak was grown here at Sol as well?" Montana asked, breaking the silence.

"She has you there!" Katalia said, raising her glass to Montana.

Istanbul glanced at a chunk of meat on his knife and shook his head. "I doubt it."

"Why is wine the only food you apply this rule to, then? Because it is convenient?"

Istanbul took his bite of steak, ignoring the question.

"Can we talk about something else?" Eiravati asked, glancing at Katalia. "Food is just so boring."

"Speaking of Eden, then," Istanbul said with a suddenly sly grin. "I hear you are having some trouble with your subjects?"

Katalia's face was utterly unreadable. "Where did you hear that, Lord Istanbul?"

"Oh, you know: here and there."

Boston did his best to feign disinterest. Eden was only a few light years away and a Nirvana stronghold. He should have heard of unrest on the planet, and yet, there had been nothing.

"Things are perfectly fine on Eden," Katalia said, topping off her wineglass. "However, thank you for your concern."

"Oh? Well, if that ever changes, I am sure Boston here could settle things for you. He is experienced at controlling natives."

Boston closed his eyes and managed to keep himself from killing Istanbul. "I do what needs to be done. Nothing more, and nothing less."

"Oh, come now, you are being modest. When push comes to shove, you can hack and slash with the best of them, yes? Like Asgard?"

"What happened?" Eiravati asked, perking up.

"One of the most brutal atrocities of the last fifty years," Montana said. "It—"

"Lady Montana," Katalia interrupted coolly, her voice of command drawing every eye to her. "Would you be so kind as to go to the bar and get us another bottle of wine?" She tapped the empty bottle on the edge of her glass. "Ours seems to have developed some leaks, and I know I can trust your taste… unlike the rest of these uncultured swine."

Montana stayed frozen for enough heartbeats to make Boston wonder if she had heard, before pushing her chair back with a screech. "Of course, Lady Vermont. It would be my pleasure."

Istanbul shook his head as she left and then went back to fruitlessly trying to flirt with Katalia. She caught Boston's eye and flicked her eyes back to where Montana had disappeared to, mouthing, "Go!"

Primitives, they were called by the sky-walkers that had deserted the mother planet. But they were hardly that. They shared the devilish ingenuity and cunning of their brethren from the sky, the same itch to explore. To conquer. To punish.

There is something about a gun that speaks to humankind. Placed in a pair of hands, gripped tight, it conveys the power of the gods, the ability to merely point and cast fire. It was, after all, built by man. So perhaps it should not be surprising that the feeling of holding one, the ease with which it becomes an extension of the body, transcends culture, transcends language, transcends thought.

So, when presented with the weapons of the enemy, the ones remembered in story and in song, eager hands griped them.

And dreamt of doing unto others what had been done to them.

BAGHDAD

Grim unease had settled between Baghdad's shoulders, an old friend from many a campaign. It was strange to find it here, clustered around a table with champagne and food flowing freely, but here it was.

Lincoln Von Chen leaned in and whispered in Baghdad's ear, "I heard about your boy launching an assault on an enclave. Good for him."

Baghdad chuckled. "You'd be the only one to think so."

Lincoln coughed and blinked eyelashes at least a dozen centimeters long, white with age. "Oh, he got suckered well and good, Pack Leader. That drop time, though!" The aged lord chuckled. "My sister could use his Wolves in the police to teach her Cats something. You taught him well."

Baghdad preened, even through his unease. "I did my best, but the Guard was a good teacher, too."

"Pity the modern Guard is not good enough for him. He deserves a few planets to conquer, not garrison work."

Baghdad had to agree. From everything he'd seen of Boston's doughy commander tonight, it was true. Boston's Wolves were well-drilled, but they'd never had an enemy to truly test themselves against.

"To peace." Baghdad raised his glass and clinked it against Lincoln's.

"May our sons and daughters never know the hardship we had to go through," Lincoln slurred in response.

Baghdad leaned back, but Lincoln motioned him closer with a crooked finger again. Baghdad leaned forward again.

"Strange business, though."

Baghdad had to agree. It still rankled that he hadn't come up with a reason for why someone would goad

Boston's Wolves into attacking nothing.

"At first," Lincoln paused for breath, "I thought it was for practice. To practice breaking into the Sinclair House Core. But the *Cortés* uses imperial encryption. Practicing on it would be of little use."

"Right," Baghdad agreed. "And it did nothing! A lot of effort just for a feint."

"Too right," Lincoln muttered and turned back to his plate.

Baghdad did the same, but after a moment's consideration, he put his fork back down. Alarm bells were ringing in the privacy of his mind, but he couldn't—

"A feint."

"Eh?" Lincoln said, creaking closer.

"It was a feint," Baghdad repeated as the whole, horrible truth laid itself out in front of him. He grabbed Lincoln's shaking arm. "When Adele took Europa. She attacked four times and retreated four times. So that the Europans would expect it. So when she attacked a fifth time…"

"They declined to commit their full strength," Lincoln finished.

Baghdad glanced around the opulent ballroom. Hundreds of high-ranking nobles were clustered around him. Almost everyone who was everyone.

And he knew what was going to happen.

Sinclair was not stupid. They knew well that they had enemies who would like nothing more than to cause a death under mysterious circumstances, so the enclave had the most sophisticated security apparatus in the Empire.

Of course, security systems are rarely designed to stop armies.

Alarms rang. Guards responded and were massacred to a man.

CHAPTER ELEVEN

Attack
CHANG

The low buzz of his comm woke Chang from a light sleep. His bunk was tucked in a corner of the Wolves' den, curtained off to give him the minimum of privacy, but the sound was enough to send him blinking to wakefulness.

"Chang."

Baku, one of the Trout who stood watch in the ship's command center, answered him, her tone all false sweetness. "Sir Glydenfeldt, could you come to the bridge? We have a situation that could use your input."

Baku was waiting for him when he made it to the bridge, opening his eyes as little as possible on the way. "Yes?" he demanded.

"I think Lord Kalif should explain," Baku said quietly and glanced at the young man sitting in the center chair.

Chang nodded to the young lord. He really was young, younger than Boston by at least a few years. "Evening, Lord Kalif. You have the watch?"

Kalif jerked his head nervously. "Lord Delaware decided someone from the family should always be in charge," he said nervously, then quickly snapped his eyes back to one of the monitors. "What is that?"

The Eel at the communications station was Malaga again, and she manipulated something on her screen. "Another erroneous security alert from the Sinclair enclave."

Chang made a show of studying the monitors, but the glittering light codes were as opaque to him as cuneiform. "You know they're false? You're sure?"

Kalif nodded. "I have a readout to the enclave security system. Everything reports fine through our house channels."

Chang raised an eyebrow back at Baku, who cleared her throat loudly. "The Wolf, Lord Kalif?"

"Oh, that." Kalif waved a hand. "One of the Wolves, Nevada, was caught sneaking back onto the ship."

"Nevada has leave. Isn't due back until tomorrow."

"No, his leave ran out at midnight."

Chang had to check himself, as his first instinct was to laugh. But Kalif gave no indication he had any sense of humor whatsoever. "Lord Kalif, that seems a little harsh."

"What?" Kalif dragged his eyes from the monitors. "Pack Leader, we have a situation here. We can deal with the Wolf later."

"Not if you intend to file charges."

Kalif gestured at the screens again. "I will, once I have dealt with whoever is subverting our sensors."

Chang thought rapidly. Once Boston was back, he'd be able to over awe the little lord, but formally filed charges would follow Nevada, even if they had them straightened out. Dereliction wasn't something you could expunge.

"I admire your courage, Lord," Chang said, planting the seed. Then he waited.

It took a few seconds for his words to register through

the lord's preoccupation, but he eventually broke away from the monitors and asked, "Whatever do you mean, Pack Leader?"

"Filing formal charges. Admitting that one of your," Chang stressed, "Wolves was absent without leave. Sticking to your principles, no matter the potential embarrassment, rather than taking the easy way out: letting it slide and no one being the wiser."

"Oh." Chang suppressed any hint of a smile as the wheels suddenly started turning in the young lord's head. "What would have been the easy way?"

"Letting the Wolf stew in the brig overnight and not filing anything. Just let an embarrassment like that disappear."

"Ah, ha." A red flush was starting to creep up Kalif's pale neck.

That was enough doubt to get the proper result. It would be best if Kalif stewed without him. "Now, if you'll excuse me, Lord?"

"Oh, yes, Pack Leader."

Baku followed Chang to the door.

"If it looks like he's actually going to log this, call me," he whispered to her. "I'm going back to bed."

BOSTON

Boston caught Montana halfway across the dining room and made pace beside her. "Lord Istanbul is a cad, my Lady."

"Odd, because the two of you seemed quite chummy," she shot back without looking at him.

"I should have broken his nose again."

That got her to react, glancing back but not dropping her pace at all. "Again?"

Boston nodded. "I do not count him as a friend."

"I hardly need you to defend me."

None of this was going well.

"If it makes you feel any better, he was relieved for Asgard."

Her eyes widened, and she stopped short, still a few feet from the bar. "That little shit ordered the punishment on Asgard?"

Boston nodded. "And he exceeded his authority to do it."

"That fucker!" She whirled back—to do what, he wasn't quite sure—but she caught herself before taking more than a few steps. "I will have to think of a suitable way to punish him."

Did he dare? "I have been trying to get his next posting taken away, but so far, I have not had much luck. Colombia is too—"

"They gave him another posting?"

"Colombia is a powerful family."

"This is what I meant about the Empire, Boston. Humanity may be 'stronger together,'" she said, sarcasm evident as she repeated Baghdad's saying, "but by subjugating the colonies, we made this happen."

"I may yet succeed in getting his posting canceled."

"One man isn't the problem, no matter how vile of a little shit he is."

"I have no answer for that."

She stared at him for a second before giving him a sharp nod. "At least you admit it." And she offered him her arm.

He followed her lead to the bar, where she had a conversation he couldn't follow with the bartender about vintages and vineyards. The planets, at least, he recognized. He, however, focused on how she kept hold of his arm.

"I wanted to tell you how sorry I was, Lady Montana."

She turned back to him, confused. "I do not blame you for Istanbul."

"No. For the night we met."

"Oh." It was tiny, almost imperceptibly so.

The room shook, and a cloud of dust and debris crashed toward them like a wave. Boston only had time to hurl himself on top of her before it broke over them.

ASPEN

"We can only accept a three-percent reduction in tariffs," Bern said, glancing back at her aunt for support that did not come. "Any less is not worth the headache."

Aspen smiled to herself as the banter went back and forth, though she let her mother and brother do most of the talking. Thus far, Bern had spotted every trap she'd constructed; she really had to admire her cousin sometimes.

If only she were the one in charge, they might actually reach a deal.

"We have not addressed the issue of restitution," Jordana said.

"Come now, Jordana, this is how the game is played." Sherah said.

"Sinclair has caused us no end of harm on Eden through your agitating," Jordana insisted. "We demand compensation for the loss of this year's harvest."

Aspen could see the situation spiraling, which was of no use to any of them. Taoiseach, her own family was just as bad as Nirvana sometimes.

Sherah shook her head. "If you cannot control your own colonials, that is your own problem. Sinclair has nothing—"

"Perhaps a break?" Aspen suggested.

Ambroos stiffened in shock; the last time he'd dared to interrupt Sherah was when he was still a babe in arms, but

Aspen knew her mother.

"Perhaps we should," Sherah agreed. "And—"

The table shook, rattling glasses and causing a pile of slates to tumble to the floor. Instantly, porters leapt to deal with the mess as Sherah glanced around the room. "Francis!"

The head of security was at her side in seconds, head bowed.

"My Lady, we have reports of some small motion at the perimeter. If you would be so kind as to move this discussion to one of the secure conference rooms, we could—"

A second tremor shook the room, and Aspen noticed Bern catch a large water pitcher that was tottering alarmingly.

"I believe a secure conference room was mentioned?" Aspen asked.

"Yes, my Lady," Francis said hurriedly. "We can escort your guests to some quarters while—"

"Nonsense," Aspen cut him off. "They will come with us." She had worked too hard to arrange this meeting to have it end so soon.

BOSTON

The shaking and the noise stopped, and Boston cautiously raised his head. Dust was everywhere, painting most of what he could see plaster-gray. Scattered heads rose through the gloom as people began to get back on their feet.

He glanced back at Montana, but she looked no worse for wear and was scanning the room, like him.

The great stained-glass window on the other side of the hall—the side where their table had been—had come down and let in the elements, including a creeping fog. Boston stared into the gloom but couldn't make out anything. Still, the hairs on the back of his neck stood at attention. Something else was wrong.

Boston turned his prone sprawl into a soldier's crouch, up off his knees, glancing around for an obvious threat, but other than the gaping hole in the side of the building, there wasn't one.

Boston pried his eyes off the likely threat axis, hunting instead for sign of Baghdad in the still-dazed crowd, but Boston couldn't find him.

A distant roar echoed in from the gloom, drawing Boston's gaze back to the window. Most nobles had probably never heard true weather before. Boston had. He'd spent days huddled in the rain, trying to tune out the sound of thunder that every day promised increased misery. It was not something he would forget.

"That isn't thunder," Montana said. He spared her a quick glance. She was crouched like him, head down, glancing along the back wall. Looking for an exit.

"I know."

He'd heard gunpowder rifles only a few times over his career. But this sounded like that.

Boston quickly cataloged their surroundings; none of it offered any cover whatsoever. Even the bar had collapsed.

"We need to get these people out of here." Boston said. But there wasn't time.

All at once, the fog pulled back slightly, and figures became visible, slogging across the rough ground toward them. Boston strained to make out details; he could see just enough to confirm the sinking feeling in his stomach. This was a prim attack. A real one.

He took a single crouching step forward toward the threat, not really thinking yet, just reacting, but froze at the feeling of Montana's hand on his arm.

"We need to go. Now." Her gaze was harsh and startlingly clear.

Boston hesitated. For the first time he could remember, the way forward wasn't crystal clear. He should charge, try to get under their fire, try to get one of the guns away from them, try—

Then, one of the figures swung a long, lethal rifle, spitting fire, and the groans around them turned to screams.

"Go."

Suddenly, moving was everything. He ran bent double to keep from presenting a target, stumbling through debris, tripping on discarded utensils, stopping for nothing. Broken glass crunched like snow under his boots.

He let her lead, her hand pulling his. Quicker than he thought possible, she was leading them toward a set of doors in the back wall.

A shout behind them was his only warning, but it was enough for Boston to tackle Montana through the doors as bullets stitched a line across the wall on either side. Boston rolled but was back on his feet in seconds, tensed, ready, but no other shots came. There was a room full of easier targets between them and the prims.

"We need to keep going," Boston hissed. "That wall is too thin." Another round of gunfire from the room behind him proved his point, adding a second line of holes at head-height.

"Fuck," Montana hissed in pain. She pushed herself upright, her foot curled into her lap. A shard of glass had cut straight through her sole. "What next?" she asked.

Boston glanced up the corridor, which was devoid of helpful signposts. "We need to get you somewhere safe so I can go back and—"

"And do what?"

Boston shrugged. "Help."

"How?"

Boston shook his head.

Montana folded her dress up and withdrew a simple blade from a sheath on her thigh. She turned the blade over in her hands a few times and then offered it to him. "There used to be things that would eat me, if I walked too far from home."

Boston took the knife, small in his hands, thinking of the tiny girl who had once brandished it at him.

Something crashed to the ground in the great hall, shaking the floor again. "We need to keep moving."

"Help me up."

Boston got her to her feet just as the lights died. It would be a blessing, making hiding easier.

"I have an ansible," Boston said, checking his coat pocket to be sure it was there. "But we need to get somewhere safer first."

Her hand firmly grasped his. "We're just going to have to improvise."

ASPEN

Aspen waited at the door to the panic room, counting. The disaster had reached the ballroom, apparently, because dusty, bloody men and women were fleeing down the hallway.

She waved, and the couple running toward them turned and slipped past her.

"Seven, six," she counted to herself, ticking off slots they had.

The doors at the end of the hall burst open, and a flood of people rushed through all at once, dozens of them sprinting away from the loud sounds behind.

Aspen took in their scared faces, their panicked looks, and decided in less than a heartbeat.

"Close the door."

The sweating guard had the door moving before the words had left her mouth.

"No, Katalia is still out there!" Bern shouted. She was panicking, tears streaking down her face.

"At this point, there is nothing we can do for them."

Bern buried her face in Menodora's shoulder as the door boomed closed. Beyond it, Aspen could hear the shouts from the crowd, the distant bangs as they reached the reinforced door.

Menodora's eyes were red, but she wasn't crying anymore. Anger seemed to be her emotion of choice. "What happened to the vaunted Sinclair security?"

Aspen refused to be goaded. "They are dying to buy time."

She left the Nirvana and made her way to where Ambroos was fighting with the computer. "Any luck?"

He shook his head without looking up. "The central computer is locked up. No signals are getting out."

"We may be in for a long wait, then."

A massive thud echoed through the small room as something heavy crashed into the door Aspen had just sealed.

"If we should be so lucky."

CHANG

The low buzz of his comm dragged Chang back to wakefulness yet again. "Baku, what's he done this time?"

The link was silent for a few tense seconds before Boston's voice filled the tiny space. "Chang, the enclave is under attack."

Cold tendrils of dread poured down Chang's spine, banishing all trace of grogginess. Boston couldn't fake that voice.

"What's the situation?" Chang thumbed the mute

button, listening to Boston's crisp report with one ear. "Voyen!" Chang screamed in a pause and threw himself out of bed.

"Yes, sir?" Voyen's head stuck out of his bunk, illuminated by the dim light of the den. A few punches at the control panel changed that, sending the lights to full power.

"Get everyone out of bed and ready for a combat drop!" Chang shouted, still listening to Boston in his other ear. "Prim attack. Real one."

That done, Chang dashed up to the bridge, the clatter of the Wolves getting ready filling the den behind him.

The bridge was little changed from his last entrance, barely an hour earlier. Baku glanced up sharply at his entry, but Boston asked something before he could respond to her.

"We're...Taoiseach, eighty minutes from a drop," Chang relayed, glancing at the orbit monitor and eyeballing their position. Boston's disappointment was palpable. "Hunker down and stay alive until we get there. Is Baghdad with you?"

On mute again, Chang faced the wide-eyed look of Lord Kalif. "The Sinclair enclave is under attack. I'm getting the Wolves ready for a drop. We need to separate from Castle High and get into a lower orbit, get us into position to drop sooner."

Kalif goggled at him. "The enclave is not under attack. Sir Glydenfeldt, are you drunk?"

"Prims are taking the place apart down there, Lord."

"No. I have the readout from the security system right here," Kalif insisted, brandishing a slate.

"Don't worry, Boston, we're coming," Chang said. Behind him, Baku triggered the general alarm, waking the crew. "Call me back in ten minutes."

"Madam, what are you doing?" Kalif rounded on Baku.

"Calling the crew to stations."

"There is no threat!"

Frustration boiled in Chang's stomach as he felt precious seconds slipping away. "We have firsthand reports from the ground."

"Be reasonable, Sir." Kalif glanced around the bridge for support but found none. "There has not been a prim attack in over a decade!"

Chang took the measure of the young man in a few seconds and made his decision. He turned to Baku. "Baku, can you see that a qualified pilot gets up here?"

"Yes, sir. We can maneuver in ten minutes." Baku stepped to another station, and rested her hand on the Eel's shoulder. "Plot us a course right down to the safety limit. Let's see how much we can shave off that drop time." Baku stepped to a different console and sounded a different alarm. "All hands, we will be separating in ten minutes. Secure all stations for zero gravity."

"No, we will not!" Kalif declared, but no one listened.

"Sir Chang, what kind of entry will you want to make?" Baku asked, completely ignoring the man in the captain's chair.

"As close to the bone as we can cut it. Five g, at least."

Baku nodded and adjusted something on one of the plotters. "Do you think we need to pass this up the chain?"

It was a good reminder. Chang toyed with the ansible in his hands. "I'll call the police commissioner's office. That should be all the cover we need."

"Call the Pike," Kalif insisted.

"By all means, Lord Kalif," Chang said. "Call the Pike."

Kalif tapped furiously at his console, and the low ring

of an open line filled the bridge. Chang watched the preparations with one eye and Lord Kalif with the other. The moment stretched.

And stretched.

Kalif began to go ashen as the call failed to complete.

"I will call—"

"Anyone you would call is already down there, Lord. You have two options. Go along with me, and risk embarrassment later—with your career and life intact. Or refuse, and explain to the Taoiseach how you let his nobility be slaughtered."

Kalif sputtered and made no answer. Chang turned to Baku. "Let me know if you need me to send a Wolf or two up here."

She nodded, and Chang left the bridge to put on his armor.

BOSTON

Together, Boston and Montana moved as silently as they could through the dark corridors. With every step, the humidity rose and the temperature fell, making the corridors cold, clammy, and damp. He'd lost all track of where they were, but they kept moving.

Montana's hand in his was a comfort. The emergency lights were few and far between, casting long, ominous shadows. Twice, they'd ducked into offices to avoid prims, but none seemed defensible enough to stay.

Stay alive. That's what they needed to do. Wait as minutes ticked off like hours as Chang and the *Cortés* raced around Earth until they could separate in a gumdrop and let gravity carry them to the right spot on the ground.

Ahead, there was a noise in the dark.

Boston froze, one foot hanging above the floor. Air stirred, and then, a shriek split the quiet gloom.

Boston pressed himself to the wall and raced forward,

pants, shouts, and crashes of heavy impacts covering their movements. He kept running until the wall disappeared under his outstretched fingers, and he stopped.

Montana ran into him, and he swayed but kept them stable. She squeezed his hand, tugging gently, and Boston slid ever so slightly forward until he could see around the corner.

The sight roiled his stomach, and Boston had to hold his breath, fighting to keep the bile from rising.

Two women lay on the ground surrounded by four primitives. The light was dim, but he could make out the gray, lifeless skin of the prims. Hear the guttural snarls as the four brutes beat the prone women to a bloody pulp.

Montana squeezed his hand again and pressed herself to him, her lips tickling his ear. "There's nothing we can do for them."

Boston drew back slowly, mind racing. "There was another corner," he started and froze as two more dim shapes stepped into the light of the nearest emergency lamp.

Montana reacted before he did. The moment he froze, she turned, saw the threat, and sprang forward, catching the first primitive by surprise and sinking her shoulder into his gut.

Boston followed seconds behind her. He picked the larger target, but this one was prepared. The brute caught Boston's punch with one hand. He refused to scream in pain as his opponent crushed his hand, a lifetime of living on a planet giving him the muscle to overcome even Boston's well-honed physique.

Boston threw himself forward, falling to his knees to avoid another outstretched hand larger than his face, and drove Montana's knife up blindly.

The other fist came around, and Boston saw stars.

Gasping for air, Boston stabbed again, and this time, connected.

The grip on his hand finally slackened, and Boston yanked himself free, turning toward the second prim, the one Montana had distracted.

Before he found the prim, a hand found his throat.

The already dim world started to go gray at the edges as Boston fought for leverage, fought to see his opponent through the gloom. His feet slid along the now-slick laminate, until his back hit the wall of the corridor.

But that was enough, gave him something to push against. He lunged forward, his lungs bursting, and drove the knife into the arm holding him.

Sweet air flooded into his lungs as his opponent dropped him with a hiss of pain, and Boston staggered forward, jabbing upward. It connected, and his hand was drenched in a warm spray. Boston took another step forward, twisting the knife, holding on with a death grip until he felt the prim collapse. Boston rolled, flinging the knife clear as the heavy primitive crashed to the ground, rattling Boston's teeth.

The silence was sudden and ringing. Boston hit the ground, rolled, and tried to clear the sweat from his eyes. A rifle lay on the ground, discarded, and Boston swept it into his hands, stock against his shoulder. The unfamiliar grip bit his hand, but a rifle was a rifle. His finger landed on the trigger just as the first of the original four primitives rounded the corner.

The sound of the rifle firing was like fireworks in his ear. The gunpowder slugs were heavy, slow, dirty, but the rifle pumped them out at an impressive clip, catching all four by surprise. They dropped, one after another, as Boston dragged the rifle across their line. Time slowed to molasses.

And then the clip, was empty, the rifle making a muted 'click, click' noise. Time sped back up.

Blood slid sickly down his face with every heartbeat, but he was alive. And the corridor was suddenly silent, suddenly empty, except for him and the dead.

"Montana," came out too hoarse to understand. Boston cleared his throat and tried again. "Montana!"

"Here." It was the smallest of sounds, but she emerged from the gloom. She was holding a bloody shoe they had found. "I'm... I'm alright," she managed.

Boston pulled her up to him, squeezing her tight. She was trembling.

"Just breathe." He kept one ear cocked, listening for anyone approaching, but there were only her sobs now, deathly silent in his ear.

"That was... you were excellent," Boston said, and it was his turn to tremble.

She sniffed. "Well, of course I was." She was already starting to recover, her eyes drier, more focused.

With difficulty, he let her go and walked over to the nearest corpse, kneeling beside it. The primitive was mostly wearing war paint with dark symbols painted onto its gray skin. Boston tugged at the thing's belt and found another few clips for the rifle.

Boston pocketed one of the spare clips and glanced around for Montana. She was kneeling over another body, her eyes closed, hand over the primitive's face. Boston approached in time to hear her mutter, "Rest in peace, fellow traveler," as she passed her hand over the man's eyes, drawing the eyelids closed. He waited as she moved between each of them, performing the same rite, following in her wake to look for rifles, knives, anything they could use.

Her task complete, Montana glanced around, eyes

glazing over slightly as they passed over the carnage the two of them had wrought. "My knife?"

Boston returned it to her hilt-first. "Can you handle a gun?"

She nodded, and he gave her one of the guns from the dead. Boston checked the corridor behind them, but there was nothing more they could do to delay the inevitable. Her hand found his again, they slowly crept back up to the corner, and Boston peered around.

The two bodies lay there, unmoving. The sprays of blood had long since ceased, but the pool had grown, and Boston again had to clamp his mouth closed. Seeing nothing down the short stretch of corridor beyond, Boston slowly edged around, his rifle reloaded, out, ready. But nothing came to get them.

He approached the pair just as slowly, wary of anything hiding, but the corridor stayed resolutely silent.

Boston glanced down at the first woman's face and immediately wished he hadn't. She was dead, small mercy that it was.

"Eiravati," he said. His voice may have cracked; there was a strange ringing in his ears.

"Katalia," Montana said, confirming his fears. "Fuck. Bern…"

"We need to keep moving."

Montana's knees were stained red with blood as she got to her feet.

A distant shot made them both tense, and Boston dropped into a crouch. Nothing emerged from the end of the corridor, though.

"How long until the Wolves get here?" she asked, voice trembling slightly.

Boston felt for his ansible and only found a ripped hole where his pocket had been. There was no way to find it in the dark. "Slag. No way to know for sure."

"Alright."

"Just keep breathing," he reminded her.

"Just keep breathing."

CHAPTER TWELVE

A New Front
CHANG

Gravity tugged at Chang's face as the gumdrop fell with the speed of an errant star. Sweat dripped down his cheeks and was fired downward onto the deck of the cabin like tiny bullets.

"Hot enough, Sir?" Dunkirk asked, managing a grunt of a laugh. "Usually, the rotting gumdrop keeps up with the heat."

"Yeah. It'll need a new paint job."

The ground was nearing at tremendous velocity, and Chang jerked as a few of the small attitude thrusters fired, targeting their capsule as close as they dared to the wall of the complex.

And then, they were on the ground, in the rain, water sleeting down over their helmets. His boots instantly sank into mud. Chang flicked at the link controls in his armor. "Boston. On the ground, ready to approach. Status?"

Mist was all there was until Chang clicked in one of the night-vision filters. Vague shapes of heat shimmered in and out view as they advanced.

Dunkirk clicked onto the pack link. "Movement, complex right. Four."

He found the figures immediately: two of them, outlined in green. The other two heat signatures had no such cladding. Chang brought his rifle up, sighting on the distant targets. Sudden fire rang out before he could squeeze. The two red figures in Chang's screen fell to the ground; the green continued their advance, each holding the now cherry-red barrels of chemical weapons.

On a hunch, Chang activated the PA in his armor. "Boston, is that you?"

One of the figures raised a hand and continued running.

Boston and Lady Von Montana stumbled out of the mist into the circle of Wolves. Boston's somber dress uniform was spattered with blood, some of it dried. Some of it his.

Anger rumbled in Chang's stomach. One death wasn't going to be enough for the slags that did this.

"Lost the ansible," Boston said, gasping. "Heard the entry. You were early."

Chang took a second glance at the pair. Boston was bleeding from a cut above his eye and favoring his left arm. The lady wore a set of boots far too large for her, and her dress was torn in several places, clinging to every curve in the rain. It was more becoming than she probably realized.

Leave it to Boston to find a woman able to keep up with him in a firefight.

"What's the situation?"

"Power is out inside the complex. We found a lot of dead Sinclair guards, but no organized resistance."

"You survived," Chang said. "That's victory enough. Baghdad?"

"Never saw him."

"Old man'll be fine." Baghdad had taught them both. "What now?"

The kid swelled, steaming from exertion. "Do what Wolves do best."

Dunkirk blasted out a howl on her speakers that Boston joined in wholeheartedly. The kid never changed, even in the middle of this mess.

Chang studied the estate through his helmet. The only lights came from occasional flashes through windows, accompanied by the sharp beats of gunfire. It had to be hell inside that building, with no sign of stopping. "We go in without splinters," he said over the pack channel. "Never know what noble will be cowering on the other side of a wall. Fists only."

"Even gunpowder will get through our armor eventually," Voyen said.

"So kill them faster than that."

More flashes lit the windows.

"Boston, if you're coming, we need to go."

The boy glanced to Montana. "You can ride the gumdrop up," Chang said, gesturing. "It'll bounce you up to the *Cortés*, and you can get passage wherever you need from there. Boston, get into armor. We have work to do."

BAGHDAD

Baghdad massaged his knee, trying not to listen to the sounds of Lord Lincoln dying beside him. The old man had done his best but had caught two bullets as they struggled to make it out of the ballroom. Blood in the lungs was a sickly sound he remembered all too well.

A sudden thunder of blows on the door made him turn. The three Sinclair porters cowering with them tensed, light glinting from their kitchen knives.

"Steady," he said quietly.

There was enough light to make out the give of the hinges. They had a few more minutes at most.

Lincoln's granddaughter, her hands slick with blood, slumped to the floor as he rattled out his last breath, then was still.

"You did all you could," he told her firmly, noticing the tears welling in her eyes.

The hammering returned on the door, and Baghdad groaned, dragging himself to his feet. Taoiseach, he'd forgotten how much he hated gravity.

"When the door falls," he told four terrified faces, "rush them. There won't be many. They aren't organized. We kill the few here, and we can find somewhere else to hide. Charge, as fast as you can."

Europa shivered and nodded. "Do you have another knife?"

He passed her one as the bottom hinge let go with a ping. It wouldn't be long.

BOSTON

"Survivor here!"

Boston's head snapped up at the call, and he loped the thirty or so feet back to where Voyen was shoveling rubble. Together, they got the man out, a portly noble who was buried under a table, bleeding slowly from the leg. "Cancun!"

His medic skidded to a stop in front of them, her case open, helmet off, bandages already in her hands. "He's going to need evac."

"He will get it."

Boston checked his HUD again. Half the Guard in the system were on their way down, police as well, but the lifters were still twenty or thirty minutes away. They'd been an orbit behind.

"No."

Aspen Sinclair knelt next to them. She'd appeared once most of the prims had been driven off, carrying a dozen emergency kits. It was unexpected help, but it was welcome.

But now, she knelt over the man and wiped his face clean.

"Oh, Dursun." Then, to Boston, she said, "The lifters will not make it in time. Do you have morphine?"

Cancun gave Boston a horror-struck look, but he nodded. Cancun retched as Aspen put the needle to his neck, and Boston had to look around the room.

He stood in a field of fallen stars, sickeningly beautiful. The broken glass and still-smoldering fires painted a strange, otherworldly scene.

His eyes were drawn to the row of bodies, two larger than the last time he had looked. They did what they could and covered the dead with tablecloths, but that was mostly for the survivors' stomachs. The prims hadn't left much of those they'd found alive.

BERN

Bern knelt over Katalia's body, disbelieving. Katalia couldn't be dead; she just couldn't be. Yet here was her body, barely recognizable. Katalia would never be caught dead looking like that; therefore, she must be.

She must have stopped screaming at some point, because she could breathe and people weren't trying to comfort her. They just let her be, let her sit there and stare.

Across the room, her eyes found Aspen.

The wraith looked perfectly at home here in the wreckage, blood smearing her arms and giving her some color for once. Passing out bandages, helping the wounded. Doing all the things that Aspen Sinclair never did.

Somewhere in her heart, she stopped screaming.

No, this wasn't random. This wasn't chance. This wasn't some prim attack.

This was an intentional, deliberate assassination.

And she knew exactly who was to blame.

BOSTON

"Haldis."

Boston glanced up and found Delaware picking his way carefully through the debris.

"Have you accounted for all of the slag?"

Boston fell in step beside Delaware as he began moving toward the remains of the stained-glass windows, where the prims had blasted their way in. "I have a pack sweeping the grounds, looking for any of them that tried to flee. We have swept the enclave twice. However, it is a big complex."

Delaware was still meandering his way across the hall, oblivious to Boston's attempts to steer him away from the elements. "Any prisoners?"

"Lord, we have not secured the area completely. You should—"

Delaware stopped short and rounded on Boston. The portly lord was panting from exertion, spittle at the corners of his mouth, but he spat again, "Did you take any prisoners, Falcon?"

"This way, Lord."

What few prims they'd managed to take alive were gathered in one of the courtyards. Fifteen prims sat under the watchful eyes of Dunkirk and three other Wolves. Sullen anger rolled off the prims, thickening the fog with an air of malevolence that made Boston recoil.

Chang jogged up behind Boston and stepped in line behind him without a word as Delaware studied the line of prims. "So, these are the scum."

Dunkirk glanced their direction, and Boston felt her

worry through two layers of helmets. The prims were sitting up, sniffing the air, taking a growing interest in Delaware's unarmored skin. Sensing another easy target.

"Perhaps we should—"

"Have you interrogated them?"

"Interrogated them?"

"To see what made them so misguided to think they could attack us and live."

"I doubt any of our Wolves speak their language. They have given no indication they speak ours."

Delaware nodded as if he had expected that answer. "Then they serve no further purpose. Dispose of them, Lord Falcon."

It was automatic.

"Yes, Lord Pike."

He focused on the little things. Switching his radio to the pack channel. Making sure the splinters would fire away from the complex. Double-checking that none of his pack were sweeping that side of the enclave so stray shots would do as little damage as possible.

It wouldn't make a difference, Boston repeated to himself, going through the motions. The prims were dead, anyway. What did it matter if it was a few hours sooner, before a herald could pass judgment? What did it matter if it was a splinter, rather than a knife, that did the job?

When the time came to give the order, he found himself frozen. His hand on the trigger. Splinter aimed between the eyes of the biggest of the slag.

And he hesitated. Again.

The moment stretched just long enough for Delaware to turn, long enough to feel Chang's question coming, and then, Boston shouted the order.

Boston took his shot, moved, fired again, his hands as steady as shaving. Almost worse, was Delaware's expression as he watched the prims die.

BOSTON

Finally, the sound of lift fans descended on the enclave, and Boston found himself again in the blood-spattered courtyard as the first of them touched down in front of him. Before it was on the ground, the rear door was dropping, and a dozen blurry figures raced out, all catlike grace and silver-flecked might. Police. They flowed around Boston and his half-pack, ignoring them completely, before disappearing into the complex.

Two more Cats descended more slowly, their armor scintillating in tiny scales no larger than Boston's smallest nail.

"Status?" the taller one asked. All trace of playfulness was gone from Lady Torianna's voice. It was frozen like ice and Boston's soul.

"We think all the primitives are dead. My Wolves are guarding the surviving Terrans, but there are large areas of the complex we have not—"

"Keep them there. The Cats will find anyone you missed. How many dead?"

"Thirty bodies so far. Without a guest list, I have no idea how many more could still be missing."

"We have the door override codes," Torianna growled, "the plans to the enclave, and the guest list. We will find everyone. No matter what."

"Thank you," Boston said as a warm wave of tiredness threatened to swamp him.

"There will be a culling for this," Torianna continued as if he hadn't spoken. "These filthy, mud-bound prims need to be reminded they exist on our sufferance, need to be reminded we are their gods."

Boston swayed but regained balance.

"No prims did this on their own. This reeks of

Nirvana." She seemed to sniff the air. "We already know they are arming colonials. They might do the same with prims."

"What are your orders, Lady Tiger?" Boston asked, finally breaking her train of thought.

"Orders?" Boston could have sworn he could hear her blink. "Lord Haldis, get some sleep. We can take it from here."

"Lady Torianna, we can still be of use in the cleanup," Boston started. "My Wolves stand ready to—"

"You are a credit to your family and your clan. Let us Cats take over."

"As you wish, Lady Torianna," Boston gave up and gave into the cotton candy at the edges of his brain.

"Yes," she replied simply. "Now, this lifter is at your disposal. Gather your flock and get some sleep."

"Of course," Boston agreed. He managed to stay on his feet until the last of the Wolves made it to the lifter and then let Chang haul him up the ramp.

BERN

Jordana stood at the head of the long table in front of a silent room. Bern couldn't remember the family dining room ever being this quiet, not with most of the house assembled. All the survivors. Her heart was still pounding. Her hands still shaking beneath the table.

"My brother, Lord Raipur, is dead," Jordana said.

All heads turned to stare at the empty chair a few paces down from Jordana.

"My niece, Lady Iolana, is dead."

Another empty chair became the center of attention.

The litany of losses continued, six in all, before Jordana's breath caught in her throat, and she glanced down at the empty seat at her left hand. Bern couldn't bring herself to look at it. "My daughter is dead."

"Murdered." Jordana continued.

A startled gasp ran around the table. They all knew it had happened, had watched breathless as people were pulled from the wreckage of the enclave. But only those who were there knew it was murder.

"I thought… primitives?" Lady Koichi asked.

"They were killed by primitives." Jordana continued, her voice like ice. "But they were murdered by House Sinclair."

Ripples flowed around the table.

"There is no other explanation. Prims could not have breached Sinclair's security systems without an alarm. Prims could not have produced so many weapons without us knowing." Jordana took a shuddering breath. "Prims could not have known there was an event tonight."

"The police should be executing them!" Taarush yelled.

"The police have already announced it was a tragic accident and blamed the prims," Jordana cut him off. "Either Chen was in on it, paid off, or too blind to see the truth in front of them. Either way, there is little point involving the police now."

Jordana raised her gaze from Taarush and stared fixedly down the long table. "We will mourn. We will plan. And then, we will destroy House Sinclair so utterly, they will cease to be remembered."

Bern managed to rise to her feet with everyone else, though her knees were jelly. Conversations erupted as Jordana stalked back toward the entry hall, straight-backed and silent.

"Jordana, we—" Bern said as she passed, managing to take a step forward, but Jordana swept along without sparing her a glance. Whatever Bern wanted to say died in her throat.

ASPEN

"We will find out who did this," Sherah said, a whiskey glass in her hand. "And then, they will know suffering."

The four of them had gathered in the secure room at the heart of the house. Grenada was still in her torn dress, but Sherah had changed into her nightclothes. But she was no less imposing for it.

"Nirvana?" Ambroos asked quietly, his fists tensed on the table. Dursun had been very special to him, Aspen remembered.

"No." Sherah shook her head. "Chen. Torriana declined the invitation at the last moment. She did it. Or she knew. Either way, we will have our revenge."

Aspen nodded. It was the only explanation that made any sense. The security failures, the timing, the feint at the *Cortés*. It was the only thing that made of sense.

"We will start work tomorrow," Aspen promised, her mind racing ahead. Arming primitives was despicable. Sinclair was the greatest house in the greatest empire known to history. To threaten that was to threaten the very fabric of the Empire, the fabric of humanity.

And she would stop at nothing until Chen was exposed for it, until they cowered under the heel of Sinclair and the Taoiseach.

BOSTON

With two more stimtabs in him, Boston was feeling more human as he dragged himself into the foyer of the estate several hours after lifting from Earth. Settling the Wolves had taken hours. Boston had gone through the whole ritual with them: each of them cleaning their armor, him double-checking everything and ordering repairs on anything that had gotten banged up. Who knew when they'd need the armor again.

"Get some rest, boy," Chang said as they paced through the door.

"You, too. You are getting too old for this."

Chang only grumbled in reply.

Despite the hour, all the lights were on in the main entryway. His grandfather rose from one of the couches, a wry smile on his face. "You look like hell," Baghdad said drawing Boston into a stiff-armed hug. "Well done."

"Yes, indeed," Montana said, rising from one of the other couches. She was dressed quite chastely in one of the house's plush robes, but energy radiated off her. She was taut as a coiled spring.

Boston found himself standing straighter despite the protests in his back. "Lady Montana, are you well?"

She nodded. "As well as could be expected. Baghdad was kind enough to offer me a ride off the *Cortés*."

"She told me much about your escape," Baghdad said. "But now that you're back, I think its best that all of us got to bed. Everything else can wait till morning. Would you be so kind as to escort Lady Montana to one of the guest quarters?"

"Of course." He offered Montana his arm.

The moment she took it, Boston was acutely aware of Montana's closeness. Her hip slightly brushing against his, her arm sliding against his.

In a rush, they were soon at one of the guest rooms tucked away in the estate, and he palmed the door open for her. She still didn't speak but kept her hand intertwined with his and pulled him in after her.

One of the few accouterments in the spartan room was a large, full-length mirror in a tasteless black frame propped against the wall of the bedroom. Montana approached it warily and searched her reflection.

Their gaze met in the mirror. Without turning, she

whispered, "We survived."

"We survived," he repeated.

He stared back into the black of shadowcasters.

"Show me your eyes."

She touched behind her ear, and then, he could see them in all their gold-flecked violet beauty. Her gaze stayed fixed on him in the mirror, as if daring him. The robe and the remains of her dress ran off her, puddling on the floor. Boston didn't spare them half a glance. She was beautiful, a battered, bruised, triumphant goddess. He approached slowly, cautiously, afraid she would bolt if he pounced. But it was her who made the first move, pulled him close, and began to wash the night away.

BOSTON

Boston woke alone the next morning. Despite a bone-deep tiredness, sleep hadn't come easily for him, and to his delight, neither had it for Montana. That they'd managed to sleep at all was a testament to how much energy he had spent in the fight.

Dressed and shaved, he padded his way downstairs in plush moccasins. The dining room was empty, as was the great hall, so he made his way to Baghdad's study.

"I'm afraid I must ask you to leave those, my Lady," echoed out into the hallway when he pushed the door open.

The fire was already lit, the room slightly warm. Montana was on her feet, a garment bag in her hands, her back to him, facing Baghdad in his favorite armchair. Chang was off to the side, his arms folded, face set in stone.

Baghdad noticed him first. "Ah, Boston. Perhaps you can talk some sense into your friend."

Montana glanced back him and then turned her gaze to Baghdad once more. "I was the one smart enough to take them with me when we left the *Cortés*."

Baghdad acknowledged the point with a nod. "You were. However, those rifles represent my best chance to figure out who tried to murder my house!"

"You have your own."

"We do not. Chang?"

Chang nodded stiffly. "Voyen messaged me this morning. The police seized everything: all the souvenirs the Wolves got away with, their armor, everything. Those two rifles are the only things left not in the hands of House Chen."

"Montana," Boston said gently and ran his fingernail along her bare arm.

She jerked away from him, a burning fury on her face momentarily terrible before she schooled it away into anonymity. But all hope of taking her back upstairs died in his heart.

"Your gallery could use a cash infusion. I am prepared to pay—" Baghdad started, but she cut him off.

"Not enough."

Boston kept a wary eye on his grandfather and watched him rein in his temper. Montana was still here, waiting, willing to deal. They just had to find the way.

"I want them." Baghdad chipped off the tiniest sliver of his frustration and gave it voice. "Someone, likely one of the great houses, tried to win this House War in a night. And in doing so, nearly killed me and Boston. They would have snuffed out our house completely. And I want them to pay for it. I want the Taoiseach to make them pay for it."

"So do I." Her voice was quiet, but Boston could hear the flames licking the insides of her brain. "And let's not mince words. It was Sinclair. I was only at this event because Aspen insisted I attend. It occurs to me, however, that Lady Sherah would have been very happy to take this opportunity to get rid of the embarrassment of a half-breed piece of slag that divorced her house."

"Lady Sherah would never do anything to make her house look weak," Baghdad countered.

"They only look weak because it failed," Montana said. "If they had succeeded in killing everyone, there would be no need for this narrative. It is a desperation move."

"One that Chen seems to be supporting," Chang said.

Baghdad considered that, then shook his head. "Torriana just doesn't want to cause a panic."

"So, what good is a rifle going to do us if it is clear to everyone this was no accident?" Boston asked, and Montana deflated slightly.

"It had to be made in the colonies. Making that here would raise too many questions. Which means it had to be shipped in and sent down to the enclave."

Montana nodded, her back still to him. "I have a few people I can talk to, have them look into any strange shipments to the surface. See if anyone has a sudden attack of memory when confronted with some cash."

"Good," Baghdad grunted. "Boston, you start looking through all your footage. See if anything stands out as strange."

Boston gulped. "That will be a lot of footage."

"So what? I will give up one of the rifles. The other stays with me. But I want a seat at the table, even if we prove it was a different house." Montana's voice broke. "If we find proof, if Taoiseach Dublin steps in, he will not just be satisfied with a slap on the wrist. Arming primitives? This is another Uprising. He will end whatever house it was, cleanse it to the bone. And I want to be the one that proves it."

Her enthusiasm was infectious. Despite

everything—the potential costs, the lives that now hung in the balance—Boston had the urge to howl. It was like going into battle.

Baghdad got to his feet and poured four glasses from the whiskey tumbler. "The bastards have gotten lazy," he said. "They don't know what real competition feels like. We've brought ourselves up from nothing."

Chang stood slowly and took the glass Baghdad offered him, knocking their two glasses together. "I thought coming home was going to be boring."

Boston joined him without a moment's thought. "You should have known better."

Baghdad offered the last glass to Montana, still standing on her own, holding the garment bag of illicit weapons. Pure fury radiated from her violet eyes, like the hottest flames.

There was a clink, and her glass rested against theirs. "We're going to burn them to the ground."

Mired in a House War, beset on all sides by rivals, by cutthroat competitors all chasing an ever-shrinking pie, it is perhaps understandable that none of them considered the real threat.

To think outside the box, one must first acknowledge that a box exists. But after so many years of complete, hegemonic domination, after so long focused on their peers as threats, the nobility never considered that the real threat lay outside their power structures. None of them conceived that someone would have so little care for the structures of the Empire that they would tear it all down around them.

Empires choose to fall. And this is how.

CHAPTER THIRTEEN

Open War
CHANG

Much later, after Boston had escorted Lady Montana out, Chang settled back on the divan and swished his drink thoughtfully.

Baghdad returned, leaning heavier on his cane now that the boy was safely away, and poured another drink for himself as well. Wordlessly, they sat across from each other, both contemplating the prior day's events. Chang had no misconceptions about himself,; he knew Baghdad and the kid were leaps and bounds smarter than him. But they trusted him anyway. It was one of the many reasons he'd attached himself like a booster rocket to House Haldis before they were even nobles.

"Taoiseach above, Baghdad, she was more eager than you to tear down Sinclair, and she used to be one of them."

"Close exposure to that nest of vipers would make anyone want to stomp them into the dirt. On the other hand, family—even former family..." Baghdad shook his head. "Of course, she's an outsider. Living with them can't have been pleasant."

"You think we can trust her?" Chang asked, swirling his glass again.

"To a point." Baghdad leaned back, a soft smile on his lips. "You can't fake that kind of hate. She isn't a Sinclair shill. She probably has games of her own, though." Baghdad sighed. "Something about this still feels wrong. Trying to destroy all the other houses? Even for Sinclair, that is a massive escalation."

"Who else could it be?"

"No one else I can think of. Which means they're better at hiding than anyone this powerful has a right to be."

They sat in silence again for a while until Baghdad clambered back to his feet. "Whatever else we do, we need to learn more about who we're fighting with. Which means you need to pay a visit to the Stowaway."

Chang's blood didn't run cold, nor did his heart skip a beat. He'd half-expected it, hoped against it, but had been steeling himself against the possibility since the attack. Since he'd begun to get an idea of the scale of the force that must be arrayed against them.

Still, it hurt. He'd give another few fingers to avoid having to go through that hell again.

Baghdad gave him a hard look. "I know exactly what it cost to pull you out of that mess last time. And I will gladly pay it again, if that's what it takes."

Ice shook in his nearly empty glass, chattering suddenly in the quiet room.

"I can control it." He said it half to convince himself.

"For your sake, I hope so."

"I'm sure they've moved a dozen times since I last… It might take me a while to find them."

Baghdad nodded.

BERN

The sameness of it all was what hurt the most. Bern hadn't slept at all, but the hours passed regardless, and now, she stalked through Castle High, her wardrobe unchanged, the people around her hurrying to their appointments unchanged, the regular announcements unchanged. But to her, everything was different. Or was it just her?

Where her center of tranquility had been was now a whirling maelstrom that she had not yet begun to harness. It was still too painful to touch. Katalia was dead, Sinclair had killed her, and no one seemed to notice.

After what seemed like hours, she reached Montana's townhouse—so unadorned, so normal, it made her want to scream. She hammered on the door, forgoing the bell, and waited. Hoping.

The door slid open, and Montana poked her head out. Bern sighed with relief and pulled her friend into a tight hug. "Thank the Taoiseach you survived."

"I missed you, too."

Bern released her grip ever so slightly but kept her hand wound round Montana's and allowed herself to be dropped onto a familiar couch.

They sat in silence for a few moments as Bern drank in the sight of Montana alive, unhurt. She couldn't have taken responsibility for another death.

"I am so sorry," they said together.

Bern blinked and then squeezed her friend's hand. "No. I am the one who got you to go."

"Sinclair would have insisted I go anyway."

"I tried to come find you and Katalia, but they refused to open the door," Bern said in a rush. "I almost killed you."

"No."

"If I had not asked Aspen for an armistice, Sinclair might never have thought to trap us down there like that."

Montana froze, whatever she had been going to say dying on her lips. She blinked several times, staring fixedly at Bern, before finally managing, "Sinclair?"

"Yes, Taoiseach damn them. Sinclair. They planned the attack. They..." Despite everything she tried, her voice hitched. "They killed Katalia."

"How..." Montana started, then bit back her words. "Why do you think that?"

And Bern explained. Explained how Lady Sherah had stalled throughout their negotiations, just waiting for the attack to start. How they'd insisted Nirvana bring far more than just the negotiating team to sell the cover of the gala. How just that morning, Sinclair had announced a massive expansion of their nascent pharmaceutical plantations on Shangri-La.

Montana refused to meet her eyes. But she listened, her mouth half-open as Bern laid out everything she had spent the long night figuring out.

"And it was their Wolves who came in and saved everyone. But only once there had been enough killing. Did you know that Sinclair ship received over fifty calls for help? And still, they waited a half hour to pass them on?"

"What if they were hacked?"

Bern shook her head. "Not a single officer from that ship was killed, and they were all down there."

"I have something to show you."

Bern bit her tongue and forced herself to wait as Montana disappeared into the bedroom and returned with a large tray, setting it gently on the table between them.

The gun on the tray gleamed like oil under the lights, radiating malice. Bern hadn't seen any fired, but she'd heard the sounds. There were still flecks of dark brown on one end, where it had been used to beat someone. Katalia had been barely recognizable.

"How did you get this?"

"Boston and I took two when we escaped. But that isn't the important part."

Montana picked up one of the tools sprinkled around the tray and applied it to a panel on one side of the gun. The inside was rougher, without finishing, but it was embossed. The Nirvana family crest lay on the inside of the panel, a few fingers across, colored in light green.

"Taoiseach above..." Bern took the panel and traced the crest with a finger. "Augustine..."

"Someone is trying to frame Nirvana," Montana said, leaning back. "It says it was made on Heaven."

One of the few Nirvana planets that retained any amount of manufacturing, Bern noted. If someone in Nirvana wanted to make guns in secret, that was where they would do it. "Those bastards."

"If this was Sinclair," Montana said, stressing the *if*, "then they went to great lengths to—"

"Of course they did! The Taoiseach would derogate any house who armed primitives or colonials! This is treason!"

"Bern, take a minute to—"

The torrent of anger in her chest finally burst through, her defenses collapsing all at once. "No, Augustine, no! They did this. Aspen sat across from me, waiting for this to happen with her little smile and her little laugh. And my cousin was killed just a few feet away. Their ambition has been growing for years, and it finally led them to do the unthinkable. Which is why we need to get you away from them."

"What?"

"Augustine," Bern said, taking her friend's hand again and squeezing it, "this is going to be horrific. We will not stop this time. Not until Sinclair pays for what they did to

Katalia. Either the Taoiseach destroys them, or we do."

"I am my own house."

"Yes. But this House War will get worse and worse until one of us wins. And without Katalia, protecting you will be harder than ever, dear. Please come stay with me. Nirvana Estate will be the safest place in the system before long."

With aching slowness, Montana withdrew her hand. "Clarisse, this is not a good idea."

Bern felt her face warm. "You can have your own rooms. You can even bar me from accessing them. You could—"

"No, Clarisse, I worked for too long to get out from under Sinclair's heel. They do not get to control me any longer. That includes forcing me to run to Nirvana like a little girl hiding behind your skirts. No."

"I just want to help."

"I know. But I wouldn't be who I want to be if I did this."

Disappointment and pride warred in Bern's stomach. Montana was everything Bern wanted to be: confident, sure of herself, and refusing to bow to anyone. In the few years Bern had been in her orbit, she had never backed down from a fight, never tried to hide her heritage, and never took slag from anyone.

And yet, it might kill her.

"If you get hurt because of me…"

"If I get hurt," Montana said, fixing Bern with violet-tinged finality, "it will be because of my own actions. Not yours."

"As you wish, Augustine." And then, the hard part. "However, I can no longer help with the gallery."

Montana nodded softly. "I understand. But we are so close…"

"I know," Bern lied. Nothing had worked yet, and nothing would make it work, not with the House War spilling into open conflict. "It just… it is just too hard right now. Menodora and Jordana are inches from disowning me as it is."

"Bern, nothing was your fault."

Bern dismissed the platitude. She knew better. "You need to wind down the gallery, Augustine."

"I will not," she said automatically.

"Without a sponsor…" She trailed off. "Augustine, you only had a few months of runway. Now, it is less. If you want to keep all this, how can you go on?"

"It is not the best time to be losing a valuable source of income."

"The risks outweigh—"

"The risks be damned. Sinclair has taken everything else from me over the years. I will not let them take my financial independence, take what I have managed to build. None of it."

Bern didn't argue further. It was fruitless. She made small talk for a little while longer, then left, angrier. The only way to save Montana was to redeem herself in Menodora's and Jordana's eyes. And that meant ending Sinclair. By whatever means necessary.

BOSTON

Though massive—the largest structure in the Empire—Castle High couldn't hold the homes of all those who worked there. It was surrounded by dozens of smaller estates—some wealthy retreats, some tenements for the large common Terran population that kept the ring turning smoothly.

Hannigan piloted their limo up to one of the docking ports of one of the smallest, oldest estates, keeping a dubious eye on the instruments.

"A Sinclair servant lives here?" he asked, peering out a window.

Montana sat on the long divan, her legs crossed under her, studying her slate, but she nodded. "Yoseif lives here. He is the buyer for the kitchens at the enclave."

The limo rumbled as they docked to the estate, and Hannigan called from the front of liner, "We're here! I'm going to keep the engines warmed up in case the docking port falls off with us attached."

Boston rose and straightened his SpaceGuard uniform. "And the police have not asked to talk to him?"

Montana shook her head. "Not that I could find. They must have their hands full talking to the survivors."

Chang gestured for Montana to precede him, but she stayed on the divan. "Coming?" Chang asked.

She gave Chang a withering look. "I would prefer that Sinclair not know exactly how you two knew to talk to him. If he sees me and tells them, we can forget about using my residual access to their systems for anything useful."

"Come on." Boston gestured, and they headed out.

The estate was on the small side, but it didn't seem to have a tram, so it was a long hike to the apartment complex they were looking for. The corridors were dim, with lights out regularly and the insistent buzz of poorly regulated power.

"This typical?" Boston asked as they picked their way around a pile of refuse in the corridor.

"Some places," Chang grunted back, wiping his heavy boot on the deck.

Moving was helping. Staying active was helping. It kept Boston from focusing on the odd feeling in his stomach. Out of habit, he rapped heavily on the door when they found it, ignoring the buzzer. "SpaceGuard, open up."

It was only a small lie.

The door slid open an inch, and the smell wafted out. It was horrendous, stale vomit and dried sweat that made him gag.

"Slag," a tired voice said from inside. "Can't say I wasn't expecting you."

"Yoseif du Li?"

The door opened wider. Yoseif was a short man, barely coming to Boston's chest. His eyes were bloodshot, and a little bit of dried vomit clung to the side of his face.

"That's me." Yoseif was almost clinging to the door for support.

"Taoiseach, what's the matter with you?" Chang asked, taking a step back.

Yoseif shook his head. "Stomach flu. Doc said to just stay in bed and stay hydrated, but..." He took a shaking breath. "Karma, I think. Come in. I have to lie down."

Yoseif retreated, leaving the door ajar. Boston looked at Chang, who shrugged and shouldered the door the rest of the way open.

The smell was worse inside. Thicker. It was a one-room space, larger than Boston's quarters on the *Cortés* but almost barren. A mattress lay on the floor on the far side of the room, with Yoseif collapsed onto it clutching a bucket.

"Tell us what happened," Boston said, keeping his distance but squatting down.

"There were two of 'em," Yoseif started. "Man and woman. Don't know what house. Nobles, though."

"When was this?"

"Week or two ago," Yoseif muttered. "Came to me and asked to add a couple crates down to the enclave. Didn't think much of it, but they paid well. Then, I saw the news.

Had to."

"What kind of crates?" Chang asked.

"Same as any other. Nirvana markings on 'em, but so're half the crates I get. Food from Eden's cheap."

"Then what?"

"Then nothing. I took 'em down, I put em where I was told, and I spent my money." He took a rattling breath. "Told ya; karma."

"And you have no idea who they were?"

Yoseif retched, and suddenly, the bucket was fuller. Boston had to close his eyes.

"One… one of 'em rotted up," Yoseif said, wiping his mouth with the back of his hand. "The man. Called the girl a name, and she shushed him. Gave me another hundred."

"What was the name?" Chang asked, leaning forward.

"Katalia." Yoseif chuckled.

It couldn't have been. She'd sat across the table from him, laughing, arguing with Istanbul. She'd been so relaxed. And she'd died! How could she—

His shock was so complete, he didn't notice when Yoseif started to choke for air.

It was hard to understand what was happening at first. Boston thought the man was vomiting again, but nothing came up. He struggled, writhing on the bed, and Boston started forward, only to be caught in Chang's strong grip.

"We need to go."

"We need to help him." Boston yanked his arm free.

"He's been poisoned. We need to get out of here before someone sees us."

Chang was right. It looked guilty as hell, standing over a dying man—a man who'd helped perpetrate one of the greatest crimes in the history of the Empire.

Boston spared another glance fpr the dying man and then let Chang pull him from the room.

BOSTON

"It can't have been Nirvana," Montana said quietly. "And Katalia died. She would never…"

"He might have been lying."

"No." Chang shook his head. "Not with his dying breath."

"He might have been mistaken," Baghdad said. "Or it might have been a deliberate ruse."

"Still, it is a nice, tight time frame." Montana leaned forward. "I can start looking for crates sent down on those dates, trace them back. It would be good to get other cargo manifests, too—something to compare to."

Baghdad waved a hand. "Boston, can you get copies during inspections?"

He nodded. "I can, but they are few and far between."

"See if you can get Delaware to assign you a few more."

Boston grimaced but nodded.

Later, as he walked Montana to the docking ring, she said little. She was on the verge of boarding her taxi before he remembered. "Oh, I have something for you." He proffered a drive.

She raised and eyebrow.

He explained, "Istanbul. Did you see the interview he gave? About fighting off the prims to try to save Eiravati and Katalia?"

Her face clouded. "I did indeed. Bastard."

"It was complete slag. He was hiding in a cupboard all night. I found it while reviewing footage. I thought you could do something interesting with it."

"I think I could. To get his posting canceled?"

"No one will want to hire a coward."

She gave him a small smile, and her hand lingered on his as she took the drive. "Let me look at it and see what I can come up with."

BERN

Sinclair was good, Bern had to admit. The way they'd pulled the wool over everyone's eyes was masterful. No one would have expected them to attack themselves, to make themselves look weak. But their response had been too well-coordinated for anything else.

Bern peered down on the throne room, waiting for the next move. The room was possessed by the same restless energy she felt, including the packed upper galleries. She could have sat in the Nirvana section on the lower level, but she preferred the view from up here.

As they did every few minutes, her eyes found Aspen in the second row back. She was perfectly poised, so much so that Bern continually felt scruffy in her presence, despite knowing better.

Every day since the attack had proven again Sinclair's duplicity, but it seemed that only her family saw it. There was the Sinclair petition to commence another two liner routes into Chen territory. Their announcement of a five-billion-crown renovation project on Tartarus, doubling the size of their factories there.

The Taoiseach sat at the center of his horseshoe table, as he had the last few days since the attack. Whether he was continuously warned of petitions serious enough to demand his attention or canny enough to read the room on his own, she didn't know. But she enjoyed guessing.

"Next business?" the Taoiseach prompted, as people scurried around the hall, preparing. There was no trace of boredom in his face; he was very much the imperial presence, ready to cast judgment.

Bern sat up straighter and refreshed her slate. Something was starting.

The Von Anker scion stepped to the front of the room,

and Bern pulled up the profile she maintained on the young man. There wasn't much. Von Anker, while still diamond-ranked, was almost irrelevant—except for their name, which carried weight even Nirvana didn't. She flicked her eyes and noted with surprise the look of horror on the face of Lord Durban, the Von Anker representative on the council.

"My Taoiseach, esteemed members of the Grand Council, I have a charge to lay against a fellow noble."

Silence was absolute without the Taoiseach even needing to call for it. Bern scanned her notes, but there was nothing—no idle chatter, no intercepted ansibles—that might indicate what this could be. It made the hairs on the back of her neck stand on end.

"You are Lord Sidon, yes? Grandson of Lord Durban?"

Durban turned a paler white. "My Lord Taoiseach, begging your pardon. If I may confer with my grandson before continuing..."

The Taoiseach shook his head sadly. "Lord Sidon has the courage to speak in front of the council and all those assembled here. We deserve to hear what he has to say."

"Thank you, your grace." Sidon bowed again to the Taoiseach. "My Lords, I do not make this charge lightly. However, with everything that has happened across the Empire in the last few weeks, we cannot afford to wait to resolve this matter.

"Your grace, some months ago, I was approached by someone who had the tax records of my family, complete with the seals of the Taoiseach's office. This person induced me to spy on my own house, reporting the movements of my elders, upon threat of releasing these documents to the public."

"Blackmail is a serious charge. Worse still, using imperial resources to do it," a low baritone sounded from beside the Taoiseach. Lord Huntington leaned forward, somehow overcoming his own gravity to speak. "Who would dare?"

Bern had one idea who was canny enough to have done so, but it was still slightly a shock to hear the name spoken out loud.

"Aspen Sinclair, my Lord."

Huntington's face solidified into granite mid-scowl. With beady eyes, he glared down at the Von Anker boy without even a quiver of a jowl.

"Is Lady Aspen here to answer the charges against her?" the Taoiseach asked the room.

"I am, your grace." Aspen's willowy form rose, and Bern snapped her gaze to her again. She was in a chaste blue-red dress, not a single white-blonde hair out of place. "The charges are ridiculous, of course."

It rang hollow. Bern started a search for business connections between Anker and Sinclair. There would be many—the diamond houses were the original nobility—but something might stick out.

The Taoiseach seemed content to let Huntington handle the interrogation, strangely enough. At least, he made no move to cut Huntington off when he rumbled to life again. "I assume you have incontrovertible proof, Lord Sidon."

"I do." The Anker boy reached into his jacket, and withdrew a slim recorder from his pocket. "I recorded her when she came to see me last."

Aspen didn't react. She was a fantastic actor, but she couldn't hide everything. And yet, there was no flicker of surprise as she waited.

The Taoiseach's face was grave. He made a small motion, and Lord Sidon approached the long, high table and, with two shaking hands, placed the recorder on its surface in front of the Taoiseach.

A gold-encrusted hand waved over the small device, and suddenly, the speakers in the room boomed to life with the sounds of a door opening and closing and then shuffling fabric.

Bern closed her eyes, trying to discern anything from the soft sounds, so it was a shock when the first voice sounded.

"Grandfather, this cannot go on! We are almost destitute. We must do something!"

It was Sidon's voice, strained, higher and smaller than when he was presenting his case. But of Aspen's voice, there was no sound.

"Boy, listen to me. You will do nothing! I will handle things."

"But your gambling losses have ruined us! We have to do something!"

"Do you hear me? Do nothing, say nothing, and let your betters handle this!"

"Enough!" Lord Durban roared, damning himself. It was his voice conversing with his grandson's, with no sign of Aspen. Bern glanced at the old man—ashen, a blood vessel working in his forehead—but kept her gaze on Aspen. Not a twitch, not a hair out of place.

Lord Huntington nodded, sending his many chins quivering. "I quite agree. The thought of my niece engaging in this behavior and having no proof! Shame, Lord Durban. I—"

Huntington fell silent instantly as the Taoiseach raised a hand. The young leader had fixed Lord Durban with a withering glare. "We allow so much latitude to our loyal subjects, our partners in running this great Empire. And we ask for so little… except not to squander the gifts given from our very hands."

Durban's Adam's apple positively vibrated. "Your grace—"

"Take your grandson and remove yourself from my sight and my council," the Taoiseach bellowed. "Before our patience wears any thinner."

Without another word, Lord Durban rose from behind the table and marched out of the room. The hall was deathly silent, even when he boxed his grandson around the ears and dragged him out of the room. Tears were streaming from the boy's eyes, but he remained silent.

The entire room watched the pair leave—except Bern and Aspen. Aspen watched the Taoiseach, and Bern watched Aspen. She only moved after Durban passed, retracing Sidon's steps back up to the supplicant platform and pausing. She kept her hands demurely clasped behind her back, waiting.

"Was there something you wished, Lady Aspen?" The Taoiseach finally decided to notice her after the doors boomed shut behind the Ankers.

"Yes, your grace. My good name has been called into question today, and I would ask you, humbly, to grant me a boon so that impression can be rectified."

The Taoiseach nodded. "Nothing that has been said today should reflect on you, Lady Aspen. I do not know what desperation possessed the boy to lay this charge against you. Ask, and it shall be granted."

"Your grace, I ask that the task of overseeing outer rim commerce be given to my older sister, Lady Grenada. I would ask it for myself, had I the experience to hold the post."

Bern froze. Shameless of her! Of all of them! Nirvana had held that post for forty years. Did she really expect—

The Taoiseach chuckled slightly, letting the floor fall out of Bern's thinking. "The same post recently held by Lord Raipur Nirvana before he so tragically was taken from us?"

"Yes, your grace."

The Taoiseach nodded, smiling softly. "You have the gall of your ancestors, Lady Sinclair." Bern's eyes went to Menodora, who was clearly clinging to her voice with her last ounce of strength. Her caution won. Even she dared not interrupt the Taoiseach.

"Your boon is granted." The Taoiseach didn't even glance down the council table.

Bern refused to let the shock paralyze her, but it was hard. Aspen walked back to her seat calmly, as if she hadn't just won a major victory, though Lord Huntington's face showed pleasure. Bern focused on Aspen. Channeled her rage, rather than let it consume her. There had to be a way to crack the defenses Sinclair had built around themselves, and she would find it if anyone could.

Bern focused the extra antennas she wasn't supposed to have on her slate onto the small portion of the floor that was occupied by Aspen. Her face may have been placid as she listened to the next several rounds of petitions that were thankfully innocuous, but Aspen's slate was the center of a wild riot of electromagnetic activity.

She couldn't read any of it, of course. Aspen—and any other well-to-do house—could pay for sophisticated encryption protocols, but the routing details couldn't be encrypted. And that was what Bern focused on.

Strangely enough, the longer Bern kept her signals centered around the patch of floor that contained Aspen, the more it looked like there were two nodes at the center of the web. An entire second comm endpoint, buried in Aspen's other traffic.

It wasn't much, but it was a start.

CHAPTER FOURTEEN

Subversion
BOSTON

Boston had gathered the Wolves in the den for the award ceremony and done his best to make it a celebration. He'd made sure the schedule was clear of operations the next day, arranged for several kegs to be delivered, and catered one of the best noodle bars on Castle High.

Still, it was a subdued room that watched Delaware and Kalif accept their medals on the monitor.

"I am proud to accept this award on behalf of the officers and crew of the *Hernan Cortés*," Delaware said, beaming into the camera as the red medal was slid over his head.

The Taoiseach solemnly nodded. "As well you should be, Lord Sinclair. The honor, courage, and quick thinking of this man here—" He indicated Kalif, sporting his own medal. "—were in the finest traditions of the SpaceGuard."

Scattered heads turned to look at Aspen, waiting patiently with her arms behind her back at the fore of the room. She made no comment, so the moment passed. Boston was sure there would have been boos and catcalls if she hadn't been there.

"Thank you. I can only hope this will inspire others to train those under their command to the same readiness, so that we may avoid incidents like this in the future."

Delaware looked like he might have said more, but the Taoiseach moved on to the next in line and began reading a new award.

"I think that will do," Aspen announced and cut off the sound from the monitors. She floated to the front of the room full of Wolves, face placid. "Wolves, to add to what our commander said, the Taoiseach has decided to offer all of you the Taoiseach's Thanks." She nodded to a stack of twenty-four slim boxes on the table. "You all did your duty admirably."

The Wolves stayed silent. Aspen let the silence stretch just a moment longer than felt comfortable, then turned to Boston. "You wanted to say a few words, Falcon?"

Boston didn't move as the room turned to look at him. "On a more personal note, I wanted to thank all of you for pulling me out of the fire down there. Without all of you, I would be dead. So would many others. I will never forget it. Now… shall we eat?"

That finally got a howl from the Wolves, and they started forward to the line of steaming dishes. Boston, however, followed Aspen as she strode purposefully toward the door.

"Lady Aspen, may I have a moment of your time?"

She paused just a moment, glancing down her nose at him, and sniffed. "If you must."

"I wonder if you might bring a proposal to Lord Delaware for me."

Aspen raised an impeccably tailored eyebrow. "Lord Haldis. First, I am not your friend. Second, I am not your ally. Third, I am not your babysitter. I warned you when you first joined the ship to not be an embarrassment to my house. Unfortunately, it does not seem to have taken."

"I have only tried to do my duty, my Lady."

"You have highlighted our commander's failings, subverted the chain of command, and made our Pike look like a fool to anyone who knows better." She held up a hand to forestall his objections. "Was it necessary to save people? Perhaps. However, there are videos of your exploits going around the system. That does not endear you to me, the family, or the Lord Pike."

Boston gaped. He hadn't seen any of the press coverage—had, in fact, been trying to avoid seeing it—but it seemed to be doing him no favors.

Aspen made to turn and continue her exit, but she glided to a stop again, this time turning to face him outright. "Also, Lord, you might consider avoiding all matters related to House Sinclair for the foreseeable future. I care very little for what my cousin does in her spare time. However, many of the family consider her to be an annoyance. That said, being a former Sinclair offers her a certain degree of latitude. If you ever became a similar level of annoyance, you would cease to be. Problems that have my attention do not persist long."

Boston stood rooted to the spot as Aspen swept out. Chang had been hovering a few feet away, not quite listening, as the Wolves caroused behind them.

Chang laid a hand on Boston's shoulder, and Boston shook his head. "That could have gone better, eh?" Chang said

"Videos?" Boston prompted. Chang would know.

Chang nodded. "Cancun posted some of the pack's helmet footage to her blog, and it got picked up by a tabloid. You and Lady Montana shooting your way out of the enclave."

Boston hid his eyes with one hand. "See that she posts no more—at least of me. Alright?"

CHANG

The boy decided to wait another day before approaching Delaware, hoping his temper would cool. In the end, they just had to chance it. Avoiding him was becoming comical, and they had to try to find a lead. And getting a look at cargo manifests during inspections was the best they'd come up with so far.

Chang followed him to Delaware's office without a word. Boston knocked loudly and entered the second Delaware shouted for them to come in. The Lord already appeared to be in a poor mood, but the boy soldiered on. Chang was able to maintain a neutral expression, but it was hard.

They both braced, waiting. But Delaware didn't say a word, just kept his eyes focused on the desk. At last, he asked, "What can I do for you today, Lord Haldis? Have you discovered another way to embarrass House Sinclair?"

Boston managed to keep his temper in check. For the moment. At least there were no witnesses to this tirade.

"You have used your position to inflate your own ego. Embarrassed me more than once. Gone out of your way to make things public that should have remained private. All in the service of your pathetic excuse for a house. You are nothing, your house is nothing, and the moment you accept that, the better things will go for you." Delaware retreated behind his desk and thumbed through a stack of slates. "I think you and your Wolves need stiffening up. Discipline has obviously fallen almost to ground level, so you will take your entire flock, and you will drop to the training fields of North Arctica, and you will stay there until I am satisfied that things have improved. Do you understand?"

"Yes, my Lord," Boston said.

"Humph." Delaware sat again with a heavy thud. "Perhaps there is hope for you."

"I wanted to ask, Lord Delaware, if you might find yourself able to assign—" Boston started, speaking in a rush to get it all out, but Delaware was quicker.

"Out!" he roared. "You have your orders, Falcon! I expect you to set another drop record getting down to those training fields!"

BERN

"Taoiseach damn it all," Bern growled and tossed her slate down on the divan. It was useless.

"What?" Montana asked, glancing up from where she was curled up in her overstuffed armchair.

They'd taken to working together on their separate projects in Montana's townhouse, the one place on Castle High where Bern didn't feel the press of Katalia's loss so badly. The one place that felt the same. And where she could escape her family.

"Aspen is covering her tracks extremely well," Bern sighed and picked up her slate again. "She seems to have five or six different net identities that she switches between at random. There is no pattern!"

"Are you sure Aspen was in on the plot?"

"Of course, she was. She was far too calm for it to have been an accident. She knew, was expecting it. Was not surprised at all." Bern tabbed through her messages, idly playing with the filters.

"I can take a look at some of them. See if I can find anything."

"That would be lovely." Bern scooted her way down the couch and extended the slate.

Just then, Montana's slate chirped. She smiled apologetically and tapped the answer key. "Boston. Yes, the video is ready."

Montana's face was fairly radiant now, and Bern's thoughts slowed to a halt. Trepidation and amusement warred in her heart.

"Why..." It was the first time Bern remembered hearing her sound unsure. "Why don't you come see it yourself? Yes. Dinner tonight? At my townhouse?"

The revelation stunned.

Bern slid back along the couch slightly, her slate forgotten in her hands. Montana said her goodbyes and turned back to Bern, still possessed of that radiant energy. "Where were we?"

Bern fought to keep her face only blandly interested. "Lord Haldis, I take it?"

The faintest blush appeared on her friend's cheeks. "Yes. I... I can't seem to decide what to make of him."

Bern set her heart aside. "Katalia thought he was a decent man. And she was a remarkably good judge."

"One minute, he is kind and caring. The next, he puts on that armor and..."

Bern felt the moment of decision, saw both paths in front of her: the selfish on, and the one that might give Montana a modicum of happiness. Or might break her again.

"You should talk to Haldis about this," Bern said, her decision made, "and make up your own mind."

Montana nodded. "I think I might."

"Good." Bern drew back and began to gather her things.

"I can look at those records, if you want," Montana offered.

"We will look at them another time," Bern lied, rising. "I should at least pretend to be engaged with the family dinner this evening. And you have a dinner to plan!"

BOSTON

Boston contemplated the entrance again. Every muscle ached after three straight days of drops and hard training on the surface before Delaware had relented. This was their last idea. And it was a horrible one.

"Nothin' to be gained by waiting, boy," Chang grunted. "Keep things focused on inspections. Don't get sidetracked by, well, anything."

Boston nodded and crossed the alameda.

Inside was a normal office foyer, a pretty secretary waiting patiently for them. She gave him a surprised look when he said, "Lord Haldis for the commissioner. No appointment," but waved them to a chair to wait.

It was far less time than Boston expected before Lord Dhaka bounded out, reaching out to shake Boston's hand. "Boston, I wanted to make sure to thank you. You saved my life down there."

Boston blinked. He couldn't remember crossing paths with Dhaka once the fighting began. "Did I?"

"Well, all of ours. Without your call to Chang, it would have been another ninety minutes before help got there. This way. The commissioner is anxious to hear from you."

The walls beyond the foyer were slate-gray unretouched metal. Normally, people went to great lengths to disguise that they were in space, but here, there was nothing.

The corridors seemed endless, and Boston saw no signs, no directions, as they wound through the strange zig-zags. Every door was lighted and behind all of them were conversations too low to hear—some quiet, some angry.

Torriana was waiting behind an unlabeled door. She stood, her arm outstretched.

"Lord Haldis," she said, shaking his hand warmly, her

grip tight around his. "How good to see you again. Please, sit."

Boston sat where indicated, enveloped by the comfortable seat. Dhaka and the Lady Tiger sat on the other side of the table, still wearing grins. At ease.

"We really do need to set up a way for you to get in touch without coming all the way down here," Torriana remarked to Dhaka, who nodded immediately.

"I will arrange something before Lord Haldis leaves."

"Good." Torriana looked every bit a Tiger, with the bright white teeth to go with it. "Now, we have a couple of questions for you before we get to whatever brought you down here, if that is alright?"

Chang's chair creaked dangerously, but what could they say? "Of course."

He could feel Chang's disapproval.

"Good," Torrianna said again and produced a slate from beneath the table. "Do you have any information on who was behind the breach of House Chen's core last week?"

"Your house core was breached?"

Torriana smiled. "No. But it is nice to know it would be such a shock."

"What about the loss of attitude control on Europa Estate last night?" Dhaka asked rapid-fire.

"Nothing." He had not even heard it had happened.

"The wipe of the computers on the liner *Ezekiel*?"

"No."

"Have either of you met, communicated with, heard of, or otherwise interacted with a Terran with the name of Gomer Williams?"

Boston blinked. The name meant nothing to him, either, and he shook his head.

"Answer audibly, please, for the recording."

Boston's heart sank. So much for an informal chat. But Torriana was still at ease, leaning back in her chair, tapping idly on her slate.

"No, my Lady. Should we have?"

"He was the Sinclair porter who put the crates of rifles somewhere where the prims were bound to find them," Torriana said.

The wall behind her turned into a screen. A Terran man was sitting bound to a chair in a pure-gray metal cell that must have been somewhere in the complex. His head was shaved, and blood dripped from a cut above his temple.

Boston's stomach turned, but he'd never seen the man before and said so.

"Pity." The screen snapped off. "He has yet been unable to identify who paid him to move the crates. Claimed to not even know what was in them."

"I see."

Chang remained silent.

Boston could feel the next question coming. There had been nothing on the news about a body being discovered, which could only mean the police had found Li first and buried the evidence. The police always knew if you were lying.

"Are either of you familiar with the effects of cadmium poisoning?"

"I am," Chang said before Boston could think. "Saw it in the mines on Paititi twenty, twenty-five years back."

"A Nirvana colony?" Dhaka broke in.

"Yes."

Dhaka made a note.

Had it been cadmium that killed Li?

"And you, Lord Haldis?"

"No, not that I can recall."

Torriana made another tick on her slate and leaned forward slightly. "Now, Lord Haldis, this is perhaps the most important question." All trace of relaxation had vanished from her; she now appeared coiled across the table from him, ready to spring the moment he ran. "Before, we spoke about House Nirvana and whether they had any access to the *Cortés*. I want you to think hard now. Was there anything that happened—the night of the attack or since then—that leads you to believe it was them?"

"No," Boston answered. And it was completely honest. It made no sense for it to be Nirvana, and every strange occurrence they'd found so far had done nothing to change that.

Torriana stared at him for a long moment, eyes unblinking. "Good." She withdrew and nodded to Dhaka. "I think that was everything we needed to know. Obviously, if anything comes up, we expect you to share it with us. Instantly."

"Of course."

"Now, what did you have for us, Boston?" Dhaka asked.

Boston sighed in relief. At least this part of the pitch, they had practiced. "I wondered if the Lady Commissioner could see herself assigning cargo inspections to the *Cortés*. All cargo inspections."

Dhaka's quill slipped off his slate. "What was that, Lord Haldis?"

But Torriana smiled, looking even more like a large cat studying a mouse. "You want to inspect all the liners? Why?"

"Somehow, those rifles made it into the system."

"And my Cats are not good enough to inspect them?" Torriana asked, her hand at her heart. But she was still smiling.

Boston glanced at Chang. "Chang and I are used to the duty, and we have a bit of a reputation for sniffing out smugglers."

"Is that because you were assigned cargo-inspection duty as punishment so often?"

"Perhaps." Boston tried a roguish grin on her, and her smile increased a fraction. "Notwithstanding, Lady Torriana, I would want to make sure we can do these inspections without any undue interference. A mandate from your office will go a long way toward that."

"And piss off Sinclair. They would accuse me of stealing their Wolves. And worse, they would have a point."

"Is there something that makes you suspect undue influence would be likely, Lord Haldis?" Dhaka asked, earning a sharp look from Torriana.

"No, do not answer," Torriana said as Boston opened his mouth. She glanced at Dhaka. "I understand. Perhaps a test. I will assign the next inspection to your ship, and we will see what you can come up with. If it works..." She trailed off. "Well, we can see about getting you some broader cover."

Boston winced. It would be hard to find anything while dealing with the handcuffs of Delaware's standing orders, but they'd find a way. They'd have to.

BOSTON

A wave of smells assaulted him the moment Montana's door slid open, spilling out into the corridor and wrapping soft tendrils around him. It smelled like nothing he had smelled on an estate in the capital.

He stepped inside and back into the colonies. Spices he still couldn't name, the heady smoke of a good fire, and, somehow, fresh air. It smelled divine.

"In here!" Montana's call issued from the depths of the

townhouse, and Boston stepped inside. Every wall was covered with art—paintings, tapestries, frescos. Some had clearly been squeezed into the space between other pieces. The room itself was just as crowded. Not messy, just packed with trinkets. The largest clear space was the divan, complete with a real fur blanket hastily thrown over a corner.

He followed his nose to the small kitchenette tucked behind the living room. Montana was flushed, red spots dotting her olive cheeks, both hands occupied with a pan and a spatula. She'd set up a contraption on top of the electric grill, and the blue-orange flicker of flames issued from beneath the pan she held.

Montana's face was alight with joy as she concentrated on the pan; with no mask to hide behind, she was even more beautiful.

"What above Earth are you doing?"

She raised an eyebrow at him, sparing half a glance from her work. "What does it look like?"

Boston was shocked. This was the closest he'd been allowed to a kitchen since he was eight and snuck in to eat raw dough.

Montana gave him an incredulous look as he explained. "How do you survive?"

Boston shrugged. "It just never came up."

"I—" But something splattered in her dish, and she returned her attention to it. Only half giving him her attention, she continued, "I learned to cook even before I came to the Empire. Though a grill like this would have made it much easier."

"How did you get permission to have an open flame in your quarters?"

Her smirk was enough answer. Before he could complain, she waved him out of the kitchen. "It will be ready soon."

Boston settled on the divan, and before long, Montana brought out a pair of plates. Somehow, she danced among the clutter and dropped down beside him, legs crossed, still holding both plates. The wonderful smells intensified as she proffered a plate. "Well, go ahead."

Boston took the smallest piece of something on the end of his fork and popped it into his mouth. The heat seared him, but the taste! He swallowed anyway, aware of her eyes on him. It tasted like being a boy again, camping with Chang in some desolate waste.

"It tastes wonderful," he said, trying to cool his burned tongue.

"Of course it does." But she was smiling. "Lemon-roasted potatoes. I was waiting months for the liner to come in from Ram Setu with them, but it was worth it."

"Potatoes?"

"How you all survive without them, I will never understand. There were years I lived off these." She stabbed one and tore into it hungrily. "Though the spices from Camelot are definitely an improvement. Try the chicken."

Boston did with gusto, and it was even better.

"The trick is to have them smoke it before freezing it for the trip," she said, without him asking. "Almost like eating over a wood fire."

She lingered over her last bites, pushing her food around her plate, before setting her utensils down and meeting his eyes for the first time that night. "I need you to tell me about Asgard."

He wasn't shocked. He'd been dreading the question ever since Earth. She was too smart not to have noticed, not to have put the pieces together. "I know you were on the planet with the Guard during the massacre."

Boston set his plate down. "I was."

"Did you have a part in it?"

He could lie. He'd checked, and who was in command had never made the news broadcasts. What the circumstances were. But as with most things, he didn't hesitate. Boston plunged in, doing the thing in front of him, even though it was terrible.

"I commanded. When Istanbul ordered the village destroyed and they charged, I was right there in line. I killed... I could not even begin to count."

"How can you say it like it was nothing?" Her voice was smaller than he'd ever heard it, and suddenly she refused to meet his eyes.

"It was not nothing."

"And yet..." She stood up and paced away from him.

"I was there to keep everyone safe."

"That's what you call keeping people safe?"

"Istanbul and a dozen other Terrans would be dead if we had let them charge. They would have been torn apart."

"So, Terrans are the only ones that mattered?" Her voice was rising along with her anger.

"That is not what I said."

"It's what you meant!"

"No, I..." How could he make her understand? "You have to do the job in front of you. Not think about the big picture, not really think about what you are doing. Because you will go insane if you do. You just... you put one foot in front of the other. And you get through it."

She scowled. "As someone you kept safe, I wish you hadn't. I wish you'd have just left us alone!"

He tottered on the edge of a precipice somehow, with her on one side and a vast gulf on the other. "And down at the enclave? Do you wish I had left you alone there?"

"That was different."

"Why. Because they were not your people?"

"Because they were killing people!"

That was it. That was the difference between them, there in a shimmering soap bubble.

"I refuse to wait until people are already dead before I defend them." Boston sat, though he did not remember standing, and rubbed his shoulder. "That is how good people die needlessly. By hesitating."

She slumped on the divan beside him. "I didn't need saving, Boston."

"I know." That yawning pit was there again, threatening to swallow him whole. "I know. And I... I just ran. I never even fired my rifle that night. I grabbed you, and I ran."

"That's not what I read in the report."

Boston huffed under his breath. "Chang changed it. Tried to make me look good. I just... no one was in danger at that point. Ducane ordered it, and I just..." Shame filled him again. "I got better. I got through it."

"What happened to that boy who could see so clearly?"

He shook his head. "Waiting hurts people, too."

"Only if there is no other way. Only when—like down at the enclave—there is no other choice." She tugged his hand into hers, squeezing hard. "How do you know when there is no other way? That you could not save more people by waiting?"

"I—"

"You never know. You never know unless you try."

They lapsed into silence, her hand still in his.

CHAPTER FIFTEEN

Contraband
ASPEN

The endless parade of court life continued even amid open warfare. Many of the events were incomprehensible to Aspen: a ball for this, a gala for that. Still, she had learned how to play the game, what events to attend, and which ones to snub. If nothing else, these events gave her an opportunity to study the other sides, even though her time might be better spent elsewhere.

It was a smaller gathering than usual, and for that, she was thankful. The fewer uninitiated she needed to ward off from trying to induce her to dance, the better. She was here for business.

And here it came. Lady Torriana approached warily and raised her glass in a greeting. It might have been warm. Her dashing silver dress uniform did nothing for Aspen, but it was so useful when people wore their ranks displayed.

"Good sol, cousin," Torriana greeted her with a thin smile, and Aspen nodded.

They let the silence linger as they evaluated each other.

Aspen cataloged the list of slights they'd presented to Chen in the last few weeks, trying to weigh which of them had caused this rise. It would tell her something about Chen's internal power structures, as they grappled with Sinclair's assault.

"I saw you were able to win another imperial liner contract," Torriana said with the same thin smile on her face. "Congratulations."

Left out was the fact that they'd broken a Chen monopoly to do it. Aspen let a genuine smile warm her face; she'd been the one to figure out what Chen was bidding and undercut them just enough to make it worth the Taoiseach's while. It was so good to have her work recognized.

"Thank you. We are very proud that we can offer the most efficient service in the Empire."

Torriana's smile thinned slightly. "Indeed."

The party turned around them, and Aspen let her gaze slip from the commissioner, hunting for an approaching ambush, but there was nothing.

"I wondered if I might ask… how are things going on Dinas Affaraon and Kazakhstan? Until recently, we had been receiving regular reports from those worlds, but they have, alas, slowed to a trickle."

Aspen did not even need to refer to her slate; she'd skimmed the latest reports from those worlds just that morning. Unrest continued to grow despite everything the local guard could do about it. "No trouble that we need concern others with," Aspen said. It was certain that Torriana had other spies on the planet, but they'd contained the ones that had been most obviously reporting on the world.

Torriana dropped her feigned smile and took a step closer. "Aspen, please, the police are not your enemies.

The only way we are going to bring the real perpetrators to justice is if we work together."

If Aspen had not known that Torriana could act just as well as she could, she might have thought her sincere. But it was impossible for Chen to have pulled off what they had without the active involvement of the police. Or at least, their willful blindness. No, it was all too clear.

"Rest assured, Lady Commissioner, anyone who has helped shape the events of the last few months will receive their correct allocation of consequences."

Torriana's flash of anger before it was schooled away to placid nothingness was proof enough that her message had been received. "I fear you are making a mistake."

"Whoever dared to pervert the natural order of things by enlisting prims to attack my house made a far greater one than they could ever have imagined."

Torriana hesitated, then shook her head. "Fly safe, Lady Aspen." The graying lady retreated, and then, Aspen was back to observing the room, hunting for someone else she needed to speak to. Despite Chen's overreach, they had still created a wonderful amount of confusion in the Empire. And in confusion, there was profit.

BOSTON

"Interstellar Transport *Star of Terra*, please cut your acceleration and prepare to be boarded by customs officials."

Boston tapped his foot on the deck and studied the *Star* as they drew closer. *Star of Terra* was the second-largest liner ever built, only recently usurped by the *Taoiseach Jupiter*. All interstellars were laid out in approximately the same way. A long central core, empty except for plumbing and a narrow walkway, defined the length of the ship. At regular intervals, spokes of containers spit off from the central axle in an octagonal pattern. These spokes stretched out three or four containers long and then terminated in a docking port, allowing whole spokes to be drawn off the vessel at once.

The front of the vessel was capped by a great hemispherical protuberance, the meteor shield. A great half-sphere of ice-clad metal, the shield ensured that any small particles the vessel struck while flitting across a solar system would harmlessly embed themselves in the ice, rather than rip through the ship and its valuable cargo.

Every other part of the ship was containerized. Crew quarters, living spaces, passenger bunks, and environmental plants were all containers that could be unloaded from the ship at will, if needed.

The pilot of the *Star* squeaked a reply, and Boston retreated from the cockpit once he was sure the *Star* would let them dock, leaving the approach to their Eel pilot.

The back of the cutter was built just like the Wolves' den on the *Cortés*, and his flock were working their way into their armor.

"Forsake it all, Lord Haldis, this is becoming a pattern," Dunkirk said, struggling with her armor. "Last-rotting-minute operations."

"At least we had a whole day's notice this time!" Gault shouted from the back of the den with the rest of 3rd squad.

Boston ignored the ribbing. "Voyen, do the briefing." Taoiseach damn it all, he was tired.

"Copy that, Lord," Voyen said, a breath of professional air. "Alright, Wolves, we do this by the numbers. 1st pack gets the front, 2nd pack starts at the eleventh ring, and 3rd pack, the thirtieth ring. Two minutes per container. Make sure you check all the—"

Boston felt the moment of decision on them. While he'd asked Torriana for a chance, he still had to make sure they found something. And that meant not doing things according to Delaware's standing orders. It meant trusting the ten years he'd spent doing this

"Sorry," Boston cut off the pack leader, who fell silent instantly. "Pack Leader, we are going to try something new today."

Chang vibrated to attention and took the center of the room. His helmet was on, but Boston thought he was smiling.

"Would you care to tell them how?" Boston asked.

Chang's voice confirmed it; he was definitely grinning from ear to ear. "I was doing this slag long before you got put into a test tube. I know all there's to know. First, start with the cargo manifest. Compare it to the list in the ship's computer. Any container with something that doesn't match up, open it. And then, open a few crates in the container. Don't just settle for reading labels."

Chang cleared his throat and continued, "Then, look at the individual crate masses. Every atom in those containers has been accounted for, so it damn well better match. Make sure there aren't any oddballs, too. If crate five weights half of what the rest of the crates do, give it some extra attention. This is a game of smarts. You need to think like someone trying to hide something and then look where they'd look. Think sneaky."

"Are we looking for something specific?"

"No, Dunkirk," Boston said hurriedly. "Just contraband. Most smuggling is about trying to escape taxes. Rich houses trying to stay rich. Today is our chance to ruin their day."

Above, lights flickered from red to yellow—the pilot telling them they were getting close.

"Alright, Wolves, go hunt!" Boston yelled, and they howled in response, heading for the leeches.

"Lord Haldis," Voyen said, stepping closer and using a private channel, "it will be very clear from my report that we used a different method than our last inspection."

Boston did his best to read a faceless helmet and settled on something close enough to the truth. "You let me worry about that, Voyen. I doubt the Pike could be more pissed at me than he is already."

Voyen somehow managed to convey skepticism without a word.

BOSTON

Boston flicked his smallest finger inside the armored gauntlet and a burst of pure oxygen puffed his face, enough that he could get his breath back.

"Alright! Container 2570," he said as they trudged to a stop at the end of a spoke. "Anyone want to wager anything on this one?"

"Damn, Lord Falcon, you owe us about a rotting month's pay already. Do you really want more?"

"Sure. I feel lucky about this one."

And the strange thing was, he did. This container met every one of the criteria Chang and Boston had ever seen. It was buried deep in the spoke, right next to the rim. It was a Sinclair-owned container but with cargo that was registered to a relatively small company within the Sinclair family empire. And it was unevenly loaded; one of the crates was five kilos heavy.

"You know the drill. Break out the scanners," Boston said but stopped himself from repeating the same instructions he'd given for the last thousand containers. It felt like a thousand, at least.

Nevada ran his XRI over the surface of the first crate and studied the output intently while Dunkirk and Cancun stood by, waiting to lever the next one off its stack. Nevada tapped the slate, then shook his head. "Nothing."

And on to the next crate. And the next.

"You think we'll see any real action soon, Lord?" Cancun asked as they moved a crate around.

"Why? Are you bored, Cancun? The enclave was not excitement enough?"

"No, I, uh, I am thinking of putting in for a leave, actually."

"Planning a trip?"

"Cancun's decided to go become a real doctor," Dunkirk said, cutting Cancun off.

"Shut up!"

Cancun struggled to unseat one of the retaining straps, and Boston lent his shoulder to the effort. The clamp popped free, and then, the crate was slowly drifting upward.

"Come on, explain yourself, Cancun."

"I was thinking of applying to the Joint Fleet Doctor program."

"And demote yourself to be a rotting Gull." Dunkirk said.

"It's technically a promotion!"

"To be a Gull. Gulls aren't wolves."

"If it is something you want to do, Cancun," Boston said, derailing the argument before it devolved further into inanity, "I would be happy to recommend you."

"Only if we aren't getting deployed soon," Cancun insisted. "I wouldn't want to run out on everyone."

Boston was impressed. "I appreciate the sentiment. It does seem unlikely we will be deployed anytime soon, though."

"Oh." It sounded more than a little disappointed.

Before Cancun could continue, Dunkirk dropped a crate onto her foot, producing a truly impressive torrent of invective on a link none of the Wolves thought he was monitoring.

"I'd heard some bad things about Eden," Cancun said when the curses had stopped.

It was the second time someone had mentioned Eden, but Boston still couldn't find any official reports, and he'd looked. "What have you heard?"

"My aunt's a superintendent in a factory out there. Said they've had some strikes. Terrans pushed around, that kind of thing. She said they were bringing in some Guard to help."

"Really? Not that I heard."

There was a rap at the door of the container, and Boston stepped back to open it. Chang poked his head in just enough to close the comm link.

"You find anything?" Boston asked on a private link.

"Not even a misplaced shipping label. It was a good idea, but there's nothing on this boat."

"Forsake it all." Delaware was going to go ballistic, and this time, with cause. Boston's veins ran with ice; he could just see Delaware's bloated face as he yelled.

Chang hit Boston heavily on the back, making his teeth rattle. "Cheer up. You're in zero gravity again. How're your hamstrings?"

"Hundred and ten percent," he lied.

"Last one," Nevada announced on the pack link, and then, he got to his feet. "Not a thing. Every readout was the same. Nothing but grain."

"Slag." Boston sighed. "Alright, pack it up. I will buy everyone a round when we get back to Castle High. Assuming there is a bar open this time of morning."

Boston started to stomp out, but he kept turning Nevada's words over in his head. He paused, one foot on the threshold of the container. "Nevada, could you please repeat what you just said?"

"Every one of the scans was the same," Nevada repeated. "Absolutely nothing."

"Then how is one of the crates five kilos heavier than the rest?"

"Uh." Nevada glanced back at the crate. "Uh."

"Don't just stand there," Chang barked. "Crack it open!"

Dunkirk tossed a crowbar to Cancun, and the two of them reached down and levered the lid of the crate off.

Cancun's gauntleted hand reached in and came back trailing fine kernels. "Grain. Just like the manifest said."

"Dig around a little bit."

"The grain'll go everywhere," Cancun said. "It'll take hours to clean up."

"Good point." Boston's frustration broke. "You may as well dump the crate and save us the trouble of caring."

"Lord—"

"Dump it!"

"Yes, Lord!" Cancun flicked the crate up like it weighed nothing. Grain flooded out—or rather, the container stopped, and the grain didn't, shooting up in a dense clump until it hit the ceiling. It was an explosion, and the kernels were flung in every direction. In seconds, the wall of grain slammed into Boston, each kernel clattering on his helmet like a raindrop. He started laughing—he couldn't help it—as the cloud thinned slightly, letting him see again.

"Any sign of contraband?"

A chorus of nos answered him, including Dunkirk's expressive, "Less than the clothes on a colonial."

"Well then," Chang said, but Boston cut him off.

"Dump another one."

"Boston, that's—"

"Crack open another one." There had to be something

here.

Dunkirk joined Cancun in flipping the next crate, though with considerably less enthusiasm. Maize flooded out again, washing over the Wolves.

The container rang with the high-pitched crash of a dropped pitcher, setting Boston's teeth on edge. "Slag. Who broke their visor?"

Something tapped against Boston's leg, more massive than any maize kernel should be. His hand shot out and caught the object before it drifted away. As gently as he could, he brought it up to the light for inspection.

"A book?" Chang asked.

"An old book," Boston said. He peeled back the cover. The inner page was better preserved than the front, and he could make out the title and the publisher's mark. "This was printed on Earth."

"It'd have to be two thousand years old," Dunkirk said.

They stared at the flaking book in Boston's hands.

"Chang, see if you can find a container that will hold pressure. I want to get this back under nitrogen purge." Boston spared one eye from the thin volume to look at the remains of what must have been an expensive display case. The glass shards floated slowly downward.

"Dunkirk, Cancun, Nevada, I want to put eyeballs on each of the crates. Carefully!"

The Wolves delicately began to unload the rest of the crates. The rest of the flock wandered in, helping where needed but otherwise just standing and watching as more and more valuables were unearthed. Eventually, someone remembered to start taking pictures.

Boston's visor darkened as a flashbulb went off. When it cleared he stared at the sheer magnitude of their find. The whole wall of the container was covered in antiquities:

an old rifle, more books, paintings. The book from the broken case was placed delicately in a plastic pouch and strapped to Boston's hip. A feed from his suit kept nitrogen flowing over the folio.

"And then, these forsaken things," Dunkirk said, handing a clear bag to Boston. Sparkles filled the bag: diamond gems.

Chang whistled. "How much is all this worth?"

"More than any of us have ever seen in one place, myself included. Slag, this has to be the biggest find in the last twenty years."

"Just one of those things could set one of our Wolves up for decades," Chang said, nodding at the diamonds. "Buy a nice villa in the colonies, no questions asked."

Boston rolled the bag around in his hand. He couldn't even feel the weight of them. Gems were the easiest thing to smuggle, tucked away in any nook. It was hard to prove they were real, mined on Earth. No other planet had had life long enough for them to be natural, though they could be produced industrially.

Boston handed the small bag to Dunkirk. "Make sure all of these get photographed; I want a complete record of it all."

"Of course, Lord Haldis."

Boston glanced over at Chang. "Any chance you already called this in?"

"Nope. That pleasure is all yours." Boston could hear him grinning again.

"Wonderful."

CHANG

As predicted, Delaware was not amused.

"Just what did you think you were doing, Lord Falcon?" Delaware shouted, standing mere feet in front of Boston. Red veins bulged from his neck, but he showed no signs of slowing down or of giving Boston a chance to explain.

Chang focused on keeping his hands from curling into fists inside his arm. Just that was threat enough, since he could punch with the force of a limo on full burn. Keeping his mouth shut wasn't a problem. The armor was soundproof, so he could call the Pike as many names as he could think of in perfect safety.

Boston was drowning, though. He kept trying to respond, which just fueled the Pike's rage. At least Chang had found reasons to deploy all the Wolves around the ship, so they didn't have to see this. He had a watch party at every docking latch and several along the spoke. No one was getting near the container without him knowing. And because he was just as sneaky as the next smuggler, Dunkirk was magnetized to the outside hull.

He took a little pleasure in tracking Lady Torianna's party as they approached, very carefully not giving Boston or Delaware any notice she was coming.

Lady Torianna swept in like a wave on the sea, fast and energetic. She was just in her undress uniform, but she moved with the grace of someone used to zero gravity, firing out of the small maintenance tunnel like a shot in a cannon. She hooked both hands around the door frame and flipped herself up and over, landing crouched on the ceiling, knees bent, ready to fire off again.

Chang braced at attention, gratified to see Boston only a millisecond behind him. Delaware took a second to understand what was happening, following her flight with his piggy eyes, mouth slack.

Torianna observed the room for a moment and then dropped, flipping in midair to land on the deck with them.

"The three of you can relax," Torianna said, still facing the other wall. "No need to hold onto ceremony on my account."

"Lady Commissioner?"

"I heard what was going on from the *Star's* captain and decided I needed to see this for myself," she said, tactfully not mentioning that Boston had called her—even before Delaware. The woman knew what she was doing.

"Well, I... welcome, Lady," Delaware said finally, drawing himself up.

"Can we see it?"

"Of course. This way." Boston gestured and led both of them into the container. They'd moved the grain and the remains of the crates out and just left the haul. There were a few more books now, all gingerly secured to keep them out of the way. Three enormous chunks of petrified wood—the rarest substance in the Empire—made up the base of the stack. Ancient tools, a non-functional rifle with House of Eire markings, and several crates almost entirely filled with furs were stacked on top.

Torianna reached out and caressed one of the rifles. It was an ugly thing, only half the size of the splinter Chang wore across his back, with exposed components everywhere and a rough black tarnish all along one side. But it was emblazoned with the sigil of House Eire, the family that had birthed Empress Adele before she took the throne.

"I am almost glad my Cats were called away to other duties and I had to ask Lord Delaware to supply someone to inspect this freighter," Torianna said, moving deeper into the container. "You seem to have a nose for this, Lord Haldis."

"All it took was following procedure," Boston said, straight-faced. The boy's mouth was going to get him a bloody nose—if he wasn't shot. Chang couldn't be prouder.

"Do you have an explanation, Lord Delaware?"

"I think the Lord Falcon explained well enough, Lady—"

"No, no." Lady Torianna continued her examination of the contraband without looking up. "About how this contraband ended up in a Sinclair container, on a Sinclair ship."

"No, Lady Commissioner." Delaware swallowed heavily. "I had not yet begun to look into that."

Torianna eyed him coolly over an ancient folio. "I suggest you have Lady Sherah contact my office at once, then. If the true perpetrators cannot be found, the fines will be assessed against the house, you know."

He swallowed again. "I do."

"Good." She flicked her eyes to Boston. "The Taoiseach is in your debt, Lord Haldis. Between the lost taxes, illegal weapons, and," she bent over the petrified wood and rubbed a long nail against it, "recovered historical treasures, the Taoiseach's coffers have swelled considerably this night. Congratulations."

"Thank you, my Lady."

"We may have to make your helping the police a more permanent arrangement. Clearly, someone is doing something wrong."

"If I may, Lady, one of my Wolves will explain."

"Nevada, get in here!" Chang barked, correctly interpreting where this was going.

Nevada bounded into the room and slid to a stop next to Boston at attention.

"Tell the Tiger what you found."

"Yes, Lord." Nevada dropped to a knee and opened one of the emptied crates. "My Lady, I found a projection matrix on the inside of the crate." Armored gauntlets ripped away at the inner liner, revealing circuitry. "It was designed to muddy our XRI return so that when we scanned the crates, it showed only hash—just what you would expect from grain."

"A sophisticated technique?"

"Yes, my Lady."

"One of the crates was a little heavier, which made us want to search this container. I guess they just couldn't get it to balance. We only discovered it by opening the crate."

"I wonder why the inspectors on Shangri-La did not," Torianna mused, with another pointed look at Delaware. She held the look for a moment and then shook her head, a bright smile returning. "Regardless, Lord Haldis, you and your Wolves deserve a specific reward for your efforts."

A flash of alarm crossed Boston's face, which thankfully, no one else saw. Torianna swaggered along the line of contraband before picking up the small bag of diamonds. She hefted it for a moment, checking the weight, and then tossed it underhanded to Boston.

He caught it automatically and glanced down at the small bag. "Yes, Lady Chen?"

"Your cut," she said matter-of-factly. "An excellent job, as I said, Lord Haldis." She waited for his reply, head cocked to one side slightly.

"Are you sure that is... appropriate, Lady Tiger?"

She shook her head and sighed drolly. "Lord Haldis, it is customary for those that discover things like this to share in the spoils. Do feel free to distribute something to your Wolves."

"I see."

Chang could see Boston thinking rapidly, and then, he cast an eye down the row of contraband. "In that case, I did have my eye on something else."

Torianna's grin returned, wider. "What did you have in mind?"

Chang spared a glance for the ignored Delaware, watching him as Boston and Torianna pursued the stacks. It was all the cut Chang needed.

CHAPTER SIXTEEN

Consequences
BOSTON

The family limo met them at Port Chittagong after the liner was safely docked and the seized goods turned over to Torianna's Cats. Boston stopped in a leech just long enough to divest himself of his armor and arrange for the Fish to take the rest of the Wolves back to the *Cortés*.

"Taoiseach above, I hope it is a while before we have to do that again," Boston said as the hatch closed behind him. Every muscle in his back ached.

"You taught Delaware not to ride you, at least," Chang said.

"He may hate us more now." The lecture had been bad, but the glares on the ride back with Lady Torianna had been murderous.

"He deserves it," Montana said, leaning forward off the long divan running along one side of the limo.

"Hannigan, why didn't you tell us we had a guest?" Chang demanded as he headed to the flight deck to berate the young man in person.

Boston settled heavily at the table across from

Montana, eying her warily. "How do you know Delaware?"

"He's a Sinclair," she said. "Did you get the manifest?"

Boston's stomach lurched as they disconnected. It then plummeted into his shoes as Hannigan poured on the hydrogen. "I did. Not that there was anything illegal in this shipment."

"Yes, I know." Montana held up her slate, showing the crates and crates of contraband. "Following Cancun's vlog is easier than getting you to answer a comm, apparently."

He ignored the jab. "Think it will lead to anything?"

"Hard to say. Those crates were hidden from the inspectors, just like the guns were. It is better than reviewing helmet footage for the third time, at least."

Something cramped in his calf, and he bent double, squeezing hard. "You are not the one who needs to do the legwork."

"Shall I kiss it and make it better?"

"Hold on to that thought." Boston reached for his bag and drew out the small packet of diamonds. "I had another idea for an approach: building a network."

He tossed her the small bag, and she opened it gingerly. Light sparkled in her face as she wormed out the first stone. It was as big as her fingernail and glittered in the overheads.

"How did you get—"

"They were lost in transit."

"You stole them?" Her voice was an odd mixture of reproach and wonder.

"How much did you say it would take to set up a network for ourselves?" He pressed the rest of the diamonds into her hand. "Untraceable. Easy to hide. Everything we could want."

She shook her head even as she extracted the rest of

the diamonds, weighing them in her hand. "This is wrong."

"I tried telling Torianna that, but she insisted I take my cut."

Montana fixed him with a hard look. "And that makes it right? How many other things do you just go along with because everyone else does them?"

That stung. Her face softened a micrometer, but words didn't come. "Still." She looked down at the diamonds again. "This could change everything. Give us a fighting chance."

"Selling them will be a problem."

"I might know someone."

"Good enough. But I have something else for you." Boston swept a hand out toward where he'd gently set down his bag. "This one is a little less useful and more battered. We will never be able to sell it, but I thought you might appreciate it just for the sentimental value."

Montana reached out and dragged the bag over. Boston watched the way her eyes narrowed as she opened the back, her lips tightening, then going slack as she pulled the book out.

"Verne." It was a gasp. "From Earth?"

Boston nodded, and she dropped the book back into the bag. "Boston, that's worth—"

"I know, but it is too rare. No one would ever buy it without knowing where it came from. But I thought you might appreciate it."

"We had one. When I was a girl," Montana murmured. "Everything was sealed up on the colony ship. It was preserved. Felt only a few hundred years old when I read it."

"You like it."

"I—" She tore her eyes away from the book. "This is

amazing."

Boston shrugged. "I only had to steal it."

BERN

Terraforming was the technology of the ancients. The ones who had actually lived on the surface of a world and bent their minds toward studying just how theirs was collapsing around them. Dotted across the colonies there were still ancient, imperfectly understood machines whirling away, attempting to make their worlds more livable. More like Earth of Old.

Still, there were pieces of the puzzle that were understood, and Bern nodded at all the right points as they were explained to her. The Marx Brothers World-builders, Sir Marx explained, knew more about the lost art than anyone else. And if Nirvana needed additional support in maintaining the Sun Shield over Camelot, this was the best place to come.

He was almost giddy at the prospect of her business, fawning over her, offering a plate of Dearworth Delicacies from Olancha. She noted that he had to unwrap them, as if they were a precious thing to be conserved, rather than kept sitting on a plate, ready for every guest.

She focused on his mustache, trying not to laugh as it wobbled a decimeter on either side of his face.

"What about delivery times?" Bern pressed out of habit. "If we decide we need the support, how long would new fabrication take?"

"We have a line set up—" he started, but she cut him off. She'd done her research, after all.

"Surely, you must have material in stock?"

"Ah," Sir Marx said, suddenly not meeting her eyes, "I am afraid all our inventory is spoken for at the moment, but rest assured..."

He continued prattling on, and she listened with one

ear, casting her eyes around the office while he talked. He gestured to a slate, but the real prize was on a small desk at the back of the office a fiber terminal that would give her physical access to their internal networks.

Only a little later than she'd hoped, there was a knock at the door. A harried junior clerk poked his head in, gulping visibly as his senior turned red.

"Leon needs you down at the docks," the assistant said.

Marx gave her a sweet, entirely unbelievable smile. "This will only take a moment," he said, rising calmly.

She nodded, carefully not noticing him swat at the clerk, muttering, "Carl, you idiot!" as the door closed.

She waited three rapid-fire beats of her heart before she made her move.

Her satchel came out, and she connected her slate to the thick fiber-optic, jacking into the spare port at the terminal. It was a fairly expensive security system, but it was from a company sponsored by Nirvana. The house core opened for her in seconds.

She began cloning the core, sucking dry the entirety of the data stored in the background, while she hunted for the prize. Aspen had used four different comm codes in talking to the company, and Bern dumped all of them into her slate's ready memory.

It took barely a minute before she was back in her seat. All evidence of her infiltration gone, she pulled up the messages and paged through them.

Marx didn't seem to be aware that four of the people he was talking to were Aspen. She'd done a masterful job of making her voice and tone sound different in each one. All four were buyers, it appeared. Bern did some quick math, between the four of them, Sinclair was buying millions of crowns of terraforming equipment.

They were after a planet. A new colony, the first in twenty years. But which one? And why now?

When Sir Marx came back into the room, Bern was able to tell him, "I think I have all I need," with a smile.

CHANG

Chang didn't glance around furtively, didn't hunch, did nothing out of the ordinary as he marched down the corridor. He knew better, had done this too many times to do anything different. But it felt different. He felt the creeping dread in every extremity, like walking on a high-gravity world. Every step took more energy, but he did it anyway.

It was just a random shopping complex up in the poorer part of the estate, closer to the hub. The overheads were lower, the gravity lower. But it was still Castle High.

"The bastards," Chang muttered to himself under his breath. The last time he'd frequented the Stowaway, it was in one of the tenement complexes, a solid forty-five minutes' bus ride away from Castle High in a higher orbit. The bastards hadn't had the gall to set up their little base so close to the police back then. But now, they had. Chang wondered if anything had changed, or if they'd just grown bolder.

Gambling wasn't technically illegal. But gambling anything more than a pittance was the curse of death for your career, your prospects. The Taoiseach had no tolerance for it, especially among the nobility. Leaving things to pure chance was obscene. Games of skill—like the game of Empire were tolerated—celebrated even, but—

He spotted the first lookout and ignored her. Just a woman selling bonsai trees, three or four racks of them spilling out into the corridor. Nothing to see here. But she watched him too intently, and no matter how many soft snips he heard, the tree didn't change shape.

He kept going down the corridor. The shops on either side were vacant, but he could still feel eyes on him as he approached the bar.

He still had friends who could control themselves enough to dabble, to not need to be saved, so he had the passwords when challenged. And he submitted amicably enough to the searches, having done the smart thing and left all his electronics in a locker. Not that he was worried about being tracked, it would have been riskier to carry them around these thieves.

The room was different, but the sound was the same: the soft tinkle of the slot machines, the rapid ticking of balls bouncing in roulette wheels, whizzing around as fast as his heart.

It was early—not that you could tell time in a place like this—and only the poor die hards like him were around at this hour. Early enough that he might be able to get an audience. Chang tightened his grip on himself and strode out into the casino.

He found Malmö exactly where he expected; in a booth in the small bar area attached to the casino. His muscle had changed, but he waved Chang over anyway. There was an odd, happy smile on the tiny man's face.

"I heard you were coming in, and I couldn't believe it. How are you?"

He shook hands, made pleasantries, and sat, waiting politely for Malmö to hop up onto his cushions. That was the trouble with Malmö: he was always friendly, always reasonable. Until you were in too deep. He made it easy to believe that it was going to be a shame to do all the terrible things he was going to have to. But he'd do them anyway. With a sad little smile.

"There's a tourney tonight, I could get you in, even

spot you the entrance fee, if you wanted," Malmö said.

"I was looking for a different kind of favor."

"Anything for a friend."

Chang leaned in. "Remember the kid I was bringing up? Well, there's a girl in his life now."

Malmö smiled. "There always is."

"I want to check her out, before things go too far. Make sure the boy isn't sticking his dick in a centrifuge."

Malmö waved his hands. "Say no more. What's the dame's name?"

"Montana."

Malmö froze. It was subtle—he had an excellent poker face—but Chang could read at least that. And Malmö knew it, too.

"I'm sorry, I can't help. Professional courtesy, you understand?"

Chang nodded.

Malmö's face shifted though. "I could play you for the info though. Then it's not me telling you. It's just the will of the universe."

Saying yes would have been easy, would have given him the information he needed, but Chang knew he couldn't. Knew that just one hand, one spin, would never be enough. It was the hardest thing he'd ever done, walking out without what he'd come for, but he did it. He was no closer to understanding just what the hell Montana was doing on the side. But for the first time, he was sure there was something.

BOSTON

"One more drink! One more drink!"

Boston didn't join in the chant, but he did help himself to his tankard as the Wolves pushed Edinburgh closer to the bar. Then, 2nd pack raised the long meterstick and drank together as the rest of the flock cheered around them.

"Drink up, Wolves! You earned it!" Boston shouted and slapped Gault on the back. A week after their raid, it was still all anyone wanted to talk about in the bars.

Boston wandered through the packed room, keeping an eye on the flock, but most of them seemed to be burning off their prize money in good spirits. It helped that he was dolling it out slowly, making sure none of them spent it all at once.

Plus, Istanbul's video had released today, making it a good day—a very good day. He hadn't seen it, but it was out there. Soon enough, it would be seen by someone important enough to cut Istanbul off at the knees.

Chang was arm wrestling in the corner with Accra, 3rd pack's gunner. A knot of Wolves—most of 1st pack—had congregated around a booth, heads bent in intense conversation.

When he meandered over, he saw that Cancun's head was slumped on the table, her blonde fuzzed head resting on the surface. "What happened?" Boston asked.

Five faces turned to look at him. Voyen patted Cancun's back and answered for the table, "Cancun's application join the Joint Fleet Doctor program was denied."

"Ah." It was a shame Cancun was a good medic and would be an even better doctor, but the service only picked a few Terrans a year. "I am sure they will reconsider you next year, Cancun."

Cancun turned a bleary eye to him from the table and shook her head.

"It wasn't rotting MedCore," Dunkirk said, cracking her knuckles alarmingly. "Delaware refused to send it on."

"Slag," Boston said under his breath. MedCore probably didn't even know she'd tried to apply.

"The rotting Pike just gets off throwing his mass around."

"Enough, Dunkirk," Boston said, trying to forestall anything else he'd have to ignore hearing. "Let me see if I can do anything about it."

Cancun shook her head rapidly. "No, Lord, that's not necessary. I… I don't want to be a bother."

"You deserve the chance, Cancun."

"I… I…" she stuttered helplessly, then slumped back on the table, head down.

"Thank you, Lord Haldis," Voyen said patting Cancun on the back again. "Cancun appreciates your support."

Cancun nodded, banging her head on the table.

"It is what I am here for."

"Haldis!"

A shout from the door made all of them look up, and Istanbul stormed in. All signs of revelry cut off as if a switch had been thrown, letting Istanbul stalk forward in silence.

"You forsaken rat! Taoiseach damn you. You will pay for this!"

Boston opened his mouth for a sharp retort but saw Chang shaking his head rapidly behind Istanbul. He bit back the reply he wanted to give and settled for "What the rot are you talking about Stan?"

Istanbul pursed his lips as if he tasted something vile. "You know exactly what you did, Haldis. You ruined me!"

"I have no idea what you are talking about!"

Istanbul was now standing nose-to-nose with Boston. For all his vanity, Istanbul's muscles were real, and Boston knew the only thing holding him back were the witnesses.

"You know," Istanbul said. "You and that mongrel! You faked that video of me on Earth and released it!"

"It sounds like you have no proof, Stan."

Montana had made sure he wouldn't. The footage hadn't come from Boston's suit, and he'd made sure not to pull it with his command authorization. As for Montana's, she knew what she was doing. Boston had no doubt the video had hopped through enough servers by this point to make tracing it back to her impossible.

"I wonder if the Condor will agree?"

Boston shrugged. He'd been conscious of the flock drawing around him, it was time to end this before it became violent. Again. "I am sure the Condor will find the truth, Stan. However, I think it is past time you left."

Faced with the crowd of Wolves behind Boston, Stan had little choice. But he apparently could not resist one final dig. "I am not done with you yet!"

BERN

"I need your help, Augustine."

Bern dodged two Terran workmen who were wheeling a large partition wall through the room. Montana's new space was extremely large—three or four times larger than the last gallery attempt—and busy with people. Everywhere Bern looked, Terrans were cutting, gluing, or assembling.

Montana missed a step halfway through explaining her plan. "Anything, Clarisse."

"Do you have somewhere more private?"

She nodded, and made a right turn, eventually leading her to a small office. The double set of tumblers on the door gave Bern some comfort, which was redoubled by the thin copper mesh that formed a complete Faraday cage on the inside. Bern waited slightly wide-eyed as Montana secured the door.

"What do you need, Clarisse?"

"Sinclair is trying to take another colony."

Montana snapped her head up, suddenly attentive. All

trace of the happy woman vanished, replaced with a smoldering intensity.

"How do you know?"

Bern explained her suspicions. "How this is connected to the prim attack, I have no idea. But we need to stop them. We cannot give them another win. I refuse!"

Montana nodded sharply. "We need to keep another planet from falling under the boot of the Empire."

Bern's heart fell. She'd known this would be the sticking point, but it was still hard. "I wish we could. However, Jordana wants to take it from them. Colonize it first. Be the first to bring the petition to the Taoiseach and take the fuel right out of their tanks. Make all the money they must have spent be for nothing."

Montana was breathlessly still. "But either way, this planet gets subjugated."

"Augustine." Bern dropped to a half-crouch and reached for her hand. "Not every first contact has to go as badly as yours. It might not be the worst thing for them to join the Empire."

"What a wonderful euphemism."

"They are off on their own, wherever they are," Bern tried to remind her, "without the resources of the Empire to draw on in times of need. There are a half dozen colonies that would not have survived if the Empire had not found them."

"The lack of choice is the problem."

"If you are unable to bring yourself to help, I will understand," Bern said, finding in the moment that it was true.

Her friend waited a long moment, her eyes downcast. Then, "You just need to know what planet they are going to try to settle?"

"Yes!" Bern squeezed Montana's hand tighter. "I am

not asking you to help with the colonization or convincing the Taoiseach. Just find me what planet they want. I will handle everything else."

Montana was quiet for a long time, looking nowhere but at the floor. "For no one but you, Clarisse."

CHAPTER SEVENTEEN

Out of Control
BOSTON

They settled into a rhythm under Lady Torianna's command. Three times a week or so, a liner would dock, and Boston would set the Wolves loose on it. Free of Delaware's insistence on clearing the liner faster, they usually found something. And all the while, they collected manifests that went into the black hole of Montana's analysis.

And the House War raged on around them. Every day brought a new shot fired, a new way the great houses tried to make the others suffer.

"This way, Lord Haldis."

Boston stepped into the Condor's office warily, his trepidation at being summoned at odds with the awe he felt for the man who held the office. He'd thought his confrontation with Istanbul had escaped official notice—until the summons had been delivered this morning.

Condor Jame Riyadh Von Dearworth was almost as old as Baghdad, had conquered Olancha, and had headed the SpaceGuard for as long as Boston could remember. The man waiting for him was exactly what Boston had pictured.

He stood easily as Boston approached the massive desk covered in slates and fixed Boston with a flinty gaze, which didn't waver a millimeter.

Boston braced at attention a foot in front of the desk and waited.

"Seldom have I received such a mixed set of reports regarding a Falcon," the Condor said quietly once the door behind them slid closed. "In fact, I hardly believe some of them could possibly be describing the same officer. Brawling on the alameda. Personally leading Wolves to defend against the worst primitive incursion in a generation. Disrespecting a senior officer in front of witnesses. Overseeing the largest contraband seizure anyone can remember."

Boston kept his mouth clamped shut and fixed his gaze an inch above Riyadh's shoulder.

"I would be well within my rights to have you drummed out of the Guard. Let you flounder trying to run your house. Baghdad seems to think you have hidden depths, but then again, he is your grandfather. We may have found the one thing that old bastard cannot be objective about."

Riyadh emerged from behind his desk, moving with care but without obvious discomfort, and poured himself a drink. "Did you have to destroy the boy so utterly? You may answer."

"The boy?" Boston asked, not able to help himself.

Riyadh stared him down with cold gray eyes. "You would do well to avoid lying to me."

"Istanbul is not fit to command," Boston said, praying his read of Riyadh was correct.

"He is not."

Boston waited for something more, but Riyadh seemed content to wait for Boston to speak. "Lord, he was supposed to leave for Olancha in a week."

"Do you think so little of the Guard that you thought we would not notice?" Riyadh continued before he could reply. "We were sending Istanbul to Olancha because Olancha is one of the most well-defended colonies in the Empire. Unlike on a small world, there are people there who could watch him. Keep him in check. See if there was anything salvageable under the weight of that boy's ego."

"There is not."

"I will now have to take your word for it, instead of the word of people I have worked with for years. People I trust."

Boston had no answer for that.

"Now, Istanbul will be sent somewhere where he will likely have less oversight."

"Lord, he—"

Riyadh waved a hand, silencing Boston. "I am not immune to politics, Lord Haldis. No one, least of all his family, wants Istanbul here now, where he can continue to be a laughingstock. He will be exiled to the colonies. Just not where I wanted him. Congratulations."

A hot ball of lead settled somewhere in Boston's throat.

"And now, I need to find someone else to take the Olancha post. It will not be you, Lord Haldis."

"Yes, Lord."

Riyadh continued his appraisal. "You have made yourself too necessary here, it seems. Lady Torianna has nothing but praise and seems to have her claws quite deep in you. And I have too many other things going on to fight her on this."

"Whatever the Empire requires."

"Repeat that to yourself as many times as is necessary." Riyadh finally stopped his pacing and settled behind his desk. He leaned back in his chair and pointed at a map of the Empire projected on his wall. "What do you see?"

Boston flicked his eyes to the familiar winged shape of the Empire's jump map. A dozen small orange dots were interspersed among the blue dots of imperial planets.

"Each of those is a problem I am watching," Riyadh said. "Something is happening out there. Small things, for now. Little embers blowing in the wind that I have not been able to find a pattern for. Yet. However, I suspect I soon will be needing smart, capable officers to solve problems for me. You could be one of them... if you ever grow up."

"Thank you, Lord Condor."

The briefest touch of a smile touched Riyadh's face. "Last thing, Lord Haldis." He held out a hand. "Thank you for what you did on Earth. You saved a lot of lives."

Boston took the firm grip, blinking furiously at the sudden whiplash.

"Now get out of my office. I have work to do."

Boston started to walk toward the door, but paused, his hand on the threshold.

"Yes, Lord Haldis?" Riyadh said without looking up.

"My Lord, I would not normally ask, but..."

"Speak, Haldis."

"One of my Wolves... She applied to the JFD program, and our commander denied her application. I was wondering if she could be reconsidered."

Riyadh finally looked up from his papers, face carefully blank. He waited a few long seconds, then nodded. "Give the details to my aide and go, Haldis."

ASPEN

Destruction is one of those most human activities. Nature can destroy things, but it is impersonal, unemotional. Nature never punishes, is never vindictive.

No, twisting the knife is a purely human vice.

But it was one Aspen never allowed herself. She watched even the most logical individuals give into their emotions and did her best to steer them back to the path of logic. Of taking the most direct path to their goals.

Even Sherah seemed more prone to engage in petty rivalries these days, as Sinclair had to fight harder and harder to keep its position atop the pile. To prove that they were most deserving of being the premier family of the Empire.

And yet, there was little choice when the rats circled.

"It is too clean," Ambroos said. "It lets Torianna retire in peace after everything she has done to us."

"It takes a major piece out of Chen's hands and puts it in ours," Aspen corrected him. "What do we care if Torianna is not herself punished? From the sidelines, she can do nothing."

He shook his head, and Lord Huntington nodded his agreement. "She has levied millions in fines on us in the past month alone. She deserves to suffer."

The fools.

"Whether she deserves it or not, it will be more effort for us to hurt her."

"I—"

"Enough!" Sherah shouted. "Neither of you have been able to resolve things. Now, we try it Aspen's way. And get our leverage on Augustine, while you are at it. She has been making too big a wake recently."

Aspen shrugged. "As you wish, Mother."

BAGHDAD

"Taoiseach above," Baghdad whispered, watching the catastrophe play out on the projector.

The four of them were gathered in the study, watching billions burn. An entire estate, a massive Chen factory on the edge of the system, was slowly falling apart as explosion after explosion wracked its fragile arms.

"How could this happen?" Boston asked, giving voice to his thoughts.

Baghdad shook his head. "Torriana will have to answer that. Something like this, on her watch? And unlike the attack on the enclave, this has to be sabotage. Everyone will know it was one of the other houses."

Nothing like this had happened in Baghdad's long memory. An estate was sacred. No one, not even the most depraved, risked going after the infrastructure that kept them all safe. Kept the air in.

"This isn't working," Baghdad said, realizing it in the moment. "Things are spiraling out of control. We need to find out who was behind the attack on the enclave. And soon."

"Inspecting the liners is a good plan," Montana said. "I am slowly piecing together how the crates must have moved."

"Too slowly. We need to get to the bottom of this soon, before this gets worse." Baghdad gestured at the frozen image of the exploding estate.

"The only way to work faster is to get more records all at once."

"And how do we do that?"

"All the houses keep these records. We would be able to access them from a house warehouse computer."

"And the chances of any of the houses just giving them to us?"

Before the question was fully out of his mouth, she

was shaking her head. "It will never happen. Even if they are completely innocent, the proprietary information they'd lose by opening their books would destroy them. Not even the police could demand them."

He waved a hand, silencing her. "I understand." Baghdad nursed his drink, looking for other ways around the problem, but he couldn't see them. "We need to consider more direct action, then."

It was the only way, it seemed.

Montana leaned forward on the divan and raised an eyebrow at him. "What do you have in mind?"

Baghdad sighed heavily. "Crime. Plain and simple. But it would put Boston and a few people he can trust in the warehouse. Any ideas?"

The boy grimaced and nodded. "I think so. We inspect the liners. We could do some smuggling of our own. Seal me up in a crate, in armor, on the liner. Ship me to the Dearworth warehouse. When no one is around, I get out, find the information you need, and then get back in the crate. Get shipped out again in the morning. Is that approximately what you were thinking, Grandfather?"

"Indeed." Baghdad was pleasantly proud the boy had put it together so quickly.

Montana rubbed her hands together thoughtfully, refusing to meet Baghdad's gaze.

"Something you wish to add, Lady Montana?"

"It seems risky."

"Very much so. But it has a reasonable chance of success, I think."

Boston nodded in agreement, and Chang made one of those non-expressions that indicated he didn't hate the idea.

Baghdad considered the problem. "We'll probably want to send in four of you. Chang, Boston, and two

Wolves you can trust. Just to cover eventualities."

"I see."

Still, her gaze was distant. "I didn't think you'd consider something like this."

"That," Baghdad nodded to the collapsing estate, "makes me consider everything."

Montana was silent for a few more moments. "The Sinclair warehouse is most likely to have what we need. That is, if we still agree they are the most likely to have done this?"

Something about her voice was raising the hackles on the back of Baghdad's neck. She was clearly hiding something.

"Sinclair will likely react more violently than anyone else," Chang pointed out.

"Yes, I know. But they have something of mine that I need back."

Baghdad raised an eyebrow and waited for her to continue. She squirmed, to the point where Boston brushed a soothing hand along her arm.

"They are holding some of my crates that I need for the gallery opening."

"You'll forgive me for thinking that somewhat less important than finding the bastards behind this."

Her eyes flashed with anger. "Yes, I know that," was bitten off at the end. "They... they are not normal crates."

"Ah. Some of your pagan art?"

Chang gave him a nod only he could see.

"You knew?" she eventually managed.

"Of course."

Her canniness reasserted itself in mere moments, and Baghdad again found himself impressed. "You investigated me?" she asked. It was slightly less than a question.

"The moment you started seeing my house heir."

"You never told me," Boston said.

"I never needed to! I liked what I found," Baghdad grunted. "She saw an opportunity, took it, and was careful about it. The laws about pagan art stopped making sense generations ago. No one cares anymore."

"Except the law has not changed," Boston said through clenched teeth. "Especially now. Sinclair could throw you to the heralds any second."

Montana shook her head. "They do not want that. They sent Aspen. She just wants me back under her thumb. Making it public will be more embarrassment for Sinclair than they want to admit. If we get the crates back…"

"It's your decision, boy. You're the ones who're going to be sticking your neck out. You and Chang."

But Boston had already made up his mind. Baghdad could tell he had the moment the question had been raised, even if he hated what he was helping Montana cover up. He made a show of considering before nodding sharply. "We will help, of course."

CHANG

"I know we are asking a lot," Boston said, looking at Voyen and Dunkirk across the narrow table. "This is a bad option, but it is the best one we can find."

The four of them were in the small breakfast nook,. Even Montana had made herself scarce for the moment of the approach. Getting them to the estate without telling them what was going on had been delicate, but they were seasoned Wolves. Chang doubted this would be their first time stepping outside the law to do the right thing.

Hopefully, it wouldn't be the last.

"You really think a diamond house was behind the attack?" Voyen asked, rubbing the stubble on his chin.

"Slag, boss, of course they were. The whole forsaken thing was too neat! I rotting told you that. No prim's got weaps like that."

"This will help us get proof."

Voyen nodded slowly. "Alright then, Lord Haldis. You've done a lot for us these past few months. You can count on us."

Dunkirk nodded emphatically. "Never been rotting shipped before. It'll be some story to tell in a couple years."

"Ha," Boston chuckled. "A few decades, perhaps. However, the plan relies on the two of you staying on the liner to explain our absence. I was going to ask who you suggest taking with us."

Dunkirk didn't hesitate for a second. "Take Cancun and Nevada. Cancun's sweet on Lady Montana. She'd help her for a kiss on the cheek. And Nevada's good at getting into places he shouldn't. Might be helpful."

"I agree with my second," Voyen said with a curt nod. "They'll back you up. And keep their mouths shut."

BOSTON

"What time do you have to leave for the liner?"

Boston checked the chrono again. "Another hour." They'd picked a liner that was going to dock in the middle of the night to make it less likely someone would notice four fewer Wolves coming back. He'd spend longer locked in a crate, but it would be doable.

Montana snuggled closer to him, resting her head on his chest. Boston's satin sheets rustled. "Thank you for doing this. I never thought... it is a huge risk."

"I never thought we would be in this position. But between the House War and everything else..." Riyadh's words still stung. "It feels like everything is falling apart."

It took her a moment to respond, and when she did,

she was barely audible. "The houses have gone to war before. This is no different."

"Still... Sneaking into another house's property... Using Wolf armor to do it..."

She let the silence stretch, and he felt the urge to fill it. "It feels like we are beset on all sides."

"You have at least one ally, Lord Boston Dublin Kun Haldis. And that is more than I ever thought I would find."

"What about Bern?"

"Bern is... complicated. And she'd never do something like this—throw away all the rules."

He chuckled at that. "Well, you know, you have an ally, too, Lady Von Montana."

She stiffened and pushed herself up slightly, rolling to face him, but keeping her eyes downcast. "Call me Tana." Her eyes snapped up to meet his. "Just when... Just with us. You can call me Tana."

"Alright. Tana." He tested the word and found that he liked how it sounded. It was a simple name for the beautiful and powerful woman in his arms. "Why Tana?"

Montana retreated a little, but he wound an arm around her as she settled back onto his chest. "It was the last word my mother ever said. Or so my father told me. They thought she was trying to name me."

"It suits you."

"I think so, too."

BOSTON

"Run the brief, Chang."

Chang sighed loudly over the comm. "Alright, Wolves, listen up. Just in case you fell and hit your heads over the last couple hours, we're here for two things and two things only: Lady Montana's crates, where we switch her paintings with the ones we brought, and the main computer terminal. Nevada'll download the info we need, then we get gone."

"Make sure not to unroll the paintings we find. They could be damaged," Boston said, repeating the instructions Montana had given him.

"Any questions? Good, no, 'cause none of you are idiots. Who wants to be first out?"

"I got it," Boston said softly. He reached out and unlatched the crate. An unseen motor hissed, and the lid retracted, giving Boston an unimpressive view of overhead lighting. It was switched off, naturally, but clicked on when it detected motion in the room.

There were no alarms. Boston cautiously raised his head out of the crate, but there was nothing out of the ordinary. There must have been five hundred containers in the warehouse, towering three or four high.

"Pop 'em."

The three other crates slid open, and the armored Wolves scented the air, checking Boston's assessment. Their small corner of the warehouse was deserted, but the towering containers made it hard to see very far.

"Nevada, main security bunker, one level up. Chang, Cancun, spread out and check the main floor."

The Wolves scattered, with Boston following a few steps behind Nevada. He was continuously amazed at how quietly a Wolf could move in armor, even over a metal floor. They moved slowly, using telltales to scan around corners for signs of Sinclair workers, but made it to the bunker without difficulty.

"Sure you can get in, Nevada?"

The Wolf replied in his nasally voice without turning, "Aye, Falcon. Most places skimp on the internal protections. If you're already inside, they're easy pickin's."

The security bunker was up a small catwalk that

overlooked the wide-open warehouse floor. Boston walked up to the door slowly. The all-glass walls told him that there wasn't anyone in the room, but he was still careful, watching for any signs of motion.

He stepped inside first, glanced around, and waved Nevada in.

Nevada went straight for the main console, pushing the light office chair out of the way so he could kneel in front of it. With dexterity in Wolf armor Boston could only marvel at, he tapped away at the keyboard rapidly.

"Aight, let's see what we have here," Nevada mumbled to himself, and Boston kept watch out of the glass. "Unix system. That's good. I—"

"Slag. Freeze."

On the factory floor below, a pair of Terrans in Sinclair colors had just meandered out from behind one of the containers. In the zoom of his helmet, he could read their nametags as they ambled down the aisle, talking animatedly.

Boston didn't breathe until they turned another corner and disappeared behind a container, neither one apparently looking up to see them in the security bunker.

"What the hell are they doing here?"

"Let's see. Worklogs..." Nevada said, resuming his rapid typing. "They aren't in the computer, so they're doing something fishy. Probably something off-book that no one wants to get out."

"Sounds familiar." Boston knelt too, getting most of his body behind the console so he was invisible from the floor. "Find what we're looking for?"

"Records from a few months ago will take a while. They need to be retrieved from cold storage. Say an hour to wade through it all," Nevada said, still typing. "But I found the crates we're looking for. Quadrant three, ninth container in the third row."

"You catch that, Chang?"

"We're going."

"You good?" Boston asked Nevada, who waved him away.

Boston retraced their steps back down into the mass of containers, heading for the quadrant Nevada had indicated. He moved slowly, checking each corner, but saw no other Sinclair workers on his way.

Chang and Cancun were already in the aisle when he arrived, and he joined them in combing through the stacks, looking for the one. Twice, they had to duck into a cavity when Cancun's telltales warned them someone was approaching, but no one came down their aisle.

"Found it," Cancun whispered, kneeling in front of the door of one container.

Boston hustled to her side. "I agree. This is it. Nevada, can you open it?"

The door to the container clicked open with a hiss, and Boston hauled it open, letting Chang and Cancun peer inside.

"Well?"

Chang's voice was oddly distant. "See for yourself."

Boston now knew what Aladdin felt when he found his cave. Rows upon rows of golden bars formed a wall on either side of him, shining in the reflected light from his helmet lamp. More somethings sparkled down the narrow aisles, diamond flashes of light.

Montana's crates, with her sigil stamped upon them, lay piled neatly at the very front of the container, set slightly apart from the mass of gold.

"Is it real?" Cancun asked.

Chang hefted one of the bars from the top of the stack and turned it in his hands. "Weight's right." Chang panned his gaze over the stacks, loudly not asking. Then, he voiced what was running through Boston's head; "A few bars each seems fair, considering the risk we're taking tonight."

"I—"

"Someone's coming!" Cancun said urgently.

"Inside!" Boston pulled her into the container and tugged the door until there was only the thinnest strip visible. His heart hammered in his chest. They had no back-up if they were caught, no weapons. They could escape, but the plan of shipping themselves back would never work if Sinclair knew there were intruders.

"Here," Cancun whispered, and proffered her mini-cam. Boston threaded it out through the bottom sill and flicked it on.

All of them were treated to a view of the aisle they had just vacated, with Aspen Sinclair walking serenely down it, her head bowed, listening intently to a Terran worker walking with her.

"My Lady, we can't possibly clear all these crates tomorrow! It was supposed to be hard to access this area. We need to excavate three rows just to get the mover in here. We—"

"What I am hearing," Aspen said, "is that you have failed to plan appropriately. Half our supplies of terraforming feedstock are in these containers. I requested they be readied for transport to Olympus two months ago. And yet..."

"My Lady, we haven't used a terraformer in thirty years! We can't just—"

"You are a warehouse, yes? Your function is to hold things until they are needed. They are needed."

The warehouse supervisor deflated. "Yes, my Lady."

"Show me your plans. I may be able to suggest

additional efficiencies," Aspen said, pacing past the container. "And I must say, I note quite a bit of sloppiness in this operation, supervisor. Containers left open, crates not put away."

The supervisor sputtered. "My Lady, we had no idea you were coming. How could we—"

"That was rather the point."

Boston waited, listening intently as they continued past. Eventually, they left the camera's range, and Boston waited, not moving, not risking the slightest sound.

"About the bars, Boston," Chang said the very moment it was safe to do so.

"Sinclair would notice a few bars missing. And the whole point is for no one to know we were here."

"Forsake it all, they're already trying to get your girl arrested. What could be worse?"

"I will put nothing past Sinclair at this point. A few gold bars each is not worth that risk. I want all of it."

Chang gave Boston a look he knew all too well, even with layers of armor between them. "Now how're we going to do that? I may have the strength of ten men, but not ten thousand."

"Nevada."

"Yes, Lord," Nevada whispered, still waiting in the control room.

"Do you see the work orders for this row in the computer? Apparently, a bunch of these containers are being moved."

They heard frantic tapping. "Yeah, I do."

"Can you add one?"

"I ... can. But..."

"Can you have this whole container shipped out? And hide it, to make it look like all the other moves? There is no way the workers know what is in this one."

Nevada's grin was audible. "I sure can, Falcon. Where do you want it sent?"

"Some public dock where we can go pick it up."

"It'll take me—"

"We have all night. Satisfied, Chang?"

"I knew there had to be a reason I liked that little fledgling when I met him," Chang chucked. "Damn sure doesn't think small."

"Isn't it wrong?" Cancun asked, her voice small and unsteady. "I mean, stealing?"

"It is absolutely wrong," Boston agreed. "And if we were here as SpaceGuard, I would never allow it. However, we are not. We are already breaking the law, infringing on another house's sovereignty. Trying to figure out whether they or a different diamond house committed treason. Larceny will be the least of our problems."

Cancun nodded ever so slightly.

"Now, swap the paintings in case something goes wrong and get buttoned up."

CHAPTER EIGHTEEN

Victory?
BERN

"This is wonderful, Augustine! Everything we talked about."

Bern spun on her heel, trying to take in the riot of color that was the room. Larger by three or four times than their last attempt, with regal white partitions to break up the space, it had something to catch her eye in every corner. It was almost more a carnival than a stuffy gallery.

Statues and paintings covered every wall, and they had more than their fair share of onlookers, but the center of attention was the live demonstrations. Montana had done it somehow: gotten colonists from across the Empire together to stage her exhibition.

"And more," Montana said, wrapping her arm around Bern's and tugging her forward.

They approached one of the colonists, stepping over the small rope partition. "Clarisse, this is Manila."

Bright pastel-green eyes peered out from beneath shocking black hair as the small woman put down her sketchbook. She was shorter even than Montana, spindly, with doll-like features and huge eyes.

"A pleasure, Mistress," Manila said, bowing low to Bern.

"Manila is from Olancha," Montana explained and waved at some fantastically detailed sketches spread around the walls in her little nook. They were quite intricate, with the softest shading between them, though all were black and white.

"Where did you learn to do this?" Bern asked in wonder.

Manila shrugged. "I just always could. From the moment I picked up a pencil."

Montana walked her slowly around the whole perimeter of the gallery, showing off the hundreds of sculptures, paintings, and a few more live demonstrations. Bern was drawn, along with the crowd, to a circle of five shirtless men taking turns slamming large hammers into a chunk of metal on the floor around them. It rang with every impact, drawing every eye.

"What are they making?" Bern asked as they hung at the back of the crowd. There was something captivating about the way they moved, glistening with sweat, keeping perfect time as their hammers went round and round in a blur of silver.

"They're blacksmiths. This is just a little show. I wasn't able to get a forge on the alameda. But they make things like this." Montana indicated the intricate statues around them, all twisted metal, sharp lines, and beautiful engravings.

Bern glanced around the packed space, the hundreds milling through it, and the little red squares saying a piece was sold hanging everywhere. "I just wish we could have done it together."

"Clarisse, this is what you and I planned. Even if

someone else paid for it, we did this together."

"The special pieces, too?"

Montana grinned and grabbed Bern's hand again. "Come see."

She was led into a maze of partitions, where the aisles were more sparsely populated. They threaded between a few people still admiring the mostly sold paintings. Montana had arranged for internal partitions in this space, making it seem smaller, more intimate, and more like a labyrinth.

They entered a small blind alley still dotted with paintings, and she led them to the very end. With a quick glance behind them, she pressed one of the panels, and the false wall swung inward. Montana pulled her in quickly, then pushed the wall closed.

They were on the inside of a box of partitions, and here too, there were pieces. Mostly paintings, but a sculpture dominated the center of the room: a nude man with a sling across his back, staring defiantly into the middle distance. It reached almost all the way to the ceiling, though the partitions rose high enough to hide it.

"Augustine!" Bern gasped, clamping a hand over her mouth. "How did you get this here?"

Montana's smile was smug. "All it took was money. The rest was easy."

"Still..." Bern paced around the statue. Someone had castrated it—more the pity—but the marblework was impressive. It must have weighed half a ton. "Where is it from?"

"Camelot, actually. It is a re-sculpture of one that used to stand in Capri, the capital city on Camelot, but it was destroyed ages ago. I saw them sculpting it on my tour of the colonies a few years ago and commissioned another one."

"Thinking ahead?" Bern asked, not able to help the smile on her face.

Montana shook her head. "Not at the time. I just thought another should exist."

Here too was another small red square.

"You managed to sell this, too? To whom?"

Montana's smile could have eaten the whole statue. "Lady Koichi's son. He wants it shipped back to his manor on Eden. Though he let me know it would have fetched a better price if it had been intact."

"Good for little Taarush," Bern mused, glancing back at the statue. "I never knew he had a streak of rebel in him. I wonder how he plans to get it back to Eden."

"Speaking of Eden..."

Something in Montana's voice made Bern turn, eyebrow raised. Her violet eyes were downcast. For the first time in Bern's perfect memory, she looked guilty.

They were alone. There had been other patrons in this special area, but they'd slipped away. Actually, not quite alone, as Lord Haldis emerged from another one of the hidden doors and walked briskly toward them.

"A few days ago, my Wolves and I smuggled ourselves into the main Sinclair warehouse and accessed its computers," Boston started. "It let us download the last six months of their shipping records. Every crate that had come through the place."

Bern's heart quickened. "And?"

"And we traced the weapons that were used at the enclave. Sinclair shipped them in —"

She'd known it all along, but still, it felt like a shock. Finally, some measure of justice.

He continued, "From Eden."

The bottom dropped out from her stomach. "Eden?"

Montana nodded. "I went over the records three or

four times Clarisse. The guns came from Eden. I'm sure."

"We also heard that, whoever set up the attack was using Katalia's name."

"My cousin did not!" It came out as a shriek.

"We know, trust us," Montana said, brushing her hand on Bern's arm.

"Every time we dig deeper the trail leads back to Nirvana. And that means either someone in your house was behind it, or someone is trying to frame you."

Anger roiled hot and sharp in Bern. Her hands were shaking. There was a ringing sound just on the edge of her hearing.

"Either way, the answers are on Eden," Montana said quietly. "Please, Clarisse, we need access to the house records there. We need to see what is going on."

It wasn't fair. None of it, none of it. Katalia could have granted that request with a swipe of her hand, but Bern couldn't.

"If I had the power…" Bern said quietly.

"In exchange," Haldis said, "we know the name of the planet Sinclair will try to petition for. You were right."

Taoiseach above! The chance to hurt Aspen, to wipe that smug little smile off her face—it was impossible to pass up. "Done."

She had no idea how, but she would manage it. If she had to drug Taruush and drag him to the archives, she would manage it.

"Olympus. Sinclair is after Olympus."

"Olympus." It was their world. A world on the fringe of the Empire, where the terraforming had been almost perfect. Covered with Earth-transplanted species. Second only to Camelot in biologics. And it was *Nirvana*. Would have been years ago, if not for the ban on new colonization.

"Those bastards." Bern balled her hands into fists, knowing what Aspen had tried to do: take advantage of her again. Ruin her. "Thank you, Augustine." She touched her shoulder. "Thank you."

"Boston managed it, not me."

She nodded to Haldis, blood still boiling. Taoiseach, they would pay.

"How far are you going to take things with Sinclair?"

"I have no idea." She really didn't. They would pay until she didn't hurt. "As far as it takes to make clear that we will not be dictated to. They do not have exclusive rights to the Empire—or to anything else."

"Do you have a plan, at least?"

Bern found herself smiling. "Not at all. And it feels wonderful."

BOSTON

"Good evening, Lord, Lady. If you would be so kind?"

Boston had almost walked right past the gilded man before he stepped out of the alcove. The herald's face was slack, uninterested, but he presented them with a small golden bauble. One of the many ways the Empire ensured that access to the highest levels was limited only to nobles.

"My apologies." Boston offered his hand. The golden ball extracted its pound of flesh from his palm, making him grimace, but beeped happily when he released it.

The herald nodded, unimpressed, and offered the ball to Montana. "Just a moment," she said hurriedly, bringing her clutch out and rummaging in the small volume.

"Montana? What?"

She waved him away, and he stepped back and waited patiently until she announced, "Got it!"

A small golden chip no larger than her fingernail sat on her palm.

"Here you are," she said.

Without a word, the herald inserted the chip and into the bauble in his hands. Nothing seemed to change, but he offered it to Montana again.

Montana then grabbed the orbit, squeezing it with white knuckles. It took longer—too long, measured by heartbeats—for it to test her blood and produce a timid, if still happy, beep.

"Is there anything else?" Her voice was resigned, but the herald shook his head, lights reflecting against his golden skin.

"No, my Lady. Please, go ahead."

Boston waited until the herald was a few steps behind them before stepping close again. "What was that?"

Montana's face could have been carved from stone. "My blood is impure."

"Tana, you know I think differently."

She gave him a small, pained smile. "Not everyone agrees with you. I have to walk around with that damn chip and summon a herald if I need to get in somewhere. I can never control my own citadel core. Never pilot an interstellar."

Boston tried to offer more sympathies, but she brushed him off. They entered the overlook late; the debate was already raging among the council.

"It is too soon to begin colonizing again!" the Dearworth representative on the council declared loudly. "We have only just healed the wounds caused by the rebellions of the Von Anker. We are still too spread out."

Bern stood at her place on the petitioner's dais, the perfect picture of a humble supplicant. Only her eyes gave away her sharpness to the keen observer.

Another man seated near the end of one of the table's arms banged his fist on the table. "We regularly hear reports of loyal Terrans killed in the colonies, and it was only a few years ago that we were forced to stamp out malcontents on Olancha. We are not ready to colonize more planets. We should wait. Another thirty years, another generation, and they will be ready."

The Taoiseach raised his hand, and silence fell across the table. "I would like to hear from Lord Huntington."

All eyes turned to the Sinclair representative. Even larger than Delaware, his complexion grew ruddy as every eye turned to face him. The position he must be in! Knowing he'd been betrayed and desperate to find a way out.

"The colonies are cowed," Huntington said slowly, carefully. "All the members of my family who serve say the same: The colonists are done rebelling. They have tried, and we have crushed them time and time again. While there are still scattered malcontents, they are in the minority, unorganized, and no threat.

"However," he turned his gaze to Bern, "that does not necessarily mean this proposal is the right one to grant."

"Oh? But it is the one before us."

Huntington nodded stiffly. "It is. It is my well-educated opinion that, at the present time, there is no great risk in returning to colonization. We show them how much better they can be if they join us in the goal of returning to Earth. And for the most part, that dream has been accepted in the colonies just as much as it has been here at Sol."

"Then you are for this insanity?" the Dearworth representative demanded with a bristle.

Huntington shook his head and did perhaps the only thing he could do. "Sinclair abstains."

Even the Taoiseach's glare couldn't control the whispers that raced around the room like wildfire.

"I am hesitant to grant this," the Taoiseach said slowly.

"The Uprising was not so far away as many of the younger members of our great families would believe. It occurred in no small part because we did not give ourselves time to rest. To recover from the strain of bringing so many of the great unwashed masses into the light. It would be the height of folly to push out again, before we had the chance to recover from those wounds."

He paused, considering, but continued, "But it is noteworthy that two of our greatest houses agree here. I will grant the proposal. And Lord Huntington? If Sinclair wishes to put forth a proposal to consider for another planet, I will consider it."

Huntington's face darkened, but he nodded wordlessly.

BAGHDAD

Baghdad considered Lady Bern's back as she slowly retreated from the petitioner's dais. Today, he'd chosen to sit on the floor, as was his due as a house lord, and the show had been worth it. Huntington looked ready to gnaw off his own arm, but Nirvana had played the game masterfully. They would have their planet, and Sinclair had nothing to show for it.

The Taoiseach's normally stern face had hardened slightly as the maneuvering around him became clear, but he had played his part, allowing Sinclair to ram a liner into their own foot. Though he clearly was not happy at the prospect.

Baghdad spared a glance toward the upper hall, where Boston and Montana were making an inconspicuous getaway. And yet, he wasn't the only one to have noticed. Aspen Sinclair was watching them go as well.

"Next, we have Lord Wallace Delaware Von Sinclair with a petition," the Taoiseach said loudly.

Baghdad found the portly lord almost immediately as

he rose, ashen. A sheaf of printings was clutched in his hand, not quite trembling.

"Your grace, I—" Delaware said without moving toward the front of the room.

Then, Aspen was on her feet, touching Delaware's shoulder lightly. "Your grace, I asked my dear cousin to yield his time to me, if that pleases you."

The Taoiseach shared a rather too genuine smile and nodded. "If that is alright with Lord Delaware."

"Oh yes, your grace," Delaware said, sitting immediately.

Aspen floated toward the petitioner's stand hands empty, unconcerned by the eyes of the crowd. The canny ones knew what had just happened. Baghdad suspected Lord Delaware had been about to petition for the same planet. What could Aspen have come up with in the few minutes she'd had to think?

In the end, it was nothing. Nothing that needed saying, nothing that needed doing, but a nothing that brought cheers and patriotic fervor to the mouths of all those assembled.

Baghdad watched, admiring the mastery of it. Aspen had somehow managed to save her house from the largest embarrassment of an age.

And yet, as she turned to leave the dais, her cold eyes found him. Baghdad had very little doubt that she knew exactly who the architects of her defeat today had been.

And that her retribution would be swift.

BOSTON

"Get to Eden as quick as you can," Baghdad said, pacing the study. "The first liner."

Montana nodded. "I have a cabin reserved, leaving in a few hours. Bern will follow in the morning, but I can do some prep work before she gets there."

Baghdad nodded sharply, then turned to Boston. He couldn't remember seeing his grandfather this rattled.

"Be on your guard. Don't let Chang out of your sight for a moment. They'll be coming for us."

Chang waved a hand. "They were coming for us already."

Baghdad shook his head and stared at the fireplace, lit with a warm glow. "We were a sideshow at best. But now, now we have Sinclair's attention. Be on the lookout for assassination attempts."

"You think they would?"

Baghdad hurled his glass, shattering it against the wall. "I think Sinclair destroyed ten million crowns to make a point to Chen!" he roared. "Killing you would be nothing!"

Boston felt the cold steel of battle harden in his gut. They'd be ready—for anything.

Of course, being ready for anything was a fallacy. Especially when facing a plan laid out over years.

BERN

Another of those tiny moments was dawning, the ones that herald the largest of catastrophes. And this one started with static on a comm line.

"I am so sorry I could not get away till tomorrow," Bern said earnestly. Suddenly, she had a planet to plan the colonization of.

"Clarisse, it's no trouble." The ansible wavered slightly, letting a high-pitched crackle through the filters. "It's just been so nice to be on a planet again. Feel the sun on my skin."

"I am sure." Taoiseach above, she wished she was there. But this was too important to waste even a second. "We will get into the archives and finally—"

The call dropped with a pop.

Bern blinked and rubbed sleep from her eyes. It was the middle of the day in Eden's capital but still the middle of the night on Castle High. She tapped the reconnect icon, mentally calculating the cost of the inter-system call.

The connecting icon spun and failed. She tapped it again and encountered the same result.

"How odd."

Next, she tried the family concierge at the retreat on Eden. That didn't go through either. Neither did the central exchange on Eden.

Bern tossed the covers back, donned one of her night robes, and went in search of answers.

The operations center never slept. On the lowest deck, where the gravity was weakest, a dozen technicians kept watch over the entirety of the family holdings—every planet, liner, and estate.

It was more crowded than she expected, and Bern entered as quietly as she could, staying back from the knot of people clustered around one of the main holos. Bern's vague sense of unease redoubled as she saw Jordana there, awake, listening intently.

"The militia was fully engaged here, here, and here," the watch officer said, pointing out places on a dense street map. "They'd called up their reserves and were mobilizing to defend the armories, but we lost contact a few minutes later."

Jordana's face was stony. "Where are our ships?"

"The *Attila* is still three weeks away."

"Can they hold?"

The watch officer's face went slack. "Hold?"

"Yes." There was no mercy in Jordana's gaze. "Can they hold the planet until the *Attila* arrives?"

"Jordana."

The graying tyrant turned to face Bern, along with

every other person in the room. Bern paused just a heartbeat, her throat dry. "The ansible is down. There is no holding or hiding this. Call the Taoiseach. Before someone else does."

Jordana jerked her head, just once, the only acknowledgment of Bern's suggestion. Then, she turned back to the watch commander. "Get me Castle High."

BOSTON

The bridge of the *Cortés* was bedlam when Boston arrived. The Fish, usually so calm, were a hive of activity, moving from station to station, talking in hushed tones. There was no panic, but even the air felt wound tight.

Delaware sat in the center of the whirling chaos as they readied the ship to depart. He barely glanced at Boston as he entered, but the flash of anger was hard to miss. Still, Boston presented himself, saluting, not a hair out of place.

"You and your Wolves have been returned to my command for the duration of this emergency."

"Yes, Lord. I understand we are heading for Eden?"

Delaware's eyes were narrowed to slits. "Indeed. I expect you to be ready for an immediate combat drop when we reach Eden. And no mistakes this time."

"We will be ready."

"I hope so, Lord Falcon." Delaware swiveled his chair away, focusing on one of the bridge screens. "This is our moment. Our chance to crush the colonial scum under our boots and prove to them again our right to rule. I will not have it tarnished by anything."

"Yes, Lord Delaware."

Delaware waved him away, and Boston headed for the Wolf den.

BOSTON

One moment, space above Eden was empty. The next, it was filled with the silent, plummeting mass of the *Cortés*.

Boston had spent most of the last few hours in the Wolf den, pouring over the maps of Eden they were able to downlink before the ship slipped beyond the reach of ansible and into the null dark space between dimensions. He'd surfaced just once, joining the briefing in the dining room.

"We will drop the Wolves when we are still hyperbolic," Delaware declared, standing before the assembled officers, his jowls quivering in self-important excitement. Behind him, the map of the city center appeared. "We will not know exactly where the bastards are concentrated until we reach Eden. Once we have intel, we will target the gumdrops, together, for the largest concentration of insurgents."

The assembled nodded. It was the way: use the overpressure of the gumdrop's impact to steal the tempo and crush the opposition as quickly as possible.

He hated to do it, but Boston cleared his throat, and Delaware ground to a halt, his eyes closed. "Yes, Lord Haldis?"

Boston pointed to the display behind Delaware. "Lord, if we come in at that speed, we will cause significant damage to the buildings around wherever we drop in."

Before Delaware could reply, Lady Aspen glided to the front of the room. "Lord Falcon, I commend you for being concerned with limiting the property damage on Eden."

Boston flushed. Dealing with collapsing high-rises was not something he was looking forward to.

"However, there may be hostages on the surface. The situation was rapidly deteriorating, and a fast transit gives you and your Wolves the best chance of making a difference. I am sure no one would wish us to delay even a single instant." Her expression was merciless. "If, in the end, Nirvana must repair a few more structures to clean up whatever small mess your Wolves make while resolving the situation, I hardly think anyone will care."

"Well said." Delaware nodded, wresting back control of his meeting. His eyes strayed to the monitors. "I want these animals wiped off the face of Eden. Any of them that have taken up arms against the Empire are to be put down with extreme prejudice."

Boston had heard variations of this order before. Had always saluted and bounded away to carry out his orders with a light heart and a heavy boot. But something felt different this time. Hating every moment of it for the first time, Boston did his duty. "Of course, Lord Delaware."

And the *Cortés* continued its headlong dash toward Eden, falling faster and faster as Eden's gravity dragged it down. The circle of the planet in the distance was still small, no larger than an outstretched thumb, but it was already swelling.

The three gumdrops suckered to the bottom of the ship separated smoothly, spinning off on their own trajectories in the dark. Seconds later, the *Cortés* engaged its engines and began pulling away to the right, decelerating so it wouldn't hit the planet.

That was Boston's job.

BOSTON

The ground was exactly the hellhole Boston had expected.

The three gumdrops descended into the atmosphere of Eden like shooting stars, streaking fire in the middle of the day. Windows broke across half the city—at least those that were still intact to begin with. And in the wide boulevard where they descended, the overpressure, the noise, and the heat turned the street into an apocalypse.

There wasn't time to see it, wasn't time to think about it, thank the Taoiseach. The flock moved in a silent tide at full sprint, covering each other in turns by reflex. At first, it was all broken concrete and red paste, but as they got farther from the gumdrops, it became bodies Boston was running past.

Government House was the center of the riot, three streets back. And it was two streets before they saw their first armed colonial.

"Splinter!" Nevada shouted while tagging the colonial holding the burnished steel splinter on SnipeNet. Without another word, without another second wasted, the flock took a knee from mid-run, and shots rang out.

A splinter could cut through a meter of stone or fifteen meters of flesh and bone. Boston sent his first shots of the day through the man before he'd gotten the splinter sighted, just a microsecond behind Chang and Dunkirk.

The figure detonated like an overstressed balloon, and the crowd behind him melted. Sudden screams cut through Boston's sound filters, but there was still no time. They were up and running for the square again.

Tunis, 2nd pack's scout, paused for a second, popping the cover of his whirligig and throwing it into the air with a heave. The little copter was out of sight immediately, but a small video appeared in Boston's visor, showing them the square on the other side of the line of buildings they raced down.

Gallows had been set up in front of Government House. There were five derricks, four already with bodies swinging on them. A crowd of colonials watched, cheering, shouting, as a woman was strong-armed up onto the derrick under heavy guard. Rifles and worse gleamed at various points in the crowd, but there were no sentries posted, no one facing the way the Wolves would come.

More chained people dressed in the remains of business attire waited on the building's front steps.

They had the video for less than a second before Boston started issuing orders, his voice a breathless rush. "Save the woman. Cancun, Dunkirk, run and get to her. Gault, take three more and see if you can reach the other hostages. The rest of us, advance by threes. Take out anyone with a weapon. Worry about the others after. Ready?"

No one dissented.

"We're ready," was the only response he got from Chang.

"Then go."

They poured out into the next intersection and into the square. For a few seconds, there was nothing to mark their passage, but then, the front rank of three Wolves—Chang among them—dropped to a knee, their splinters at the ready, and took their shots.

It was slaughter.

For the first time, Boston found himself taking an extra beat with his shots, doing his best to aim upward slightly so that his splinter met stone, rather than just flesh.

But dozens still died with each squeeze.

And he had to keep moving. Keep his spot among the Wolves, keep driving forward.

It became his heartbeat. Beat. Three splinter cracks, and dozens more dead. Run. Drop. Beat.

"Wolves!" was a scream that isolated itself in the din.

The crowd around them ceased milling and started running. Like a dam breaking, the torrent of people sprinted as fast as they could in every direction except toward the Wolves.

"Cowards," Dunkirk panted and broke for the derricks, Cancun on her heels.

The still-living prisoner had dropped to the ground, her hands over her head. Her guards broke and ran, still carrying their rifles. A few shots from the Wolves collapsed them like overripe fruit.

"What do you want to do about the running ones?" Chang asked, keeping his head low. There was no cover as they advanced across the square; an organized defense could have skewered them. But there was no sign of organization anywhere, just a blind rage. And fear.

Boston's free hand trembled, but he gave the order he knew he had to. "Blow away anyone carrying a weapon. Let the rest run."

His voice was steadier than his stomach, having just ordered the deaths of probably half those fleeing. He turned from the carnage and focused on the derrick.

Cancun had dropped beside the woman and was administering first aid. Dunkirk watched over her from a kneeling position, her head on a swivel, splinter only slightly lagging. Gault had gotten the crowd of prisoners moving back toward relative cover along the front of Government House, tucked on the side of the stairs so they would only take fire from one side.

With difficulty, Boston forced himself to glance up at the four they'd been too late to save. The first two were clearly nobles; they were a foot taller than the other two swinging beside them, both men, both dressed in rather conservative business suits. Fortunately, Boston knew none of them, though the second might have been the governor. It was hard to tell through the swelling.

"Voyen, see if you can cut them down."

Voyen climbed the derrick gingerly, the whole thing swaying with his weight, but sparks erupted from the front of his armor as someone opened fire with an automatic. He dove, going through the floor, as Boston's splinter swung toward the source.

The open doors of Government House were blown off their hinges, but someone had done their best to build a barricade. Lethal barrels protruded from the gaps.

Keeping low and moving obliquely toward the doors, Boston ran until he was with Chang again, tucked against the marble stairs. They provided cover from gunpowder, though a splinter could penetrate them if the colonials knew where to shoot.

"You'll want to hear this," Chang said. He shouldered a colonial in a brown uniform that had taken shelter with them forward.

Reluctantly, Boston dialed down his audio filters, and the screams swung back into perfect clarity. But he focused on Chang's man—his tanned skin, brown hair, and short stature. The man drew himself up at Boston's notice and snapped a half-decent salute, one end of a handcuff dangling from his wrist.

"Major Field, from the colonial militia, Master Falcon." Field was breathing heavily. He was heavyset, but he seemed alert.

"Proceed, Major."

"They hit the armory first. Yesterday, mid-afternoon. A hundred men jus' showed up, all armed with gunpowder rifles. They stormed the place before we could do anything. My unit got called up to help, but it was over when we got there. The mob kept growing, kept passing out guns. The good 'uns. We didn't stand a chance."

"Thank you, Field." Boston nodded to him. "You did what you could. Stay down and wait for us to give the all-clear."

Field nodded and took a few steps toward the rest of the recently liberated prisoners. Boston noted that several of them wore the same torn brown uniforms, and they arranged themselves on the outside, surrounding the other colonists. Protecting them.

"We need to end this," Boston sighed, looking at the feed from the whirligig. If the planetary armory had well and truly fallen, the rebels in the building could be armed with dozens of splinters. Even a glancing blow from one would be enough to rip through Wolf armor.

"Algiers, get a breaching charge ready. We blow a hole in the wall to the east and take them from behind. Gault, keep your pack here. Get them if they try to run."

Boston left Gault and his pack, finding the small side door Algiers had selected. Chang shadowed him, staying on their engaged side. Just in case.

When the charge blew, Boston was second through the hole.

CHAPTER NINETEEN

Eden
CHANG

The riot was over.

Chang paced through the wreckage of what had been the throne room of Government House, eyes peeled for any new threats, but really watching Boston. The boy was... different, with none of the happy adrenaline that came after a fight.

And his helmet was still on. The air probably stank of blood and death, but Boston had insisted on removing his helmet on every other world they'd traveled to, cocky slag. Not doing so now was different, and it worried him.

"Chang, Nevada. Pike's on his way down."

That was the last thing they needed: another giant target prancing around for any colonial with a gun they'd missed. One of the Fish-brains on the *Cortés* should have stopped him, but none of them had the courage. Apparently.

Boston took the news better than he expected. He shook off his lethargy and shouted, "Major Fields!"

The mud-uniformed colonial snapped to attention

across the room and positively dashed to Boston's side. Boston had a fan in this one, it seemed. "Master Haldis!"

"There will be a lifter landing in the square. Ensure that the crowd is pushed far back."

Fields's face whitened slightly, but he nodded and saluted again. He waved two other militiamen to him, and they raced from the great room, headed back in the direction of the square.

Boston, though, deflated slightly and remained where he was. "Such a waste."

It was barely audible, quiet enough that Boston might not have noticed he said it out loud. Still, it was enough to set Chang's teeth on edge.

"You going soft on these slag?" he asked, afraid of the answer.

Before he could respond, lift fans screamed in the courtyard, and Boston waved him off.

With difficulty, Chang got the Wolves, Boston, and even the militia organized to receive Delaware. The Wolves, he organized into rows, standing at attention, when Delaware burst through the doors.

Chang had never seen the heavy man swagger, but he was certainly doing it now. Delaware walked in like he had personally conquered the planet, gleaming in his dress uniform. Still, the effect was spoiled somewhat by the look of disgust as he beheld the devastation.

Lady Aspen followed him, and she was the opposite of Delaware in every way. She wore her ship suit, bare at the elbows and knees, and she had not even deigned to wear shoes. She viewed the dismal scene without a blink or flutter of an eyelash.

"Excellent work, Falcon. Any prisoners to deal with this time?"

Chang winced.

Boston's voice was robotic. "The militia are handling them."

Delaware shook his head. "No matter. Did any of the governor's cabinet survive?"

"No, my Lord. We have identified the bodies of Governor Xavier, Lieutenant Governor Kahina, and the rest of the cabinet. Many of them were killed in the riots, but the governor and his lieutenant were hanged."

At "hanged" Delaware's expression became queasy again, but the Lord drew himself up with his massive bulk and rallied. "A terrible thing."

Delaware glanced up and down the line of Wolves, eyes passing blankly over the colonial militia and the few scattered members of the colonial administration that had started to arrive.

"Who is the ranking member of the administration left?"

Chang stepped forward and gestured toward the woman they had saved from the derrick. "Lord, this is Khedive Lahore, the elected leader of the colonials."

"I take it we have you to thank for our rescue, Master Sinclair?" Lahore asked, her accent as clipped and aristocratic as Montana's.

Delaware inflated again. "Correct." He glanced around the room once more, only going slightly pale at the sight of the gore. He seemed to be steeling himself for something, and Chang tensed. Whatever it was, it wouldn't be good.

"I expect an imperial herald to arrive tomorrow morning," Delaware said. "She will conduct the ceremony transferring Eden from the stewardship of Nirvana to Sinclair. The Taoiseach has asked me to serve as temporary governor until Sinclair can appoint one formally."

Shock rippled around the room, and again it was the Khedive who found the courage to speak. "But Master

Sinclair, Eden has been a Nirvana holding since—"

"No longer." Delaware really was sneering now. "A simple riot only eight hours from Castle High that ransacks the capital and ends with the governor and cabinet dead, the planetary ansible destroyed." Delaware tutted. "Nirvana has obviously mismanaged this planet. Their incompetence has embarrassed their ancestors, the Empire, and the Taoiseach himself. That will be corrected."

Stunned silence greeted the announcement. Delaware took it in with ill grace and then turned away from the group of colonials to face Boston. "Lord Falcon, arrange a party of militia to clean up the receiving room. We should make things presentable for our guests."

"As you wish, Lord Pike," Boston said.

In the privacy of his helmet, Chang allowed himself a grimace. It was worse than he expected.

BOSTON

Boston paced. Paced through the muck and the blood and the bodies, his anger wrapped around him like a black cloud. Or perhaps that was just his armor.

No one approached him. No one came within half a block of him as he paced around the large Government House. Ostensibly, he was patrolling, but...

Delaware. Governor of a planet Boston had conquered for him. Rot it all. Delaware! Other than Istanbul, Boston was sure there wasn't a man who deserved it less.

He almost didn't see her. Almost marched past unseeing on his circuit. She was just a dim shape like a hundred other Edenists trying to put their lives back together.

The blowtorch of her gaze softened slightly as she walked up to him and put a hand on his armored chest. "I'm glad you're safe."

He unclipped his helmet. The warm air felt good on

his face. "I should be saying that to you."

She shook her head. "I was never in any danger. I could pass as being from this planet."

She fell into step beside him. It was one of the things he enjoyed about her company: She was comfortable with silence.

But he could still feel her anger, frustration, and pain as they walked. All around them were Edenists. A woman knelt over a chest-less body, rocking back and forth, silently weeping. She was oblivious to them, but her companions weren't. Boston's armor did nothing against the glares.

For once, her feelings mirrored his.

"This was all such a waste." The words just slipped out, slipped out and crystallized the thoughts that had been swirling in his head, precipitating fully formed on his tongue. "All of this. None of it needed to happen."

"I know."

"There was nothing I could do!" Taoiseach above, it sounded like a whine, but it was true. There had never been a moment to stop, to wait, to give people a chance to breathe.

"I believe you."

"Nirvana knew, though!" That was what made it worse. "They knew for months that things were spiraling out of control here. They could have stopped it. A show of force, a shipment of food, something, anything to head off this disaster they saw coming. But they did nothing!"

He remembered giving the order, firing his splinter, knowing that hundreds would die. "Everyone tells me I am my father's son," he choked out, his tongue thick in his throat. "They talk about the hero of Camelot. They talk about how he died saving the Taoiseach." Streaks of fire ran down his cheeks. "My father died because he waited.

He wanted to be sure, to make sure an innocent was not going to die. So, he waited until he had no other choice, and the bomber was right on top of him. And he died for it, and so did the seven other Wolves in his pack."

They left the Terran part of the city suddenly. They turned a corner, the pavement ended, the trees lining the walk disappeared, the buildings shrank, and the bodies disappeared. So did the people. They were suddenly alone. Boston plodded on, too full of energy to stop, even in heavy armor on this heavy world.

"And I told myself I would not make that same mistake. Not let people I cared about die because I hesitated." He looked down the ruined street. "I just never knew what it would cost. Taoiseach damn them all. If this is how the great nobles treat the colonies, then of course they rebel! They are right to!"

He suddenly missed her presence at his side and glanced back. She'd stopped, eyes narrowed at him. But before she could say anything, a convoy of militia teslas turned the corner and thundered past them. A dozen Edenists hung onto the outside of each of them, all in the same brown uniforms as Major Fields.

Boston waited until the convoy had faded and he could hear himself think again before he turned back to Montana.

he was close to him again and planted a thin finger in the center of Boston's armored chest. "You don't mean that. But you should. The Empire isn't right. Just because it is in power. Just because it's reality. That doesn't make it just." Montana shook her head. "You look around and see an aberration. I look around and see the norm of every day on every planet in this entire fucking carcass of an Empire."

Her anger chilled him. "It can be better."

"I understand why you have to believe that. But it isn't true. This is as good as it gets. I learned that lesson ten years ago."

"We can make it better. You and I. We can be better than all of this."

"We can be better, yes. Can the Empire?" She shook her head. "We can try..." Her voice finally cracked in a sob. "We can try to change things with everything we have. I just don't know if we can. But you have to hold tight to that anger." Violet flames flickered in her eyes. "You have to remember this. Hold on to it and never forget it."

"I am going to remember today every time I close my eyes," Boston said. And he knew it was true.

BERN

A day after the attack, the planet was still so confused that when Bern arrived, all she had to do was state her intentions in a clear voice, and her needs were met. Shuttles were prepared for her; the archives opened for her. She did not even have to flash her family ID or explain Montana's presence at her side. The colonial archivists fell over themselves to grant entry. The fact that Bern did not actually have access was noticed by no one.

The archives had survived the violence completely unscathed, buried deep as they were under Government House. Apparently, the mob had not cared that the offices were the real seat of power and instead focused their destruction on the far more opulent—and public—upper levels.

"Really? Dhaka?" Montana asked passing over another hard drive.

"Yes, Dhaka."

Montana shook her head. "I just never imagined you settling down."

Bern huffed and pulled her hair back into its bun again. This was something she wanted to talk about, but Montana could be painfully oblivious at times. "The family has been after me to marry for a while now. And this just seems easier."

Montana, for the first time Bern could remember, looked a little sheepish. "When did all this happen?"

"Over the last few days," Bern hedged. "Before all of this. However, I suspect it will still seem like a good idea. We need allies more than ever now."

Montana nodded and tapped another query into the computer.

The door to the conference room they'd commandeered slid open, and three porters wheeled in carts of additional storage disks. The search was proving daunting; most of the drives were not connected to a core, so only the indexes could be searched. They were forced to scan each drive individually for the data they needed.

Bern stood, intending only to stretch her legs, but the lead porter, distinguished by her saffron-colored sash, waved frantically to the group. Suddenly, all of them were bowing, and Bern pulled herself up short. "Please, there is no need for that."

"As you wish, Mistress Nirvana," the lead porter said, bringing her torso almost parallel to the floor, before she waved her three companions back to their work.

A fourth man entered, pushing a cart overflowing with sweet pastries, seared fish strips, and cheeses. The porters descended on it, filling out the far end of the table in an instant before standing back in a line, braced.

Montana stood off to the side, her disapproval evident.

"Will that be all, Mistress Nirvana?" the lead porter asked, her voice tipping up an octave at the end.

"Yes, thank you."

"What are your names?" Montana asked, catching the lead porter halfway through a dismissal wave. She visibly swallowed and then replied in the same almost sing song voice, "This is Axel, Karl, Gerolf, and Hein."

"And you?" Montana pressed.

The porter flushed before replying, "Senior Porter Fieke. Was something not to your liking, Mistress?" The middle-aged woman seemed genuinely concerned.

"No, I just wanted to know what to call everyone. Thank you, Fieke, everything looks lovely."

The matronly woman nodded primly and made several crisp gestures to her porters, sending them scattering.

"You aren't being punished?" Montana asked, returning to their earlier conversation.

"Punished?" Bern sought Montana's eyes over the terminal. "Augustine, no. Dhaka is a perfectly pleasant person. Far better than I could have been saddled with."

"Just so long as you are going to be alright."

"My mother and father had a perfectly amicable marriage, as you know. Not everyone is like your adopted parents."

Bern broke off as the conference room door slid open and Aspen stepped in.

She wanted to launch herself across the room at her. Aspen had that placid look on her face, like nothing could faze her, like Xavier's and Kahina's deaths were nothing. And that was just the few they knew about so far.

"Good sol." Aspen nodded to them, watching with calculating eyes.

For once, Montana was calmer than she was.

"Since the news is only a day old, I suppose you, Cousin Bern, might be forgiven for not handing in your access down here. However, Cousin Montana, I think you were never welcome in these halls. I must ask you both to leave."

"You will have to have us forcibly ejected," Bern found herself saying.

Aspen blinked and raised an eyebrow. "Why cousin, whatever could be so important as to drive you to that?"

"We are looking for evidence of who attacked the enclave on Earth."

For a few moments, Bern could not believe her ears, but Montana had said it.

Aspen's placid expression wavered, and she fixed Montana with a searching look. "What?"

"We are trying to find out who killed Katalia," Bern answered for her, "and you will not stop us."

"On the contrary. How can I help?"

BOSTON

"I am not going to kill anyone today."

That was his mantra, and so far, the day had let him keep it. Their only orders were to patrol and to keep the Edenists under control, so Boston split the flock into half packs and set them on ever-widening circuits through the city. It spread them out, but it made sure they were close, should trouble flare. He'd been able to control things with harsh glances and, at worst, overly loud shouts from his helmet speakers. But every hotspot could turn worse.

Like now.

They ran as quickly as they could through the crowded streets, trusting in their armor to keep them safe from any would-be attacker. People were just blurs, and Boston felt several stones turn to dust against his armor, but he ignored them and the people who threw them.

Finding the mess was easy enough. It was down one of the innumerable small alleys in the city. Even here, three blocks from the worst of the riots yesterday, debris was everywhere. Two burned hulks had been dragged across the road, effectively blocking all traffic. Delaware's driver must have turned down the alley to avoid the mob and been trapped.

Delaware's tesla was stopped just behind the logjam, surrounded by a growing crowd of Edenists. The street was filled with the sounds of a mob: incoherent shouts, aborted chants, the stamp of feet. But it hadn't turned violent, not yet.

Boston skidded to a stop on the broken cobbles, Dunkirk an inch behind, and tasted the mood of the crowd. The stench of fear and hunger was everywhere, balanced on the knife-edge of catastrophe, but no one had any weapons he could see.

Militia surrounded the tesla, but none of them had any rifles, either. They kept the mob at bay with riot shields overlapped in a stiff phalanx. It was a symbolic wall, nothing more, but it held.

"Major."

Major Fields, in a clean uniform that was no less mud-colored, gave him the barest hint of a nod. "Can ya' happen to give us some assistance?"

"Dunkirk, can you move the hulks?"

She turned to face the burned-out teslas, sizing them up. "I think so, Lord. It will take me a minute to get purchase."

Boston left her to her work, then turned back to the mob blocking the tesla's retreat. Some of the noise had died down at their approach, but the stench of fear redoubled. Everyone knew what Wolves had done yesterday.

His radio chimed, and Chang's panting filled his helmet. "We're still ten minutes away. Gault might beat us, but it'll be close."

"It will be over before you get here."

Chang cursed and kept running. "Don't do anything stupid. Do you hear me, boy?"

Boston waved Abuja and Cancun forward on either side of the tesla and then approached the front. Here the crowd had pressed the militia right up against the bumper, but the wall held. For now. He was head and shoulders taller than the shields, though, and felt the anger of the crowd focus on him.

"All of you have better things to do with your time!" Boston shouted with his speakers dialed all the way up. "No one needs to get hurt if you all disperse peacefully!"

"When is the bazaar going to open again?"

Boston picked the man out of the crowd in an instant. He was better dressed than most in the crowd, but his tunic hung off him like he was a scarecrow.

"Soon," Boston shot back, hoping it was true. "We are doing everything we can to get things running again."

Behind him, screeching cut through the shouting as Dunkirk shouldered the first of the hulks out of the way.

"Go home to your families!" Again, he kept his voice pitched conversationally, even if it was ear-shatteringly loud. "I have better things to do with my—"

"Falcon!"

Boston didn't want to turn, but he had no choice. Delaware had stuck his head out of his tesla window. There was no fear in his face.

"As soon as the car moves, walk backward slowly," Boston told Field, turning his gain way back down. "Nothing that looks like we are running. Orderly."

Field nodded sharply, and Boston moved around the car to where Delaware waited.

"Lord Delaware, get back in the car."

"You do not give me orders, Falcon!"

"I am trying to keep you alive."

"Just kill them and be done with it." Delaware glanced toward the crowd. "Seven or eight splinters, and the problem will be over."

Gorge rose in his throat. He'd expected it, but—

"What are you waiting for?"

Boston's hand raised to his splinter, armored gauntlet gripping the stock. After he drew, he would have seconds before the crowd charged. It had to be perfect.

Boston hesitated.

And he couldn't do it. He relaxed his hand, bringing it back down to his thigh, clenched in a fist. "No," he finally told Delaware's incredulous face. "We can resolve this peacefully."

"Lord Falcon!"

Boston ignored the shout and paced to the front of the tesla. The driver was clearly terrified, gripping the leather-wrapped steering wheel with white-knuckled force.

"When she moves the last hulk," Boston said, flicking to where Dunkirk was setting up, "you drive. Slowly. Creep."

Wide eyes stared back at him. "No. Im'ma gun it."

"You will not!" The tesla rocked as the driver flinched away from him. "Advance slowly. They will charge if you gun it, and we will all die. So we go slowly. Together."

A spike in shouts made Boston turn just in time to catch a brick sailing toward him. He had just enough time to brace before the perfectly flung brick slammed into his helmet.

It shattered into dust, parts of it falling neatly to either side.

"No damage. Hold," he managed to get out on the pack channel. Despite his protests, he tasted blood and had to rely on his armor to stabilize him for a few heartbeats.

The crowd watched, waiting for a reprisal, but the shouts died down slightly when Boston resumed his pacing without any repercussions. Boston took his position again at the back of the car, steadying the militia, and got ready to move.

"Clear here, Falcon!" Dunkirk announced as the last hulk crashed out of the way.

"Slowly! Move back."

Silently, the electric six-wheeler began to creep forward.

Field took the first step, bringing the line of shields back, and waited for the other militia around him to do the same. The crowd pressed forward into the space immediately, but no one fell. Still, it was terrible to hear their yells, feel the press of an animal made out of men.

The next step was easier, everyone moving together, as the tesla inched forward. The crowd still advanced, but less hungrily, less needy for space. First a car length, then two, they slowly pulled away.

It took five excruciating minutes to reach the end of the alley. Boston's gaze was never still; he swept every window, every corner, every junction, looking for another threat, but there was blessedly nothing. When they hit the main road, it was deserted. Even the sounds of the crowd behind them were muted now.

"Stop! Stop now!" Delaware shouted from inside the car, and the driver screeched to a stop.

Boston stepped around to where, yet again, Delaware was sticking his head out of the window, bottled rage inside the six-wheeler.

"Lord Haldis. I am giving you a direct order to go back and eliminate the hostiles."

He should have ignored it. Pretended he couldn't hear.

But he couldn't. The anger that had been roiling since he'd dropped onto this forsaken wreck of a planet slipped its chains and was in his mouth before he could stop it.

"Did they teach you nothing?" Boston yelled. He was at the window of the tesla in seconds, slamming an armored fist into the door hard enough to dent it. "That will just make it worse! Every one of them we kill, we make two more rebels! No. Get back in that tesla so I can keep you alive! Driver! Go!"

Delaware recoiled like he'd been shocked, but the window came up. The driver took the opportunity to sprint for the compound, gunning the engine up the boulevard.

"Can you and your men retreat from here?"

Field nodded sharply. "We'll be fine. Go if you have to."

Boston started running after the tesla, and the half pack formed up on him without a word, heading toward the safety of the cordon around Government House.

BOSTON

"Excellent work," Boston said once they were back safe in the compound. "Really, Dunkirk, Abuja, Cancun," he said, doing his best to look each in the eye. "That could have been a lot worse than it was."

Boston had shucked his helmet as soon as they were in the compound. His head was still swimming slightly—whether from stress, anger, or the blow to the helmet, he wasn't quite sure. But uncanned air felt good, cool on his cheeks.

Delaware was still in the process of extricating himself from the car, which Boston was trying not to notice. The large dent in the door apparently interfered with the swing of the hinges, so two Edenist porters had to drag it open.

Delaware stood and glanced around, buttoning his

coat. He seemed different, calmer, all the visible anger gone from his face.

"Haldis."

Boston and the Wolves came to attention as Delaware approached. "Your splinter, Falcon."

The bottom dropped out of Boston's stomach, replacing his anger with an aching emptiness. He complied, unstowing the long-barreled rifle from his back, where it had been for the entire engagement.

It weighed more than a hundred pounds, but he offered it one-handed to Delaware. Delaware glared, and Boston let the end of the rifle drop to the ground. Delaware reached out and grabbed the end.

"You, Falcon, finally stepped over the line."

"Lord Delaware, as I tried to explain, I—"

Delaware waved something in front of Boston's armor at chest height. With a searing wrench, his armor moved without him moving. His arms came together behind his back, and something popped in his shoulder, making him see stars.

"Lord Haldis!" Dunkirk shouted and took a step toward him as he swayed.

"Haldis is under arrest."

"What?" Dunkirk exploded, but Boston shook his head through the pain.

"Disobeying a direct order in a combat zone carries heavy penalties, Lord Haldis. I will make sure the herald tears out your throat for this. And you have no one to blame but yourself."

He couldn't speak. Couldn't breathe. The pit in his stomach just grew deeper and deeper. Delaware jerked his head toward the Government House, and Boston was compelled to follow.

CHAPTER TWENTY

Aftermath
ASPEN

Aspen spent most of her attention on her searches, cross referencing what she'd been told against her own investigations. And somehow, it all made sense. She hadn't found a single shred of evidence that they had tried to mislead her.

It was infuriating. Infuriating that someone else had been able to trace the movements of crates inside her own house. Infuriating that no one else had looked. Everyone had been too focused on the outside.

So, she searched, letting the unformed data crystallize into information in her hands. Nirvana's records were just as detailed as she'd expected, and she took little mental notes, watching how they operated. Even if nothing else came from this, even if they couldn't prove that Chen had been behind these attacks, she would have gained something.

All conversation had died when she entered. She accepted the suspicious looks and the occasional snide remark without reacting in any way. They were warranted.

But, hours into their search, Aspen became aware of an even deeper silence from the other side of the room. Both of her companions' heads were bowed over a screen in silent wonder.

"I take it you have found something?"

They started, like they'd forgotten she was there, and then, both faces hardened into near-identical harsh, impassive glances. It was a confirmation of a sort.

"Tell me."

Glances were exchanged, and Aspen rose to her feet, causing them to start.

"Tell me," she repeated.

"Can we trust you?" Bern asked, eyebrow up.

"So, it is someone in my house." Aspen had begun to wonder, begun to consider the possibility as house after house was removed from her list of suspects.

"You may have a conflict of interest," Bern said as Montana stayed silent.

"I do not."

They didn't believe her. That much was clear.

"You—both of you—need to understand something," Aspen said, taking a few paces back to try to ease their heart rates. It wouldn't do for one of them to do something rash. "Sinclair is the most preeminent house in the Empire. We deserve to rule beside the Taoiseach. However, whoever set those animals on our kind..." Aspen shivered. "Whoever did that perverted the natural order of things. They armed primitives. They armed colonials here on this planet. They fueled an uprising against the Empire. And that, I will never stand for. Never."

She flicked her eyes to Bern. "Whoever it was that did this—Chen, Nirvana, or some malcontent in my own house—I will see them dead. By my hand or the

Taoiseach's."

Aspen paused, waiting, but it was Montana who finally spoke. "It was a small Sinclair company. They paid for the shipments, paid Nirvana to hand them off back to Sinclair at the enclave. We have the complete chain of custody now."

She nodded. "And the owner is sealed by the house?"

Nods.

"Give me the name."

Aspen pulled up her house database access and waited. But when the name came, she didn't even need to type it in. She knew it by heart, having seen its paperwork a hundred times.

"Delaware," Aspen said quietly.

Never in a million years would Aspen have believed that he had the drive to accomplish something like this. Delaware, a wretched, sidelined, no one.

But it fit.

Aspen turned her eyes to Montana. "Did you know that Delaware was aligned with your mother's husband? That he lost most of his influence in the house when Orlando and your mother disappeared?"

Montana went slightly white, but she nodded. "I did."

"And you are sure?"

Bern answered this time. "Come look at the records yourself."

Aspen nodded. She would. She would make sure there was no possibility of deception, have the porters pull copies of the data again, confirm there had been no tampering. But she already knew. It made too much sense.

"Has the herald arrived yet?"

BOSTON

The walk to the Government House grew longer with every step. It was lucky the armor was doing the walking for him; with his arms clasped tightly behind his back, Boston couldn't have kept his balance.

A pair of lifters in the courtyard meant the herald had already arrived. Delaware set what must have been a terrible pace for him, shuffling furiously in the heavier gravity of Eden.

Would the herald understand? Could the herald, the Taoiseach's personal representative, known throughout the Empire for their lack of mercy, understand? Would he even have the chance to explain?

But he hadn't added any more blood to his hands. Eden wouldn't play behind his eyes every time he closed them, like Earth did. Like Asgard did.

The herald appeared on the steps of Government House as they approached. She glittered under the rays of Eden's star, every bit of exposed skin burnished in lustrous gold, with a headpiece made of golden curls and a golden cloak flying behind her in the light wind. Only her eyes were the pitch-black of shadowcasters.

Delaware stopped the moment she appeared and dropped to one knee. "I welcome you to Eden, Lady Herald." The voice demonstrated more grace and poise than Boston had yet seen from the older Pike. Boston didn't have to see his face, though, to know it was contorted in the same smug smile Boston had come to hate.

"Thank you, Lord Delaware. We are very pleased to be able to render unto you your reward for all that you have done for the Empire."

Delaware rose a fraction, knee still on the ground but no longer bent double. "I only did my duty, your grace."

The herald nodded. At some hidden signal, others poured from Government House—nobles and Terrans, but no colonials that Boston could see. Bern and Montana stood together in the front, impassive.

Light flared as the herald drew a sword from a thin scabbard on her hip. She slowly brought the sword down, placing it on one of Delaware's shoulders, about to bestow a blessing.

"Lord Pike Wallace Delaware Von Sinclair, for your actions here at Eden... For your actions on Earth... For all of that, I charge you to die."

It came faster than Boston could think. The herald reversed her grip on the sword, raised it, and sent it flying back across Delaware's neck.

All Boston could do was close his eyes as hot blood splashed against his cheek. He flailed, but his armor stayed locked in place, holding him up. He blinked his eyes open—he couldn't help it—and his gaze went straight to Delaware, who had both hands pressed over his neck, his mouth working soundlessly.

Blood still seeped from the wound, painting a wide arc around the lord. With a slow inevitability, Delaware toppled to the ground all at once, landing with a meaty thud.

The quiet wind was the only sound until the herald spoke again. She made some small movement and drew Boston's gaze.

Her face was utterly expressionless. Somehow, she had avoided discoloring her golden toga with blood, and her eyes stayed fixed on the body as she cleaned the blade of her sword with a golden cloth. Boston started at the sharp snap of the sword returning to its scabbard.

The herald then spun on one heel and faced the still-silent crowd. "Wallace Delaware was guilty of treason against the Empire. Blinded by his ambition, he attacked his own people and committed the cardinal sin of arming colonials and primitives, using them as tools to embarrass, attack, and discredit his enemies. Such acts deserve a thousand deaths, and yet, one is all we can ensure."

The herald's voice was surprisingly strong for someone so small, and she addressed the crowd without hesitation. "Eden will remain a vassal of House Nirvana, now and for always. We will rebuild. We will put down any remnants of the rabble he incited. And we will retake Earth as one people, under the banner of House Eire."

The herald turned back to face Boston and the Wolves, and he felt her black gaze fall on him. "Why is Lord Haldis restrained?"

Boston couldn't speak. He tried, but his tongue refused to form the words. The blood still dripped off his cheek.

Then, Dunkirk stepped up next to him. She removed her helmet, blonde fuzz rippling in the wind, and faced the herald fearlessly. "Delaware had him arrested, your grace."

The tiniest tilt of the herald's head demanded more.

"Lord Haldis tried to stop Delaware from eliminating some colonial witnesses to the riot. He wanted to interrogate them. Delaware wanted them dead—perhaps to cover up his crimes." Dunkirk lied with accomplished speed and not a single quaver in her voice as she faced down the embodiment of the Taoiseach.

The herald focused on Dunkirk for seven or eight beats of Boston's heart, and then, his armor unlocked. White stars burst behind his eyes, and he dropped to his knees as his arms were freed. His shoulder throbbed.

Dunkirk levered him back to his feet.

"Find Chang. We are getting off this rotting planet," Boston said through gritted teeth.

BAGHDAD

It was all over except the medals.

Baghdad clapped loudly with everyone else gathered

in the ballroom as Boston bent his head to receive his, a scarlet starburst around his neck. Baghdad repeated the phrase to himself. It was over.

The Taoiseach had moved faster than Baghdad had ever seen. Heralds and police had stormed the Sinclair Estate, searching its computers, flaying anyone who had helped Delaware. Three Terrans had been beheaded.

"How could one man have caused so much chaos?" Chang muttered in the lull as the Taoiseach moved to the next in line and started singing Aspen's praises with a worrying honesty.

"He never could have without the House War."

Still, Baghdad couldn't help the itch between his shoulder blades.

The Taoiseach was sure Sinclair knew nothing else about Delaware's plans. Otherwise he would not be lowering a twin of Boston's medal over Aspen's shoulders.

"All she did was call the herald," Chang grunted, following Baghdad's gaze.

A stamp of his foot brought silence for a few moments.

"There is one other thing you should know," Chang said.

Baghdad tightened his grip on the cane in his hand. He knew there would be something.

"Got a note from a Fox I know who got stuck cleaning up the mess on Eden. Some slag-ridden idiot took until now to notice that two entire gumdrops—with the sets of armor and splinters to go with them—are still missing."

"Missing?"

"Yep. Building was destroyed, but they didn't find any pieces of the gumdrops in the wreckage."

"You could conquer a colony with that."

Chang considered, then nodded.

The Taoiseach was placing a medal over Montana's

neck now.

"Did you ever find out who was using Katalia's name?" Baghdad asked.

"No. Did the heralds?"

Baghdad's eyes found Aspen again. She was standing primly in the center of the stage. "Not unless you or Boston told them you'd talked to Yoseif."

Chang shook his head.

"Then Delaware had a partner. One we don't know about."

Bern got her medal as well, and the Taoiseach faced the crowd, the picture of a pleased monarch, and raised his voice further. "Three cheers again for our heroes!"

The crowd erupted into shouts once more, an elation Baghdad couldn't feel. The Taoiseach then launched into speech, praising all four on the stage again.

A chair scraped behind them, and Baghdad tensed as someone new sat. In the middle of the speech. Why would—

"Sir Haldis, so good of you to leave this row open."

Baghdad turned a micron, but it was Chang's whispered, "Slag, Istanbul," that identified the voice for him.

"Indeed, dog. Make a scene, I dare you."

Chang tensed, ready for just that, but Baghdad laid an arm on his knee. "Speak your piece, Lord Istanbul."

"I just wanted you to know who was responsible for this."

Baghdad's mind whirled. Istanbul? But there had been no evidence, none at all, that the Colombia were involved with Delaware. How could—

"Tell Boston our debt is far from settled," Istanbul whispered and then slunk away.

"Chang, what—" Baghdad started, but the Taoiseach's

speech reached its crescendo, drawing his attention back to center stage.

"There is only so much the Empire can do for each of you to thank you for putting your lives at risk to bring this traitor to justice, and our thanks is only the first of the rewards. However, for one of you, we can do more today. Lord Haldis—"

Baghdad tensed.

"Two weeks' time is the anniversary of your family's elevation to the nobility. And on that date, I will welcome you as the new head of House Haldis."

BOSTON

Boston held his glass in numb fingers. All his elation had drained out of him. Now, he just felt empty, like his glass.

"You knew this was coming," Chang said quietly.

"We did," Baghdad agreed, settling into his chair with a creak. He looked tired. More tired than Boston could remember. "I still have leads though you'll find none of them very appealing, Boston."

"For getting out of this?"

Baghdad's face fell. "For a bride."

That felt worse.

"We could see if Nirvana will let their scion marry. She was impressive as all hell today," Chang said.

Baghdad shook his head. "They like us, but not that much. Not their last bachelorette of this generation."

"Change the subject."

The two old men were silent for a few beats of Boston's heart.

"We have to consider our alternatives, Boston."

And Istanbul. That burned worse. He'd never expected that stuck-up little prick to understand him so well. To understand how to *hurt* him so well. "Forsake it all!"

Before he could begin his tirade, the doors to the study

burst open and Montana stalked in. Every motion was angry; Boston could almost feel the heat rolling off her.

"Are you alright?"

Montana shook her head. "Drink first."

"I see you have news as good as ours?"

Montana gave him a blazing glare and nodded. "Aspen. She did it, the little fuck. I'm going to be derogated in three days. Stripped from the rolls of the nobility, cast back out as a common Terran."

Boston rested a hand on her shoulder, but she ignored him. "I have become an embarrassment to the Sinclair dynasty," Montana smoldered quietly, ignoring his sympathy. "More than an embarrassment. A public embarrassment. Before, I was unknown. No one cared that I had divorced my family. Now, though… Now, they want me gone."

"I am confident you can meet this challenge, Lady Von Montana." Bagdhad said after a moment's silence.

"Are you? Wonderful. I have worked too hard for too long to be in the position I am now. I will be nothing if they succeed. Worse than nothing. Lose everything that gives me the tools to—"

"Unlike yourself, I still remember what being common feels like. As does Chang," Baghdad said cutting her off, flushing at his collar. "All of us in this room lost tonight, and I trust you will remember that better, in future."

Montana's violet eyes blazed, and Boston took her hand in his before she said something truly unforgivable. She glanced at him, giving him the barest glimpse of the explosion imminent. But she choked it back, squeezing his hand until her knuckles were white.

"Of course, Lord Haldis." Her eyelids fluttered, revealing a still-smoldering but dimming fire. Then, she glanced around the room. "Forgive me. The night has been trying."

"For all of us."

She nodded. Voice tight, she asked, "How did the Taoiseach decide tonight was the night you would take over?"

Boston explained. He was glad that he held her hand firmly in hers; she might have tried to find Istanbul and drive her knife through him herself.

"Well then." She glanced down at her glass, as if seeing it for the first time, and knocked back the amber liquid. "Well then. Our problems present some interesting… synergies."

Hope dawned, hard and terrible in Boston's chest.

Baghdad was able to speak before he was. "Now that… That just might have some merit to it."

"What does?" Chang asked, glancing between them, confused.

The room was silent, and Montana's gaze was everywhere except at him. When she spoke, it was almost too quiet to hear. "What do you say, Boston? Will you let me marry you?"

Chang interrupted before he could make so much as a sound. "She is too much of an outcast."

"She was just given a medal in front of the entire court." Baghdad nodded, leaning in. "Take me through it."

"We'd need a honeymoon," Montana said breathlessly. "We could have the ceremony, induct Boston to the head of the house, and then leave. No one could complain." She extended a finger, then a second, worrying her lip. "And when we get back, we can handle things together. Boston would stay in the guard, and Baghdad could tutor me in putting the house in order."

"How long would you be gone?" Chang asked.

"A long time." Her eyes were closed, calculating.

"Long enough for Baghdad to plan a transition. The *Taoiseach Jupiter* leaves in a few weeks on her shakedown cruise. We could get the Taoiseach to give us cabins. Do a long run out to the rim and back."

"A good excuse not to take over the house immediately," Baghdad agreed.

Montana extended a third finger. "It will end my derogation. There would be no point, with me marrying you immediately after. Thwart Sinclair again. And finally, Boston, we are phenomenal in bed. Say that about any of the other possible candidates."

"But… marriage."

"Do you not want to marry me?"

"I do." He found himself grinning. He leapt off the divan and dropped to one knee beside her. "Everyone, everything, is coming down against us right now. Let us turn that back on them. You and I. Together?" Boston asked with a grin. "What in the whole rotting universe could stop us?"

Her eyes sparkled. "Nothing."

"Then it is settled," Baghdad said, getting to his feet. He paced in front of the divan, cane forgotten. "We can announce it tomorrow."

"I'll need something to do," Chang said.

"I'll speak to the Taoiseach about the *Jupiter* and see if we can slip her launch date some. This can work," Baghdad continued without noticing Chang's tangent.

"Do we have anything else to talk about?" Boston asked, tugging Montana to her feet. "Otherwise, I think we have an engagement to celebrate."

"No, by all means," Baghdad said, and Montana tugged Boston toward the doors.

BOSTON

Later, Boston savored the warm buzz that suffused his

entire body after strenuous exercise, his arms wrapped around Montana. "So. Wife," he said into her ear.

"Fiancée, at this moment."

"Fiancée," he repeated. The word sounded good in his mouth.

"Possibly. My certainty is fading."

It was dark, but Boston could make out the shape of Montana's face, her eyes fixed on the wall away from him. "What? You no longer think we are good in bed?"

She kicked him hard in the shins, making him pull her tighter. "House Haldis needs to stop being an outcast."

"Tana," Boston said almost silently, but she shivered under him the way she did every time he used the name. "We will make it happen together."

"Lady Montana is the woman who will help House Haldis rise to power," she said quietly. "Not Tana."

"Well then. Tomorrow, I will announce to all of Sol that I am marrying Lady Montana. But it is Tana who I want to spend the rest of my life with."

"Do you really mean that?"

"Absolutely."

"Then… can I make a request?"

"I will be happy to rub your feet."

"No!" She whacked him again. "Boston, be serious."

"Alright." He put on his most serious face in the pitch-black of his bedroom. "What is it?"

"I want to make a request for our first stop on the *Jupiter*."

"She will probably have a set shakedown cruise to fly."

"I think whoever her captain is would make a diversion for us."

"Perhaps. Where were you thinking? I was rather looking forward to a long run first, though. Six months or so with no ansible, no way to get news from Castle High." He savored the idea. "That is exactly what I need right now."

"Mmm, me too," Montana purred in his ear. "But I... I want to visit where we first met."

"The Taoiseach's Grand Hall?" Boston asked, trying to see her face in the dark. "But we just... oh. You want to see your birth world."

She nodded slowly. "I know I am not supposed to think of it as home, but I..."

Boston pulled her tighter. "Tana, of course you do. I still think of the hovel I was born in as home, before we built the estate. I would love to see where you grew up, the places you played as a child."

"Then we can go?"

"I will talk to the captain as soon as we find out who they are. We even have some spare cash, so we could pay for it if we need to. Chang will dig the coordinates out of the database and make sure they are in the *Jupiter's* computer before we launch."

"Thank you, Boston," she breathed and rested her head against his chest. She stayed there until he drifted off to sleep.

BERN

It hurt more than Bern expected, watching Montana be married to Lord Haldis.

She clapped, she smiled, she did all the right things. It helped having Lord Dhaka on her arm, offering chaste support whenever she needed it. Strangely, that made the ceremony easier, forcing her to keep herself together with a close observer.

The party was more difficult. It was held in one of Port Chittagong's small ballrooms, where Montana and Lord Haldis could make their escape to the liner with ease.

Bern watched the increasingly inebriated performance with bemused grace, especially when her fiancée was drawn into a drinking contest with some of the SpaceGuard present. At least tonight, inter-service rivalries appeared to be paused.

Bern sat down at one of the recently vacated tables and found her slate in her hands. She scanned the news feeds out of habit, but there was nothing new. Had been nothing interesting since Delaware's death, as the House War had slipped into ugly stalemate. Even Jordana didn't seem to know what to do. Delaware was dead, but she wasn't whole. None of them were.

She settled for running another search through the shipping records. It had been her habit for weeks, constructing ever more convoluted queries, hoping to find some clue as to Delaware's partner.

So focused was she on the slate that she failed to notice the elder Lord Haldis settle into a chair beside her.

"Enjoying the evening, Lady Nirvana?"

"Does it look it?"

"No."

A question had been burning away in the corners of her mind for days. "How can one man have done this?"

The elderly gentleman considered that for a moment, his face pensive. Then, he sighed and settled lower on his cane. "We all bear responsibility. Delaware was able to do what he did because we all expect scheming to be the norm. I just hope the diamond houses learn the right lesson from this and de-escalate, rather than give in to paranoia."

"That is unrealistic."

He smiled softly. "Perhaps."

"There must be things we are missing," Bern said after a long moment of silence.

"Such as where the Nirvana gumdrops are."

Bern blinked. "Gumdrops?"

He gave her a sharp look. "Friends of friends in the Guard have become increasingly concerned that a significant amount of Guard equipment went missing from Eden during the fight. The armory was destroyed, of course, but when searching the wreckage, they did not find remnants of the heavy equipment. Specifically, two gumdrops, complete with Wolf armor and splinters. And they were never used by the rioters. At least, as far as we know."

"How is it possible we do not know of this?" Menodora and Jordana had not mentioned anything like it.

"Paranoia?'

It was too likely an answer for her to dismiss. "And they are not on the planet somewhere?"

Baghdad looked perplexed. "They must be. Unless you think they were shipped out?"

She blinked at him. She hadn't meant to suggest that, but… "There has been a lot of traffic to and from Eden the past few weeks. And very little of it inspected."

Even as she was speaking, she began programming another query. This one focused on recent traffic from Eden, rather than historical.

Baghdad eyed the query over her shoulder and tutted approvingly. "A brilliant idea, Lady Nirvana."

She put the slate on the table. "I will have the results auto-forwarded to you. It may take a while."

"Not to worry. I should be hosting, regardless." He offered her a hand to pull her to her feet, though he leaned heavily on his cane to manage it. "Let me introduce you to some of Boston's other friends. It will do you some good, I think, to be distracted."

He really was quite perceptive. "As you wish."

BAGHDAD

Baghdad left Bern with some of the Wolves, who were telling shameless and probably very embellished stories of Boston's first few years in the colonies.

He found the newly married couple not too far away, apparently taking a respite from dancing and talking with Yilan, Hannigan's sister, who had been convinced to wait tables for the night.

"Enjoying yourself, Lady Haldis?" Baghdad teased as he approached.

"I am indeed, Lord Haldis," Montana replied, flushing as she entwined herself in Boston's arms. "I am told all our cargo was loaded on the liner. Nothing is going to delay our sail."

"Wonderful. Though I think you've earned the right to call me Grandfather."

"Lord Haldis, I'm... Thank you."

"Think nothing of it. You've made him happy." Baghdad gestured to Boston. "And not incidentally, you will be a tremendous asset to the house."

"I have trouble articulating how much I have enjoyed the last few months, getting to know the family."

"Ha. We'll soon fix that," Baghdad said, catching Boston's eye. "But... I have something for you." Baghdad patted his pockets, searching, and finally withdrew a small box covered in soft felt. "This was my wife's. She had hoped to pass it on to our daughter, but since that was not to be, I'd like to give it to you."

He extended the box, and Montana took it with trembling fingers. The lid flipped up, revealing a necklace covered in glittering rubies and sapphires. It formed the shape of a series of shooting stars.

Montana picked it up carefully and drew the silver chain around her neck, the magnetic clasp binding behind her head. She looked down at the necklace for a few moments and then back at him, her eyes sparkling with tears. "Thank you, Grandfather. I love it."

She half turned, showing it to Boston, who nodded. "It suits you, Tana."

"Tana?" Baghdad asked.

"Oh…" Montana glanced back at him, still blinking furiously. "It was my name for many years. They lengthened it to Montana when I came to the Empire. I was told it was my mother's last word. She died in childbirth, I think, but my father thought she was trying to name me. It was a word in his people's language."

"What does it mean?"

"It is a little complicated." Montana hesitated. "Something to do with fire and flames, but my father's people used it to refer to meteor showers. There was one the night I was born. There were a lot of meteor showers."

Boston lifted a hand and rested it on Montana's shoulder. She leaned in toward the touch, and his hand glided down around her waist to pull him into a light embrace.

"It suits you."

"Thank you, Grandfather." She visibly seemed to pull herself together and turned to face Boston. "Now, I think I need another dance."

BAGHDAD

The party wore on. Baghdad circulated as best he could, being a good host, making sure no one seemed out of place. When Boston wasn't dancing, he was entertaining his myriad of friends, introducing Montana to them all. Bern seemed to be Montana's only guest, though she was firmly ensconced among the Wolves, now flirting shamelessly with Dunkirk and Cancun.

His slate chimed.

Baghdad maneuvered himself to one of the sparsely populated tables on the edge of the party and sat. It felt good to get the weight off his knee.

Baghdad withdrew his slate from its sling and opened the message. It was exactly as Bern had promised: a copy of her query on the Nirvana records. But what was disquieting was the result. A single massive shipment of three whole containers had been dispatched from Eden to Sol a week after Delaware's passing. Three containers was plenty large enough to hold a pair of gumdrops and all their associated equipment. But the shipment had never officially been unloaded, just transshipped somewhere.

It probably had never even been inspected, just loaded onto a waiting liner.

Baghdad stared at the result, trying to puzzle out the meaning. The company name that had ordered the shipment was unfamiliar, not one of Delaware's aliases. Meteor Enterprises. But it had been paid for with the same cash cards, had been routed the same, confusing way.

For all Baghdad's experience in running the house, interstellar commerce was not his forte. His eyes found Montana across the ballroom. She was standing back as Boston drank from a comically long beer glass. And it was suddenly very inconvenient that their expert in such matters was about to be incommunicado for six months.

As much as he hated to, he had to do it. He zipped across the room and asked Montana, "Could we have a word in private?"

She nodded, unconcerned, and separated herself from chatting with one of the waiters. She led him out of the ballroom and to one of the small conference rooms that dotted the area around it. Parties were not uncommon just before a liner left, but with so few passengers on the *Jupiter,* they had the place to themselves. She chose one far enough from the ballroom to give them some privacy.

"I'm sorry to distract you tonight, but I need some help unraveling these."

"Of course, please."

He handed her the slate and explained the search. Her eyes went wide as she examined the results.

"I wonder if the heralds have found this yet," he said.

"I'm reasonably sure they haven't," Montana said, not meeting his eyes.

"How can you be sure?"

"Because if they had, I'd have been arrested."

CHAPTER TWENTY-ONE

Ember

MONTANA

She was so close. That was what fucking burned, acid chewing at her throat, searing her veins—she was so close! Only to have it all collapse here, with only hours left until she was gone.

"What?"

He didn't understand yet. That was a relief, but it was also a curse. He hadn't recognized the name of one of her shell corporations. But as soon as he tried, he'd be able to find her.

Gently as she could, she tugged the slate out of his hands and tossed it on the table. Realization, heartbreaking and fierce, was rising in his eyes, and he swayed forward. She was not quite sure what he intended; he might not know himself. But she was.

Her knife was where it always was—carefully wrapped on the inside of her thigh—and it was in her hand before he could react.

"Don't do anything rash, Baghdad." She let her voice slip, losing the practiced aristocratic accent that had been beaten into her as a girl. That was a joy, too.

Her new grandfather-in-law stared back, shocked, but his eyes focused on the knife in her hand. She noticed how he shifted his weight, gripped his cane tighter. The old wolf was still a soldier.

"Explain yourself," he demanded.

Could she? Was there anything she could say to that hard face, those searching eyes, that would get her out of this mess? She doubted it. Any lie she told now… No. He would see through it, would have seen through it if he'd had the slightest inkling that she was more than just a smuggler, more than a woman making a doomed attempt to salve her conscience. And she'd cultivated that, as much as she dared.

The truth though, would get him killed.

Baghdad made a slow motion toward the table, and she raised the knife again, making him freeze.

"Don't, Baghdad."

He gave her a sour look before putting his hands together on his cane. "Why don't we talk this out?"

"There's nothing to say."

Baghdad glowered at her. "At least let me sit."

She jerked her head in a nod, and he slowly sank into one of the chairs facing her, careful to keep his hands visible.

"I wonder if I can reason it out," he muttered to himself.

"You're welcome to try." She needed time to think, damn it.

"What did you say Tana meant?"

She had to smile. Gods, what this man could do if he could see past the prejudices the Empire had forced onto him.

"Could Tana mean Ember?"

"Some translations do."

"Then you were the one helping Delaware stir up the colonies, Ember?"

She nodded, and gods above, it felt good to admit. "We had different goals, but yes. Everyone assumed Ember was just a superstition."

"I did." At least he did her the courtesy of not lying now.

"I wasn't lying when I said Tana meant meteor shower in my people's language. But it was tied up with superstitions about where meteors came from. I was already known as Tana in some circles, and when people started using Ember, it seemed harmless enough."

"Still," he shook his head, "remarkably shortsighted of you, to use your own name, when planning a coup."

"I used Katalia's name when I needed to. But that's not what this is."

"It must be. Delaware had grander ambitions than ruling Eden. He planned to take over Sinclair, take over the Empire, for all practical purposes. He's everything you hate about the nobility. Boston never would have backed Sinclair against the Taoiseach just because—"

"That's not what this is!" she yelled.

"Then tell me."

Could she? Could she make him understand? Was there a version of tonight that didn't end in tragedy?

Realization dawned in his eyes halfway through her thought. "The colonies," he muttered.

"Not 'the colonies,'" she corrected. "Stars, all of you nobles. 'The Colonies' don't exist. Not as a bloc, not the way you think of them. Even Boston does it."

"And how does putting House Sinclair in power help anyone, colonial or not?" She could see she'd awakened his anger, but he had it under iron control, seeking to understand before he decided to lash out. "You divorced them. You hate them! Why help them?"

"Sinclair isn't supposed to win the House War. They're supposed to be destroyed by it." Saying it out loud felt so right.

Baghdad gaped at her. It was the first time she could remember seeing him so dumbstruck, but he didn't argue with her, didn't try to convince himself she was kidding. It made her respect him all the more.

"For what they did to you?"

"This isn't about me. This is about every planet the Empire is subjugating!"

"An uprising."

"A rebellion," she corrected, hating the look of disgust that crossed his face.

"Humanity is stronger together," he said, repeating the same catechism he'd thrown in her face months before.

"Strength isn't the only important thing, Baghdad."

"The Empire has its flaws—" he started, but she cut him off.

"The Empire is a blight on the face of the universe."

He shook his head, but she pushed forward. "You know this, even if you won't admit it to yourself. You see all the fucked-up shit that goes on out there, and you hate it. So does Boston. It's the only reason I don't hate him. It isn't your fault. You were conditioned by it, brutalized by it, just like I was. You just don't know there is an alternative. I do. And now, you do, too."

That was all he needed to see her question. "You want me to join you?"

"Yes." Her voice was a whisper. "Yes, Baghdad. Gods, yes. Help me make something better."

Baghdad's lips worked wordlessly. "How do you expect me to trust you? Or expect me to forgive anything you've done?"

Hope flared like a distant nova in her heart. He wasn't saying no.

"This… this wasn't how things were supposed to go," she said, resisting the desire to wring her hands. Even now, he made her feel like a misbehaving child. "I had a different plan, a worse plan, before I met you all. You, Bern, Boston, all of you are better than this Empire that has you in its clutches. We can make it better."

He eyed her levelly. "The Empire has given me and my family everything."

"No, it only takes. Takes your souls, your morality, your dignity. Out there, Boston will see that. I will make him see it. All you'd have to do is let us." Her voice was a whisper. "Wait a few hours, just until the *Jupiter* passes light speed. Then, nothing can stop me."

He hesitated, and she thought she had her chance.

"You'll cause chaos," he breathed. "Anarchy."

"I know."

"No. You've never seen chaos," the old man said. "You've no idea what it will be like. Even if you succeed, millions will die."

"I'm not naive. In the forest, fire burns and kills and destroys, but it's the only way to make new things grow. It's terrible but necessary. And I'm not afraid of it."

"We can fix it," he said, and she felt him saying no. "Taoiseach damn it all, you've done half the work, starting the House War. Exposing Sinclair. We can fix it from the inside, together. You don't have to tear it all down!" Baghdad raised his head and made her stare him down. "We can find a way. The three of us, the four of us. But not by burning it all down. Adele was trying to make things better, I know that. We can, too."

It broke her heart. Still dignified, still grand, clinging

to his principles even though he must know they would get him killed. It was almost enough. But he was wrong. He had to be wrong.

"No," she whispered and cast her hope into the fire. "I'm sorry, Baghdad. Half measures aren't enough. They'll never be enough. As long as the Empire exists, it will strangle anything else that tries to grow near it. It all needs to burn."

He rose slowly, leaning heavily on his cane. He'd gone sallow sometime during their conversation. "And Boston?"

"I—" she started, but the door burst open behind them.

"Augustine, what—"

She had just enough time to turn, to see Bern behind her, a look of horror slowly dawning. And then, Baghdad made his move.

She felt the cane slam into her knees, taking her legs out from under her. His hand reached for the knife and she let herself fall to stay out of his grip. Somehow, her elbow found his stomach, and she dragged him down with her.

He was so light. She'd remember that for the rest of her life: how he seemed like a twig in her hands, though no less ferocious for it. And how suddenly the end came... with her knife embedded in his stomach.

She rolled off him, gasping for air as Bern rushed forward and pressed her hands to the gaping wound in Baghdad's side.

"Well played," Baghdad coughed. And she thought he meant it.

"Augustine, what did you do?" Blood welled up from between Bern's fingers, staining them as red as her soul.

Baghdad gurgled as blood filled his lungs. "I hope... it's worth it."

"It will be," she whispered

And then, he was still.

It was the hardest thing she had ever done. Reaching up to close his eyes. Whispering the benediction over someone she'd killed. Someone she knew. She—

"Augustine, what the Taoiseach is going on?"

Bern's eyes were wide, terrified, darting between the knife in her hands and the dead body on the floor.

She barely thought the maneuver through, but her body reacted like she'd been rehearsing it for days. She lunged, more careful with the knife this time, and got her arms around Bern.

Bern tried to struggle, but she was weak, weak like all of them that had grown up outside the well of a planet's gravity. Even slick with blood, even fighting as hard as she could, Bern was no match for her.

Her friend froze at the touch of warm steel on her neck.

"What the rot is happening?" Bern gasped, trembling now.

She hated this. She hated feeling like this. But it had to be done. What she was doing was more important than anything. More important than any of them.

"It wasn't supposed to be like this," she whispered. Bern tossed a hand back, reaching for her hands, but she missed. "I was going to just move messages for the colonies. Give them a chance to organize."

"What is this?" Bern whispered, terrified. "Is this about the colonies?"

"There is nothing else," she whispered. Her hand was trembling so much, she nicked Bern's neck, and blood welled up against Bern's ivory skin. Against the silver blade, her father's blade. The one she'd just used to kill the only other person to ever treat her like a daughter.

She couldn't do it.

She threw the knife away, heard it clatter against the wall, and Bern let out a startled woof of air and started to dart away. But she was faster. She grabbed the wrist of the arm that was still wrapped around Bern's throat and pulled. Bern's hands shot up, frantically tugging on her arm, but Bern didn't have the strength.

It felt like years until she stopped struggling.

MONTANA

The first thing she did was slit a strip of fabric from the bottom of Bern's dress and use it to bind her friend's hands. Her breathing was steady, if shallow, and she dragged Bern up into one of the chairs, then bound her ankles together.

She wiped her hands on a dry part of Bern's dress and then pulled out her slate, tapping out a message. She ignored the body as long as she could, but eventually, had to look down at it. His suddenly small form.

She was covered in blood, her dress saturated with it in places. She suddenly couldn't stand it anymore and pulled off the tattered thing, draping it over Baghdad. The chemise she wore under it was revealing, designed to suggest, but it was enough. Barely.

She stifled a scream.

"Lyoness," she gasped. The name of her home.

"Khan, Bell, Darla, Kerr." Her brothers and sisters.

"Lake and Ike." The couple who lived closest to the river.

She made it through all forty-nine names of her mantra before the trembling stopped, before she was able to breathe again. She was the only one now who knew those names. Most of the faces were still clear, but some were getting hazy. It had been hard enough to tell Cal and Theo apart when she saw the twins every day.

A sharp rap at the door made her start, and she sprang

for it, getting her hand on the handle just soon enough to prevent it from being pushed open.

"It's us." Manila's urgent hiss was the only thing that could have saved her, and she cracked the door just wide enough for them to slip in.

Manila and Diego contemplated the room wordlessly for a moment. "Fuck, what did you do?"

"Fuck off, Diego," Manila said and rested a hand on her shoulder, careful to avoid the worst of the blood stains. "Are you okay?"

She nodded jerkily. "Is everything loaded?"

"Almost," Diego rasped. Gods, she hated listening to the voice he'd been left with, as if he were gargling rocks. "Everyone else is safely hidden away. We should be, too."

"I know, but we need to deal with this."

Manila held up a bag. "I brought you another dress. And some things to clean up with."

"Wha?" Bern stirred in her chair.

"You left one alive!" Diego started forward, pulling another knife from under his waiter's tunic.

"No!" She almost screamed it and reached Bern before he did.

Another chunk of Bern's dress went into her mouth, muffling the start of a scream. Bern stared back with one eye, the other blocked by an errant shadowcaster.

"We won't hurt you," she promised. "You'll spend a few hours locked in this room, and then, you'll be free."

Bern's eyes were wide. She tried to speak, but nothing clear came through the gag.

"Clean up," Manila instructed, handing her a set of rags. "We need to get you back to the party, and we need to get to the ship."

She nodded and began.

MONTANA

She was aflame. So close she could taste it, vibrating with nervous energy.

Diego and Manila had gotten themselves hidden back in the cargo containers. The eight members of her team that she'd managed to smuggle into Sol were all there, with enough food and oxygen to last them the nine-month trip.

"I thought he would come see us off."

Boston hung wistfully at the boarding tube, the last connection back to Port Chittagong. Chang and everyone else had said their goodbyes when they left the party. It was beyond time to have it sealed, but Boston had worked his charm and gotten a few more minutes.

She ran her fingers over his shoulder. He liked that, she'd learned. "Baghdad and Bern had their heads together last I saw them—some new Sinclair machination they were dealing with," she lied. "I asked, but they said they did not want to distract us. Wanted us to focus on the honeymoon."

"Good of them," he said wistfully.

Behind them, the klaxon sounded, and Boston withdrew from the doorway. They were about to leave.

"We should tour the ship, get to know the place."

It took six hours for the liner to accelerate to the velocity she needed to slip beyond the stars. Six hours pinned in normal space, still in reach of communications with Sol. Six hours where things could still go wrong.

But they didn't.

She focused on learning about the liner. Anything to keep from screaming from the stress. Every mile they slid farther from Earth was one closer to freedom, but every second was one where the body could be discovered. One where Bern could finally work her way out of her bonds and call for help.

She didn't look at the container with Diego, Manila, and the others when they passed. She didn't look at the container that held the gumdrops, the splinters, the armor.

Boston lit up when he saw the engine room, their elderly, distinguished, and above all enthusiastic captain at their elbow the entire time. Boston crawled through ducts, inspected gages, touched everything he could get his hands on. And she feigned indifference. Feigned not hanging on every word of how the FTL drive worked.

Every word about how things could go wrong.

She couldn't unsee his face. Unsee the horror, the shock, the fury he'd shown her.

She felt a yawning chasm open in her stomach, but she clamped down on it, focused on breathing, on feeding oxygen to the flames that burned in her heart.

She fed her hope into the fire, too. Everything she'd half-wanted, all the might-have-beens and fantasies became fuel. She refused to fail now. Not when she'd given everything.

Her heartbeat in the kilohertz, they ended the extensive tour on the bridge. Where she always knew they would.

"Lady Kun Haldis." Boston bowed and let her precede him. It was probably the fifteenth time he'd used her new name on the tour, but it still made her miss a beat every time he did.

It was sparkling, immaculate, a marvel of engineering, and Boston gloried over every detail. But her eyes were only for the large golden sphere at the front of the room.

It was the same as the one that had dotted Castle High. That gave nobles access to rooms, that had even been at her wedding. Behind the ornate finish and mysticism, it was nothing more magical than a DNA-testing machine, keyed to gene markers common to Terra.

The captain, Colombia, noticed her gaze. "It is impressive, is it not, my Lady?"

She allowed herself to approach. Feel the hum of the thing. Feel it judging her. "So, this is what has kept the colonies in check all these years."

Colombia chuckled. "I think the Guard has had something to do with that, has it not, Lord?"

Boston, thankfully, made no response, and she was able to focus on not reacting to Colombia. Still, she couldn't resist the slightest needle. "Oh, no doubt, Lord. But this is what we have that the poor colonists do not: the power to fly between stars."

Her palms itched to touch it, but she resisted. She knew what would happen, what had happened the first and last time she'd dared. It had thrown her across the room, a warning to be received only once. She was only seventeen at the time.

Colombia made a show of checking his screens and nodded to himself. "Crew, make ready for transition!"

She ignored the flurry of shouted orders, the dramatics to make everyone feel like they were about to be a part of something important. It would be, but not for any of the reasons they knew.

"Would you like the honors, Lord Haldis?"

Boston grinned. "She is your ship, Lord Colombia. I would never stand in your way."

Colombia waved a hand. "There will be plenty of time for that later. Consider it a wedding present."

Boston grinned wider, a boy allowed to play with a new toy, and stepped up to the sphere. "Whenever you feel like it."

Boston pressed his hand to the sphere, and her heart stopped.

An hour could have passed while she waited for his

hand to connect. A year, before he grimaced at the prick of his skin. An entire age of the universe, before she felt the telltale hum of the deck under them, and the stars winked out of the view ports.

They were away. And nothing could stop her now.

She waded through the last of the formalities, floating, and finally allowed herself to be led to their quarters. She could have sung, she could have danced, but she didn't. Her control was absolute.

For a little while longer.

The moment the door to their quarters closed, she was in his arms, clawing at his shirt, ripping at his dress pants, divesting him of everything that reminded her of the Empire. Everything she hated. Until he was just him.

"I wish you had not needed to change out of your dress," he found time to whisper. "I was looking forward to tearing it off you."

She forced herself to meet his gaze, the desire in his eyes making her flush. It took her a moment to find her voice, to bring a smile to her lips.

"I'll make it up to you," Ember promised.

ACKNOLEDGEMENTS

Writing this book took ten years, more or less. In that time, I forced most of my friends and family to read a host of very bad drafts. Hopefully, the final result is some consolation that it was worth it. I couldn't possibly list everyone, but all of you have my thanks for putting up with me.

What I needed was professional help, and much too late, I got it in the form of Andy Meisenheimer, Elisabeth Chretien, and the rest of Dan Alexandar's team at NY Book Editors. Among everything else, they helped me *understand* the feedback I had been getting from readers all this time.

The story of the Eire Empire will continue in Book 2, *Sparks*, not as soon as any of us would like.

Want to find out more about the Empire?

Visit eireempire.com